JUNE FRANCIS's maiden name was Nelson, and although she can't lay claim to the famous Lord Admiral, she can boast of at least six mariners in her ancestry who came from far and wide. June's mother worked in service and her tales of the old days have inspired several of June's thirty published novels.

By June Francis

It Had to Be You

JUNE FRANCIS

Allison & Busby Limited
13 Charlotte Mews
London W1T 4EJ
www.allisonandbusby.com

First published in Great Britain by Allison & Busby in 2011.
This paperback edition published by Allison & Busby in 2012.

Copyright © 2011 by JUNE FRANCIS

The moral right of the author is hereby asserted in accordance with
the Copyright, Designs and Patents Act 1988.

All characters and events in this publication,
other than those clearly in the public domain,
are fictitious and any resemblance to actual persons,
living or dead, is purely coincidental.

All rights reserved. No part of this publication may be reproduced,
stored in a retrieval system, or transmitted, in any form or by
any means without the prior written permission of the publisher,
nor be otherwise circulated in any form of binding or cover
other than that in which it is published and without a similar
condition being imposed on the subsequent buyer.

A CIP catalogue record for this book is available from
the British Library.

10 9 8 7 6 5 4 3 2 1

ISBN 978-0-7490-0959-5

Typeset in 10/14.2 pt Sabon by
Allison & Busby Ltd.

Paper used in this publication is from sustainably managed sources.
All of the wood used is procured from legal sources and is fully traceable.
The producing mill uses schemes such as ISO 14001
to monitor environmental impact.

Printed and bound by
CPI Group (UK) Ltd, Croydon, CR0 4YY

Dedicated to my husband John, whom I met in a Liverpool cinema in the Fifties and who much later joined Clayton Le Moors fell runners and introduced me to the beautiful Lancashire countryside.

PROLOGUE

January 1952

'Granddad, I don't think we should go to the pictures this evening,' said Emma Booth, drawing aside the curtain and gazing out over the darkened garden. Earlier in the day the River Calder had frozen over and the fells were white with frost. As the sun dipped to the horizon, its dying rays glistened on the hoary pavement out front.

'Why, lass?' asked Harold Harrison.

'Because it's going to be really slippery outside and I don't want you falling and breaking an arm or a leg. You're not as young as you were.'

'Just because thou's only twenty-one and I'm in me eighties, lass, doesn't mean I'm any more likely to do that than thee.' He chuckled. 'In fact, if I remember rightly, last time the river froze over and we got out the skates, I stayed on me feet and it was thee that went sliding along on thy bottom.'

Emma smiled. 'That was different and it was a few years ago when Gran was still alive. She was partnering you, if I'm not mistaken.'

A shadow crossed Harold's face and his chin dipped onto his chest and for several minutes he was silent. Then he jerked up his head and said, 'I still want to go and see Fred Astaire and Ginger Rogers. I always come out wanting to sing and dance when I see one of their films.'

'This one hasn't got Ginger Rogers in it, Granddad. It's Jane Powell, although she's a good singer and can dance OK.'

'No Ginger Rogers!' He pursed his lips and then his wrinkled face relaxed into a smile. 'I bet I still come out singing. After that performance of *Life with Father* at the church school a few days ago I need cheering up. The acting was good but there wasn't one dramatic moment in it. I'll put on me boots and I'll be alreet, lass. I need cheering up and so do thee.'

Emma decided it was a waste of time arguing with him – and after all, the cinema was on the first floor above the Co-op, so they didn't have far to go. She put the last dish away on the dresser and took off her apron.

'OK. We'd best get ready, then, but make sure you're well wrapped up.'

'Stop fussing, lass. I'm not a three-year-old,' said Harry, rubbing his hands together and grinning, obviously happy that he had got his way. He hurried over to where his coat, muffler and cap hung on the back door, humming a tune as he put them on.

It did not take Emma long to get ready, and after banking up the fire in the black-leaded range with some slack, she pulled the front door closed behind them. The air was so cold that it seemed to take bites out of her face and she clung to her granddad's arm, not so much because she needed steadying, but to slow him down. If they took it easy they were less likely to fall. They arrived at the Co-op in one piece and were soon making their way upstairs and, in no time at all, were seated in front of the big screen.

The lights dimmed and Emma settled down to being taken out of herself, knowing that it would be just the same for the dear, old, white-haired gentleman beside her. Life had been tough since her grandmother had died five years ago. Still, there was little point in complaining. They were better off than many: her grandfather owned the cottage in which they lived, and with his pension and her small earnings, they could enjoy the occasional outing such as this one.

It was trying to snow when they emerged from the cinema a few hours later with a crowd of chattering, happy cinema-goers, but Emma knew that it would not dampen her granddad's spirits.

'Now, lass, that film didn't lack dramatic moments,' he crowed.

Before she could prevent him, he set off ahead of her, singing one of the hit songs from the film called 'How Could You Believe Me When I Said I Loved You When You Know I've Been a Liar All My Life'. Then the rhythm seemed to get into his feet and he began dancing. She hurried after him, smiling as her 'teenage' grandfather capered along the road. Then suddenly her smile vanished because one of his legs slid from under him and he went flying, falling heavily. His head hit the kerbstone and by the time she reached him he was lying in the gutter.

Her heart thudded in her chest as she knelt beside him and realised that he had lost consciousness. 'Granddad, Granddad,' she cried, a sob in her voice as she gently lifted his head onto her lap.

'I'll go and get the doctor,' said one of the cinema-goers and hurried off.

Emma remained where she was, scarcely aware of the cold, damp ground as she hugged the old man to her, tears trickling down her cheeks. In her head she could hear him saying, *Now, lass, that was a dramatic moment!*

CHAPTER ONE

Emma watched as snowflakes as large as halfpennies swirled down from a loaded grey-yellowish sky onto the coffin. Foolishly, she felt glad that she had dressed her granddad in his best Sunday worsted suit, vest, long johns, white shirt and waistcoat, as well as the plaid scarf and old tweed cap that had seldom been off his head. Visualising him clad in warm clothes had somehow helped her to cope with this moment, as his earthly remains were lowered into the cold earth.

Her friend Lila Ashcroft had understood but teased her, saying she was surprised that she hadn't put in his favourite dancing clogs as well. Emma's eyes had filled with tears, thinking that it was dancing that had finished off her last and dearest remaining relative. At least he had died happy, she thought, and hoped he was dancing in heaven.

The vicar's voice broke into Emma's thoughts as he intoned, 'Earth to earth, ashes to ashes, dust to dust; in sure and certain hope of the Resurrection to eternal life, through our Lord Jesus Christ, who shall change our vile body, that it may be like unto His glorious body, according to the mighty working, whereby He is able to subdue all things to Himself.'

Emma brushed back the chestnut hair that fell to her shoulders beneath the baggy, black, hand-knitted beret as she bent to pick up a handful of soil and the tears rolled down her cold cheeks. She dropped the earth onto the coffin and thought back to the evening when her grandfather had died. He had never regained consciousness, so she had not been able to say a proper goodbye to him. She was going to miss him so much, but at least she could be thankful that he had been spared the lingering, painful illnesses suffered by his wife and only daughter.

'You all right?' asked Lila, slipping a hand through Emma's arm.

Emma did not reply but took a handkerchief from a pocket and mopped away her tears. She thanked the vicar and turned away from the graveside, thinking to return tomorrow on her own. She spoke to those who had come to support her and invited them back to the house for a cup of tea and a bite to eat. Then she walked on ahead with Lila towards the church gate. Once outside they quickened their pace.

'So you're all alone in the world now,' said Lila, her fresh complexion flushed with cold. 'That's so sad.'

'I don't need reminding,' said Emma, turning her coat collar up against the falling snow.

'Sorry,' said Lila meekly. 'It's just that I don't know what to say.'

'You could say nothing.'

'Sorry.'

Emma sighed. 'I'm sorry, too. I don't mean to be rude but you're lucky, you know. You've still got your mam and dad. I know your dad was crippled in the war but at least he's still around.'

'I know, but I wish I'd had grandparents as well. Yours were always so welcoming and your granddad was such a laugh. I wish Mam was not always at me dad when she gets home because of his model-making. It isn't his fault he can't get paid employment and has to occupy his time in some way – and he does get a war pension, so he's not living off her the way she'd have you believe. She really goes on at him sometimes.'

'I know.' Emma heaved another sigh. 'But it's still better than having to live alone. I don't know what I'm going to do without Granddad. The only fault I could find with him and Gran was that they would never talk to me about my dad. When I asked about him, she would just say that she'd hardly known him and he was dead and that was it.'

'It's hard, but at least you can remember your mam,' said Lila.

'Aye, but she didn't talk about him either, and I was only five when she breathed her last – and I can't say my memories of her are happy ones. Frankly, I felt that she resented me,' murmured Emma. 'But then she was really ill. I do remember from a photograph of her when she was young that she was lovely, but I've no idea what my dad looked like. There are no photos of him anywhere, not even on their wedding day.' She sighed. 'After Mam died, I used to try and eavesdrop on Granddad and Gran's conversations to try and find out whether they talked about my parents when I wasn't there, but they never did.'

'Perhaps he was killed in the war,' suggested Lila.

'If he was, then he would have been alive when Mam died in '36 and surely he would have come to the funeral.'

'Perhaps something went wrong with their marriage.'

'It's a real mystery.'

'If your grandparents never talked about him it could have meant that they didn't approve of him,' said Lila.

'Aye, I suppose so, but I think it's also possible he and Mam had a blazing row and he just walked out, never to return. She had a real tongue on her sometimes, didn't want me bothering her when I wanted to be with her and have her tell me a story or to talk about Dad. She took after Gran. I certainly suffered from the sharp edge of Gran's tongue when she was teaching me all she knew about bottling and baking and how to make a proper Lancashire hotpot. Yet I'd still have her back, because I know she loved me despite the way she'd slap my hand if I made a mistake.'

'Mam and Dad might remember your dad,' said Lila, pensively.

Emma shot a glance at her friend's plump, pretty face. 'I never thought of that. Would you ask them for me?'

'Aye, I'll do it when I get home.'

Suddenly, Emma became aware of voices to their rear and realised she and Lila had slowed their pace whilst talking and must hurry up. She needed to get the kettle on. She put on a spurt and instantly Lila protested that she couldn't keep up with her.

'Sorry, but the sooner we get there the sooner it'll be over with,' said Emma. 'I've an awful lot to think about and do now that Granddad's gone. Thank God, he encouraged me to take that correspondence course in bookkeeping, not that I've managed to pick up many clients; it's been a full-time job looking after him and doing all that Gran used to do for the last five years. Still, everything has to change now.'

They arrived at the house and Emma put her hand through the letter box and drew out the key on the string and opened the front door. She ushered Lila inside. The front room had seldom been used since the death of her grandmother and, despite the fire burning in the grate, the air still felt chill. The dark, heavy oak furniture made the room appear even more gloomy on this winter's day and Emma decided to light the candles in the candelabra that the old woman had bought at a house-clearing sale between the wars. The candelabra was of Georgian silver and, when she was eight years old, Emma had been given the job of polishing it weekly. It had always had pride of place on the dinner table every Sunday in her grandmother's day, but unless Emma could find a way of improving her finances, then she would have to take it into Clitheroe and pawn it. It wasn't as if it was a family heirloom, like the embroidered white cotton tablecloth with a crochet border. She would never part with that because it had been made by her great-grandmother Harrison and was only brought out on special occasions such as this one. She sighed, thinking that her grandfather had always enjoyed a good get-together.

At one end of the table Emma had set out crockery and cutlery, and the rest of the space was taken up with plates of sandwiches, pies, scones and cakes – the latter sweetened partially with grated carrot because sugar was still on the ration – all made by Emma, herself. The ingredients had been paid for from her granddad's savings that had been hidden away in a metal box beneath a floorboard in his bedroom.

She hurried through into the shabby kitchen where it was much warmer. She put on the kettle, looking out at the garden. At the moment the hens were providing her with only a few eggs, and the only vegetables were bedraggled-looking sprouts that were swiftly being buried beneath the falling snow. At least all that whiteness outside was reflecting light back into the kitchen.

There was a knock on the front door.

'I'll go,' called Lila.

In no time at all both rooms were crowded with those who well remembered both her grandparents from way back. Folk were told to help themselves to food and tea and Camp coffee. There were only a few men present because it was a working day, but those who were there could be heard discussing whether the weather meant that the football and horse racing would be cancelled. Most of the women had known Emma's grandmother as a faithful member of the Women's Institute and a reliable source of jams, scones and cakes and pickles for various fund-raising events. Several of them asked Emma if she would be leaving the village and seeking a job in nearby Clitheroe. She told them that she had made no plans concerning her future.

'Delicious scones, Emma,' said the vicar's wife. 'I never realised you had such a light touch with pastry.'

Emma flushed with pleasure. 'Gran taught me.'

'Then she taught you well.'

'She not only taught me how to bake, but to preserve and bottle, knit, crochet, and make rugs. It was Granddad, though, who taught me how to play the piano and saw to it that I did a bookkeeping course.'

'Then you'll make some man a good wife one day,' commented the vicar, who was standing at his wife's shoulder.'

His words startled Emma because marriage was something she had not thought about with having to look after her granddad. She was glad that the vicar did not appear to expect a response from her. She had always been rather in awe of him, having had little to do with him over the years, aside from listening to his sermons on a Sunday and shaking his hand at the church door after the service. Even so, he'd been very supportive when it came to discussing the funeral arrangements, and she gave a half-smile before saying wryly, 'I've no one in mind, so I'll need to find more bookkeeping work in order to support myself.'

He smiled. 'Well, if you need a character reference I will happily provide one for you. Your grandparents always spoke well of you and you have proved yourself a loyal granddaughter.'

Strangely, instead of delighting her, his praise made Emma want to go out and do something wild and reckless. But she thanked him and was relieved when he moved away to talk to one of his other parishioners. Shortly after, her guests began to depart and she breathed a sigh when she waved the last one off before going into the kitchen, where she found Lila washing the dishes.

'There's no need for you to do that,' protested Emma. 'I can do it later. Let's have another cup of tea and something to eat.' She'd had the forethought to fill a couple of plates for the pair of them and had placed them on the dresser out of the way; otherwise, what with her having to talk to people and Lila keeping their cups filled, both might have had to forgo food altogether because the buffet had been consumed in no time at all.

They sat down at the table. 'I'm going to have to go home soon,' said Lila. 'Mam wants me to prepare supper with her being at the hospital.' She paused to finish off a sandwich. 'By the way, did I tell you that she was sorry she couldn't get away for the funeral?'

'I didn't expect her to be here. She has a job to do and bosses will only give you time off for funerals if it's family. You could only be here because the mill's closed down for the week.'

Lila's smile faded. 'I'm wondering if it's the beginning of the end and I should start looking for another job. The home market for cotton goods is really slack at the moment and it's not that good abroad either.'

Emma looked at her with concern. 'But it has happened before and things have improved. Don't you think they will this time?'

'I feel as if there's change in the air,' said Lila gloomily. 'There's much more competition since India got its independence and is making its own stuff. And more fabrics are being made from taffeta and nylon these days.'

'Well, let's hope things buck up,' said Emma in a bracing tone, placing another log on the fire. She thought about how the local newspaper had said that the cost of coal was going up by four pence a bag and she wondered how she would keep warm once her coal reserve and her logs ran out. She recalled her granddad telling her that when he'd first started work as a calico printer at the factory in Barrow, coal had been eight pence a hundredweight. Since the war, and what with a Labour government getting voted in, the miners' wages had increased, and rightly so, but it meant the cost of living had gone up again. She wondered what this year would bring now that old Churchill was back as prime minister. She guessed that she was going to have to pray for an early spring.

'So what are you going to do about money?' asked Lila.

'I'll decide that after I've sorted out Granddad's papers. There's loads of stuff in his bedroom. At least he had several insurance policies, though they were only for tuppences, sixpences and one for a shilling a week. Fortunately he made a will after Grandma died and left the cottage to me, so I don't have to worry about having a lawyer to sort things out.'

'I wish I could stay and help you,' said Lila.

'I'll be fine. I'd have to scrutinise everything myself anyway, to make sure I don't miss anything that could be important.'

Emma's gaze was suddenly caught by the cat crawling out from beneath the sofa. It walked stiff-legged towards the fireplace and stretched out on the rag rug and rolled over. At least she was not completely alone in the house but had Tibby for company. Emma bent over and tickled the white fur on the cat's tummy and she purred.

'You're soft with that cat,' said Lila, smiling faintly. 'A dog would have been much better company. You could have taken it for walks and it could have caught you a rabbit for the pot.'

Emma glanced up at her friend. 'She's a good mouser. Besides, cats are more independent. You can't just leave a dog to fend for itself if you have to go away anywhere.'

'I suppose you have something there. Mam would never let me have a pet. But what about the hens? Doesn't she chase the hens?' asked Lila.

'Not since she was pecked a couple of times,' replied Emma, thinking she was going to have to buy some chicken feed if she were to keep the hens. Although, right now she was wondering if she could afford the expense of feeding them. The roof was leaking and the window frames hadn't seen a coat of paint for several years.

Soon after arranging with Lila to meet the following morning, Emma saw her friend out, then she put the kettle on for another cup of tea. She hurried upstairs and hung the black astrakhan coat that had once been her grandmother's in her own wardrobe. It was freezing in the bedroom and she wasted no time carrying the cardboard boxes from her granddad's room downstairs to the kitchen.

She leant over to the wireless perched on a shelf in the alcove next to the fireplace and fiddled with the knobs until she recognised the signature tune of *Workers' Playtime* coming from a factory somewhere in Britain. It was a programme that had started during the war to encourage productivity and still featured famous singers, musicians and comedians of the day. Her granddad had really enjoyed singing along to the music. She felt the tears well up again and this time she allowed herself the luxury of a good cry. Then she mopped her face and drank her cooling tea before turning her attention to the boxes.

Each had a label stuck on with the contents written in her grandmother's neat hand. It had been heart-wrenching watching the old woman slowly succumb to the painful form of arthritis that had eventually affected her heart and killed her, but her grandmother had never complained.

Emma took the top from the old chocolate box with a pair of fluffy white kittens depicted on its lid and soon discovered that the contents were a mishmash of old bills, postcards from various seaside resorts, and letters. Perhaps her granddad had rifled through them after the death of her grandmother and that was why they were in such disorder. The ink had turned to sepia on some of the letters tied up with yellow ribbon. There weren't many of those and they proved to be addressed to 'Ma and Pa'.

As she began to read them Emma realised that they had been penned from the front by her dead uncles during the Great War. She read no further, unable to bear their poignancy. She did not want to dwell on the sadness in her grandparents' lives right now. They had suffered so much, first in losing both their sons and then their only daughter, who had been born late in life to them. It was a relief to turn to the next box which proved to contain

23

more bills going back years to the last century. It was interesting discovering the different prices of goods but she knew that she must not waste time.

She reached for the next box and here she found birth and death certificates, as well as her grandparents' marriage certificate. There was no sign of her parents' marriage certificate or her own birth certificate. What she did find were the deeds to the house, which proved to be an interesting document. Apparently the house had been used as a shop and tea room in her great-grandmother's day.

Emma rose and placed the document on the table, knowing she had to keep it with all the certificates in a safe place. Then she returned to her task of sorting. Now she came across birthday cards, some addressed to her mother, Mary, during her girlhood, others belonging to her grandparents and uncles, and there were several that were addressed to Emma. One was made from stiff card and appeared to have been hand-painted. It was in the form of a number three with tiny teddy bears, dolls, flowers and birds filling up the space. It wished her a happy birthday and was signed *love Daddy* with three kisses.

Her heart seemed to flip over. 'Oh!' she exclaimed, thinking that her father must have made this himself. Had he been here for her third birthday, or had it been sent from somewhere else? There was no envelope. She sat, clutching it against her and wishing she could remember him. What kind of man could make something like this and yet part from his wife and never send his daughter another birthday card?

She rose from the chair to place it on top of the deeds and certificates before continuing with her task, listening with only half an ear to the jokes of Charlie Chester on the wireless. Shortly after, she switched off the programme and made another cup of tea before resuming her place and taking the last box onto her knee.

It was at the very bottom of a pile of old newspapers, one dated 1918 proclaiming that the guns had fallen silent along the front, that she found a single letter. It was dated August 1940 and began *Dear Mrs Harrison* . . .

The address on the top right-hand side was in Liverpool. The paper was stained as if at one time it had been affected by damp and yet the newspapers above it were perfectly dry. Had someone cried over this letter? Her gaze went swiftly to the bottom of the page to the signature of a Mrs Lizzie Booth. Emma's heart gave a peculiar lurch. Could this letter be from her father's mother? She began to read its contents and soon realised her mistake.

Dear Mrs Harrison,
    This will be the last time I will write to you, if I receive no reply to this letter.

Perhaps you are no longer living at this address but I would have thought if that was so, then the new tenants would have returned my husband's letters, as well as mine. But perhaps you have received them and chosen to ignore them. But what I have to say now concerns my husband's daughter, Emma. I am sorry to inform you that William was killed at Dunkirk.

Emma had to pause and take several deep breaths before rereading that last sentence again and continuing.

In his final letter to me he asked that I try once more to persuade you to allow Emma to have some contact with us. He so wanted his two girls to grow up knowing each other. Is that too much to ask? I beg you not to ignore this letter. I am certain that it would be of benefit to Emma to get in touch with me and for her to meet my daughter Betty.
Yours sincerely,
Mrs Lizzie Booth

Emma reread the letter twice through a blur of tears. So it was true that her father was dead! How long after her mother's death had he married again? How old was her half-sister? Perhaps it had been one of those quick wartime weddings. Yet it seemed her father had not forgotten about Emma after all and had wanted to see her again. Why had her grandmother kept this information from her? His widow must have badly wanted to fulfil his last wishes if she had persisted in writing to this address despite her previous letters being ignored.

Emma felt hurt and angry, believing it was too late now to do anything about it. She wondered if her granddad had known about the letters. Somehow, she thought not. With trembling fingers she folded the letter before putting it on top of the birthday card her father had sent her. Or was it too late? Aye, it was too late to get to know her father but perhaps it was not too late to meet her half-sister and stepmother. Maybe that was why her grandmother had not destroyed the letter but had intended her to find it one day?

Emma knew that she could not ignore her discovery. How odd it felt thinking about having a stepmother. It reminded her of those stepmothers mentioned in fairy tales. Yet the little she knew about Lizzie Booth from reading her letter convinced Emma that she was in no way similar to the wicked stepmothers in *Cinderella* or *Snow White and the Seven Dwarfs*.

A faint smile twisted Emma's lips. It was possible that Lizzie Booth had given no more thought to her when she had not received a reply to this letter. But what if she had not forgotten her? What if Emma went to visit the address in Liverpool and explained matters to her? She felt a stir of excitement as well as trepidation at the thought of visiting the city. The furthest she had ever travelled was to the Lake District and Blackpool, and always in the company of her grandparents.

Of course, it would cost money to go to Liverpool. Could she afford the trip? Probably not, and yet she felt that she must go. She glanced towards the window and saw that the snow was still falling. Obviously it would be sensible to wait until the weather improved. It might also be a good idea to talk to Lila's parents about her mother and father before making the journey to Lancashire's premier port.

CHAPTER TWO

The next day when Lila called round to the house, Emma asked her whether she had mentioned her father to her parents. 'I did as it happens,' said Lila, smiling.

'What did they say?' asked Emma eagerly.

'Mam said that your da', William Booth, was a handsome devil and could charm the birds from the trees. Apparently he spoke just like them announcers on the wireless. He never actually lived here, you know.' Lila's grey-blue eyes sparkled with enjoyment at dropping this gem of information. 'Although, it turns out that his great-grandparents were from this area. They were married in the parish church but lived up the hill in Wiswell. When

29

the mill at Barrow closed down for a while during the last century, they left in search of work and they ended up in Liverpool.'

Emma was stunned. 'So my dad came from Liverpool?'

'Apparently.'

Emma was silent, thinking about her stepmother's letter. 'I've met a few Scousers on the fells and they certainly didn't talk BBC English.'

'There are bound to be posh areas in Liverpool as well as slums,' said Lila. 'Think of shipowners, doctors and the like.'

'Even so,' muttered Emma, frowning. 'How would an ex-mill worker make enough money in the big city in Victorian times to end up speaking posh? Anyway, Gran and Granddad Harrison certainly weren't well off.'

'Your granddad owned this cottage, so he wasn't on his uppers.'

'No, but it was left to him, and Granddad had to continue working until he was an old man and he didn't have that much in the way of savings. He had to eke out his money with living so long.' She gnawed on her lip, digesting this new information. 'If my dad was from Liverpool, I wonder how he and Mam met? Did your mam say?'

'She was a bit reticent about that. I mean, I think she would have told me if Dad hadn't given her a look.'

Emma pondered on that nugget of information and then said firmly, 'I must talk to your parents. I found something yesterday and I'd appreciate their thoughts on what I've discovered.'

Lila smiled. 'Well, you're in luck. Mam's changed shifts and will be home this afternoon.'

'I'm made up about that,' said Emma, her eyes lighting up. 'I'll get my coat.'

'What did you find by the way?' asked Lila curiously, watching her friend put on the Great War-style black astrakhan coat trimmed with rabbit fur over the shop-bought black jumper and skimpy black skirt that Emma had bought for the funeral of her grandmother. Lila knew that her friend had not had any new clothes since then, although she was not alone in that. Their families had all had to make do and mend during the war and its aftermath.

'A letter from my stepmother.'

Lila's jaw dropped. 'What stepmother?'

Emma glanced at her over her shoulder. 'The one my dad married after my mother died and who lives in Liverpool with my half-sister.'

'Blinking heck, Em, I'm sure Mam doesn't know anything about a stepmother. What was she doing writing to you?'

Emma pulled on her black beret and flicked back her chestnut hair. 'She wrote to Gran, telling her that my dad was killed at Dunkirk. By the sound of it she and Dad had written before and their letters had been ignored. Apparently my dad wanted his daughters to grow up knowing each other.'

'Blinking heck, who'd have believed it!'

'I'm thinking of going to Liverpool to look them up.' Emma reached for her bag and put it over her shoulder.

'I'd do the same if I were in your shoes,' said Lila, almost enviously.

'There's the cost of the fare, of course,' said Emma, grimacing. 'So perhaps it would be more sensible just to write to her.'

'But it's an adventure, Em! Just think of going all the way to Liverpool! I wouldn't mind going there myself, only me mam and dad wouldn't let me.'

'Then in that case, your mam's hardly likely to encourage me to go,' said Emma dryly.

Lila puffed out her rosy cheeks and then let out a long breath. 'It's different for you. You're going to see relatives, not just to have fun.'

'You're right. I'll see what your mother has to say,' decided Emma, 'although we're both old enough to do what we please.'

'I know we are but it's difficult to go against your parents when they've brought you up and you're their only chick,' said Lila.

As they trudged through the snow along the road in the direction of Wiswell, both girls were silent. Emma was conscious of the beauty of the surrounding countryside. She tried to imagine what it must be like living in a bustling, crowded, smoky city without a field or hill in sight and where people were strangers to each other, but she found it difficult because it was beyond her experience.

At last they arrived at the Ashcrofts' house and Emma could see Lila's father's face at the window. Pity for him touched her heart. He seldom went outside the house because he had difficulty walking. They went inside and he gave Emma a nod. She murmured a greeting and hung her coat over the back of a chair and sat down whilst Lila went in search of her mother.

Emma glanced about the overcrowded room at the various knick-knacks and wooden models set on every available surface before her gaze came to rest on Mr Ashcroft again. He now seemed completely unaware of her presence and she watched his slender fingers working with glue and matchsticks. He spent most of his days either gazing out of the window or making models from matchsticks whilst listening to music on the wireless. A cigarette smouldered in an ashtray at his elbow.

Emma thought his models were brilliant but Lila had told her that her mother was getting fed up of them, complaining that they would soon be running out of space to display them. Right now it appeared he was making a model of the nearby ruined abbey before it had fallen victim to Henry VIII's dissolution of the monasteries. At the moment the model was a creation of delicate tracery and beauty. There was a box of matches on the coffee table close to hand and Emma picked it up to see how many there were left in it.

'So, Emma, Lila tells me you want to speak to me,' said a woman's voice, startling her so that the box of matches slipped from her fingers and disappeared from sight.

Emma looked up and saw Mrs Ashcroft standing in the doorway, wiping her hands on a dishcloth. Her hair was several shades darker than her daughter's and she had determined, strong features with a hooked nose.

'That's right. What's Lila told you?' asked Emma in a rush.

'Apparently you've got a stepmother and a younger half-sister living in Liverpool. Well, I know what I'd do, lass, I'd stay where you are. I've only been to Liverpool twice in my life. Once to catch the Isle of Man ferry to go on my honeymoon and secondly to meet the troopship that brought Jack here home from Burma. It's noisy, dirty and there's so many people you wouldn't believe it. There's prostitutes, thieves and drunks staggering about, aside from the sailors from all parts of the world. It's not the kind of place for a well-brought-up country girl, as your mother—' She stopped abruptly.

'What were you going to say about my mother?' asked Emma swiftly.

'I didn't intend saying anything,' said Mrs Ashcroft, sitting down in a chair. 'But now I've started I suppose I'd better tell you.'

'Jane!' Mr Ashcroft gave his wife a warning look.

'It's too late for that, Jack,' she said. 'Emma should have been told years ago and then it wouldn't come as a shock to her.'

'What should I have been told?' asked Emma, paling. 'Is it that my parents weren't married and that I'm-I'm—'

'Of course not!' said Mrs Ashcroft, looking shocked. 'I was going to say that your mam ran away to Liverpool when she was only eighteen, and when she came back it was with you and she was already suffering from the consumption that would kill her. I will add that she was wearing a wedding ring, as well as a lovely diamond-and-emerald engagement ring.'

Emma's shoulders sagged with relief. 'So I'm not a bastard child.'

Mrs Ashcroft clicked her tongue against her teeth. 'No need to use that word in this house, but you understand, Emma, why you're best staying away from such a sinful place.'

'Surely there must be some decent people there?' protested Emma. 'Lila told me that you met my father and that he spoke posh.'

'Of course there are decent people there, but

how will you be able to judge which ones they are when you've had no experience of life in the big city? You could end up in trouble.'

'Stop frightening the lass, Jane,' said Mr Ashcroft. 'Liverpool's not as bad as you make it sound and at least she'll find plenty of life there. I met several Scousers in the army and I got on with them OK. We used to have a good laugh, despite them coming from a poor background.'

'You're a man and so it's different for you,' said his wife scornfully. 'Emma might be twenty-one but she's an innocent girl. So there is life in Liverpool, but it's not the kind of life Emma's used to. Her mother, Mary, soon found that out when she started mixing with actors, artists and musicians and the like.'

'You make it sound like Sodom and Gomorrah,' said Mr Ashcroft. 'It's a city like any other and there's talent there. The comedian, Arthur Askey, came from Liverpool and so did John Gregson, the actor, and Tommy Handley from *ITMA* on the radio. You should let the girl find out for herself what it's like.'

His wife's lips thinned. 'She'll regret going there if she does. Mark my words,' she said darkly. 'Her grandmother would have wanted her to have nothing to do with her father's second wife and daughter, otherwise she would have told Emma about them.'

'Be that as it may,' said Mr Ashcroft, his lean face stern. 'Her grandparents are dead and the lass needs to learn to make her own decisions.'

'Thank you, Mr Ashcroft, for your advice,' said Emma, despite feeling inadequate to make grown-up decisions after all that his wife had said. 'And you too, Mrs Ashcroft,' she added hastily. 'But what did you mean when you said that my mother mixed with actors, artists and musicians?'

'I'd rather not talk about it but I suppose I must,' said Jane Ashcroft, folding her arms beneath her bosom.

Mr Ashcroft swore beneath his breath.

His wife glared at him and then turned back to Emma. 'Your father being an artist wasn't of any use at all to your mother. I'm sure nobody was buying paintings during the Depression.'

'But you said that she had a lovely engagement ring,' protested Emma. 'He must have earned some money.'

'Maybe he did but your mother ended up having to sell that ring.'

'But my father must have had some talent,' insisted Emma. 'I found a lovely birthday card from him that was hand-painted. You met him and so he must have visited my grandparents' cottage.'

'But he didn't stay, did he?' said Mrs Ashcroft. 'Forget about him, Emma. He's dead and picking over the past will do you no good.'

Emma found her fists clenching. 'Why did my mother leave him and come back here with me? I know she was ill but—'

'Perhaps she realised her mistake in marrying him. He was a charmer, as I told our Lila, but it was your grandmother who cared for you and Mary in her final days. Your mother knew she'd be forgiven just like the prodigal son because your grandparents were good, caring Christians. You should let that be the end of it. After all, he mustn't have wasted much time finding someone else if he had another child before he was killed at Dunkirk.'

'Enough, Jane,' warned Mr Ashcroft. 'One would think you had something against the man. Now, put the kettle on and make the lass a cup of tea before she has to go out in the cold again.'

'It doesn't matter, Mr Ashcroft,' said Emma in a low voice, shrugging on her coat. 'I'll have a cup of tea when I get home. Right now I need time to think, so I'll go now and see you again sometime.' She left the room.

Lila hurried after her. 'I'm sorry about that, Emma. Mam really sounded like she had a knife in your dad. I can only think it's because she knew your mother well before she ran away to Liverpool.'

'Maybe that was it,' said Emma, her face serious. 'As it is I've learnt quite a bit about my parents this afternoon.' She tucked her scarf inside her coat. 'I'll see you soon.'

She opened the front door and went outside. Before she had set foot inside the Ashcrofts' house, she had been dithering about going to Liverpool because of the expense. Now she was determined to see her stepmother and half-sister. Surely Lizzie Booth would be able to provide her with some answers about her parents? After all, her father must have talked to her about his first marriage for her to know about Emma. She would wait until the insurance companies paid out what was due to her from her granddad's policies and the snow was all gone before making a move. In the meantime she would need to find more bookkeeping work in order to support herself.

CHAPTER THREE

It was almost three weeks since Emma's visit to the Ashcrofts' house and she still had not made up her mind about when to visit Liverpool. She had thought much about what her grandmother's feelings would be if she were alive and concluded that her reasons for preventing Emma from going to Liverpool no longer existed. Obviously the old woman had feared that if Emma had known the truth, then she might have followed in her mother's footsteps and built herself a life in Liverpool and stayed there.

There came a sudden hammering on the door and Emma lifted her gaze from the numbers on the page of the open ledger and dropped her pencil. The noise had a pattern to it that she recognised and, pushing back her chair, she hurried through into the front room and opened the door. As she had expected, Lila stood on the step.

'What's all the commotion?' asked Emma.

'The king's dead!' Lila's pretty plump face was flushed and her grey-blue eyes were shiny with tears.

Emma sighed. 'I know. It was on the wireless.' She beckoned Lila inside.

'I feel really upset. In fact, everyone I've spoken to is upset,' said Lila, going through into the kitchen. She was about to sit down in front of the fire when she noticed hanks of wool on the chair. 'Where's that come from?'

'I found it in a cupboard upstairs in my grandparents' old bedroom. Gran must have bought it at a bargain price but never got round to using it.' Emma gathered up the multicoloured wool and moved it to the table. 'I thought I'd use it up,' she added.

'You know what the king dying means,' said Lila, sitting down in the chair. 'Change.'

'Obviously. Granddad always said the king was a man who knew his duty, unlike his brother who was born to the role.' Emma put on the kettle. 'King George stuck by us throughout the war, when he and the queen could have easily gone to Canada with the princesses.'

'The queen's not the queen anymore, Princess Elizabeth is. She's already on her way home from Africa with the Duke of Edinburgh. Imagine how she must be feeling with having been so far away when her father died. She'll want to be with her family right now. It's at times like these that you need your family around you.' Lila dabbed at her eyes as her tears welled up again.

Emma thought of her half-sister and stepmother. She still hadn't done anything about contacting them but Lila's words caused her to wonder whether her father had brothers and sisters. Maybe they were still alive! And what about her stepmother, she must have family somewhere?

'Princess Elizabeth is going to have little time alone to mourn her father with her having to fill his shoes,' mused Lila, leaning back in the chair. 'I wonder what kind of queen she'll make?' Her face brightened. 'There'll be a coronation, and that means parties.'

Emma nodded, just able to remember King George VI's coronation the year after her mother died. There had been parties and she still had a commemorative mug on the dresser. 'A coronation will take time to arrange because they'll be inviting heads of state from all over the Empire as well as other countries,' she said.

'Most of them will probably have to attend the king's funeral, as well,' said Lila. 'You can bet there'll be a lying-in-state for people to go and pay their respects.'

'But that'll be in London and all the newspapers will be full of it,' said Emma, her expression thoughtful. 'I might be best leaving putting an advertisement for bookkeeping work in the *Clitheroe Advertiser and Times* until the king's funeral is over. In the meantime I think I'll go to Liverpool. I might also buy myself a new outfit in the new midi style. I want to make a good impression and the blacks I have are so shabby. A new coat is out of the question but I think I must have a new frock.'

Lila's eyes widened. 'So you're definitely going to go?'

Emma nodded. 'Death can come so suddenly. Think of Granddad! What if my half-sister were to die before I got the chance to meet her because I delayed trying to find her?'

'But she's younger than you,' said Lila. 'You're being really cheerful.'

'We both know that the young can die as well. Remember Joan who died of scarlet fever?'

'Aye, and I also remember Mam telling me about an outbreak of diphtheria that killed hundreds of children.'

'Thank goodness, a vaccine was discovered that's saved thousands of children's lives,' said Emma.

Lila agreed. 'What will you do if your stepmother

43

asks you to live with them?' she asked.

Emma shook her head. 'I can't see that happening. Besides, my home is here.'

Lila looked relieved. 'I'm glad you feel like that, because you're my best friend and I'd miss you.'

Emma smiled. 'I'd miss you, too. Besides there's a possibility that we mightn't hit it off.'

'But you might, and if that was the case then you'd want to see more of them,' said Lila.

'Probably, but my doing so would all depend on how often I'd be able to afford to travel to Liverpool.'

'Or them coming here. I would love to get a peek at your half-sister and see if she looks like you,' said Lila.

Emma removed the steaming kettle from the stove. 'There's a thought,' she murmured.

Lila sighed. 'I envy you making your own decisions. I really should be sticking up for myself and doing what I want instead of doing what Mam wants all the time.'

'But you can't be doing that while things are so uncertain at the mill. Unless you find yourself a husband, of course,' Emma added with a smile.

'Mam's always discouraged me from having a boyfriend.' Lila grimaced. 'Perhaps I should start looking for another job in Clitheroe and I might meet someone there. But in the meantime, do you want to go to the pictures tonight? *The Man in Grey* is on, with James Mason and Margaret Lockwood. I love him. He has a real menacing air about him and sends a shiver down me spine. So what d'you say?'

'OK! But it'll probably be the last time for a while,' said Emma.

CHAPTER FOUR

Emma hitched her bag higher on her shoulder and stepped down off the train in Lime Street station. Jostled by other passengers as they forced their way past her in their haste to get to the ticket barrier first, she was spun round and felt her bag slide down her arm. She felt disorientated, what with the noise of hissing steam from the engine, the voice over the Tannoy announcing the time of the train to London, hurrying feet and people calling to each other. Then suddenly she realised her shoulder bag had gone and her heart began to bang inside her chest.

'Don't panic, don't panic,' she whispered to herself. 'It's probably on the ground.'

She stood stock-still and dropped her gaze, but her bag was not there and people were beginning to swerve to avoid her. One man swore, telling her to get out of the bloody way. Hurriedly she stepped aside and moved towards the edge of the platform, wondering if her bag had been kicked into the gap between the train and the edge. She knelt down but could see no sign of it. Could someone have snatched it? Her purse, hanky, library book and the letter from Lizzie Booth were inside it; her heart sank. At least there was not much money in her purse, but even so . . .

Emma felt sick as she rose to her feet and stood, dithering, trying to make up her mind what to do. This was a really bad start to her trip to Liverpool and she could not help recalling Mrs Ashcroft's warning. Fortunately her return ticket was in her coat pocket. She looked towards the barrier and beyond to where high upon a wall was an advertisement for Taveners Fruit Drops and a huge clock, the hands of which stood at a couple of minutes past eleven o'clock. There was nothing stopping her from going home right now. Yet she was reluctant to do so after all the effort she had made to get here. She tried to cheer herself up by thinking that her bag might have been kicked along the platform and someone had picked it up and handed it in at the lost property office.

Her spirits rose slightly and she headed in

the direction of the ticket barrier and there she told the ticket collector what had happened. He commiserated with her but told her bluntly that he doubted she would get it back. Still, he directed her to the lost property office before turning to the next passenger waiting to get through the barrier.

Emma soon discovered that no shoulder bag answering to her description had been handed in and, feeling down in the dumps, she turned away. Oddly, her thoughts now were of her mother and she wondered how she had coped in this huge, bustling station when she had come to Liverpool all alone. Had she already known someone in the city? Perhaps someone she had met walking on the fells. Maybe Emma's father on Pendle Hill? Had she fallen in love at first sight with him and followed him here? The thought of her parents meeting in such a way caused Emma to feel quite emotional.

'Yous all right, queen?' asked a voice.

Emma lifted her head and brushed away a tear with the back of her hand and turned to regard the owner of the voice.

The woman was wearing a figure-hugging red suit that had seen better days and a tatty white fur hat. Her make-up had been applied in a slapdash fashion, so that she looked a bit of a clown. Emma knew there was no way she could explain to her the real reason why she had felt so terribly sad all of a sudden. Instead she said in a trembling voice, 'My bag's been stolen.'

'Shame. Some people have no conscience,' said the woman, who smelt of drink but had kind eyes. 'Lost everythin', have yer?'

'I've still got my ticket home because I had that in my pocket, but I came here for a special purpose and don't want to go home yet.'

'I gathered yer weren't from round here. Woolly back, aren't yer? I had an aunt who lived up Blackburn way and she spoke just like yous.'

'I was born here, though,' said Emma swiftly. 'My dad was from Liverpool but he was killed in the war.'

The woman heaved a sigh. 'So was my fella. So where were yer aiming for, queen?'

'I came here to find my half-sister. I had a letter with the address on but that's gone, too.' Emma sighed.

'Can't you remember where it is?' asked the woman.

'Oh aye! It was Whitefield Road,' she replied.

The woman smiled. 'Ha! Yer'll need to get a tram or a bus that goes up West Derby Road past the Grafton dance hall and the Palladium picture house. Ask the conductor to put yer off at Ogden's tobacco factory.'

Emma squared her shoulders. 'I've no money, so

I'll have to walk there. Can you tell me which is the quickest way to go?'

'It's a bit of a walk, girl, and yer could get lost. It's getting a bit foggy outside.' The woman screwed up her face and dug into her pocket and produced a sixpence. 'Here yer are, queen, have this one on me.'

Emma stared at the coin on the grubby, white-gloved hand and was touched by the gesture. 'I can't take your money.'

'Why not? My money not good enough for yer?' said the woman belligerently, jutting out her chin.

'It's not that,' said Emma hastily. 'I-it just seems wrong. You don't look like you have much money to spare.'

The woman smiled. 'Looks can be deceptive, queen.' She took Emma's hand and pressed the sixpence into her palm.

Emma returned her smile and thought of fairy godmothers in disguise. 'Thanks. I really appreciate this.'

'Glad to hear it. Yer can get the number 12 bus in Lime Street or the 11 tram. Just cross the road. They stop in front of the lions guarding St George's Hall.' She jerked a thumb. 'Just go that way. You can't miss it.'

Emma thanked her again and headed off in that direction. Although still upset about her bag being stolen, her spirits were lifted by the woman's kindness, which belied what Mrs Ashcroft had said about the citizens of Liverpool. She only hoped that when she reached her stepmother's house she would receive a warm welcome there, too.

As Emma came out onto Lime Street, across the road she saw a blackened building that reminded her of the Roman or Greek temples depicted in her children's encyclopaedia. Spotting the lions the woman had mentioned on their plinths, she waited for a gap in the traffic in order to cross the road. She stood there for what seemed ages, hovering on the pavement, not prepared to take her life in her hands like some people who darted between vans, cars, buses and trams. Then she saw several people gathered on the kerb together, and as they swooshed forward onto the road, she decided to go with them.

On reaching the other side she joined a queue at a bus stop, aware of a feeling of nervous exhilaration. What if she got on the wrong tram or bus and ended up getting lost with only a couple of pennies to her name? Then a number 12 bus came along and she had no trouble getting on it. She found a seat downstairs and soon found herself having to repeat her destination several times to the conductor. He was obviously having some difficulty understanding her accent. Eventually he must have got the gist of what she was saying and told her that he'd give her a nod when it was time for her to get off.

She wiped a hole in the condensation on the window with her glove in an attempt to see the route the bus was taking, only to discover she could see very little. Still, there was no going back now she had come this far.

On leaving the bus, the conductor pointed her in the direction she should go. Fortunately she was not alone and followed in the wake of several other people along a cobbled lane. A large red-brick building loomed up on her left but she could see only a few yards ahead. The fog appeared to be getting thicker. Perhaps she should turn right round and go back into the city centre. What if she really did get lost?

Eventually she came to the end of the lane and was faced with a road going in two directions as well as another road that forked off the main one. She stood for several minutes, filled with indecision. Then she saw a woman, wearing a mackintosh and a headscarf, come out of a street and hurry in her direction.

'Is this Whitefield Road?' called Emma.

'What's that you're saying, girl?'

Emma repeated the question and the woman nodded. Then she disappeared into the fog. Emma crossed the slippery cobbles to the other side of the road, where she noticed a pub and a shop next to an open space and then a street called Rothwell Street. She crossed to the other side of it and walked along the pavement, peering at numbers above shop doors that were firmly closed against the weather. At least she appeared to be going in the right direction if the numbers were anything to go by, she thought. She passed a couple more streets, called Harewood and St Albans, and came to a row of long gardens with walls and gateposts but no gates. She could see what she assumed were houses looming through the fog.

Emma's heart lifted as she came to the number on Lizzie Booth's letter. She walked between gateposts and up a path that was uneven and slippery underfoot. The next moment she went flying and all the breath was knocked out of her. She lay gasping, unable to move. Then she tried to get to her feet, only to almost faint because of the pain in her foot and ankle. Emma waited until the world steadied before looking to see what had caused her fall. She noticed that the path was broken in places and moss and tufts of dead-looking grass had taken root in the cracks.

Now she was closer to the house, she could see that the front door was boarded up and so was the ground floor window. She could have screamed after coming all this way to discover that the house was derelict. She tried to get up again but the pain was so bad that she sank to the ground once more, unable to put her weight on her foot. Now she really did have a reason to panic. Were people living in the other houses? Would they hear her if she cried out? Of course, there were shops nearby but they were definitely too far away to hear her shout for help. Yet surely someone was bound to pass this way sooner or later, so she should try. This she did, but the fog seemed to simply swallow up the sound of her voice and no one came.

She was really beginning to panic now because she could feel the damp seeping through her clothing. She must try and get up. If she could reach the gatepost and lean against it, she was more likely to be seen by a passer-by. She managed to stand but still could not put any weight on her damaged ankle. Her eyes tried to pierce the curtain of grey but all she could see was a stunted tree not far from one of the gateposts. She wobbled and stretched out her arms to help her keep her balance. What if nobody came and she ended up freezing to death? She shouted again until she was hoarse and beginning to feel quite desperate.

Then suddenly she heard a mournful wailing and a cold trickle of fear ran down her spine. What if the house behind her was haunted? She remembered that Liverpool had been bombed during the war. Could her half-sister and stepmother have been killed? Regret, disappointment and sadness mingled with her fear at the thought that she would never meet them.

She shivered and dug her hands into her

pockets. Instantly her fingers made contact with a box of matches. How had they got there? She remembered the story of *The Little Match Girl* that her granddad had told her when she was small. That little girl had been out in the snow and had kept lighting the matches to warm herself. In the end she had died after having a vision of her grandmother in heaven.

Emma began to strike the matches and at the same time to try and call for help. When a male voice shouted, 'Where are you?' she almost jumped out of her skin.

'I'm in the garden of this derelict house,' she croaked. 'I've hurt my ankle and can't walk.'

'Stay where you are!' ordered the voice.

Emma thought that was a daft thing to say when she'd just told him that she couldn't walk. She remembered Mrs Ashcroft's words and thought how vulnerable she was to attack right now. Then a figure loomed up through the fog and she realised that it belonged to a very tall policeman.

'What on earth are you doing in here, miss?' he asked, gazing down at her.

'I came in search of my stepmother and half-sister who used to live here. I didn't know the house was derelict,' she replied, tilting her head so she could see his face.

'You're not from around here, are you?' he said, offering her his arm.

'No.' She reached out to him but lost her balance and yelped with pain as she fell against him.

The next moment he had swung her up into his arms. 'I think it'll be easier if I carry you. Put your arm around my neck and hang on.'

She would have preferred to stand on her own two feet but knew it would be stupid to say so in the circumstances. 'Y-you're not taking me to the police station, are you? I haven't done anything wrong.'

He grinned. 'First stop, the newsagent's nearby. Need to get a bit of light on you and have a look at that ankle. Mr Mason also has a telephone if I need to make any calls.'

'Thank you,' she said shyly, 'but I really don't want to go to hospital.'

'Who said anything about hospitals? I doubt we'd get an ambulance coming out in this weather,' he said. 'Besides, it could be just a twisted ankle or a sprain and I can deal with that.'

She clung to him as he carried her to the block of shops the other side of St Albans. It was a relief to get indoors out of the cold. She found herself being stared at by the man behind the counter. 'Sweeping girls off their feet now, Constable,' he said, pausing in his task of placing packets of Woodbines on a shelf.

'Very funny,' said the policeman, not sounding amused at all. 'Where's the chair you generally keep here?'

56

Mr Mason did not answer but lifted a chair over the counter and allowed it to slide slowly from his hands onto the floor. 'What's happened to her? Who is she? Haven't seen her round here before.'

'That's because she's from somewhere else,' said the constable, lowering Emma onto the chair.

She sighed with relief and was now able to get a proper look at her rescuer. He appeared to be in his early twenties, and whilst not exactly having the looks of a matinee film idol, he was good-looking and had the bluest eyes she had ever seen. Her heart seemed to flip over as he met her gaze and she lowered her eyes swiftly to her swollen ankle. 'I'm not going to be able to get my shoe off,' she said in dismay.

'You'll have to, miss. I've done a first aid course and would like to have a butcher's at your ankle and foot and then put it in cold water. That should help to get the swelling down.' He glanced at the shopkeeper. 'What about it, Mr Mason? Can you fetch a bowl of cold water for the young lady?'

'Certainly. As long as there's no mess made on my shop floor.' The newsagent disappeared through a curtained doorway into the back.

The constable removed his helmet, revealing fair hair cut in a neat back and sides. After placing his headgear on the counter, he lowered himself onto one knee and took Emma's foot into his hands.

'Now, scream if I hurt you,' he said.

Emma thought if he had intended raising a smile from her, then he had succeeded. 'I'll try not to.'

He glanced up at her and grinned. 'I'm glad you haven't lost your sense of humour. So what's your name and where d'you come from?'

'My name's Emma Booth and I live in a village near Clitheroe. I came in search of my stepmother and half-sister as I mentioned to you earlier. The last address I had for them was that derelict house.' She drew in her breath with a hiss as he eased off her shoe.

'So you mean to tell me that you've come all the way from by Pendle Hill to find them?' His fingers moved gently over her ankle and foot.

She trembled with the effort of not crying out and gasped, 'You know it?'

'Lovely scenery. Good walking country. I think you've only sprained it but I'll know better after the swelling's gone down.' He placed her foot on the floor. 'The house of the garden you were in didn't receive a direct hit, from what I remember being told, but was caught in a bomb blast.'

'Are you saying that those inside might not have been killed?' asked Emma eagerly.

'Could be.' He straightened up. 'I don't come from round here and I wasn't a policeman during the Blitz.'

She gazed up at him with a hopeful expression

on her face. 'C-can you help me find out what happened to them?'

He rubbed his nose. 'I suppose I can try. Tell me their names.'

Her spirits rose. 'My stepmother was a Mrs Lizzie Booth and her daughter's name was Betty Booth. I've never actually met them. My mother died before the war and my father remarried, only to be killed at Dunkirk. My grandparents brought me up and now they're dead.'

'Tough luck! My dad was killed at El Alamein.'

Before she could commiserate, there came footsteps and a voice said, 'Here's your water, Constable. How's it looking?'

'Well, she's not going to start quickstepping around the Grafton dance floor any minute now,' he replied, taking the bowl from Mr Mason and putting it on the floor. 'Now, Miss Booth, you're going to have to take off your stocking if you're to place your foot in here.' He indicated the bowl on the floor. 'Mr Mason and I will look away.'

'Thank you,' murmured Emma, blushing as she hastened to undo her suspender button and remove her stocking. She gritted her teeth against the pain as she did so and then gasped at the coldness of the water as she placed her foot in it.

The policeman turned his head and watched for a few moments before speaking to the shopkeeper in a low voice. Emma attempted to wriggle her toes, which proved difficult, and wondered how long she was expected to keep her foot in the water. How was she to get home? She should never have come to Liverpool but stayed safely in her cottage, thought Emma, feeling woebegone.

The constable's voice interrupted her thoughts and she looked up at him, thinking again what lovely blue eyes he had. 'I've asked Mr Mason here, Miss Booth, if he remembers your stepmother and her daughter but he wasn't here during the war,' said the constable, adding gently, 'It is eleven years since the Blitz in Liverpool.'

'I realise that now but I just didn't think about Liverpool having been bombed before I set out,' said Emma, withdrawing her foot from the water, only to submerge it again when the policeman raised his eyebrows. 'I should have stayed at home,' she said gloomily. 'My bag was stolen with my purse in it as soon as I set foot in Liverpool and now this had to happen.' Her voice shook.

'It's not your day, is it, Miss Booth?' said Mr Mason, shaking his head.

'That's an understatement if ever I heard one,' muttered the constable. 'I tell you what, Miss Booth. When you feel able to make a move, I'll take you to the police station. You can report the theft officially and we'll see what we can do to get your bag back.'

'I doubt you'll be able to get it back,' said Emma,

grimacing. 'How far is it to the police station?'

'A mile or so. I have my bike locked up not far away. I'll be off duty soon and can fetch it and give you a ride there. It'll be warm in the station and you can have a nice cup of tea and a bite to eat. I'll strap up your foot and then we'll sort out how to get you back home.'

Emma was not going to argue with him, despite wondering how she was going to stand when her ankle still hurt and her foot was half-dead with cold. Perhaps he would sweep her off her feet again. The thought brought a flush to her cheeks and a warmth to her body. She could only mumble how much she appreciated all he had done for her. She told herself that he was only doing his duty but she had never received so much attention from an attractive young man before and was rather looking forward to a ride on his motorbike.

An hour or so later, when Emma caught sight of the constable's bike, she was lost for words because it proved to be only a pushbike. She did not have the nerve to ask how she was supposed to get comfortable on it as he lifted her up onto the crossbar. Whilst she clasped her shoe and stocking with one trembling hand and the bar with the other, he swung up into the saddle and pushed off from the kerb. The bike swayed and Emma almost dropped her shoe as she made a grab for his tunic. His front lamp sent a shaft of light through the fog and she clung to him with her heart in her mouth as he pedalled off down the road into what she thought of as 'the Unknown'. Presumably he knew exactly where he was going, but she could not help wondering what would happen to them both if they were to crash into a vehicle. Was what he was doing legal? She felt even more anxious when they reached the end of the road and she could see lights from moving vehicles shining through the fog.

To her relief he dismounted but kept a hand on her back to steady her as he waited for an opening in the traffic. Then he ran with his bike to the other side of the road, whilst she prayed fervently that a vehicle wouldn't suddenly appear out of the fog and hit them.

When he mounted the bike again, it occurred to Emma to question whether he did this kind of thing often. He seemed quite competent, so perhaps she should stop worrying and have some faith in him. They spun round a corner and then suddenly he was pedalling smoothly and humming a tune beneath his breath. It took her only a couple of moments to realise that the song was 'A Bicycle Made for Two'. If the day had not already begun to take on a dreamlike quality it would have done so then. Never mind what Mrs Ashcroft might think of such antics, what would her grandparents have had to say about her riding through the fog on a policeman's crossbar? She felt a giggle rising up inside her, reckoning that if her granddad had still been alive and she had told him of the events of her day in Liverpool, then he would have said that there had been some real dramatic moments. Perhaps she should relax. No doubt once she returned to her village, life would resume its usual humdrum routine.

Emma sat in front of a roaring coal fire with a steaming cup of tea in one hand and a sausage butty in the other. Her foot was propped up on a stool, and as she alternately sipped the tea and took bites from the butty, she was mesmerised by the flickering flames in the fireplace. She was glad of this moment alone. Her ankle felt so much better now and she was able to wriggle her toes and rotate her foot a little, despite it still being painful.

The door opened and the constable entered. From a conversation she had heard earlier between him and the desk sergeant, she now knew that his name was Dougie Marshall. 'So, Miss Booth, how are you feeling now?' he asked, smiling down at her.

Emma felt a flutter in the region of her heart and was glad she had bought a new frock. It was of black broadcloth with a detachable pleated white gilet and a black tie and there was plenty of material in the skirt. 'Much better now, thank you.' She wanted to add that she didn't know what she'd have done without him. If he hadn't come along and rescued her she might have frozen to death. He was her hero! But she felt too shy to say so.

What she did say was, 'I-I'm wondering what happens next. I have my return ticket home but I think I might find it difficult getting on and off the different trains. And what about my stepmother and my half-sister? Do you think you'll be able to find out what happened to them?'

'I'll certainly try,' said Dougie. 'Some of the locals might be able to help out. Leave it with me and I'll see what I can do. You said that your stepmother's name was Lizzie Booth?'

She thought what a good memory he had. 'That's right. You've taken my address in case my bag is found, not that I'm holding out much hope. I don't know what the librarian will say about my library book.'

'You've reported it stolen to the police, and if you give the copy of the form I gave you to the librarian, you shouldn't have to replace it,' he said. 'Now, I think it's probably best that you stay here for the night. With a bit of luck the fog will have dispersed by morning. The way you moved your foot just then, your ankle should be much better in the morning.'

'You mean I-I'll sleep here in the p-police station?' she stammered.

He grinned. 'Yeah! We can give you a nice warm bed in a cell. I can't see you having any villains for company tonight the way the weather is. It won't cost you anything and we'll even give you breakfast.'

She decided there was no point in worrying about having no nightie or toothbrush and thanked him. Her only concern was the hens and Tibby but no doubt they'd survive her being away for just one night. As for herself, she'd been fed and was warm and safe and she was going to have a heck of a lot to tell Lila when she saw her.

CHAPTER FIVE

Emma eased herself down from the carriage and limped along the platform to the ticket barrier. Her ankle throbbed, but at least she had managed the trains and there was only the walk from the station through the village to her cottage. Then she'd probably need to relight the fire in the range before she could make herself a cup of tea and put her feet up. She was feeling cheerful despite not having found her sister and her shoulder bag being stolen.

She had spent the journey feeling slightly euphoric. Dougie Marshall had accompanied her to Lime Street station and had told her he would definitely be in touch. She couldn't get him out of her head. Every time she thought of his blue eyes smiling kindly into hers and his sweeping her off her feet she felt a warm thrill. Surely she couldn't have fallen in love at first sight? She told herself she must not read into his behaviour more than his simply doing his job as a policeman. And yet he had held her hand after he had helped her into a carriage for what had seemed longer than was necessary. Perhaps he was attracted to her? She sighed; she must get him out of her head because she had so much else to think about during the coming weeks.

Emma had not gone far after leaving the station when she was hailed by Lila's mother. She wished she could pretend not to have seen her because she was in no mood for an interrogation, but already Mrs Ashcroft was crossing the road towards her.

'You're limping, Emma. What's happened to you? Lila dropped by at your cottage last night and found it all in darkness,' said the older woman. 'She let herself in and stayed for a while, hoping to see you. When you didn't arrive home she fed the cat and hens.'

'That was kind of her,' said Emma, grateful to her friend. 'I had a fall and had to stay in Liverpool, so if you don't mind, Mrs Ashcroft, I don't want to stand about.'

'Perhaps I should come with you,' said Lila's mother, gazing down at Emma's foot. 'Twisted your ankle, did you? It looks a bit swollen. Maybe

I should take a look. I don't suppose you had it X-rayed?'

'No. A kind policeman saw to it for me,' she replied casually.

'A policeman!' exclaimed Mrs Ashcroft sharply. 'I knew you'd get into trouble.'

Emma had an overwhelming urge to shock Lila's mother. 'Aye. He took me to the police station and put me in a cell.'

Mrs Ashcroft gasped. 'You never were!'

'I were,' said Emma, forgetting her grammar. 'Now if you don't mind letting me get on? I need to rest my ankle.'

'I'm coming with you,' said Mrs Ashcroft, taking hold of Emma's arm. 'You lean on me.'

Emma was driven to say, 'What about Mr Ashcroft? Won't he be waiting for you at home? And what about your job at the hospital?'

'I don't have to be in work until later. Your grandparents would have wanted me to look after you, now you're all alone. A young woman of your age is vulnerable to all sorts of temptations and dangers.'

'I don't think anyone is going to attack me here,' said Emma firmly.

'Were you attacked in Liverpool?' asked Mrs Ashcroft, sounding as if she would almost enjoy hearing that Emma had suffered an assault.

Emma gave her a look and changed the subject.

'You haven't asked me if I found my stepmother and half-sister.'

'If they'd welcomed you with open arms, then I doubt you'd have come limping home. You would have stayed there for a few days to recuperate,' said Mrs Ashcroft.

Emma hoped that was what would have happened if her stepmother and half-sister had been there. 'The house was derelict,' she said. 'Constable Marshall said it was bombed during the Blitz.'

'They're dead, then,' said Mrs Ashcroft with a jerk of the head. 'It's probably just as well, Emma. You'll be able to settle down here again now.'

Emma frowned, not liking her family written off so easily. 'The house was still standing and Constable Marshall believes they're alive. He's going to try and trace them for me.'

Mrs Ashcroft looked put out. 'Was this policeman a young man? You sound like you're going to be relying on him rather a lot.'

'He's in his twenties and it's part of his job to help the public find missing persons,' said Emma coolly.

'There's no need to take that tone,' said Mrs Ashcroft, sounding affronted. 'I'm only thinking of what's best for you, Emma. Can you really afford to be going back and forth between here and Liverpool if this Constable Marshall finds your stepmother and half-sister?'

'Surely that's my business,' said Emma.

Two spots of colour appeared in the older woman's cheeks. 'You sound just like your mother and look what happened to her.'

Emma was really annoyed by that remark. 'She met my father, that's what she did. I wouldn't be here if she hadn't gone to Liverpool and married him, so I'm grateful that she did.'

'But she brought you back here,' said Mrs Ashcroft promptly. 'There's no doubt in my mind she believed this village to be a healthier place to live and she hoped to make a recovery. Your father might have followed her here but he didn't stick around, as you know.'

'Perhaps that was because Gran didn't make him welcome. If his great-grandparents once lived here, maybe the two families quarrelled and Gran couldn't bring herself to accept my father. She could be stubborn and found it difficult to forgive a slight or a wrong done.'

'What an imagination you have,' said Mrs Ashcroft with a sniff. 'But don't go expecting too much of strangers, Emma. They can let you down.'

'If you mean Constable Marshall,' said Emma, 'he was kind to me, so naturally I think the best of him.'

'As long as that's all you do, Emma. You're far too young to know your own mind yet when it comes to choosing a husband.'

'A husband!' Emma gasped. 'That's a bit of a leap! I hardly know the man. You're being ridiculous to suggest that I'd be thinking about marriage so soon, even though I'm not as young as you like to make out!'

'Don't be insolent!' Mrs Ashcroft's eyes flashed. 'When a girl is on her own, with very little money, it can be very tempting to accept the first man who asks her to marry him.'

Emma tilted her chin. 'I intend to support myself and not trust to a man to do it for me, even if it means pawning the coat on my back and every stick of furniture I have.'

Before Mrs Ashcroft could respond to that comment, Emma limped away. She was still angry when she reached the house. It was a relief to get inside out of the cold and go into the kitchen. Instantly, she heard Tibby mewing outside the back door. She let her in, but when the cat stropped Emma's legs she picked her up. 'Now you must be careful, Tibby. I don't want to be falling over you and I need to get the fire lit,' she said, placing the cat in the front room and closing the door on her.

Emma took a pair of walking socks out of her boots by the back door. She removed her shoes and put on the socks and an apron over her new frock before setting about lighting the fire. Within the hour the kitchen was feeling much warmer; even so, Emma had draped about her shoulders the shawl that she had made for her grandmother's birthday before she died. The old woman had called it her 'Joseph' shawl because Emma had used up oddments of leftover wool to crochet the garment. She had kept it for sentimental reasons and because it really was warm.

She made a pot of tea and let the cat back into the kitchen. There was no fresh milk but fortunately she found a tin of condensed milk in the larder. Her granddad had been partial to it spread on bread, and Emma remembered her grandmother making coconut ice for the church fete. She was hungry and fancied some coconut ice but had to make do with a slice of stale bread toasted and spread with home-made blackberry jam.

She poured herself a cup of tea and stretched out on the sofa. Instantly Tibby jumped on her lap. Emma was glad of her company. She had calmed down now but she could not forget what Mrs Ashcroft had said about her parents' marriage or of her seizing hold of the first presentable man. She thought of Constable Marshall and felt a warm glow.

Then she frowned. For all she knew he could already have a serious girlfriend. He could even be married, although she doubted that young married men went round giving girls rides on the crossbar of their bikes. What would it feel like to be kissed by him? She imagined the feel of his mouth on hers and recalled the strength in his arms. Then she thought of all the jobs that needed doing in her cottage and how handy it would be to have a man about the place. How practical was her Liverpool policeman?

She pulled herself together. What was she thinking? She must stop such thoughts right away. It was Mrs Ashcroft's fault for putting romantic ideas into her head. She found herself wondering if Mr Ashcroft had been the first man to propose marriage to Lila's mother when she was no longer a spring chicken, and she had accepted him because she was on the shelf. Or perhaps they had been in love and blissfully happy once upon a time, but the war had destroyed that happiness? She thought about what Mrs Ashcroft had said about her parents and her mother coming back home with her. What could have gone wrong with their marriage? How long had they been married before Emma was born? Where exactly had they tied the knot? Emma would like to visit the church or the registry office where they were married. No doubt, somewhere in Liverpool, there would be a record of the marriage and her birth.

Emma knew she had to visit the city again but right now she must find more work and so needed to place an advertisement in the *Clitheroe Advertiser and Times*. Reluctant as she was to go out in the cold again, she must write a piece out today and post it, as well as do some shopping.

* * *

Emma was frying potato scallops that evening when she heard a rat-a-tat on the back door. 'It's not locked,' she called.

Lila opened the door and stepped inside. Her expression was a mixture of concern and excitement. 'Are you all right? Mam said you'd hurt your ankle and spent the night in a police cell. What on earth happened?'

Emma chuckled. 'I tripped over in the fog, but fortunately this gorgeous policeman came to my rescue.'

Lila's eyes widened. 'Gosh. What was he like? Tall, dark, handsome . . . ?'

An imp of devilry seized Emma. 'Very tall. He made me feel like a shrimp. Especially when he swept me off my feet and carried me to the nearest shop,' she said, her eyes sparkling. No doubt this information would find its way back to Mrs Ashcroft.

'You're pulling my leg,' said Lila.

'It's the gospel truth!' Emma was beginning to enjoy herself. 'He even gave me a ride on his bike. I sat on the crossbar and I had to hang on to him very tightly in case I fell off. He was really strong. I'd never experienced anything like it. We could only see a few feet in front of us. It was thrilling, frightening and exciting all at the same time.'

'How old is he?'

'I'd say only a few years older than us.'

Lila sighed. 'Gosh, I wish we had a bobby like him around here.'

'It would probably be too quiet for him with it being just a matter of making sure none of the men are drinking after hours or day trippers driving too fast through the village.'

'You're forgetting about sheep and hen rustlers,' said Lila with a giggle.

Emma smiled. 'You're right. I should tell him that it's a bit like the Wild West out here but he knows Pendle Hill, so will be familiar with the area and would guess I was telling a fib.'

Lila pulled a face. 'Shame. Anyway, I expect he'll be looking for something more exciting in terms of crimes to solve and criminals to catch. Maybe he'll want to be a police inspector.'

'No chance of doing that here.'

'Will you be seeing him again?'

'He said he'd be in touch. Did your mother tell you that I didn't find my stepmother and half-sister?'

'Aye.'

'The house was derelict, but Constable Marshall is going to try and trace them for me.' Emma began to flip the scallops onto a plate. 'Are you hungry?'

'I've eaten. Is that all you're having?'

'I had a big breakfast at the police station,' said Emma.

'That must have been hours ago.'

'So, I need to lose some weight.'

Lila stared at her. 'You're short of money after buying a new frock and going to Liverpool, aren't you?'

'I'm fine. Nothing for you to worry about,' said Emma lightly. 'It's just that I have to make my money last until I get some more work.'

Lila sat down and rested her arms on the table. 'If Mam didn't make me hand over me wages, I'd give you a loan. So what else happened? Did you get to look in any of the shops?'

Emma shook her head. 'I told you it was foggy, and I'd lost my bag, so I had no money. You know, I never gave any thought to Liverpool having been bombed before I went there. Stupid of me. I didn't get to see the River Mersey either. I'm going to have to go there again but it might not be till summer.'

She was thoughtful as she ate her supper.

'And if your policeman gets in touch?'

'Whether he gets in touch or not,' murmured Emma. 'There are things I need to find out about my parents.'

Lila frowned and stood up. 'Why can't you leave the past alone?'

'Because I'm curious!'

'It was curiosity that killed the cat,' said Lila, shaking her head. 'I'll have to go. Is there anything I can get you? You'll be wanting to rest your ankle.'

'It's good of you to offer but I'll manage,' said

Emma. 'By the way, thanks for coming in and feeding the hens and the cat.'

'It was the least I could do. See you soon.'

Emma saw her friend out and then, after she had gone, switched on the wireless so she wouldn't feel so lonely. She listened to *The Goon Show*, remembering how her granddad had enjoyed the adventures of Neddie Seagoon. He was always falling prey to the schemes of Hercules Grytpype-Thynne and Count Moriarty. She could almost hear the old man's throaty chuckle as he laughed at the antics of Spike Milligan as Eccles and Peter Sellers as Bluebottle in their attempts to rescue Neddie. She must visit the family grave again soon.

It was to be more than a week before Emma was able to visit the churchyard. She knelt on a sheet of newspaper by the family plot and removed dead greenery before emptying the dregs from the water container. Then she half-filled it with fresh water before placing the first of the daffodils from her garden in the container. She spent several minutes, thinking of her grandparents and her mother, before getting up from her knees and wrapping the dead plants in the newspaper. On her way to the church gate, she passed the verger who was pasting a sheet of paper on the church noticeboard.

'How are you getting on, Emma?' he called. 'Still missing ol' Harry?'

'Aye, but he'd want me to get on with my life.'

She brushed back a strand of chestnut hair. 'At the moment I'm waiting for a reply to an advert I put in the *Clitheroe Times*. I need more bookkeeping work.'

He nodded. 'No doubt you'll also be waiting for a letter from Liverpool.'

His knowing about her trip to Liverpool came as no surprise as there was a flourishing grapevine in the village. 'That's right.'

'Well, I can't help you there but I'll have a word with the vicar, if you like, and see if he knows anyone who needs a bookkeeper when he's visiting in the parish.'

Emma had not forgotten the vicar's offer to provide her with a reference, but she had never thought of asking for his help in finding a job. She thanked the verger and then hesitated before asking, 'Do you remember my mother?'

'Of course I remember Mary. We were at school together. She was right pretty and had a way with her that had us lads vying for her attention. She had a lovely singing voice and was often chosen to perform solos.'

'I never knew that,' said Emma, astonished. 'In fact I know very little about her. My grandparents hardly ever spoke about her after she died.'

'Perhaps it was too painful. She had an ambition to sing professionally but they didn't want her to leave the village.'

'So she ran away,' said Emma softly.

'Aye, well, she had a determined nature; she wanted to be somebody.'

'Things mustn't have worked out for her on the stage if she married my father,' said Emma.

'You mean she must have given up her dream,' said the verger, looking thoughtful. 'That's not necessarily true. She left when she was only eighteen and didn't return until several years later. I remember seeing a poster up outside a theatre in Manchester, advertising a variety show and she was on the bill.'

Emma's eyes widened. 'Did my grandparents know?'

'I didn't keep it a secret, told my mam about it. You can bet the news went round, but your grandmother wouldn't have gone to see her. According to my mam, she didn't hold with the stage. Singing in church was one thing, but going around the country, performing in public and for money was quite another.'

'That's sad,' murmured Emma. 'What a shame Gran couldn't have been proud of her. I imagine, though, that Granddad would have gone to see her perform if he'd been able to.'

'Aye, well, it would have been more than his life was worth to go against your gran.'

Emma knew what he meant. 'At least Mother came back here with me when she was ill and was allowed to stay, so Gran must have forgiven her.'

'Or ol' Harry put his foot down. She brought them a granddaughter. I remember Mam saying that must have gone a long way to healing the breach.'

Emma could see why that could be true and smiled. 'I mustn't keep you from your work any longer but I'm glad we had this conversation.'

He grinned. 'It brought memories back – but you don't want to go delving into the past too much, lass,' he warned. 'You don't know what you'll find and you can't change matters. You're only young and you've your life ahead of you, concentrate on that.'

'I'll do my best.' She waved and went on her way, knowing that, despite his advice, she still intended finding out more about her parents if she could.

She was halfway along the street when she noticed a tall, fair-haired man standing outside her front door. She felt a stir of excitement. Could it be Constable Marshall come to visit instead of writing her a letter? She quickened her pace.

He must have heard her footsteps because he turned his head and watched as she approached. 'Constable Marshall, I didn't expect to see you here,' she called.

'I fancied a trip into the country, Miss Booth. I see your ankle is much better now,' he said, smiling.

'Aye, it's fine now.' She smiled up at him in

delight. 'Call me Emma,' she added. 'I hope you haven't been waiting long.'

'No.' He watched her as she pulled the key through the letter box. 'That isn't very sensible, you know.'

'No one is going to break in here,' said Emma. 'I've nothing worth stealing.'

'Even so, it's no fun discovering someone has been in your house and rifled through your things,' he warned.

'OK. I get your message,' said Emma, opening the door. 'You'll come in, of course, and have a cup of tea,' she said, smiling. 'I've been baking, so I can offer you fresh scones with home-made jam.'

He grinned. 'Sounds good to me, and you can call me Dougie. Why stand on ceremony? I don't know when last I tasted a home-made scone. Mam goes out to work and she doesn't have time for baking.' He wiped his feet on the mat and followed her inside.

Emma didn't doubt for a moment that some of her neighbours would have spotted this new arrival and could imagine that, before nightfall, the news would be spread all over the village that Emma Booth had entertained a strange man in her cottage. The thought made her chuckle.

She led him through into the kitchen and offered him a chair before putting on the kettle. Then she sat down and stared at him expectantly. 'So what news have you for me?' she asked.

He had been gazing about the room, but now he gave her his full attention. 'The bad news is that Mrs Lizzie Booth was killed in a road accident a couple of years ago. The good news is that your half-sister was not involved.'

Emma was thankful about her half-sister being safe but felt sad that she would never get to meet her father's second wife. 'What happened to my half-sister after her mother's death? Was she put in an orphanage?'

'No. Mrs Booth had a sister. At the time of her death she and your half-sister were living with Mrs Gregory and her children.'

'So Betty is living with her aunt and cousins?'

He nodded and took out a notebook. 'Her aunt is a Mrs Elsie Gregory. She was widowed six months or so before her sister's death but has since remarried her husband's brother. She has a son who's away doing his national service and there are two daughters, one's working and the other is still at school.'

Emma was relieved that Betty hadn't been left all alone in the world. 'Do you think her aunt will allow me to see Betty?'

'I didn't get to meet the family,' said Dougie. 'I received the information from a police station in Bootle. I can't see any reason why she shouldn't.'

'So where are they living?'

'Out past Bootle, which is north of Liverpool. In an area called Litherland, near Seaforth. You might have heard of Seaforth . . .' said Dougie, his blue eyes meeting Emma's.

'No,' she said.

He looked surprised. 'But you've heard of Gladstone?'

'Aye. He was a prime minister in Victorian times.'

'Well, his family had a big house in Seaforth. In fact, there's a big dock there called Gladstone Dock, named after his brother.'

'I see.' Emma frowned. 'So the Gregorys live near the docks?'

Dougie shook his fair head. 'No. I just thought you might find it interesting about the dock and the Gladstone family. It's history, isn't it?'

She smiled. 'Aye, it is. Where do the Gregory family live exactly?'

'A mile or more from the docks, the other side of the Leeds-Liverpool canal, in a large Victorian house with a garden,' said Dougie, leaning towards her. 'I went and had a look for curiosity's sake. If I were you, I'd write to the aunt, introducing yourself, and say that you'd like to meet your half-sister.'

'You think writing is better than going there?' she asked, getting up and removing the kettle from the heat.

'Think, Emma, what happened last time you went in search of your half-sister. It's not a good idea to spring surprises on people you don't know. I've heard of cases where the last thing people want is the past being dragged into the present. It can ruin some people's lives.'

Emma wondered how many times people were going to tell her to leave the past alone. 'How can I ruin Betty's life? I only want to meet her, not take her away from her family.'

'I'm just giving you my opinion, you don't have to take notice of it,' he said stiffly.

She flushed, realising she had offended him. That was the last thing she wanted to do after he had been so helpful to her. 'Of course, thank you. I really do appreciate what you've done for me in coming all this way to tell me,' she said awkwardly. 'If you give me her address, I will write to Mrs Gregory.'

He smiled. 'Sensible girl. That way you're less likely to get hurt.'

Emma was not so sure about that, because she knew that if Mrs Gregory wouldn't allow her to see her half-sister, then she would be hurt. She spread blackberry jam on scones and then made tea.

'These scones are good,' said Dougie, after taking a bite out of one. He looked surprised.

She flushed with pleasure and offered him another and sat opposite him to drink her own tea. 'I should have given you a napkin,' she said.

'It doesn't matter, as long as you don't mind crumbs on the floor,' he said. 'What are you planning on doing if Mrs Gregory allows you to meet her niece and you'd like to see more of her? Will you stay here or consider moving to Liverpool?'

Emma did not know what to say as the last thing she had in mind was to leave the cottage that had always been her home. 'I don't know yet; so much depends on my getting enough work to support myself. I'm a freelance bookkeeper and have just a couple of small-time clients. That was all right when Granddad was alive and we had his pension and savings, but without them . . .' Her voice trailed off.

'You haven't thought of making money from baking scones?'

'You are joking!' said Emma, smiling.

'No. These scones are good. May I have another one?'

She offered him the plate, flattered by his comments. 'There's already a perfectly good bakery in the village,' she murmured, 'and there's also the Co-op.'

'Never mind them,' said Dougie, leaning forward. 'I was thinking more of you doing what you are doing now. Providing tea and scones for visitors in your own home.'

'What visitors?' she asked, taken aback.

'Tourists who come to the area to visit the ruins

of the abbey and walk the fells,' he replied. 'I bet there'll be quite a number of motorists visiting the countryside from Easter onwards. You're nicely situated here.'

She found it difficult to take his idea seriously. 'I'd have to sell an awful lot of teas and scones to make a living from it.'

'Part-living. You'd have your bookkeeping, as well, don't forget.'

'Even so . . .' Suddenly she remembered what was written in the deeds of the cottage about the house having being used as a shop and tea room. 'What if I decided to move to Liverpool?'

'Finding somewhere to live in Liverpool would be difficult. Lots of homes were damaged or destroyed in the Blitz.' Dougie swallowed the last of his scone. 'Anyway, this is a lovely place and surely you have friends here? Still, you have to make your own decision. Do you bake anything other than scones? Are you any good at cakes, and in particular, Lancashire specialities?'

Emma was touched that he should be so keen on helping her with suggestions to support herself, but a bit hurt that he wasn't encouraging her to move to Liverpool closer to his home. 'I can make Chorley and Eccles cakes, but I'd have to save enough coupons to buy the dried fruit needed. That's one of the difficulties with your idea – so many commodities are still on ration. Sugar is just one of them.' She sighed. 'Before the war my grandmother used to make the best coffee-and-walnut cake I've ever tasted. It didn't taste the same once she ran out of coffee and had to use Camp coffee with chicory.'

'What about Lancashire hotpot?'

Emma did a double take. 'It's a big step from providing visitors with tea and scones to a hot meal.'

'I'm thinking of the walkers who, after tramping the fells in the rain, are cold and wet, as well as being as hungry as a hunter,' he said, his hand hovering over the last scone. 'They'd be made up with a bowl of steaming hotpot.'

She passed the scone over to him. 'I don't know if it's feasible. I have a roof that leaks and need money to repair that before I could spend out on tables and chairs and the like.'

He nodded. 'I understand that, but if you really want to have a go, then you have to make it happen. Life doesn't hand things to us on a plate. We have to work for them.'

'I don't mind hard work, Dougie,' she said earnestly, 'but I do need capital to finance this venture and I don't have any money to spare.'

He frowned. 'It's a blinking shame. But I wouldn't forget my idea, because you never know what's round the corner. Now, how about showing me your village?'

'It would be a pleasure, Constable Marshall!' She knew that all eyes would be upon them but did not care. She would be proud to be seen with him. She collected the crockery and carried it over to the sink, thinking she would wash up later.

Once outside Emma hesitated, wondering which way to take him first. 'When you walked from the station, you'll have seen how small my village is compared to Liverpool,' she said.

'Yes, but I haven't seen all of it. Do you have a cinema?'

She nodded. 'And an assembly room for dancing and concerts. During the war the wounded soldiers used to be brought over from Calderstones hospital. The villagers would put on entertainment for them. I remember thinking how it really brought the war home to me. Up 'til then it didn't seem real because we weren't a target for the bombers and we seemed so far from the action going on elsewhere. You must have seen so much in Liverpool.'

'The port lost a lot of men in the Battle of the Atlantic.'

'But your father wasn't one of them.'

'No, I remember him telling me that he hated the sea.'

'I love the river here, especially when it freezes over and there's skating,' she said dreamily.

'So you can skate.'

Emma nodded. 'My grandparents loved to skate. Have you ever been on the ice?'

He grinned. 'Not wearing skates. Went through the ice on Stanley Park lake for a dare when I was a kid. I fell through it and thought I was a goner.'

'That must have been scary,' said Emma.

'It was, but fortunately I was rescued by a copper.'

She stopped in her tracks. 'Is that why you became a policeman?'

'Yes. I decided I wanted to be there to help people when they were in trouble.'

Emma thought that was rather noble of him. 'You've never wanted to be anything else?' she asked.

'No,' he said firmly. 'Now, why don't you show me the ruins?'

Emma was happy to do so, because she would be away from prying eyes in the abbey grounds. Once there, she had the feeling that he wasn't overly impressed with the ruins and was disappointed by his reaction.

'When next you come to Liverpool, you should see St Luke's, it's a bombed-out church at the top of Bold Street,' he said. 'Its walls have been left standing as a memorial to the people of Liverpool who were killed during the Blitz.'

'I'd like to see it,' she said, finding it hard to believe it could possibly compare to her local ruined abbey.

'Then perhaps we can make a date sometime and I can show you round Liverpool?' said Dougie.

Emma flushed with pleasure. 'I'd really like that. I'll need your address, so as to let you know when I'm coming.'

'Okey-doke!' He took out pencil and notebook and wrote on a leaf of paper and handed it to her. 'Is there anything else?'

Emma realised that they were back at the cottage and it was time for him to go. 'Aye,' she said. 'Can you tell me where the registry office is in Liverpool?'

He nodded. 'There are two. I'll show you when you come.'

Emma looked forward to keeping that date with him, but first she needed to write a letter to Mrs Gregory and post it as soon as possible.

CHAPTER SIX

'Oh, hell!' exclaimed Elsie Gregory, chewing on her lip.

Her hand shook as she reread the letter from Emma Booth and then her knees gave way and she had to sit down. How she wished her husband, Owen, was still alive, but he had died just over two and a half years ago of a muscular wasting disease. She had married his brother, Teddy, last year and she had never spoken to him about the troublesome times with her sister and the fact that Lizzie had a stepdaughter. Marrying Teddy had been a mistake, but when her son, Jared, had left to do his national service, something he had deferred until he finished his apprenticeship, she had missed having a man about the place.

'What's up?' asked Teddy, glancing up from an old American comic he had taken from a pile that he had found in a cupboard in Jared's bedroom.

Elsie darted him a look. Lizzie had never liked Teddy but, after she had been killed in that terrible road accident here outside the house, her sister's opinion of him had not seemed to matter when he had started visiting regularly to console her in her second bereavement. She had been glad of his company because she'd been in a bit of a state.

'I've just received this letter,' she said, then stopped, not knowing how to go on. Should she tell him or shouldn't she? She remembered Owen saying that the rickets Teddy had suffered from as a child had not only stunted his growth but had affected him in other ways, too. He was certainly nothing like his brother: he had never had a long-term job, but a series of odd jobs, and she remembered Owen slipping him money, even when he could ill afford it when the children were younger and times hard. Before she had married Teddy she had felt sorry for him, reasoning that he could be forgiven in the circumstances for having a chip on his shoulder, but she hadn't realised just how aggressive and bossy he could be at times. Owen had been the man for her and Teddy wasn't a patch on him.

'Well, spit it out, woman,' he commanded.

Elsie took a deep breath. 'Y-you remember our Lizzie's husband, William Booth?'

Teddy's eyes darkened. 'Of course I bloody remember him. She would have married me if it weren't for him getting in there first. I could never work out why she should want to marry a nancy boy artist.'

'Well, I thought like you at first,' said Elsie, fiddling with a corner of the letter, thinking he was kidding himself if he believed Lizzie would have ever married him. 'I remember saying to her, "Who wants to buy pictures during a depression?" but actually he'd sold several pictures before she married him. We both knew his first wife, Mary. She used to lodge a few doors away from us when she was appearing in the theatre.'

'I didn't know he'd been married before!'

'Yes, well, there were things our Lizzie wanted kept quiet. Anyway, as it turned out, not only did his pictures sell but his family had money. You'll remember how nicely spoken he was. Not the least bit like some of those arty types our Lizzie used to mingle with.' Elsie's face softened with the reminiscence. 'She loved the music hall – she once sang on a cruise ship with a girl who went and caught polio later.'

'Will you get on with it, woman,' snapped Teddy. 'What's all this got to do with the here and now?'

Elsie hesitated and there was a long silence

before she managed to say, 'This letter is from William's daughter from his first marriage. She wants to meet Betty and would like to get to know her. Apparently she only recently discovered that her father remarried. Her granddad died suddenly and she found a letter from our Lizzie, sent during the war, telling the girl's grandmother about Betty and that William had been killed at Dunkirk.'

'So what's the problem?' Teddy rustled the pages of the comic. 'Is she asking to take Betty off your hands?'

'I couldn't just give our Lizzie's daughter to a stranger,' said Elsie, shocked.

'You make it sound as if Betty's only a little girl, but she's fifteen, older than your Maggie.'

'She doesn't say anything about having her live with her,' said Elsie. 'Besides, Betty is settled in school here. It would be wrong to send her off somewhere else when she'll be doing her school certificate next year and then she can get a job.'

'I see.' He smirked. 'You're thinking of her earning some money at last.'

Elsie flushed angrily. 'That has nothing to do with it.'

'No?' He looked disbelieving. 'Where does this girl live?'

'In a village up Lancashire.'

He held out his hand. 'Let's see the letter.'

She hesitated before handing it over to him and

watched his lips move and his forefinger follow the first line of writing. Then he gave up and handed it back to her. 'I can't understand the girl's writing. So what's your problem?'

Elsie took a deep breath. 'Money.'

Teddy stared at her. 'What do you mean by money?'

'William entrusted money to our Lizzie,' she said in a low voice, glancing over her shoulder towards the door. 'No lawyers involved. He wrote it in a letter and trusted her to do what was right for Emma. He wouldn't have any truck with banks and kept his money in a safe in the house. After he was killed, she opened a bank account and in it went.'

His jaw dropped. 'Bloody hell! What kind of sum are we talking about here?'

'A lot.' She paused and swallowed. 'You know how ill Owen was and how he couldn't work in the end. Well, our Lizzie was very fond of Owen. He was the brother she had never had, and she grieved to see him suffering and me so dragged down by it all, and with the kids to support.'

'You don't have to give me the whole sob story,' growled Teddy, putting down the comic. 'Get to the point!'

Elsie cleared her throat. 'Lizzie suggested that we bought a big house and we all lived together. She would loan the money that was Emma's to Owen and she would provide the other half of the asking price out of her share of his money as his widow. She had actually managed to sell a couple more of his paintings after the war and that brought money in, too.'

'She always did have it cushy,' said Teddy, his eyes dark and resentful.

Elsie did not agree but did not say so. 'It goes to show that she made the right choice when she married William, that's all,' she said, springing to her sister's defence. 'Anyway, Lizzie's idea was that when the time came and the children left home, we'd sell this house and move to somewhere smaller. She would go up to Lancashire and see if Emma was still alive and give her the money that she was owed.'

'Bloody hell, that's complicated,' said Teddy, rasping his fingernails on his unshaven jaw. 'So you've known about this other daughter of William's all this time. Why have you never mentioned her and why have you never told me about the house not belonging to you? Or does it belong to you now Owen and Lizzie are dead?' His mud-coloured eyes raked her face.

'It doesn't, not really,' said Elsie swiftly. 'Anyway, getting back to my story. After Lizzie was killed, I was in no state to be worrying about William's daughter, so I put her out of my mind and forgot about her. I thought it likely she was dead.'

'You wanted to believe that,' said Teddy, smirking.

Elsie went as red as a beetroot. 'This is our home! How could I go selling it to hand money over to a stranger?'

Teddy stared at Elsie for what seemed a long time before saying, 'I never thought you could be so devious. If I were you, woman, I'd ignore the bloody letter and get on with your life.'

'You mean not even mention it to Betty?'

'Of course bloody not,' he said, sounding exasperated. 'You know that girl is just like Lizzie, and once she gets something fixed in her head she won't let it go. If she knows that she has a half-sister, she'll want to meet her.'

Elsie dug her fingernails into her palm. 'But it doesn't seem right.'

He gave a nasty little laugh. 'Not right, woman? Your conscience doesn't seem to have bothered you much so far, if you've kept this from Betty all this time. Forget the other girl!' He tore the letter in half and flung it on the fire.

Elsie made no effort to prevent the letter from turning into ashes, despite feeling sick with guilt. Knowing that Owen would never have countenanced his brother's actions and would have been dreadfully disappointed in her, she told herself that she had to put her own family's needs first.

CHAPTER SEVEN

Emma shifted the bucket with her foot a couple more inches to the right to catch the water that was leaking through the corner of the ceiling in her bedroom. She felt like screaming and made the decision that she would no longer put up with this inconvenience every time it rained. She would sell the furniture in her grandparents' former bedroom and move her possessions into there. She didn't know why she hadn't done it before. Perhaps it was because it still felt very much their room. She hadn't even felt up to getting rid of her grandfather's clothes but decided she would do that tomorrow. Then, sometime during the coming week, she would visit the second-hand shop in

Clitheroe. The bedroom furniture was solid oak and well built and ten times better than the new utility stuff that was in the shops these days.

She went downstairs and switched on the wireless and had just settled in a chair with her knitting when she heard a tapping on the kitchen window.

'Come in,' she called, guessing it was Lila whom she had not seen for several days.

The door opened and in came her friend. 'I had to come,' said Lila, removing her dripping hat and placing it on the draining board. 'I hear you had a gentleman caller last weekend.'

A smile lurked in Emma's brown eyes. 'You've taken your time coming to find out about him. I thought you'd have been here within hours once the news got round.'

'I haven't been well,' said Lila, removing her raincoat and hanging it on one of the hooks on the wall. 'I've had a cold and I didn't want to give it to you.' She pulled a chair up to the fire and sat down opposite Emma. 'Was he your policeman?'

'Aye.'

Lila linked her hands and placed them between her knees and leant forward with an eager expression on her face. 'Tell me everything! What did he have to say?'

Emma told her the bare bones of her conversation with Dougie, and when she had finished, Lila said,

'So what are you going to do?'

Emma set aside her knitting and put on the kettle. 'I took Dougie's advice and wrote a letter to Betty's aunt, asking if I can see her.'

Lila smiled. 'That makes sense. So this Dougie, will he be visiting you again?'

Emma's eyes were dreamy as she murmured, 'We're planning to meet up next time I go to Liverpool, so I'm praying that I'll hear back from Betty's aunt soon.'

Lila wriggled her shoulders and said excitedly, 'I bet you're chuffed with him coming all this way to see you.'

'Well, he didn't have to come,' said Emma.

'No, so he must like you,' said Lila. 'So when will you be going to Liverpool?'

'It depends on what the aunt has to say, and money. I'm still waiting for some response from my advertisement in the newspaper. I also need to get rid of Granddad's clothes and some furniture, so I'll have to go into Clitheroe and see a second-hand dealer.'

Lila's eyes were instantly alert. 'What furniture?'

Emma told her and Lila reacted by suggesting that she advertise the furniture for sale in the local newspaper, too.

'But it'll cost me more money to do that,' said Emma reasonably.

'But the dealer is bound to try and diddle you

because you're a woman and a young, inexperienced one at that. You could get your money back by cutting out the middle man.'

Emma hesitated. 'I'll think about it.'

'I could ask at work if anyone is after buying some bedroom furniture if you want me to,' said Lila. 'There's not much to be had in the shops, and what there is isn't quality stuff according to Mam. It seems to me that there's always someone planning a wedding in our place, so you could be in luck.'

Emma's face lit up. 'Thanks! That sounds really promising. I'd appreciate you doing that, although I wouldn't know how much to ask.'

'Barter,' suggested Lila. 'Start at a price you'd like to get and then be prepared to lower it if they're not prepared to pay it. It's what Mam does when she has time off and we go to the market in Clitheroe.'

'I'll try it,' said Emma firmly.

'That's the ticket,' said Lila, glancing over Emma's shoulder. 'The kettle's boiling, by the way.'

As Emma made the tea, Lila called over to her, 'So is there anything else Dougie said that was interesting?'

'He suggested that I open up my house after Easter to provide tea and scones and the like to day trippers,' said Emma.

'Blinkin' heck! Your baking must have really

impressed him,' said Lila, grinning. 'But you're not taking him seriously, are you?'

Emma was disappointed by her friend's reaction, despite her own initial response to Dougie's suggestion. 'I'm sure he wasn't joking, although, just like you, I have my doubts whether I could make it work. Then I remembered that my great-grandmother kept a shop and had a tea room here in this very house.'

'You don't say!' exclaimed Lila, glancing about her.

'My guess is that she probably only opened up the place as a tea room in the summer,' said Emma, handing a cup of tea to her friend. 'But she must have made some money from it to go to all that effort. If the weather was good, she'd have been able to put chairs and tables in part of the back garden. I've space to do that, despite the hens and the vegetable patch.'

Lila stared at her. 'You're beginning to believe that you could do what this Dougie suggested.'

'Why not?' Emma pursed her lips. 'If I sell the furniture, there's nothing stopping me starting off in a small way. I could start by putting out a couple of chairs and one table out front to attract passing trade. If I were able to earn more from my bookkeeping, as well, then maybe I could manage to get some repairs done to this cottage.'

'You mean you'd set out a table on the pavement?'

'Why not? I've seen pictures of that done in other places.'

Lila looked doubtful.

Emma sighed. 'Anyway, I won't be doing anything until Easter.'

During the next few days Emma made her plans and waited to see if they would come to fruition. She decided to do what Lila had suggested and placed an advertisement for the furniture in the FOR SALE column of the *Clitheroe Advertiser and Times*.

Another week trickled slowly by and it felt to Emma as if she was forever waiting for the postman to call. When at last someone came to view the bedroom furniture, she had still not received a reply to her letter from her half-sister's aunt. She did not have much confidence in her bartering skills but the engaged couple who called at the house appeared just as inept as she was. Even so, a price was reached that satisfied the three of them. The husband-to-be promised to call round in a couple of days' time with transport and the money.

He was as good as his word, and soon Emma was gazing about the empty space in the main bedroom and wishing she could afford to repaper the walls. Setting that thought aside, she knew that she was going to need help to move her furniture and bed into here. Perhaps if she dropped a few hints in church on Sunday, the verger might assist her. Until then she would stay put and write another letter to Mrs Gregory. It was just possible that the first one had gone missing in the post.

The verger and his son were quite willing to shift furniture for Emma, and furthermore, the vicar spoke about arranging for her to visit a farmer out Wiswell way, who needed someone to sort out his paperwork for the taxman. Someone whose fee was not exorbitant. So a day later, Emma accompanied the vicar to the farm and came away with a battered account book and a couple of tins stuffed with invoices and bills of sale. Two days later, she had a response to her advertisement and visited a woman who had recently been widowed and left in sole charge of her husband's small business. She told Emma that she was hopeless with figures and employed her on the spot.

As Easter came and went, bringing with it unseasonable weather, Emma filled in columns of figures and added and subtracted, trying to keep her mind on the job and not think too much about her plans for a tea room and the absence of a reply from Mrs Gregory.

The days passed, the weather improved and soon the hedgerows were fragrant with hawthorn blossom. Emma had still not heard a word from Mrs Gregory, or Dougie for that matter. She felt hurt where Dougie was concerned and annoyed with the woman who didn't have the good manners to reply to her letter. She did not believe that both her letters could have gone astray and came to a decision. Disguising her handwriting, in case Mrs Gregory should pick up the letter first, she penned another letter to her half-sister. She could only hope that, if the aunt did see the letter, then she would not notice the postmark. It was a chance she would have to take as she had no other option.

CHAPTER EIGHT

Betty Booth was returning from visiting her friend, Irene Miller, when she spotted the postman about to go up the drive to her aunt's front door.

'I'll take the post,' she called, hurrying towards him. 'It'll save your legs!'

He turned and smiled at her. 'It's not your birthday, is it?' he teased, handing over several envelopes.

'No, my birthday was in November,' she replied, flicking a ginger plait over her shoulder, wondering if there was a letter from her pen pal in Canada. Her former English teacher had come up with the idea of having a pen pal; a sort of hands-across-the-sea-reaching-out-to-the-Empire to get her pupils practising writing about themselves in letter form and learning about other people's lives.

There was no blue airmail envelope for her but there was a letter in her cousin Jared's handwriting addressed to his mother. He was doing his national service with the Liverpool King's Regiment and had recently been stationed in Berlin. All the females in the household missed him but they all knew that Uncle Teddy was glad to have him out of the way. It would have been odd if the quick-tempered old git hadn't resented his tall, attractive nephew who had a charm that the older man would never possess. With Jared away, Teddy thought he could lord it over the females in the family and this more than irritated them all. There was something about him that gave Betty the creeps.

Suddenly she noticed an envelope addressed to herself, and squinting at the postmark she was only able to make out the Lancs part of it. She placed the envelope up the sleeve of her cardigan, thinking to read it once inside the house. Hopefully she would have it to herself for a change. She hurried up the drive, breathing in the fragrance from the wallflowers her aunt had planted last September, on the warm breeze. She stood on the doorstep and reached inside the letter box, found the key on the string and dragged it through and opened the door.

As she stepped into the lobby, all was quiet, which probably meant that Uncle Teddy was putting in a few hours as a bookie's runner this Saturday. Her eldest female cousin, Dorothy, was a sewing machinist and worked half-day Saturday. As for Betty's Aunt Elsie and her younger cousin Maggie, they had gone into Liverpool. They really enjoyed roaming around the shops and Maggie always managed to wheedle something out of her mother.

Betty placed the rest of the post on the sideboard and then flopped into an armchair. She kicked off her shoes and curled her legs beneath her before tearing open the envelope. She took out two sheets of paper and flattened them on her knee, and then looked at the address written at the top right-hand side and saw that it was a place near Clitheroe, in Lancashire. She wondered who could be writing to her from there and began to read.

My dear sister, Betty,

This letter will most likely come as a surprise to you. Especially if, like me, the truth was withheld from you. I never knew you existed until a few months ago, after my granddad died, when I found a letter from your mother amongst his belongings. It was one that informed my grandmother of the death of my father and yours, William Booth. If I had known of this letter earlier I would have tried to find you.

My own mother died of consumption when I was five years old and it was my grandparents who brought me up in this village in the Lancashire countryside. I did visit Liverpool in February shortly after the king died to try and find you, only to discover that the house where you had lived was derelict. Fortunately a policeman did some detecting for me and discovered that you were living with your aunt. I have written to Mrs Gregory twice but she has not answered my letters. I presume this is because she would rather we did not meet. Perhaps she considers it too painful for you to be reminded of your parents in this way. I don't know. Still, I would like to meet you but will understand if you feel you cannot go against your aunt's wishes. On the other hand, if you feel, as I do, that your mother and our father wanted us to get to know each other, then please get in touch with me at the above address.
Warmest wishes,
Your half-sister
Emma Booth

Betty was flabbergasted. She reread the letter and her mouth widened in a smile as she remembered a conversation with her mother years ago. She folded the missive neatly and placed it back in its envelope and thought back to the day when she had started primary school. She had clung to her mother's hand, begging her not to leave her. Lizzie had hugged and kissed her and told her that she had to be a brave girl. Betty had not wanted to be brave all on her own and had cried to her mother, 'Why do I have to be an only child? Why did my daddy have to die? Why couldn't I have had a sister?'

'You have cousins,' her mother had replied.

'That's not the same,' Betty remembered saying.

After a moment's hesitation her mother had said, 'Well, you do have a sort of sister. She was your daddy's daughter from his first marriage.'

Betty recalled her astonishment. 'What kind of sister does that make her?'

Her mother had hesitated again before saying, 'You could say that she's your half-sister.'

'How can I have just half of a sister? Does she have a mummy?'

'Emma's mother died and so I married her father,' her mother had answered.

'Does that mean she's an orphan?' Betty had asked.

Her mother had nodded and told her that her sister, Emma, was several years older than her and lived with her grandparents up north and that was why they had never met. It was a long way away, and besides, Emma was all the family her grandparents had.

Betty felt tears prick the back of her eyes as they often did when she thought of her mother. They had dearly loved each other, and Betty knew she would never forget that terrible day she had come home from school to be told that her mother was dead. Aunt Elsie had done what she could to comfort her but she was grieving herself after the double blow that had struck the family in the years since the end of the war. And then she had shocked them all by inexplicably marrying Betty's lovely Uncle Owen's ignorant and rude-mannered younger brother. Betty gnawed on her lip. There were times when he looked at her in a way that made her shudder. If Betty had had her way, she wouldn't have allowed him in the house. He just wasn't good enough to fill his brother's shoes. He didn't have a proper job and she doubted he gave any money to Aunt Elsie towards the housekeeping. Sometimes she wondered how her aunt managed to provide for the lot of them, although her aunt and Dorothy both had jobs. No doubt Jared still helped out by sending money home to his mother.

But what was she thinking about allowing her mind to drift like this? Her half-sister wanted to meet her and Betty certainly wanted to meet Emma. But why hadn't her aunt mentioned the letters and why hadn't she written back to her? What could be the harm in the pair of them meeting? It was not as if Emma was suggesting that she went and lived with her. Betty rather thought that her aunt might have liked the idea, because she got really vexed when her niece went on about being an artist like her father.

Betty had her mind set on trying to get into Liverpool's School of Art after leaving the grammar school in Waterloo next year. Betty's art teacher had told Aunt Elsie that she had talent, but her aunt had said that she didn't want her niece messing around with paint but to get herself a proper job and earn some money. When Betty had argued with her, Elsie shook a finger at her and said, 'You're a very fortunate girl. Your mother and I never had the opportunity to go to grammar school and I'll not have you wasting your time with arty people. You want a decent job, so you can meet decent men. You're bound to marry because you've got a way with you, just like your mother.'

Betty felt a familiar anger. She had worked hard to pass the scholarship, so it wasn't as if it had been handed to her on a plate. And how was she fortunate when she was an orphan? She was definitely in no rush to settle down, marry and have babies. She wanted to make something of herself, not be some man's slave.

She uncurled her body that showed all the signs of burgeoning womanhood and got to her feet.

She was hungry. Pocketing the letter, she hurried into the kitchen and checked to see whether there was a loaf in the bread bin. She cut a slice of bread and spread it with shop-bought plum jam. If Aunt Elsie had been there she wouldn't have been allowed to eat between meals. Her aunt just didn't take into consideration how hungry a growing girl could be.

Suddenly she caught the sound of the key being scrabbled up the door, clinking as it went through the letter box. Swiftly she swallowed the last of the jam bread and wiped the corners of her mouth and poured herself a cup of water. She was calmly drinking it when her aunt and younger cousin entered the kitchen, carrying several shopping bags.

'What have you been up to?' asked Elsie sharply, dumping two bags on the table and staring at her niece.

Betty's eyes widened. 'Whatever do you mean, Aunt Elsie? I haven't been up to anything. I'm standing here, minding my own business, drinking a cup of water. What's the harm in that?'

'Don't give me cheek! You've got that look on your face. It's the same one our Lizzie used to wear when she'd been doing something she shouldn't.'

Betty was astounded at this mention of her mother. She found it difficult to believe that Lizzie had ever done anything wrong. Her mother had been one of the most sensible and kindest people she had ever known. She thought bleakly, why did God have to take the good ones like her mother and Uncle Owen? Why couldn't he have taken Uncle Teddy or her Aunt Elsie, instead? She was always up in the air about something. It showed in her restless movements and her twitching face. No wonder she looked older than her age: crow's feet at the corner of her hazel eyes and grooves going from her nose to her chin. Her hair was no longer the natural gingery red that ran in her side of the family but was going grey. She was busty and had legs straight like tree trunks and they were mottled with sitting too close to the fire during winter. She wasn't at all like Betty's mother.

'Well, are you going to tell me what you've been up to?' demanded Elsie.

'I've been round at Irene Miller's house, listening to records,' said Betty. 'Her brother, Jimmy, who's in the merchant navy, has just brought her the latest Johnnie Ray from America. It's called "All of Me".'

'I wish you wouldn't waste time with her,' said Elsie, frowning. 'And why listen to that caterwauling rubbish? He wails "cry-i-ing over you",' she sang in quite a decent voice. 'Mario Lanza! He's the one you should be listening to.'

'You like "Because You're Mine" don't you, Mum?' said Maggie.

'That's right, love,' said Elsie, giving her younger

daughter a look of approval. 'You know a good singer when you hear one.'

'I think he's great,' said Maggie, heaving a sigh. 'I like Danny Thomas, too. Remember him in that film last year with Doris Day?'

'*I'll See You in My Dreams*,' said Betty. 'He sang "It Had to Be You".'

'That was a lovely song,' said Maggie.

Betty leant her back against the table and folded her arms across her bosom and smiled. 'You're a romantic. There are plenty of singers with voices just as good as them. Frankie Laine, for instance.' She began to sing 'Mule Train'.

'I can do without you belting that out,' said Elsie, emptying potatoes onto the table. 'You can start peeling these, Betty.'

'OK,' she said, opening a drawer and taking out the potato knife. 'But what about his version of "Jealousy" and that one he sang with Jo Stafford, "Hey, Good Lookin"?'

'Enough!' cried Elsie, putting her hands to her ears. 'I've a blinding headache coming on. Maggie, you fry the sausages. I'm going to take some Aspro and have a lie-down.'

'There's a letter for you from Jared on the sideboard,' said Betty.

Her aunt's expression altered. 'Why didn't you say so straight away?' She hurried out of the kitchen, picked up her son's letter and went upstairs.

'I'm going to have to put everything away, as well as cook the sausages now she's gone,' complained Maggie. 'She should have come home from town when I suggested. She got all hot and bothered and I thought she was going to faint.'

'I heard her talking about hot flushes to next door the other day and something about "the change",' said Betty.

'What's that?' asked Maggie.

'Something women go through when they reach her age. I think it means they can no longer have babies.'

'I don't get it,' said Maggie. 'Why should she go all faint because she can't have babies anymore?'

'Don't ask me!' said Betty. 'Your mother never tells us girls anything. It was your Dorothy who had to tell me about periods when I started with them.' She changed the subject. 'Did your mother buy you anything new?'

'Only white gloves. I lost one of the pair she bought me at Christmas. She was a bit narked about it to be honest. I felt guilty because she said she didn't want to be spending money out on gloves for me again,' said Maggie gloomily.

'If she's so short of money, she should make you do without,' said Betty firmly.

Maggie looked annoyed. 'I have to have a pair of gloves to go to church.' She placed several packets on a shelf in the larder. 'Remember Dad?

Until he got ill, he was really generous when it came to finding ways to provide us with pocket money.'

Betty recalled how they'd had to earn their shilling by making him a cup of tea or going to the shops for his cigarettes or evening *Echo*. Fortunately, since her mother's death, she had found herself a little job doing messages for an elderly widow down the road. This she kept quiet about because she was convinced her aunt would take the money from her if she knew about it. As it was, Betty had managed to save her shillings and had them hidden away in an old sock beneath her mattress.

Fortunately, her aunt didn't set foot in Betty's bedroom as she was expected to keep it clean and change the bedding herself. As soon as their evening meal was over, she planned on going up to her room and writing a reply to Emma's letter. She decided not to mention it to Maggie, just in case she went and told her mother. This would be Betty's secret.

Emma was hoeing the vegetable patch when she heard the squeak of the postman's bicycle brakes and then footsteps approaching the front of the house. She dropped the hoe and raced up the garden and into the house, wondering whether it was another response to the second advertisement she had placed in the *Clitheroe Advertiser and Times* or if it was a reply to her letter from her half-sister.

On the mat lay a single envelope. She snatched it up, noticed the postmark and wasted no time in opening the envelope. Inside was a lined sheet of paper that looked like it had been torn from an exercise book, with handwriting that slanted to the right in bright-blue ink. A lot of words had been crammed onto the single sheet. She recognised the address on the right-hand side and her gaze went swiftly to the signature at the bottom. It was from Betty!

Dear Emma,

Thank you for your letter. It was a real thrill to get it. My mum had told me that I had a half-sister living with her grandparents, but I was only little at the time and I'd almost forgotten about you. Anyway, I'm not going to gabble on because there'll be no paper left and I don't want to run out of ink. I'd like to meet you and suggest that we do so outside the Forum cinema on Lime Street in Liverpool next Saturday. You can't really miss it as it's on a corner, and if you come out of the left-hand side of the railway station and go down towards Lime Street, it'll be dead ahead of you. I hope one o'clock will be OK but don't write back, just turn up. I mightn't be as lucky in getting my hands on your letter before my aunt does next time.

Look forward to seeing you,
Betty Booth
P.S. I don't mean this coming Saturday, but
the next.

The postscript made Emma smile and convinced her that her sister really did want to make certain that she arrived at the appointed spot on the right day. A week gave her plenty of time to prepare and it was good that Betty was making allowances for her not knowing Liverpool that well. It was obvious that she hadn't told her aunt about Emma writing to her.

The question now was whether she would have the time to meet Dougie as well as Betty. She decided to write and let him know that her half-sister had been in touch and tell him the time and the place where they were meeting. If he was not on duty, then perhaps he would suggest a rendezvous later in the day? It would be lovely if they could spend time together. Her heart that had been racing after her dash up the garden now seemed to bounce inside her chest just at the thought of seeing Dougie again. She was going to have to keep her fingers crossed that it would happen. Life had taken on a whole new and exciting direction from that which she would have envisaged a year ago. She could not wait to see both of them.

* * *

'Where are you off to?'

Betty almost jumped out of her skin at the sound of Teddy's voice. She had not realised he was in the house. Did she dare pretend she had not heard him and wrench open the door and go out?

'Are you deaf, girl?'

He seized her by the shoulder and Betty stiffened. 'Let me go! I've an appointment that I must keep,' she blurted out.

He spun her around and she saw that he was wearing a towelling dressing gown but his short bowed legs were bare and hairy. He was only the same size as her but of stocky build and there was an expression in his muddy grey-brown eyes that made her feel uneasy.

'That isn't an answer. Meeting a boy, are you?'

'No!' she said indignantly. 'But even if I was, it's no business of yours. You're not my real uncle. Uncle Owen was that!'

'Don't you give me bloody cheek. You're just like your mother, the way you speak to me.' He ran his hands down her back and pulled her against him.

'Y-you know nothing about my mother,' she stammered, her knees beginning to tremble even as she struggled.

'That's right, fight me,' he said against her ear. 'Lizzie thought herself above me and went off with that bloody artist. A lot of good it did her. Both of them are dead now.'

'Don't talk about my parents like that,' cried Betty. 'Let me go!'

'Not bloody likely. We don't often have the house to ourselves like this, do we, girl?' His voice had sunk to a hiss, reminding her of a snake.

She couldn't speak, terrified of what he might do to her. Then there came the sound of voices outside on the step and he released her abruptly, causing her to fall against the wall. 'One word, girl,' he whispered, slapping both her cheeks lightly, 'and you'll regret it. I'm the man of the house and my word goes.'

He made for the stairs and scurried up them in no time.

Instead of waiting for the front door to open and facing her aunt and cousin, Betty turned and ran through the house and out into the garden. Her heart was hammering against her ribs as she made her way along the side of the house. She peered around the corner to see if Elsie and Maggie had gone inside. There was no sign of them, so she wasted no time running towards the bus stop on the main road. She prayed that if she was late at the meeting place, her sister would wait for her.

Emma had read the poster advertising the film *Reluctant Heroes*, showing at the *Forum*, several times. She had arrived too early, hoping that Betty might be early, too, as Emma had arranged to meet Dougie early evening.

'Emma?' A hand touched her arm, startling her.

She whirled round and saw a freckle-faced girl. She was wearing a navy blue gabardine mackintosh that was unbuttoned to reveal a blue and white gingham frock. She looked older than Emma expected, despite the ginger hair tied in bunches and the navy blue beret.

A warm feeling welled up inside Emma. 'Aye, I'm Emma Booth. I take it you're Betty?'

Betty smiled. 'That's me. I know I'm late and I was worried you mightn't wait.'

'After coming all this way, I'd have waited quite a while, luv,' said Emma. 'Ever since I found out about you I've been wanting to meet you.'

'As soon as I read your letter I felt the same. I've always wanted a sister. We don't look like each other, though, do we?' said Betty. 'I take after my mother's side of the family.'

'I think I must get my looks from our father,' said Emma. 'My mother was blonde and more fragile-looking than I am.'

'Do you have a photo of our father?' asked Betty eagerly.

Emma shook her head. 'I hoped you might have one.'

Betty frowned in thought. 'I'm sure there's one of him with Mum somewhere. I remember seeing it when I was younger. Maybe Aunt Elsie has it in the box where she keeps the insurance policies, old birthday cards and things.'

'I'd be really pleased if you could find it. I do have a birthday card Dad made for me when I was three,' said Emma. 'I thought you might like to see it, so I brought it with me. Maybe we can go somewhere, so we can sit and talk?'

'What about Lyons café across the road?' suggested Betty. 'My cousin Maggie goes there with my Auntie Elsie when they come into town. I do have a couple of bob, so I can pay my way.'

Emma smiled. 'That's all right. I think I can afford to treat my little sister.'

Betty's eyes lit up. 'Thanks! I appreciate that because I don't get much in the way of pocket money since Aunt Elsie married again. But I do have a little job.'

They crossed Lime Street and went inside the café and sat down at a table and picked up a menu. A waitress came over to the table with a notepad and pencil and gazed at Emma expectantly.

'A pot of tea for two,' she said.

'Anything to eat?'

Emma looked at Betty. 'What would you like?'

'Seeing as you're paying you choose.'

'What's your favourite cake?' asked Emma.

'Chocolate, but I don't expect you to buy that because it's dear. A scone will do me. After all, you've had the cost of the journey,' said Betty seriously, leaning across the table towards her.

'That's very thoughtful of you,' said Emma,

smiling. 'But if you ever come to visit me, I'll make you a chocolate cake as good as my grandmother used to make before the war.'

'You like baking?' said Betty, interested.

'I'm good at it and I know I'm the one who shouldn't be saying that. The proof is in the tasting,' said Emma. 'Right now I would like to taste what the scones are like here and see if they match up to mine.'

She gave the order and watched as the waitress moved away before taking Lizzie Booth's letter and her father's birthday card from her bag. She slid them across the table towards her half-sister.

Betty picked up the card first and inspected it. 'It's good! I like art, you know, but my aunt wants me to have what she calls a *proper* job. I don't know why she thinks money can't be made from studying art.'

'You must take after our father.'

Betty blushed. 'I like to think so. What do you like to do?'

'I earn money from bookkeeping. I also enjoy knitting and crochet work, as well as cooking, of course.'

'That's creative. Mum was a good cook,' she added, gazing down at the letter open on the table. She felt a catch at her heart as she recognised her mother's handwriting and for several moments could only see the words through a blur of tears.

'Are you all right?' asked Emma in a gentle voice, placing a hand over her half-sister's on the table.

'It's just seeing Mum's handwriting suddenly like that,' said Betty, her voice unsteady.

'I still get upset about Granddad. It's so hard when you lose someone you've known and lived with all your life. I got the impression that your mother Lizzie was a kind and thoughtful person. I would have liked to have met her.'

Betty lifted brimming eyes to Emma. 'You do understand. She was the best person I ever knew and very different from her sister, my Aunt Elsie. She gets all wound up if I mention Mum, so I don't get to talk about her often. I sometimes feel that if I could talk about her more she wouldn't seem so dead.'

'Do you dream about her?'

'Sometimes.'

'Was your mother pretty?'

'Oh yes!' Betty took a handkerchief from a pocket and wiped her eyes. 'She didn't have freckles like me and her hair was a much nicer shade of red. I sometimes wonder whether Aunt Elsie was jealous of Mum and that's why she doesn't like to talk about her.'

'It's possible that your aunt just might find it too painful to talk about her. After all, they were sisters and must have been fond of each other, if your mother decided the pair of you should move in with her family.'

Betty stilled. 'I never thought of that.'

'Is your aunt unkind to you?'

'Not really. We just don't always see eye to eye. Although she's been more difficult since she remarried.' She fell silent, toying with her handkerchief.

Emma waited for her to go on, but when Betty did not continue, she said, 'Would you like to see a photograph of my grandparents? I've one of my mother, too.'

Betty nodded.

Emma took the photos out of her bag and slid them across the table. Betty picked them up and scrutinised them. 'I think your granddad has an interesting face. I'd like to draw him.'

Emma's eyes lit up with pleasure. 'That would be really nice. Keep the photograph. I've others of him at home. He had a lot of sadness in his life but he never let it get him down. He had a good sense of humour. The last time we had a night out, we saw a Fred Astaire musical. Granddad loved singing and dancing.'

Betty smiled. 'I like musicals. Gene Kelly's on in *An American in Paris* at the Majestic cinema and there's a matinee this afternoon.'

Before Emma could comment, the waitress appeared with their order. The letter, the card and the photographs were set aside whilst they drank their tea and ate their scones. Emma could not help comparing them to her own feather-light ones. These scones were fine, and if people were prepared to pay for them, then perhaps she *should* put a couple of chairs and a table out front when the weather was good. She looked forward to seeing Dougie later and discussing the subject with him.

When they had finished eating and drinking, Betty said, 'My elder cousin Dorothy said that *Picturegoer* gave *An American in Paris* a really good write-up.' She hesitated. 'Do you fancy going to the pictures? The cinema is only about a twenty-minute walk away.'

Emma hesitated. 'I did plan on seeing someone else whilst I was in Liverpool.'

'Oh!' Betty's face fell. 'Best forget about it, then.'

Emma thought, who was the more important, Dougie or Betty? She would never have met him if she hadn't been desperate to get to know her half-sister. 'No, if you say it's not too much of a walk, then we could go and see what time the film finishes. I'm not meeting my friend until quarter to five.'

Betty said, 'I didn't realise that you had friends in Liverpool.'

'He's the policeman who helped me to find you.'

'So you became friends because of me,' said Betty, grinning. 'Is he tall, dark and handsome?'

Emma laughed. 'He's certainly tall, but he's fair

127

and blue-eyed. I'll pay the bill and we'll go.'

As they took a short cut through Lime Street station and then up the back of the Empire Theatre into London Road, Emma asked how Betty's cousins had felt about their mother marrying again.

'Jared had already left to do his national service when the wedding took place. I'm sure my aunt wouldn't have married Uncle Teddy if Jared had still been at home. Trouble was that he couldn't put it off any longer as he had finished his apprenticeship.' Betty sighed. 'The day your letter came, one for my aunt also arrived from him. His regiment is being sent to Korea,' she said in a low voice. 'It was news that his mother, his sisters and I have been dreading.'

'When will he be leaving England?'

'Next month.'

'What is he like? Does he have your red hair?' asked Emma.

Betty shook her head. 'He's tallish, has dark-brown hair and is attractive to look at more than conventionally handsome. I'll bring some photographs next time we meet. He's clever, too, and can make me laugh. He followed his dad into the building trade. My uncle had his own little business until he took ill, and then there was just no money and Jared had to go and work for someone else so he could finish his apprenticeship. He served his time as a plasterer but he can do other jobs to do with building.'

'He sounds a very useful man to have around,' said Emma, thinking of her leaking roof.

'He is! Jared attended the Liverpool School of Art as part of his studies for his City & Guilds examinations,' said Betty earnestly. 'That's when I started thinking that perhaps I could go there, too.'

Emma smiled. 'If you're that keen, you should go.'

'Easier said than done, because my aunt is against it,' said Betty, frowning. 'But I'm determined to have a go, even if it means that I have to have an ordinary job to earn money and go to night school when I'm older.'

'That's the ticket,' said Emma encouragingly. 'Tell me what else you're interested in besides art and musicals. What subjects do you enjoy at school and what about your girl cousins? What are they like?'

'I like geography and I wish I could be better at French. I'd like to go to Paris one day and see the paintings in the Louvre,' said Betty with enthusiasm.

'Is that why you want to see *An American in Paris*?' teased Emma.

Betty said, 'You're quick off the mark, aren't you? Gene Kelly is an artist in the film, so it's not just that I want to see it because of the Parisian background and the singing and dancing.'

'Well, let's hope that we get to see it and it

finishes in time for me to meet my policeman,' said Emma.

'Yes, let's hope,' said Betty, linking her arm through Emma's. 'I do like you. I wish we could have met years ago.'

'Me too,' said Emma, touched by Betty's words. 'I'm sure you and my granddad would have got on.'

'Do you like living in a village?' asked Betty.

'It's all I've ever known.'

'Are people different in a village?'

'I presume you mean different from townies, and that's something I can't really answer because I've never lived in a town,' said Emma. 'I have a friend whose mother thinks Liverpool is sin city.'

Betty looked taken aback. 'I've never thought it was that bad, although I suppose there is a fair amount of crime, just as there is in most ports and big cities. Occasionally you read in the *Echo* about robberies and fights on the streets, caused by gangs of youths or men. Mum used to say that none of us are perfect.'

Emma said, 'My granddad often said that we've all sinned and fallen short of the glory of God, so we shouldn't judge people.'

'I suppose judging people is something that all people do, though,' said Betty.

'In a village most people know each other and are interested in what's going on in each others' lives,' said Emma.

'But that happens in neighbourhoods in cities,' said Betty. 'My aunt worries about what the neighbours think.'

'My mother ran away to Liverpool, but not because she'd done anything wrong. I never knew about it until recently, but I bet it was the talk of the village at the time.'

'Why did she run away?'

'Because she wanted to go on the stage, and eventually she did,' said Emma, smiling. She changed the subject. 'So how far is this picture house?'

They had already passed the TJ Hughes store, so Betty said, 'Not far now.'

Shortly after, they had bought their tickets and were seated in the auditorium of the Majesty cinema. The lights dimmed and the opening title and credits came up on the screen. They had missed the B-movie but both were soon caught up in the foot-tapping music of Gershwin, and, although the film had what Emma thought of as its darker moments, Betty was obviously enjoying every minute.

When they came out of the cinema, they were both humming 'Our Love is Here to Stay'. It was only when they reached London Road and there was a clock on a wall outside a shop that Betty said, 'Gosh, look at the time!'

Emma saw that the hands stood at twenty to five. 'I'm going to have to go!' she cried, breaking into a run.

'When will we meet again?' asked Betty eagerly, keeping up with her.

Emma glanced at her. 'I can't afford to come too often.'

'What about the first week in June?' suggested Betty. 'It's half-term. We could meet during the week.'

'OK!' said Emma. 'Write to me and let me know which day and the time and meeting place.'

'Will do,' said Betty, slowing her pace. 'See you then.'

Emma raised a hand in acknowledgement and put on a spurt. She had arranged to meet Dougie in Lime Street, only when she arrived outside the railway station, there was no sign of him. Her heart was thudding in her chest with her dash along London Road and she felt an acute disappointment because he was not there. She could only think that he must have got fed up of waiting for her and gone. What must he think of her? He had every right to be angry. Emma had always prided herself on her punctuality. Now, due to her being late, she might never see him again. She could have wept.

CHAPTER NINE

'You're really going to go through with this?' asked Lila, watching Emma place a notice in the front window of the cottage.

'Why not? It's worth a try.' Emma was not going to confess to having the collywobbles about this venture.

'The weather forecast isn't good,' said Lila tentatively.

'That's why I haven't put a table and chairs outside. It said showers, which means that people from the towns and cities will be hoping for spells of sunshine and head for the seaside or the countryside. Some are bound to come and visit the abbey over this Whit bank holiday weekend. I want to be prepared. The food won't go to waste because what's over will feed me for a few days.'

Lila shook her head. 'Mam thinks you're mad. She said you're young enough and bright enough to train to be a nurse.'

Emma's eyebrows shot up. 'Why should I do that? I already have qualifications in bookkeeping. Besides, in my opinion, nurses are born, not made. It was enough for me to cope with looking after Gran when she was seriously ill and dying by inches. It isn't where my gifts lie.'

'You are fortunate,' said Lila. 'Some of us can't pick and choose what we want to do with our lives. Mam decided for me. She said that I didn't have much of a brain and could earn reasonable money at the mill, so she pushed me into that job.'

'That's a terrible thing to say to a daughter,' said Emma indignantly. 'You never told me that at the time, and no wonder. I think not only is it insulting those who work in the mill, but she hasn't given you a good opinion of yourself. Most people can succeed at a whole host of different jobs, if they get the opportunity and the right training. Anyway, you should put yourself forward to be a nurse. I'm sure coping with your dad must be good training.'

'I did suggest it at one time but Mam said I hadn't the patience. Anyway, I don't want to be a nurse now. Besides, we're talking about you, not me,' said Lila. 'Do you really think you're going to make a profit serving teas?'

Emma shrugged. 'I feel I've got to give it a try. Besides, I'm not as desperate as I was for money earlier in the year. I've another client. The money isn't marvellous, because I didn't like charging her too much, but at least it's regular.'

'Who is it this time?'

'A little old lady in Clitheroe. Her brother died suddenly and she wants to keep on the sweet shop which he owned. She's always done most of the serving behind the counter anyway, whilst he had another job. Fortunately for me he did all the paperwork and she doesn't have a head for figures.' Emma frowned. 'Which, when you think of it, is all wrong. There must be lots of women who are good at arithmetic, so in any business or family both men and women should know what's what when it comes to balancing the books.'

'Mam has control of the money in our house,' said Lila, twirling a strand of light-brown hair around a finger. 'She had to when Dad was away fighting in the war. I reckon most arguments between husbands and wives are over money. Most men don't want their wives knowing what they earn. You're lucky, Emma, having control over your own money.'

'I just wish I had more of it to have control of,' said Emma with a wry smile as she went outside to check if her notice was straight.

It looked quite professional and she felt proud of her handiwork. Perhaps she had inherited some of her father's artistic talent after all. She had embellished the wording with sprays of blackberries and strawberries advertising both jams available to have with locally made cream on her home-made scones. She had also made a pan of Lancashire hotpot using breast of lamb. She thought of Dougie and wished he could see her now. She had sent him a letter, apologising for being late for their meeting in Liverpool. She had not heard back from him and was disappointed.

'Right, then,' said Lila, clapping her hands together as she came up behind Emma. 'I'll have a cup of tea and one of your scones with strawberry jam and cream. And I'll tell you what, Em, I'll take a chair and the card table outside and hopefully it'll encourage trade.'

Emma chuckled. 'Good idea, but what if you get caught in a shower?'

'I'll come back inside. I suppose what you really need is a wrought iron table with a big umbrella,' said Lila thoughtfully. 'Ones just like you see in posters of Torquay or Rhyl at railway stations.'

'Perhaps one day I will have huge striped umbrellas and wrought iron tables,' said Emma, her brown eyes sparkling. 'But right now you sit outside and enjoy the fresh air and I'll serve you there, miss, but I'm not charging you. You're my friend.'

Lila shook her head at her. 'Now you're being daft. You're doing this to make money. I can afford to pay for a scone and a cup of tea. What are friends for if not to be a proper support? I think your prices are very reasonable.'

Emma flushed. 'I've based them on prices I saw in Lyons café in Liverpool and a tea shop in Clitheroe.'

'I see,' said Lila, picking up a chair and taking it outside.

As Emma put on the kettle, she thought how pleasant it would be to just sit outside and watch the world go by. She liked watching people and was interested in what made them tick. Remembering her stolen bag, she frowned, thinking about what it was that turned some people into thieves, wife beaters and murderers, and others, like Dougie, to become policemen. She wondered if he ever got scared when he came up against a violent criminal. She sighed. Would she ever see him again? It was too late to write to him about her being in Liverpool this coming Wednesday. Betty was meeting her off the train. Maybe on Tuesday she would write and tell him that she'd taken his advice and was turning her house into a tea shop.

By the end of the day, Emma's hopes of her venture being truly launched successfully were dashed. Several of the villagers had called in to encourage her and have a chat, but only one other, besides Lila, had sat down and paid for a cup of tea and a scone. There had been no day trippers at all. As she sat with Tibby at her feet and a bowl of hotpot and a couple of scones on the table in front of her, she felt full of gloom.

She hardly slept that night, filled with indecision about whether it was worth trying again tomorrow. Dawn came early, around four-thirty, so she got up, let the cat out, and went for a walk along the river. The birds were madly twittering in the trees and she saw a water vole and a kingfisher and the sight lifted her spirits. The air had a slight chill to it, but the sky hinted that the day might turn out fine. Her walk had done her good and she felt more hopeful. When she arrived back at the house, she decided to make a fresh batch of scones before breakfast and go to early communion for a change.

There were no hymns and she missed having a good sing with the congregation at the later service. She prayed for Betty, wondering whether she went to church. If she did, Emma could imagine her singing her head off, belting forth such hymns as 'Hills of the North, Rejoice'. It was one of Emma's favourites, although it was an Advent hymn, so wrong for this time of the year. 'Come Down, O Love Divine' was more appropriate for Whitsuntide.

She decided to make puff pastry and put a crust

on the hotpot and turn it into a pie. It was just after twelve, and while she was listening to *Two-Way Family Favourites*, which linked servicemen stationed in Germany with those at home, a husband and wife entered her front room. They told Emma that they were from Manchester and that the sun had woken them early and so they had set out in their Morris Minor for a walk on the fells and then had decided to come and have a look at the ruined abbey. They had already done a four-hour stint on the hills and were thirsty and very hungry. They wanted something more substantial than scones and tea and their eyes lit up when she mentioned her hotpot pie. They scoffed it in no time at all and also ate a couple of scones each and left a generous tip. She wanted to ask them to recommend her to their friends but didn't have the nerve, so she just thanked them and waved them off as they drove away.

For the next hour she was convinced that visitors to the abbey and walkers would call in, but, except for a lone woman dressed in tweeds who was from down south and doing a tour of northern ruined abbeys and castles, there was no one else. Not even Lila dropped by, so Emma shared the remains of the hotpot with the cat and told herself that it really was early days yet. The whole of the summer stretched before her, and, pray God, business would improve. She reminded herself that there was still tomorrow which was bank holiday Monday.

She rose early again the following day and decided to make lentil soup and Chorley cakes, knowing the latter would keep in a sealed tin for several days if she had no customers. She was delighted when, about eleven, one solitary cyclist called in, wanting a sandwich. She could only offer him egg or crumbly white Lancashire cheese with her home-made chutney. The chutney brought forth the question whether she had a jar to sell. Taken by surprise, she offered him one of her remaining two jars and he gave her a florin for it, saying it was the best he had ever tasted. When he had left, she danced round the kitchen. Such frivolous behaviour was brought under control when Lila entered, via the garden, and asked how business was going.

Emma smiled. 'I've just sold a jar of my home-made chutney.'

'Good for you. Dad likes chutney.' Lila sat down and yawned.

'Late night?' asked Emma.

Lila gave a wry smile. 'A disturbed one. Mam did an extra shift at the hospital. They had trouble with one of the patients going completely crackers. Dad had a bad night, too, with his leg giving him gyp and he wasn't pleased with the lunch I made him either. Mam's off today and is resting in bed, so I thought I'd get away.' Lila yawned again.

'What have you got to eat? Anything nice?'

'Lentil soup or Chorley cake.'

Lila wrinkled her nose. 'You know what I really fancy?'

Emma gave her an enquiring look.

'Chocolate cake,' said Lila.

Emma remembered Betty wanting chocolate cake at the Lyons café in Liverpool. 'I'll tell you what. I've some cocoa, so I'll make a small one, but while I do so, why don't you go back home and bring your dad here for some soup and a sandwich?'

Lila stared at her. 'It is a smashing idea but he can't walk without being in pain and the wheelchair has a wonky wheel.'

Emma grimaced. 'Sorry! I just thought it would be good for him to get out.'

'It would, but it's really difficult pushing him in that wheelchair.'

At that moment someone called, 'Emma, are you in?'

To her amazement, she recognised that voice and rushed into the front room. She stared at Dougie from starry eyes. 'Fancy you coming here today! When you didn't answer my letter I thought I'd never see you again.'

'Sorry about that, but life's been a bit hectic,' he said ruefully. 'And to be honest, I owe you more than one apology. I didn't turn up at the meeting place either. One of my twin brothers ended up in hospital and Mam needed me. He's still there and, as I decided the other twin was less likely to get into trouble if I kept my eye on him, I've brought him with me.'

Suddenly, Emma noticed a sullen, spotty-faced youth lounging against the door jamb. 'Is that him?'

'Aye, this is Norm,' replied Dougie, with a long-suffering air. 'Say hello to Miss Booth, Norm,' he added without looking round.

'Ciao,' said Norm, raising a hand languidly.

'Hello,' said Emma, presuming 'ciao' was Liverpool slang. 'Please, sit down, both of you,' she said, pulling out chairs.

They both sat down at a table and sniffed the air. 'Something smells good,' said Dougie.

'It's my home-made lentil soup,' said Emma, beaming at him and rubbing her hands together. 'Would you like some?'

'Too right I want some,' said Dougie, returning her smile.

'Does your brother want a bowl, as well?'

Norm nodded.

'Two soups coming up, then,' said Emma, almost skipping out of the room.

Instantly Lila pounced on her. 'Did I hear you say the name *Dougie*?'

'Aye, he's here,' she whispered, 'and there was me thinking I'd never see him again and he's come all this way to say sorry.' Emma's face glowed.

Lila stared at her. 'You've really got it bad, haven't you?'

'I don't know what you mean,' said Emma loftily, setting about heating up the soup on the range and fetching bowls and spoons. 'He has one of his brothers with him,' she added.

'So you're feeding them both?'

'Aye.'

'I hope you're charging them. I know your soft heart but you are in business to make a living out of this,' said Lila.

Emma glanced at her. 'Dougie is a friend.'

'A friend you haven't seen for at least a couple of months and didn't answer your letter. You must be realistic,' said Lila.

'He had a reason for that,' said Emma hastily, 'and keep your voice down.'

'You have to charge him,' said Lila earnestly.

'I offered the soup to him. He didn't ask for it,' said Emma.

'Even so,' said Lila. 'It was his idea that you did this and so he should support you by coughing up.'

'What's going on?'

Both girls started at the sound of Dougie's voice.

'Nothing,' said Emma hastily, glancing over at him standing in the doorway. Oooh, he was so tall and strong-looking! 'Do you want bread with your soup?' she asked.

143

'Yeah! And I'll pay for it,' he replied, shooting a frowning glance at Lila.

She had the grace to blush and mumbled an apology and looked away.

'You don't have to pay,' said Emma, taking a loaf from the bread bin. 'You're here as my guest.'

'No, I'm not,' he said firmly. 'I arrived here uninvited. It would have been difficult for you not to offer us your home-made soup when our tongues were almost hanging out.'

'I wouldn't deny that but even so . . .' Emma shifted uncomfortably from one foot to the other.

Dougie walked over to her and brushed her hot cheek with his lips. 'No arguments, Emma. I can afford it more than you can to give it away.'

Before she could say anything else, he had returned to the front room and closed the door firmly behind him.

Emma glanced at Lila and picked up the bread knife. 'He heard you. How embarrassing is that?'

'I'm sorry. I was only thinking of you,' said Lila, staring out of the window. 'Besides, it forced his hand, didn't it? He said he could afford to pay. Anyway, Em, you know what they say – the way to a man's heart is through his stomach.'

'I don't need to be told that,' said Emma, 'so will you be quiet and let me get on with what I'm doing!'

'I'll go if you like,' said Lila, glancing over her shoulder at her.

'You don't have to. What did you come for, anyway?' asked Emma, placing bread on a plate.

'You've forgotten already! I needed to get away from my parents and I came to see how business was going. As you now have customers, I will go,' said Lila, opening the back door.

Emma realised her friend was hurt and was about to call her back when she heard a hissing noise and saw that the soup was about to boil over. She had to let Lila go so she could swiftly remove the pan from the heat. She filled the two bowls she had put on a tray with the plate of bread before opening the door and carrying the food into the front room.

Dougie stood up and took the tray from her. Norm, who was sitting back in the dining chair with the front legs off the floor, immediately sat forward and crashed into the table. 'Will you be careful!' roared his brother. 'It's a wonder it wasn't you that fell off that bloody wall.'

'You'd have liked that, wouldn't you?' retorted Norm, thrusting out his chin. 'Our Pete was always your favourite.'

'I don't know where you get that idea from when I spent years not knowing which one of you was which,' said Dougie, placing a bowl of soup in front of his brother. 'Now, shut up! I don't want any more arguing in front of Emma. She has enough to contend with having been left on her own to fend for herself and trying to get a business going.'

'Don't worry about me,' said Emma, slightly shocked by the angry exchange, unaccustomed as she was to hearing brothers arguing. 'I-I'll make a pot of tea, shall I?'

'Yes, you do that, Emma,' said Dougie in his normal voice when addressing her.

'Is there any butter?' asked Norm.

Before Emma could answer, Dougie said, 'Some things are still on ration, you know.'

'But this is the country,' protested Norm. 'They have cows in fields, so they should have butter.'

Emma understood his logic. 'I might be able to find you some.'

'But you'll put it on the bill, Emma,' insisted Dougie.

'I really wish you hadn't overheard what Lila said,' said Emma, hurrying from the room.

When she returned with the butter, Dougie smiled and said, 'So that was your friend, Lila. I thought as much.'

'I know she shouldn't have said what she did, but we've been friends for most of our lives. She feels she has to look out for me, now that I'm on my own.'

'And I suppose she wants you to make a going concern of this, so you stay in the village,' said Dougie.

'That's right. When I told her about my half-sister, Lila thought I might want to go and live in Liverpool,' explained Emma. 'It's not that she's got anything against the place, but her mother would never allow her to go there.'

'Why?'

'Mrs Ashcroft works as a nurse and Mr Ashcroft was wounded in the war and is crippled. He can walk but it's painful for him to do so. He can't work, so he seldom gets out. Lila is an only child like me, so there's no one to share the load when it comes to looking after him.'

He nodded thoughtfully. 'Does he have a wheelchair?'

'Aye, but it has a wonky wheel and so it's difficult to push, and their house is just outside the village.' Emma reached for his empty bowl. 'Would you like a Chorley cake with your tea?'

'Sure, why not?' Dougie glanced across at his brother. 'Norm, Chorley cake?'

'What's one of them?' asked Norm, handing his empty bowl and spoon to Emma. 'I enjoyed that. You can come and stay at our house any day. Mam can't make soup like that.'

'Enough,' said Dougie, frowning him down.

Emma murmured, 'So, two Chorley cakes?'

Dougie nodded.

Emma went into the kitchen, considering the compliment Norm had paid her. It had come

147

unexpectedly and she could just imagine what his mother might say if Emma turned up at their house, saying that she'd come to take over the cooking. She giggled and wondered what Dougie's mother was like. Would she welcome Emma, if her friendship with her eldest son were to develop into something more serious? She thought of the way Dougie had kissed her cheek and touched the place where his lips had rested for an instant. That, too, had been unexpected and no doubt was a spur-of-the-moment thing. Should she really be reading something into it?

She put the Chorley cakes onto plates and carried them into the other room. 'Are you here just for the day?' she asked, placing them in front of the brothers.

'No, I have tomorrow off as well,' said Dougie. 'We brought our bikes on the train, so will have a cycle round, stay in a youth hostel and then be home by tomorrow evening.'

'I hope the weather holds out for you.'

'We have waterproofs.' He took a mouthful of tea before adding, 'So when will you be seeing your sister again?'

Emma's face brightened. 'Wednesday! She's meeting me off the train.'

He frowned. 'She does realise that's the day that the men of the first battalion Liverpool King's Regiment are coming to town? There's going to be over seven hundred of them marching through the main streets of the city centre. I won't be able to meet up with you because I'll be on duty.'

Emma's expression altered. 'Surely she must know! Her cousin, Jared, is in the King's and she told me he's sailing for Korea this month.'

'That's right. The King's are leaving Liverpool for the Far East on the troopship *Devonshire*. It's scheduled to sail at six-thirty in the evening. What time are the pair of you meeting?'

'One o'clock.'

'Then you'll have plenty of time to see the King's,' said Dougie, his face alight. 'It'll be a sight worth seeing. The city's already decked out with flags and banners. I reckon it'll be a crush, though, because thousands are bound to turn out to watch them.'

Emma thought about what he was saying and asked, 'What about the soldiers' families? Will they get a good place to watch their menfolk march past before they sail?'

'Some members of the families will,' said Dougie. 'They'll be on the upper deck of the Prince's Landing Stage to see the soldiers after they've arrived by train from Wiltshire at the Riverside railway station. The soldiers will be welcomed aboard the *Devonshire* by their commanding officer and will have a short time aboard before they march through the city. Their families will be there to watch them set out.'

'So it's likely that his mother could be there and maybe his sisters, as well?' said Emma.

He nodded. 'Places would be limited, so it looks like your half-sister was not included.'

Emma agreed. 'But she'd want to see him.'

'I should imagine so, and Lime Street is as good a place as any to watch the soldiers march past. St George's Plateau is where the pair of you should get yourself a speck.'

'It wouldn't surprise me if Betty had it already worked out,' said Emma, smiling.

He asked about her sister and how they'd got on together. Emma thought she had already told him in her letter but repeated what she had written. 'I'm glad you weren't disappointed in each other,' he said.

'So am I,' said Emma. 'I think she really misses her mother, and her aunt seldom talks about her. She doesn't like her aunt's second husband, Uncle Teddy.'

'I wouldn't like Mam putting someone else in Dad's place, to tell you the truth,' said Dougie. 'What d'you say, Norm?'

'I only just about remember Dad,' said the youth, wiping cake crumbs from his chin. 'But we don't need a stepdad. It's bad enough having you on our backs.'

Dougie scowled. 'Yous two need someone behind you. I'll be glad when the pair of you leave school and get jobs. I won't be worrying what you're up to during the school holidays then.'

'Come off it,' said Norm, picking up the teapot and refilling his cup. 'You know that you like having us to boss around. More tea?'

Dougie took the pot from him. 'Emma, what about you having a cuppa?'

'Thanks! I think I will,' she said, fetching a cup.

She asked what had happened to Norm's twin that had put him in hospital. Dougie's face darkened. 'All I can say is that it was a black day when he did what he did. If I hadn't been off duty, then he could have been in really serious trouble.'

'We were only larking about,' said Norm sullenly. 'You forget that you were once our age.'

'When I was your age there was a war on and I'd been through the Blitz acting as a message boy and nearly got meself killed a couple of times,' said Dougie firmly. He drained his cup and reached inside his pocket and withdrew his wallet. 'Can I have the bill, Emma? It's time we were getting going.'

She wanted to say *Must you go?* Instead she wrote on a pad what they had to eat and drink and the cost. She tore off the slip of paper and handed it to him. He didn't say anything but handed over a ten-shilling note. 'I'll go and get some change,' she said.

'No! Keep it.' Dougie stood up. 'You're underpricing

yourself and the rest is a tip for the excellent service. I'll be recommending you to my friends and anyone I see on my travels today.'

'It really is far too much, but kind of you,' said Emma, delighted that he had enjoyed her food.

Dougie smiled. 'I'm made up that you took notice of my suggestion.'

She saw him and Norm out and stood waving as they rode off on their bicycles, wondering when she would see Dougie again. She hoped it would not be too long. She went back indoors, washed the crockery and cutlery that the two brothers had used and then waited for more customers, but no one else came that afternoon. Remembering how she and Lila had parted, Emma decided to make her friend a small chocolate cake. It did not take her long and that evening she walked to the Ashcrofts' house with it.

Mrs Ashcroft opened the door to her and stared down at her with a fixed expression on her face. 'What do you want?'

Emma was tempted to say *Thanks for the welcome* but kept a rein on her feelings. 'I've brought a chocolate cake,' she said sweetly. 'Lila was saying she fancied one. It's only small but there should be enough for you and Mr Ashcroft to have a slice too.'

The older woman's expression thawed. 'That is good of you, Emma. Come in and I'll make a pot of tea.'

Emma stepped over the threshold and Mrs Ashcroft called up the stairs to her daughter. Then, taking the cake tin from Emma, she went into the kitchen.

Lila came running. 'So he's gone, has he? Did he pay you?'

Emma raised her eyes to the ceiling. 'You're terrible! I've a good mind to take my chocolate cake back. It was embarrassing. He gave me a whole ten shillings.'

Lila's mouth gaped and then she smiled. 'So he should.'

'At least he's not tight, even if he is forgetful,' said Emma.

'What did he forget?'

'It doesn't matter,' said Emma.

Lila gave her a look and then said, 'Come in to the sitting room.'

Jack Ashcroft glanced up from the model he was working on. 'Did I hear mention of chocolate cake?'

Emma smiled. 'I promised Lila and a promise is a promise. I just hope it's good enough for my best friend.'

Lila slipped a hand through Emma's arm. 'I'm sorry I embarrassed you. Sit down and take the weight off your feet.'

Emma sat on the sofa and Lila sat next to her. 'So when's he coming again?' she asked in a low voice.

'I don't know, but he was telling me about the Liverpool King's Regiment coming to the city on Wednesday. Betty's cousin is one of the soldiers and she is bound to want to see the regiment march while I'm there,' said Emma.

'What's that I heard about the King's Regiment?' asked Mr Ashcroft.

Emma proceeded to tell him all that Dougie had told her and about her half-sister's cousin doing his national service and sailing to the Far East. He nodded. 'He should be proud to serve with them,' said Mr Ashcroft. 'The Liverpool King's is one of the oldest infantry regiments of the British Army. It was formed in 1685.'

'That's going back some way!' said Emma.

He nodded.

But before they could say any more, Mrs Ashcroft entered with the tea tray. They watched as she cut the cake and Emma waited for them to voice their opinion.

'Needs a bit more sugar but I would expect that with rationing, but you're not a bad little cake maker,' said Mrs Ashcroft, finishing her portion first. She licked a finger and gathered up the last crumbs from her plate with it.

'You're too damn fussy,' said Mr Ashcroft, leaning back in his chair and stretching out his leg with a grimace of pain. 'It was very kind of you to think of us, Emma. A very nice bit of cake.'

'I'm glad to say my hens are laying well,' said Emma, 'otherwise, you wouldn't be having the cake.'

'Well, it was lovely,' said Lila. 'Another cup of tea, Em?'

Emma smiled. 'No thanks, I'll have to be going. I've work in Clitheroe tomorrow and I'm going to Liverpool on Wednesday, but I'll be doing teas again next weekend.'

'The Sabbath should be kept holy,' voiced Mrs Ashcroft.

'There speaks a woman who's worked many a Sunday,' said her husband.

She frowned. 'My work's essential.'

'Aye, so you keep telling me,' he said dryly.

'I'd best be going,' said Emma hastily, not wanting to listen to any more family arguments. She picked up her cake tin.

'I'll see you out,' said Lila.

The two young women stood on the step for a few moments. 'So will you be seeing *him* when you go to Liverpool?' asked Lila.

'No, he's on duty. I don't know when I'll be seeing him again. I'm just hoping it won't be too long.' She jumped down off the step and made for the gate.

'Perhaps he'll come and see you again soon,' called Lila.

'I hope so,' said Emma, opening the gate and

closing it behind her before hurrying away.

She knew that she must not be forever thinking of Dougie. After all, she'd had a life here in the village before she met him. Not only was there her bookkeeping but there was a lot to be done in the garden. She must water her tomato plants that evening without fail. When the time came for her to make her special chutney she wanted there to be plenty of green tomatoes left on the plants, never mind luscious, ripe red ones. She had to get everything done if she wanted Wednesday to be clear for her trip to Liverpool.

CHAPTER TEN

'Who are you getting all dolled up for?' asked Maggie. 'You're not going to the Prince's Landing Stage to wave our Jared off.'

'No, I'm not, and neither are you,' said Betty, fastening a green, bow-shaped plastic slide into her hair just above her ear.

Maggie elbowed Betty in the ribs. 'Move over! I can't see the whole of my head in the mirror with you in the way.'

'Don't do that!' exclaimed Betty, frowning. 'I'll move in a minute. Where's your Uncle Teddy? I know he hasn't gone with your mum and Dorothy.'

'He's actually got some work,' said Maggie. 'So who are you meeting and why did you take photographs out of Mum's box upstairs yesterday?'

Betty paused in the act of putting on her dark-green jacket. 'I don't know what you mean,' she said casually.

'Oh yes you do!' cried Maggie, facing her. 'I saw you taking them because you left the door open slightly. You've no right to be nosing in that box. It's Mum's private stuff.'

Betty's expression was instantly stormy. 'Some of those photographs belonged to my mum! By rights they're mine! Anyway, Aunt Elsie is not going to miss them unless you go blabbing.'

'I won't tell her if you let me come with you,' said Maggie, reaching for her cardigan.

Betty groaned. 'Isn't it enough that we live under the same roof without you having to come everywhere with me? I want a few hours to myself.'

'I hardly ever go anywhere with you,' protested Maggie. 'So who are you meeting that you don't want my company? I thought we could go into town and watch the King's march by.'

Betty stilled. 'Why don't you go with one of your mates?' When her cousin didn't answer, she added, 'I'm going. See you later.' Betty opened the door and would have slammed it behind her if Maggie hadn't caught hold of it. 'Don't be a meanie! If you don't let me come, I'll believe you're seeing a boy, and you know what Mum will say about that.'

'I'm not seeing a boy,' said Betty, remembering

Uncle Teddy accusing her of the very same thing last time she had been in a rush to meet Emma. She thought of his unwelcome behaviour and wondered if she should have mentioned it to her aunt. She was only too thankful that she had not been alone in his company since. At least he wasn't here now, otherwise she would have thought twice about leaving Maggie alone with him in the house. She stared at her younger cousin. 'Now go and do whatever you were going to do before you decided you wanted to come with me,' she said softly.

Maggie folded her arms across her narrow chest and said belligerently, 'Go out on your own and leave me behind. See if I care.'

'Don't try and make me feel guilty. I'm going and I don't want you following me,' said Betty firmly.

Maggie stuck out her tongue and then marched out of the room and up the stairs. A relieved Betty opened the front door and went out and hurried to the main road to catch the bus. There was a queue and she was conscious of several more people tagging on behind her. When the bus came, she went upstairs and managed to get a seat at the front, so she could gaze down on people. This was an enjoyable pastime despite the air upstairs being fuggy with cigarette smoke.

As the bus headed into town along Stanley Road, she thought of Emma and hoped she wouldn't mind spending several hours on St George's Plateau, waiting for the King's to march past. They needed to be there early if they were to get a good speck. If there was time, they should make it to the Pier Head before the regiment arrived there and be able to watch the ship sail. The lord mayor would be giving an address from the balcony of the town hall in Dale Street, so that would delay the regiment.

Betty could not wait to see Emma but to her dismay, as she stepped down onto the pavement in Lime Street, she saw Maggie staring at her through the downstairs window of the bus. Her cousin smiled sweetly at her, but to Betty's relief there was a queue of people behind her, waiting to get off the bus. She wasted no time diving into the crowds that lined the pavement, hoping that her cousin wouldn't see which way she went, and made for the station.

Emma's train must have got in early because she was waiting beneath the clock. Her face lit up as she saw Betty coming towards her. She looked smart, thought the younger girl. Her half-sister was wearing a matching skirt and blouse in pale turquoise with a green bolero. 'I know I'm early again,' said Emma, 'but I didn't want to be late.'

'It doesn't matter,' said Betty, smiling. 'I've something to tell you. I hope you don't mind but Jared's regiment is marching through Liverpool centre today and I want to see if I can spot him. I had thought we could go to St George's Plateau and watch from there, but—'

'I know about it,' said Emma, tucking her arm in Betty's. 'My policeman turned up on Monday and told me. He suggested that we go to the Plateau.'

'I was just going to say that there's already crowds there,' said Betty. 'Apparently the regiment will be taking a salute opposite the Plateau. We could go window shopping along Church Street and Lord Street because they'll be coming along there on their way to St George's Hall. I'd rather avoid Lime Street if I can. It's where I got off the bus and my cousin was on it. I'm sure she intends following me but I managed to give her the slip. Trouble is,' added Betty, 'she might still be hanging around there. We could go out the other side of the station and across the road to Clayton Square. She knows nothing about you and I want it to remain like that because she'd go and blab to Aunt Elsie if she discovered who you were.'

'OK! I've brought some food and a thermos flask,' said Emma. 'We can always have a picnic on the pavement whilst we're waiting.'

As they made their way to Church Street, Emma gazed about her with interest, thinking she had never seen so many people. There were women selling flowers that Betty called 'Mary Ellens' opposite a large departmental store called Owen Owen and the food emporium, Reece's.

'They sell delicious cakes in there,' said Betty, gazing in the window. 'Mum took me once. It has a dance hall on the first floor and it used to be a favourite place to meet those in the armed services during the war. I believe they still have dances. Do you dance, Emma?'

'Aye. Country dancing mostly,' she said. 'My granddad used to enjoy prancing about.'

'We learnt some of that in school. It's fun but you can tie yourself into knots trying to follow the steps,' said Betty with a smile. 'By the way, I managed to get some photos of my mum and our dad.'

Emma was delighted. 'Have you one of them on their wedding day?'

'No, but I have one of Mum on her own, one with me as a baby and a couple of her and our dad together on a day out at New Brighton.'

'New Brighton?'

'It's a seaside resort the other side of the Mersey. I remember us going there as a family when Uncle Owen was alive. We haven't been since.'

Betty fumbled in her pocket for the photographs and her elbow caught a woman loaded down with shopping bags as they passed the corner into Church Street. The woman dropped one of her bags. 'Watch where you're going, girl,' she said crossly.

'Sorry,' said Betty, bending down to pick up the bag and its spilt contents. As she straightened up and handed it to the woman, she caught sight of Maggie a few yards behind her. 'Damn!' she exclaimed.

'Language,' said the woman.

Betty ignored her and seized hold of Emma's arm. 'Would you believe it! Our Maggie is just behind us. She's a real pain in the neck,' she added savagely.

'Is she really that bad?' asked Emma, allowing herself to be hustled along the pavement.

'She could be worse,' said Betty, her heart-shaped face flushed and irritable. 'But she's close to her mother and a terrible chatterbox. She just wouldn't be able to keep this quiet and then Aunt Elsie would probably be determined to prevent me from meeting you.'

'Perhaps we'll lose her in the crowd,' said Emma.

Betty could only hope so as they continued along Church Street into Lord Street where the devastation caused by the bombs of the Luftwaffe was more obvious. Betty paused at the Victoria Monument and faced the way they had come, searching for any sign of her cousin.

'Gosh, this must have looked a real mess during the war,' said Emma.

Betty nodded absently. 'And after. Mum brought me into town not long before she was killed. We stood on this spot. Wherever you looked it was just brick fields. She pointed out to me where different buildings had once stood. The Customs House was destroyed and the Head Post Office; the William Brown Library was almost totally obliterated, the same with the museum. Fortunately all the books and exhibits had been removed, mostly to Wales, as were the paintings from the Walker Art Gallery, but that pretty well escaped damage. Two big departmental stores, Blackler's and Lewis's, were completely gutted and, of course, the docks and warehouses and hundreds of homes were destroyed.'

'Terrible, such loss,' murmured Emma. 'My policeman friend, Dougie, said there's the remains of a church called St Luke's that's a memorial to those who died during the war. I'd like to visit that as a sign of respect to our dad.'

'If you'd mentioned that earlier we could have gone there.'

'I also want to visit Liverpool's registry office,' said Emma.

'There's one not far away from St Luke's in Gambier Terrace. It's up near the Anglican cathedral. Now that is worth a visit, although some of the stained glass windows were damaged during the war.'

'I'd like to do that another time,' said Emma. 'Right now I'm looking forward to seeing the famous Liver birds.'

'At least the Luftwaffe didn't get them,' said Betty, a lilt of satisfaction in her youthful voice. 'We'll have a look at them eventually, but right now, I think we might as well stay where we are. It's a good perch here on the monument to watch out for our Jared.'

Emma was quite content to do as Betty suggested, so they settled themselves. Emma decided that now was as good a time as any to have their lunch and unpacked egg-and-lettuce sandwiches she had brought and poured tea from a flask.

'It's ages since I've had a picnic,' said Betty, her eyes alight with interest as she gazed about her.

They both consumed the sandwiches. Suddenly Emma spotted a face that was only familiar to her because she had seen it just a couple of days ago. 'Goodness, there's Dougie's brother! I wonder where he's going.'

'Where should I be looking?' asked Betty, turning her head this way and that.

Emma did not reply because she realised that she had also been seen. To her surprise, Norm began to make his way over to her. He was not alone but accompanied by a middle-aged, plump woman with fluffy greying hair beneath a brown felt hat. 'Ciao, Emma,' he said, raising a hand. 'I didn't expect to see you here. This is my mam. We're just off to visit my twin. He's in hozzie in Heswall across the water.'

'Hello, Mrs Marshall,' said Emma, wiping a hand on a handkerchief and getting to her feet. 'It's nice to meet you.'

They shook hands and Mrs Marshall beamed at

Emma. 'And you, luv. Our Dougie and Norm have told me about you. Praised your cooking to the skies. I've always struggled in the kitchen. My fella was a better cook than me.'

Emma did not know what to say to that, so asked how Norm's twin was doing. Mrs Marshall sighed. 'Our Pete! It's going to be some time yet before he can come home. He broke several bones and one in more than one place, so it's going to be a long job. That'll teach him not to go climbing walls.' She paused to catch her breath before continuing. 'He's in a nice place, though, not far from the River Dee. It's a bit of a trek but on a day like today, it's a treat. Still, Norm is company for me on the trip and he misses his twin.' She paused again before saying, 'So what are you doing here? Was your father in the King's?'

'I suppose it's possible,' said Emma, who had not thought of that. 'I'm here with my half-sister. This is Betty.'

Betty had already risen to her feet and Mrs Marshall stared at her keenly before saying, 'I feel I've seen you before, luv.'

'Really?' asked Betty, surprised.

Mrs Marshall nudged her son who was looking to where two lads were jostling each other. 'Here, our Norm, d'you recognise her?' she asked.

Norm shifted his gaze and stared at Betty. 'You do look familiar. Could be the Millers' house that I saw you,' he said. 'Pete and I were there with Jimmy Miller not so long ago. It was ages since we had seen him but his mam remembered Ma and invited her to visit her next time we went.'

Betty smiled. 'That is probably it. I'm a friend of his sister, Irene.'

Norm grinned. 'So where do you live?'

'Over the canal bridge about half an hour's walk from the Millers. My mother was killed in a road accident and I live with my aunt and cousins.'

'Tough luck.'

'Yeah, I'm sorry to hear about your mother, girl,' said Mrs Marshall sincerely. 'But we'll have to go now, Norm. I hope to see you again sometime, girls,' she added.

'You'll give my regards to Dougie?' said Emma.

Mrs Marshall nodded. 'Ta-ra, luv.' She hustled Norm away.

Betty stared after them. 'What were the chances of that happening?' she murmured.

'I only met Norm a couple of days ago,' marvelled Emma. 'Some coincidence seeing him and his mother here. I wonder what Dougie will make of it when they tell him.'

'I can't remember ever seeing this Dougie with his brothers,' said Betty, sitting down and finishing her sandwich.

Emma sat beside her. 'Now what about these photos?' she asked.

Betty produced the pictures and Emma was able to see for the first time what her father looked like. There was a lump in her throat as she gazed at his narrow-cheekboned face and smiling eyes. He was of slender build and wore what appeared to be baggy corduroy trousers. His shirt sleeves were rolled up and between his fingers he held a paintbrush. The photo of Lizzie was another happy snap, as she was smiling too. Dressed in a wide floral skirt and a blouse with a scooped neckline, she was sitting in a field of buttercups.

'Your mother was pretty,' said Emma, returning the photos to Betty. 'And our father's not bad-looking either. I wish I could get a copy done. Do you have the negatives?'

Betty shook her head. 'Why don't you take the one of Dad? Maybe there's some way a photographer could copy it without the negative.'

'I suppose it's worth a try. Thanks, Betty.' She smiled and pocketed the photo. 'Have you finished with the one of my granddad?'

'No. I'm sketching a copy and then I plan on painting it. You don't mind my hanging on to it a bit longer, do you?'

'Of course not.' Emma rummaged inside her shopping bag and produced two slices of cake from a paper bag.

'I'm sorry I forgot the one of our Jared but hopefully you'll be able to see him for yourself,' said Betty.

She was about to bite into her cake when a familiar voice said, 'Hi, Betty, fancy meeting you here.'

She started and looked up into her cousin's self-satisfied face. 'What are you doing following me, Maggie?' she demanded tight-lipped.

'Well, you wouldn't take me with you,' she said sulkily.

Emma glanced from one cousin to the other and said, 'You'd best introduce us, Betty.'

'No! Don't tell her anything,' said Betty, scowling. 'She'll only repeat it to Aunt Elsie.'

'Mum has a right to know who you're meeting,' said Maggie, lacing her white-gloved fingers together. 'For instance, who was that lad you were talking to just then?'

'He's the brother of a friend of mine,' said Emma.

'And that's all you need to know,' said Betty hastily.

'It looked like you knew each other to me,' said Maggie. 'I'm going now and I'm going to tell Mum when she gets back.'

'You do that and you'll be sorry,' said Betty. 'Now shoo!'

Maggie's lips tightened and she turned on her heel and marched away.

'You think she'll tell?' asked Emma.

'Of course she will. That is unless I can think up

a way of blackmailing her into not doing so,' said Betty.

'Blackmail!'

'Bribe, then,' murmured Betty.

Emma was slightly shocked at this further sign that families didn't always get on. 'Perhaps I should come home with you and explain to your aunt that we've met and now we want to go on seeing each other occasionally.'

'No! She'll put a stop to it!' Betty sighed. 'At least Norm drew some of the attention away from you. Hopefully she'll think you're just a friend of mine,' said Betty, more confidently than she felt because that Lancashire accent of Emma's was quite distinctive. As she ate her cake and scattered some crumbs for the pigeons, she thought about what was best to do. 'Perhaps we'd better not meet for a while but just write to each other,' she suggested after several minutes. 'You could send your letters to my friend Irene Miller's address.'

Emma could see the sense in Betty's idea. 'I am going to be occupied during the coming weekends for some time if I'm to make a success of my little tea shop business,' she murmured. 'It's a pity you couldn't come and visit me, but hopefully we'll be able to meet here in Liverpool again in the autumn.'

'After the school summer holidays have finished,' said Betty. 'Because Aunt Elsie is bound to find plenty for me to do with her being out at work.'

With that agreed, Emma and Betty sat watching people coming and going, and waiting for the regiment to appear. It was a while before they heard the sound of a regimental band. Emma felt a thrill go through her and stood on tiptoe but there was no sign of the soldiers yet. But as the music grew louder and louder, she felt Betty hanging on to her sleeve and peering over the heads of people.

'They're coming, they're coming!' cried Betty.

Emma thought it was crazy the way her heart was beating so fast. It wasn't as if she knew any of these soldiers and, no doubt, she would have a job guessing which one was Jared Gregory. She could now see the regimental colours and then the band. People were cheering and she found herself yelling herself hoarse as the ranks of soldiers began to march past. The music was stirring and she felt so excited to be part of the crowd of people gathered there.

Betty tugged on her sleeve. 'Look, look! There's our Jared,' she yelled, pointing.

Her hand could have been indicating a dozen or more different soldiers, except there was one who glanced up at them, there on the monument, and winked at them.

'I can't believe it!' cried Betty, jumping up and down with excitement. 'Did you see him wink at us!'

'I definitely saw one wink in our direction,' said Emma, amused.

'That was our Jared! Oh, I hope he doesn't go and get himself killed,' said Betty, her voice breaking.

'Don't think like that,' said Emma, putting an arm around her.

Betty rested her head on Emma's shoulder. 'I'm tired. I suppose it's all the excitement and I hardly slept last night, thinking about today.'

'What do you want to do next?' asked Emma. 'If you're tired, then perhaps you'd be better off going home.'

'No, not yet,' said Betty, lifting her head. 'I said that I'd show you the Liver birds.' She took Emma's hand. 'Come on, let's get down from here. People will start dispersing soon and we'll be able to get away. We can go down Water Street and I'll show you the Pier Head.'

Half an hour later, Emma found herself gazing up at the birds on top of the Liver Building. 'I can't believe I'm actually seeing the Liver birds in the flesh,' she said.

Betty giggled. 'Hardly flesh but I know what you mean.'

'What kind of birds are they supposed to be?' asked Emma.

'Our Jared reckons they're cormorants and that's a bit of seaweed they've got in their beaks,' said Betty.

Our Jared again, thought Emma, trying to bring to mind the soldier who had winked at them. She reckoned he was a cheeky chappie and couldn't help smiling. 'You will bring a photograph of him next time we see each other,' she said.

'Sure, I will,' said Betty. 'We'd better go back now. I doubt we'll be allowed on the Landing Stage in the circumstances.'

Emma nodded. 'We can take our time walking back to Lime Street,' she said.

By the time they reached the railway station, the crowds were dispersing. There they hugged each other and said their goodbyes. With a slight niggle of worry, Emma watched her half-sister walk away, hoping that Maggie would not get Betty into trouble with her aunt.

Betty decided not to go straight home but instead made her way to her friend Irene's street, near the library. As it happened, Irene and some other girls had a skipping rope and were singing 'Old Soldiers Never Die' in the road.

'Want to join in?' called Irene as she caught sight of her friend.

'I'll turn the rope if you like while someone else has a skip,' offered Betty, noticing her friend's flushed cheeks, lively blue eyes and flyaway blonde hair, due to the exertion of the game. She thought that Irene was so pretty that she'd have all the boys after her in a few years' time.

'Sure,' called Irene, nodding at the girl holding the far end of the rope.

The game continued for another quarter of an hour. Then Irene was declared 'out' and she and Betty left the others to continue without them.

'Let's have a sit-down,' suggested Irene, pushing open their front door that was on the latch. She parked herself on the mat, leaving enough space for Betty to sit beside her. 'What's up?' she asked.

'I want you to come to Aunt Elsie's house with me. If you're there, then she's less likely to have a go at me.'

'A go at you! What for?'

Betty told her about her afternoon. Irene's eyes widened in surprise. 'Blinking heck, fancy you having an older half-sister and not telling me. That's great!'

'Of course it's great! But I don't want Aunt Elsie knowing I've been seeing Emma, or Maggie telling her about Norm Marshall. She might stop me from going out altogether, reading things into that chance meeting that weren't there.'

Irene's eyes narrowed. 'You haven't taken a fancy to Norm, have you? He and his twin, Pete, tried a bit of breaking and entering a short while ago, only Pete fell from the windowsill of an upstairs window. Norm had no choice but to go and fetch his big brother.'

Betty's mouth fell open. 'The idiots! Fancy doing such a daft thing when your brother's a policeman.'

'From what I heard our Jimmy saying, they did it *because* their brother is a policeman. Sheer devilment! The newspapers might say all this juvenile crime is down to boys having lost their fathers in the war, but we lost our father and our Jimmy didn't get into trouble.'

'Your Jimmy's different. He has his head screwed on right, just like our Jared.' Betty paused. 'Anyway, let's think of what we can do to bribe our Maggie into keeping her mouth shut. That's if we get to our house before Aunt Elsie.'

'What does your Maggie like?'

'Clothes, music . . .'

'You could shut her up by bribing her with the promise to take her along to the next musical evening at the Gianellis',' said Irene, shifting a little because the bristles on the coconut mat were itching her bare legs.

'You think they'd invite her?' asked Betty.

'The Gianellis welcome anyone who loves music. Especially young people, because they believe it keeps us out of mischief.'

Betty smiled. 'Shall we go, then?'

Irene nodded.

Betty was relieved to find only Maggie at home. She was stretched out on the sofa, reading the *School Friend*, and pretended for a few moments that she was unaware of their presence. Then she looked up with a start and said, 'I hope you two aren't ganging up on me.'

'Don't be daft,' said Betty, raising her eyebrows. 'We've something to say. If you keep your mouth shut about seeing me in town, Irene will ask Mrs Gianelli can you come with us to their next musical evening.'

Instantly Maggie put down the comic. 'You mean it?'

'Yes,' said Betty. 'You like Italian tenors and Mr Gianelli sings as good as Mario Lanza. It's a real treat listening to him.'

'OK,' said Maggie, her eyes alight. 'I won't say anything to Mum about you being with that woman at the Pier Head, although what the big secret is I'd still like to know.'

'Never you mind. Just don't say anything about my taking the photos either, will you?' asked Betty.

'No, but Mum might discover they've gone and, it's my opinion, she'll guess it was you that took them. Sooner or later she'll find out what you're up to without my saying a word,' warned Maggie.

'So what are you three plotting?' asked a voice from the doorway, causing them to jump.

To Betty's relief it was her elder cousin. 'Hi, Dot,' she greeted. 'How did it go?'

'Marvellous. I managed to spot our Jared, but I came over all tearful and so did Mum. She's gone for a drink but I've got a date tonight.'

Dorothy plonked herself down on a chair. Betty thought that this cousin was really nice-looking and couldn't be more different from her mother. Her hair was dyed strawberry blonde and she had green-blue eyes in an oval face with a cute nose and a Cupid's-bow mouth. She had a lovely figure and the two-piece dusky-pink costume she wore accentuated her bust and slender waist. The skirt was flared and was mid-calf length. Her hair was styled similar to the British film actress, Diana Dors. She kicked off her tan kid sandals. 'Put the kettle on, one of you, and make us a cuppa.'

Betty stood up and went into the kitchen. Irene followed her. 'So d'you think Dorothy heard anything we were discussing?' asked the latter.

'I don't know, but even if she did, I don't think she'll say anything. She and Aunt Elsie have been at odds ever since she married Uncle Teddy. He's such a creep. I think if Dot had the money and was able to find a place of her own she'd leave home.'

'That's OK, then,' said Irene, nodding. 'You'll just have to hope that you can trust Maggie, because I've no idea when the Gianellis will have their next musical evening. It mightn't be until September. They generally go to Italy for a week during the holidays and then they take their lot camping in Wales, along with Mrs Gianelli's sister and her children. Jimmy and I went with them last year.'

She paused. 'So when d'you think you'll be able to see your half-sister again?'

'Emma said autumn and that seems ages away.'

Irene could only agree. 'At least we've the summer holidays to look forward to,' she murmured. 'Perhaps if the Gianellis go camping again and ask me and Jimmy along, I might be able to wangle an invitation for you, as well.'

'What do you do there?' asked Betty curiously.

'It's by the sea, so we swim and sunbathe, and you can hire bikes and play rounders in the field where we camp. Rhyl's only a couple of miles away and there's a fair there.'

'It sounds fun,' said Betty wistfully.

'It is, and it would be more fun for me if you were there, too.'

Betty sighed. 'But it would cost money and I can't see Aunt Elsie coughing up.'

'No harm in asking,' said Irene.

'Well, don't go saying anything to the Gianellis just yet,' said Betty. 'I'll sound her out first.'

Irene nodded.

The following evening Betty broached the possibility of going camping during the summer holidays with her friend Irene. But as soon as she mentioned the Gianellis, Teddy said, 'They sound like Eyeties.'

'Mr Gianelli is half-Italian, yes,' replied Betty, wishing he would keep out of her conversations.

Teddy glanced at Elsie. 'You can't let her go mixing with wops. They were on Hitler's side during the war and they're bloody papists as well.'

'So what!' said Dorothy, without looking up from *Woman's Weekly*. 'You never go to church. Anyway, I bet his other half is English.'

'That's right,' said Betty, glancing at her cousin gratefully.

Teddy glared at Dorothy. 'You've no right to interfere.'

She flashed him a honeyed smile. 'But that's what you did, Uncle Teddy. You didn't give Mum a chance to answer Betty.'

'She'll agree with me,' said Teddy. 'Won't you, Elsie?'

Elsie did not immediately reply.

'Elsie!' he snapped. 'You heard what I said. Betty can't go off on holiday. You can bet there'll be lads there and you don't know what she'll get up to.'

Betty reddened. 'I don't know what you're talking about. It's a family holiday.'

'And do the Gianellis have a son?' demanded Teddy.

'Yes, two, but—'

'Enough said,' muttered Teddy. 'You can't go. Besides it would cost money and we can't be throwing that away on a holiday, just for you.'

'Camping! Surely it won't cost that much, Mum,' said Dorothy.

Her mother hesitated before saying, 'Betty'll need a new school mackintosh for next term and that's going to cost. Besides, if I were to let her go, then she'd have to take our Maggie with her. Fair's fair.'

'You can't afford it, Elsie, and that's that,' said Teddy. 'These girls have no sense of the value of money.'

'You can talk,' said Dorothy, lifting her head and staring at him. 'When are you going to get yourself a proper job instead of messing around just doing a few hours here and there and living off me and Mum?'

Teddy started to his feet with an ugly expression on his face and lunged towards her. 'You have too much to say for yerself, girl. If you'd had my life you'd know you were born.'

'I think I know I was born,' said Dorothy, without flinching. 'I work blinking hard for every penny I earn. You want to try piecework, that's what I have to do if I want to go out and to keep myself in stockings, on top of what I give to Mum. It's no doddle.' She stood up and tossed her magazine on the chair. 'Now if you don't mind, I'm going to get ready to go out.'

She brushed past him and left the room.

'She has a bloody cheek that girl,' blustered Teddy. 'Our Owen was far too soft with her. That's why you've got to be firm with these two, Elsie,' he added.

'They're not bad girls,' said Elsie, getting out a cigarette with a trembling hand.

'No, we're not,' said Betty, getting up from her seat. 'I'm going upstairs to do some revision. Forget I asked about camping, Aunt Elsie. I'm sorry it caused an argument.'

'That's all right, Betty. I have a week off during the holidays. I'll take you and our Maggie to Southport for a day out,' said Elsie hastily.

'That'll be nice,' murmured Betty, and left the room.

'Can I go and do my homework too, Mum?' asked Maggie, taking one look at Teddy's face and wanting to escape.

'Yes, you go, love,' said Elsie.

After the girls had left, Elsie switched on the wireless and dance music flooded out. She guessed the conductor was Victor Sylvester as she picked up the magazine that Dorothy had left behind. Her fingers trembled as she opened it.

'You should have told your Dorothy off for speaking to me like that,' snapped Teddy, hitting the open magazine with the flat of his hand. 'I'm going down the pub and I don't know when I'll be back.' He slammed the door as he went out.

Elsie wished she could turn back the clock but it was too late for that. Perhaps God was punishing her.

CHAPTER ELEVEN

'So you're off to Liverpool at last,' said Lila. 'I can't believe how quickly the summer's gone and now we're well into October.'

Emma tucked the chamois leather pouch on its string inside her brassiere. 'I would have gone in September, but the weather was so good I thought I'd grab any chance of making money at the weekends that I could. Besides I've a couple of small-time clients whose accounts I'm doing weekly now and Betty was only settling back into school then.' She frowned, remembering her half-sister's last letter mentioning she would be doing her school certificate next year. How old was she? Emma had been of a mind that Betty would have been too young to be sitting those exams just yet. When had she been born? If she was sixteen in the next nine months, then her mother and their father must have married almost as soon as Emma's mother had died.

She glanced out of the window. 'It looks like rain. I'd best take my umbrella.' As she placed it in her leatherette shopping bag, she added, 'Why aren't you at work this morning? Surely the mill hasn't closed again?'

'I've packed it in.'

'What!' Emma stared at her in amazement. 'What did your parents say?'

Lila fiddled with her hair. 'Mam's furious and Dad just looked stunned. Then this morning he told me he'd thought that I'd never have the guts to give it up and look for another job.'

'You are going to look for another job, then?'

Lila said, 'Of course! I could do with a real change from everything, though.' She hesitated. 'I wouldn't mind going to Liverpool with you today.'

'You mean you're thinking of looking for a job there?' Emma's voice rose to a squeak.

'What's wrong with that?' asked Lila, flushing. 'Although, I haven't come to any proper decision yet. But I'd like a look at the place.' She added, 'Will you be seeing Dougie as well as your sister while you're there?'

Emma remembered the last letter he had written, and although its tone had been friendly, he hadn't said anything that caused her heart to flutter and there had been no mention of seeing her again. 'I've sent him a note, telling him when I planned to go.' She sighed.

Lila said, 'So he didn't get back to you?'

'No, but then he does have a job that occupies a lot of his time. As well as that he has to think of his mother and brothers. Pete was still in hospital last time Dougie wrote to me.' She remembered the last time she had seen Betty and they'd met his mother and Norm, and how Maggie had turned up as well. According to Betty, her cousin had kept quiet about having seen them because she had promised to take Maggie along to some musical evening at the house of a family called Gianelli. Emma felt uncomfortable about what had happened with Maggie, because surely she would have wanted to see her brother march by. Emma remembered the way he had winked at them and could still see his face in her mind's eye.

'We really don't need Dougie, do we, to enjoy ourselves in Liverpool?' said Lila bracingly, rousing Emma from her thoughts.

Emma agreed. 'Can you afford the train fare?'

Lila nodded. 'I haven't been giving Mam my wage packet unopened for the whole of the summer. I suddenly thought, I'm twenty-one, what am I thinking of handing it over, just like that, at my age? I'm also doing half the housework, cooking

184

and looking after Dad, so I deserve more than I was getting. I give her what I think is a fair whack, and keep the rest for myself.'

'Blinking heck!' exclaimed Emma, even more surprised. 'You've kept that a secret. What did your mother say?'

Lila smiled nervously. 'She ranted, but I stood my ground, even though my knees were knocking. Eventually she just had to accept it. Same as me having given up my job. She hit the roof and called me a daft bitch and threatened to throw me out of the house if I didn't get another job straight away, but I think she's bluffing. She needs me there, but it's time I had a bit more life of my own.'

Emma shrugged on her coat. 'She'd have more of a fit if she knew you were considering looking for a job in Liverpool. How will they cope without you?'

Lila's mouth drooped at the corners. 'That's my problem. Dad can be a pain at times but I do worry what he might do if he were to get really down. He used to be such an active man. I did take him out in the wheelchair during the summer, just along the road, but it's not the same as him striding across the fells.' She sighed.

'It's so upsetting for you all,' said Emma, pulling on her hat and matching gloves, knitted from the wool she had found in spring.

'I probably won't look for a job in Liverpool,'

said Lila, 'but I'm looking forward to seeing the shops.'

'Well, keep a tight grip on your handbag when we get there,' warned Emma, opening the door and leading the way. 'Your mother will only say I told you so, if it were to get snatched.'

On arriving in Liverpool, Lila not only hung onto her handbag but clung to Emma's arm as if her life depended on it. They shared Emma's umbrella as they made their way through the rain to the Forum cinema. 'I don't know why your sister couldn't meet us in Lime Street station,' complained Lila.

'I didn't think of it this time,' said Emma, understanding how her friend felt in light of the horrible weather. 'Be thankful we weren't in that train crash involving those three trains at Harrow last week.'

'I know, it was awful,' said Lila, seizing hold of part of the umbrella as the wind threatened to blow it inside out. 'All those people killed! I'd have thought twice about taking the train if I'd remembered that before we set off.'

'Well, we're here now,' said Emma brightly. 'And I think I can see Betty standing on the steps out of the rain.' She lifted the umbrella higher and waved frantically, shouting, 'Betty, I'm here!'

She saw her half-sister's face brighten. Then, as Emma began to cross the road, she caught sight of Dougie. Instantly she turned in the opposite direction and barged back across the road with her umbrella held in front of her like a shield, hauling Lila with her. They narrowly missed getting hit by a van and fortunately reached the pavement in one piece.

'You're mad!' cried Lila, her face pallid as she tugged her arm free from Emma's. 'We could have been killed! What were you playing at?'

'We made it, didn't we?' said Emma in a slightly breathless voice. 'I thought I saw Dougie.'

'So where is he?' asked Lila, gazing about her.

Emma's eyes darted here and there but she could no longer see him. Her face fell. 'He's vanished.'

'Hard luck,' said Lila, shaking her head at her as she smoothed her coat sleeve. 'But next time, think twice, luv, before dragging me with you and putting our lives in danger. We both could have been killed, and how would me mam and dad manage then?'

'Sorry,' said Emma, biting her lip.

'Are you OK, Emma?' asked Betty, appearing beside her. 'You gave me a fright. I thought you were going to be hit by that blue van.'

'I know. It was stupid of me to do what I did, and all because I thought I saw Dougie Marshall,' she said crossly. 'No, not thought. I *did* see him. Maybe he saw me and didn't want to talk to me.'

'I've seen his brother a few times at Irene's house

187

and also at the Gianellis'. I did think to ask how his brothers were and I've a feeling he told me that the one you like is on a training course.' Betty glanced curiously at the woman, standing the other side of Emma.

'A course!' said Emma, her eyes brightening. 'Does that mean he could have been away somewhere?'

'Probably. I could ask Norm, if I see him again,' said Betty.

Emma smiled. 'Thanks for telling me. It's possible my letter didn't reach him until it was too late for him to arrange a meeting.'

There was a silence and then Lila said, 'So are you going to introduce us, Emma?'

'Sorry,' said Emma hastily. 'Betty, this is my friend, Lila Ashcroft. I'm sure I've mentioned her in my letters. She had some time off, so decided she'd like to come and have a look at Liverpool.'

'I see,' said Betty, sounding slightly put out. 'Seems you brought the rain with you, Miss Ashcroft.'

'I don't know about that,' murmured Lila. 'Probably it swept in from the sea and you got it first and passed it on to us.'

Emma sensed an atmosphere. It had never occurred to her that they might not take to each other. 'So, what are we going to do with ourselves now it's raining?' she said brightly.

'An afternoon at the pictures?' suggested Betty.

'That sounds sensible,' said Emma.

'I can go to the pictures at home,' said Lila, adjusting her hat which had been knocked askew by the umbrella. 'I came here to look at the shops.'

Betty exchanged glances with Emma. 'Perhaps we could go to the Tatler cinema in Church Street and your friend can look in the shops on the way.'

'That sounds fine to me,' said Emma. 'Lead on, then, MacDuff!'

'So you've read *Macbeth*,' said Betty instantly. 'I'm studying that for my English Lit. GCE. It's a bit dark, full of witches, ghosts and murders.'

'We had our own witches not far away,' said Emma. 'Ever heard of the Pendle witch trials?'

'No!' exclaimed Betty, her eyes widening. 'The only other witches I've come across are in Enid Blyton and Grimm's fairy tales, although I've grown out of them now.'

Emma said casually, 'So how old are you?'

Betty smiled. 'I'll be sixteen next month.'

'What date?' asked Emma, trying to work out the sums in her head.

'The same day as Prince Charles,' replied Betty.

Fourteenth of November, thought Emma.

Lila burst out, 'Isn't it time we made a move? We're only here for a few hours.'

'Sor-ry,' said Betty, pulling a face, 'but we've only been here a couple of minutes at the most. She led them past St John's indoor market in the direction of Clayton Square, unaware that they were being watched.

Dorothy had been shopping and, a few moments earlier, was in a hurry to get home out of the rain. Then she had caught sight of Betty outside the Forum cinema. That had surprised her because, on such a horrible day, it would have made more sense for her cousin to visit one of the local cinemas, rather than come all this way in to town. The next minute, she saw Betty waving to someone. Then her cousin bolted across the road and had stood talking to a couple of women for a while before the three of them had headed off in the direction of Clayton Square.

Dorothy wasted no time in following them. She had felt protective of her younger cousin since Aunt Lizzie was killed. Now Dorothy watched as the two women and Betty dawdled along the pavement, gazing in the windows of Owen Owen and then turning the corner into Church Street. They looked in the shop windows of Bon Marché and George Henry Lee's.

Eventually they came to the Tatler cinema, where the programme ran continuously, showing newsreels and cartoons, and stopped outside. They did not go in immediately but stood talking. Then Betty and one of the women went inside the cinema and the other crossed the road to gaze into the shop windows on the other side.

Dorothy's curiosity got the better of her and she decided to follow Betty and her companion into the cinema. She bought a ticket and was shown to a seat. On the screen was a newsreel about the queen, and the broadcaster was providing the latest information to do with the arrangements for Her Majesty's coronation next June. It still seemed a long way off to Dorothy, so she didn't take much notice. The next item of news was about the situation in Korea.

She felt a trickle of fear down her back, thinking of her brother, Jared. In his last letter, he had made her envious of the tropical climate in Hong Kong and that made the last-minute training his regiment was having to *suffer* before sailing for Korea sound a bit of a joke. She knew he was making light of the situation, so as not to worry her. Yet she dreaded her mother receiving a telegram, saying he had been killed. It would have been great if he could be home for Christmas but he still had almost a year to go before finishing his national service.

The newsreel came to an end and Dorothy looked about her for Betty and her companion. Then she spotted the two of them several rows in front of her on the left-hand side of the aisle. She divided her attention between them and the screen, while she planned how she could accidentally-on-purpose bump into them on the way out of the cinema. Who was that woman? She remembered Jared mentioning, in a letter, having seen Betty chatting to a bit of a dish dressed in turquoise and green, standing on the steps of the Victoria Monument. He had added that she was no doubt someone with whom their over-friendly cousin had struck up a conversation.

Dorothy now wondered if that was true as she sat through several cartoons, including Bugs Bunny and Tom & Jerry, until she saw Betty and the woman getting to their feet. Instantly Dorothy rose and, with a whispered 'Excuse me', made her way to the aisle and hurried to the rear of the auditorium.

She reached the exit at the same time as her cousin and her companion and feigned surprise. 'Betty! What are you doing here?'

'Watching the cartoons,' countered Betty, startled. 'What about you?'

Dorothy gave her cousin credit for her swift reaction and said good-humouredly, 'I asked first. Who's your friend?'

Betty sighed. 'Emma, this is my cousin Dorothy. She probably won't budge until she gets the truth out of me. It amazes me how I can't go anywhere without bumping into a member of my family.'

Emma smiled and held out her hand. 'I'm Emma Booth, Betty's half-sister.'

Dorothy did a double take before taking the

hand offered. 'I'm Dorothy Gregory. I'd like to know where you've sprung from.'

Emma said in a whisper, 'I think we'd better go into the foyer as we don't want to disturb people.'

The three of them left the auditorium and found a sofa and a chair to sit on. 'So what's this all about?' asked Dorothy, placing her shopping beside her chair. 'Am I to take it that Betty's father had another wife before Auntie Lizzie?'

'That's right. My mother's name was Mary Harrison,' said Emma. 'She came to Liverpool from my village near Clitheroe when she was eighteen. She met my father here and they married and had me. Then she became ill with consumption, so went back home to my grandparents, taking me with her. She died when I was about five.'

Betty took up the tale. 'Emma didn't know I existed until the beginning of this year. Her granddad died and she found a letter from Mum addressed to her grandmother. It told her that Dad had been killed at Dunkirk but his dying wish was that he wanted his two girls to get to know each other.'

'The letter was dated 1940,' put in Emma helpfully. 'So I wrote to your mother, but she didn't answer my letters, so I then wrote directly to Betty.'

Dorothy shook her head. 'I can't believe that your grandmother never told you! That was a bit remiss of her.'

Emma sprang to her grandmother's defence. 'I was the only family my grandparents had left after my mother died. I think Gran was worried that I might prefer Liverpool and living with a young stepmother and half-sister instead of two elderly people.'

Dorothy glanced at Betty. 'So how long have you been keeping quiet about this?'

Betty told her and why.

Dorothy looked surprised. 'I can't understand why Mum kept quiet about Emma writing to her.'

'I think she must have disapproved of our dad because he was an artist,' said Betty. 'You know she doesn't want me following in his footsteps.'

Dorothy frowned. 'But why should she hold that against Emma?'

Emma said slowly, 'Maybe she knew my mother and they didn't like each other?'

'I suppose that's possible,' said Dorothy. 'I remember your dad, but only from visiting their house when we lived in Liverpool. I remember now that he painted a picture for me. I had it on my bedroom wall for ages. Then we moved house and I never saw it again. Mum told me that it must have got misplaced in the move, but I bet she threw it away.' She frowned. 'I loved that picture. I reckoned he was a good artist.'

'I think so, too,' smiled Emma. 'So are you going to tell your mother about my meeting with Betty?'

'I'd rather you didn't, Dot,' said Betty hastily.

'I'm convinced Uncle Teddy will put his spoke in and say she's not to allow it. Remember how nasty he was over the Gianellis? If he knew Maggie and I were going around there for musical evenings he'd probably explode.'

'You and Maggie are spending evenings at the Gianellis'!' exclaimed Dorothy.

'One evening a week, that's all,' said Betty hastily. 'Instead of listening to records like I do at Irene's house, we have live music. Mrs Gianelli plays the piano, as well as sings, and Mr Gianelli and his son Tonio play the mandolin and the guitar. They sing in Italian sometimes. Operatic stuff as well as ballads.'

Dorothy thought it sounded worth going along to and asked, 'Who else goes?'

'When he's home, Jimmy, Irene's brother, as well as Norman Marshall. Apparently Irene's mum knew his mum during the war and Emma has met him and his brother, who's a policeman. There's a few other teenagers who come along, too,' said Betty.

Dorothy's eyes sparkled. 'It sounds fun. I think I'd better go along with you both and cast my eye over the proceedings, so that if it ever comes out that you and Maggie have been going there, I can put in a good word for you both.'

A smile flooded Betty's face. 'I'm sure you'll be made welcome. Now what about Emma?'

Dorothy glanced at Emma. 'What do the pair of you do together?'

'Go to the pictures like now or have a picnic,' said Emma. 'This is only the third time we've met but we keep in touch by letter. I send mine care of Irene Miller.'

'I see,' said Dorothy. 'I must admit I can't see any harm in your getting to know each other. But do remember Mum is responsible for you, Betty. If anything were to happen to you whilst you were out with Emma it would all have to come out.'

'What could happen?' said Betty, surprised.

'I don't know!' said Dorothy.

Emma said, 'I'll leave it to you and Betty to decide whether you want to tell your mother. After today it's unlikely I'll see Betty for a while. What I'd like to do next time is take her to see a pantomime here in Liverpool the week after Christmas.'

Dorothy smiled. 'That sounds a good idea. I enjoy a pantomime myself.' She stood up and gathered her shopping together. 'Well, you seem to have it all worked out and I don't see what harm you're doing by meeting up every now and again. I'm not going to say anything for the moment. It's been interesting meeting you, Emma. See you again sometime.' She walked away.

'She's nice,' said Emma, gazing after her.

'Yes, she's OK is our Dorothy,' murmured Betty, looking thoughtful. 'So I won't be seeing you until

Christmas is over after today?' she added.

'I'm afraid so,' answered Emma regretfully. 'Shall we go and meet Lila at Lyons now? I just hope she managed to buy something that she couldn't get at home and is pleased with it.'

Betty said ruefully, 'I don't think she likes me.'

'She doesn't know you,' responded Emma, linking her arm through her sister's. 'Not everybody hits it off right away.'

'But we did, and you hit it off with our Dorothy just now,' said Betty.

Emma could not argue with that. 'It's the way Lila is. She didn't hit it off with Dougie either.'

'Perhaps she's jealous of you,' said Betty.

'I can't think why,' said Emma.

They left the cinema and headed off in the direction of Lime Street. Emma had expected to find Lila waiting for them outside but she wasn't there. She peered through the window, thinking she might be inside but could see no sign of her.

'What do we do?' asked Betty, shivering in the rain and wind.

'Go inside,' decided Emma.

They were just about to do so when Emma heard her name being called. The next moment Lila came running towards them, her cheeks flushed and a bulging shopping bag swinging from her fingers.

'So there you are,' said Emma.

'Sorry I'm late,' said Lila. 'I tell you what – tea

and cakes is on me,' she said, smiling.

They went inside the café. Emma was relieved that her friend appeared to be in the best of moods. Whilst they were waiting for their order to arrive, Lila showed them what was in her shopping bag. Emma admired the jumper and skirt; the latter had plenty of fabric, unlike during the war and the years immediately after, when clothing coupons were needed due to a shortage of materials. Then she told her about meeting Dorothy.

Betty sat there, listening, wishing she could get as excited as Lila over what was really just an ordinary skirt and jumper. Her mind drifted and she thought about what Emma had said about taking her to the pantomime. Like Dorothy, Betty enjoyed a good panto and it would be special because she'd be going with Emma. It was something to look forward to after Christmas was over.

CHAPTER TWELVE

'You're lucky Christmas is coming, lass, I'll give you five pound for it,' said the man on the market stall in Clitheroe.

Emma was not prepared to haggle. She needed the money more than she needed her grandmother's silver candelabra and saw little point in pawning it when she could not see herself having the means to redeem it.

'I'll take it,' she said.

She would be seeing Betty, as well as Dorothy, in Liverpool on New Year's Eve. It had come as a surprise to receive a letter from her sister's cousin but she had welcomed the friendly gesture. They had exchanged letters several times since that first one. It was Dorothy who had written to say that she would purchase the tickets for the pantomime to save Emma the worry of perhaps arriving in Liverpool and having to queue up, only to discover the seats were sold out. She would like to go, too, and bring Maggie, as well. Emma was pleased with the notion and indeed was beginning to feel almost part of the family.

She had enclosed a birthday card with a postal order in a letter to Betty for her birthday in November. She had also knitted a hat, scarf and gloves as well as several dolls that she had stuffed with cotton wool and then kitted out as witches, even providing them with twiggy broomsticks. She had got the idea from having seen some witch-like figures in a Clitheroe fancy gift shop during the summer. After Easter, she planned to sell her own version of the Pendle witches in her tea room. Hopefully the day trippers would like them and they would go like the proverbial hot cakes.

Like so many people in the area, she considered the Pendle witches to have been simply wise women, who had a knowledge of herbs and a gift for healing, although there had been those found guilty of extortion by threatening to put a spell on people and using so-called black magic. The trials had taken place seventy years or more after Henry the Eighth's dissolution of the monasteries. The loss of the local abbot had created a moral vacuum and the area had become a wild place once more. Ten of the so-called witches had included two men, and they had been hanged.

Emma felt a shiver go through her at the thought of meeting death in such a way. She placed the money from the sale of the candelabra in the pouch, attached to the cord around her neck, and buttoned up her coat. She was glad that those days were in the distant past. Yet even here, in this country market town of Clitheroe, there were bound to be thieves about. The other day she had read about a boy who'd dressed up as a girl and broken into a house. The owners had left the burglar alone in a locked room and he'd jumped out of the window. Some boys had given chase and discovered the ruse. She could not imagine that happening in her own village, but even so, one had to be careful. There were still people about who were cruel and dishonest.

Emma caught the bus to her village and hurried home through a drizzle. When she arrived at the cottage she put her shopping away, placed a log on the fire and switched on the wireless. It was Wilfred Pickles and she relaxed as she made herself a cup of a tea and a bite to eat. She really enjoyed the programme *Have a Go* which involved ordinary people talking about their lives and answering questions for prizes. One of his catchphrases was 'What's on the table, Mabel?' She was his wife. Another was 'Give her the money, Barney.'

She wondered if her sister listened to the programme. At least she would soon be seeing her, as well as having a few days away from the cottage. Dot had suggested booking Emma into a bed & breakfast in Liverpool for New Year's Eve, so she wouldn't have to worry about getting the train back home late at night. Emma had agreed and was glad she had got a reasonable price for the silver candelabra. At least she had someone who cared about her, even if it wasn't Dougie, whom she had still not heard from despite the letter she had sent him after her last trip to Liverpool.

'Are you two ready?' asked Dorothy impatiently, tapping her foot on the hall lino.

'We're coming now,' said Betty. 'Maggie couldn't find her left shoe.'

'What's the rush?' Elsie came out of the kitchen, nursing a cup of tea. 'Where are the three of you going?'

Betty froze and then glanced at Maggie. It had been Dorothy who had told her sister about Betty's half-sister and that it was something she had to keep quiet about if she wanted to go to the pantomime with them.

'If I've told you once, Mum, I've told you ten

times,' said Dorothy, looking her mother squarely in the eyes and smoothing a glove. 'I'm taking the girls to the pantomime as a treat.'

Elsie frowned. 'I don't remember you mentioning it.'

'That's because you never listen to me.'

'That's a lie! Anyway, why don't I get treated?'

'This is part of their Christmas present from me,' said Dorothy, opening the front door. 'Besides, you've always said that you hate the pantomime, think it's stupid.'

'Well, it is,' said Elsie, resting her hip against the door jamb. 'Men dressing up as women and women as men.'

'Mum, I'm not going to argue with you now. We've got to go. I've seats booked. Come on, girls!' ordered Dorothy, holding the door ajar.

'But you're leaving me in all on my own on New Year's Eve,' complained Elsie.

'That's not our fault. You should have insisted on going to the pub with Uncle Teddy, instead of letting him go off on his own,' said Dorothy. 'I saw you giving him money.'

'It's none of your business,' snapped her mother. 'Now, get out!'

'I'm going. I just wish you'd never married him. He's done us no good. He wheedled his way in here, making you feel sorry for him and—'

'That's enough!' said Elsie harshly. 'You don't

know what it's like to have been married to a man and then left bereft.'

'He's not a patch on Dad,' said Dorothy.

'Shut up, right now! I don't want to be reminded of your dad and his sufferings.' Her tone brooked no argument.

Dorothy hesitated. 'We all miss him, Mum. I just wish—'

'I know what you wish. Now go!' ordered Elsie.

Maggie went over to her mother and hugged her about the waist. 'I wish you were coming, Mum. See you later.'

Elsie stroked her hair with an unsteady hand and then pushed her away. 'Go and enjoy yourself.'

'I will,' said Maggie. 'But why don't you go out and enjoy yourself?'

'I might,' said Elsie.

'What's going on here?'

Dorothy stared at her uncle and thought he looked two sheets to the wind already. 'Here he is, Mum, back already,' she said. 'Your little hero. A lot of good he'll be as company this evening. He'll snore the hours away till midnight.'

Teddy glared at Dorothy and attempted to block her way. She forced her way past him, dragging the girls with her. It was a relief to be outside in the cold evening air.

'I thought we weren't going to get out then,' said

Maggie, looking worried. 'D'you think we did right leaving Mum with him?'

'Don't you be worrying,' said Dorothy soothingly. 'Mum can look after herself. Now, let's run. We don't want to be late.'

'Let's hope Emma makes it,' said Betty. 'What is it we're seeing? I've forgotten.'

'*Jack and the Beanstalk* and I'm sure it'll be a laugh,' said Dorothy, concerned about her mother, despite the reassurances she had given to her sister.

Emma was already at the meeting place and looking anxiously about her. It was the first time she had been in the city after dark. She was trembling with nervous excitement, clutching the bag containing the presents she had brought for her sister. She had a present for Dorothy, as well, for her going to all the trouble of booking the seats and the bed & breakfast place for her.

The neon lights advertising Guinness drew her fascinated eye as she waited outside Lime Street station. She thought how coincidental it would be if Dougie suddenly hovered into view. Then she spotted Betty, Dorothy and Maggie.

'Emma, you made it!' cried Betty, flinging her arms around her.

Emma hugged her half-sister, delighted by her welcome. 'Did you have a good Christmas?'

'It was OK. What about you? Were you on your own? Were you lonely?'

Emma was touched by her concern. 'I missed Granddad, of course, but I did spend part of Christmas Day with my friend, Lila, and her parents.'

'Emma, I think you've met Maggie,' interrupted Dorothy.

Emma nodded in the youngest girl's direction. 'Hello.'

'Hello,' replied Maggie.

'Now, come on, all of you,' said Dorothy. 'You can chat on the way. We want to be in on our seats in plenty of time.'

'I owe you some money,' said Emma, as they began walking along Lime Street and past the Empire Theatre.

'It can wait,' said Dorothy. 'This-a-way.'

They crossed London Road and hurried into Fraser Street where the Shakespeare theatre was situated. People were already entering the building and the four girls wasted no time going inside. They found their seats and settled down. Dorothy had brought a bag of sweets and passed it along. Emma decided to leave the present-giving until later.

'I hope you can sing, Emma,' said Dorothy, 'because there's bound to be a singalong and they like you to try and lift the roof off.'

'Of course I can sing,' replied Emma, crunching a pear drop. 'I presume you three can sing if you've been going along to the musical evenings at the Gianellis'.'

'I have been known to belt out a tune when asked to give a turn,' said Dorothy, her green-blue eyes dancing. 'It's a pity that home entertainment will soon be on its way out.'

'What do you mean?' asked Emma.

'Have you got a telly, Emma?' asked Maggie, who was straining to hear what the elder two were saying.

'No,' said Emma, flashing her a smile. 'I've never even seen a telly.'

'Never?' chorused Maggie and Betty, looking shocked.

'Never,' affirmed Emma, her eyes amused by their reaction. 'I listen to the wireless a lot.'

'We've seen telly at a friend's house and several others have said their parents are determined to buy one in time for the queen's coronation,' said Maggie. 'I'm going to get to work on Mum for us to get one. You should get one too, Emma.'

Emma could not see herself being able to afford a television in the foreseeable future, so changed the subject. 'Any news of your brother, Dorothy?' she asked.

'Not recently. But I'm praying that no news is good news.' A shadow crossed Dorothy's face.

'There was a battle just before Christmas that the Lord Mayor of Liverpool called *Operation Scouse*. The King's Regiment was in the forefront of the fighting to rescue prisoners from the Commies.'

'That must have been worrying for you,' said Emma, remembering her first sight of Jared Gregory and that Betty had promised to show her a photograph of him.

'It was,' said Dorothy. 'It's blinking awful, but I suppose it'll all come to an end one day.' She sat up straight in her seat. 'Let's not get ourselves miserable but look forward to the pantomime.'

No sooner had she finished speaking than the fire curtain rose and the lights dimmed. Conversation ceased as the curtains opened to reveal a scene that looked as if it had come out of a picture book.

For several hours they all enjoyed the colour, the costumes, the jokes, the singing and the dancing, and were completely taken out of themselves. As they left the theatre all agreed that it had been magic.

'I wouldn't mind a goose that laid golden eggs. I don't suppose you have one in your village, Emma?' teased Dorothy.

'If only,' she said, her eyes sparkling. 'What I have got is a few little Christmas presents.'

'What are they?' asked Betty, looking pleased.

'Nothing wildly exciting. Open them when you get home.'

With a flourish Betty produced from her bag an envelope. 'And you're not to look at what's inside this until you're alone.'

Emma thanked her and pocketed the envelope before turning to Dorothy. 'Now, I owe you money for the pantomime ticket.'

'No, you don't,' said Dorothy. 'It's my present to you.'

Emma frowned. 'I can't accept that.'

'Yes, you can,' said Dorothy firmly. 'You've had enough expense getting here and you wouldn't have had to stay overnight if I'd been able to get tickets for a matinee. Unfortunately I couldn't.'

Emma decided to accept the gift with good grace. 'Thanks, that's very kind.'

There was a silence.

Then Betty asked, 'When will I see you again?'

'I wish I could say tomorrow, but I have to go back early as I've urgent bookkeeping work I must catch up on,' said Emma. 'I'll write and arrange to meet up with you as soon as I can.'

'OK,' said Betty, kissing Emma's cheek. 'See you when I see you.'

Dorothy smiled at Emma. 'I've enjoyed our outing.'

'Me, too. Thanks again and happy New Year,' said Emma, blinking back unexpected tears before hurrying away.

Dorothy was tempted to go after her and ask if

she'd like to walk around the town and see it coming even more alive as midnight approached. Yet she knew that she had to get the younger girls home. 'So-oo, I wonder when we will next see Emma,' she murmured.

'I bet it'll be months,' sighed Betty.

It was not until they were on the bus that the cousins decided to open their presents. Betty tore off the wrapping to expose a long, colourful, knitted scarf, hat and gloves.

'Sensible,' said Dorothy.

'They'll be lovely and warm,' said Betty, draping the scarf around her neck. 'But there's something else in here.' She drew out a knitted doll.

'What's it supposed to be?' asked Maggie, reaching for it.

Betty held the doll out of her reach. 'It's obvious that it's a Pendle witch. I remember Emma telling me about them. Look she's got gozzy eyes. I wonder if Emma did that deliberately to make me smile. Imagine this witch trying to cast a spell if she can't see straight. I'm going to call her Winnie.'

'How original,' said Maggie sarcastically.

'You must admit it's not your usual kind of present,' said Dorothy, chuckling. 'What else is in there?'

Betty handed over two small bags tied up with tape. Dorothy sniffed. 'I can smell cinnamon.'

They ate the biscuits on the walk from the bus to their house. Betty remembered to put the ends of her scarf beneath her coat, not wanting her aunt to notice it and ask questions. Winnie the Witch she stuffed into her bag. When they arrived home it was to find just one light on in the hall.

'Mum and Uncle Teddy must have gone to bed,' said Dorothy, surprised.

'Who's going to first-foot?' asked Betty.

'I remember when our Jared used to do it,' said Maggie.

Dorothy said in a fierce voice, 'Shut up!'

Betty sighed. 'It seems a bit tame going to bed on New Year's Eve this early. Can we be sure they've both gone to bed?'

'If he's in bed, he'll be snoring,' said Maggie. 'If he's not, then he's gone out again.'

'You two go up and listen, while I put the kettle on,' said Dorothy.

Betty and Maggie crept upstairs and stood on the landing, listening. They could hear Teddy snoring and went back downstairs. 'He's up there, all right,' said Betty. 'Presumably Aunt Elsie's tucked up with him.'

'She might have gone out,' said Maggie.

'Maybe. Even so, it seems I might have to let the new year in,' said Dorothy.

'OK! But you don't have to go yet,' said Betty. 'Leave it until just before midnight in case Aunt Elsie wakes up and comes down.'

So it was agreed. They talked about the pantomime

with the wireless on so they wouldn't forget the time. As it drew closer to midnight Dorothy made her preparations. She placed a small lump of coal, a slice of bread, salt in a twist of paper and a couple of pennies into her coat pocket.

'I'm coming with you,' said Maggie, with an air of excitement. 'You can't go on your own. You don't know who you might bump into.'

'OK,' said Dorothy, smiling down at her younger sister, 'but make sure you're wrapped up.' She glanced at Betty. 'You'd better be listening out to let us in. We don't want to have to knock loud and wake *him* up.'

Betty nodded, not wanting to rouse Teddy either.

She saw the sisters out at ten to twelve and then went and curled up on the sofa, listening to the wireless and waiting for Big Ben to strike the midnight hour. She did not have long to wait, and the strokes had scarcely finished when she heard the ships' sirens on the Mersey sounding and church bells ringing. The next moment came the noise of heavy footfalls overhead. Damn! The noise must have woken him up. Maybe it would wake her aunt up, too?

She made a dash for the front door, hoping the other two would be waiting there, only to slip on the carpet runner in the lobby. Her feet went from under her and she landed flat on her back.

'Is that you, Elsie?'

Betty recognised Teddy's voice and hastily rolled over and pushed herself up onto her hands and knees. 'No, it's me, Betty.'

'Where's your bloody aunt?' he demanded, hovering into view on the stairs.

'Isn't she with you in bed?' asked Betty, trying to avoid looking at his bowed legs in the grubby long johns.

'No, we had a disagreement and she went out.' He scowled down at her.

'Where did she go?'

'I don't bloody know. She didn't bloody tell me!'

Betty wished he'd stop swearing and go back to bed. She got to her feet, wincing as she had hurt her back when she slipped. 'I'll just wait here to let our Dorothy and Maggie in,' she said. 'They're first-footing.'

He stared at Betty. 'It's late. You should be in bed. Get upstairs.'

She shook her head. 'I have to be here to welcome them in.'

'I said *get to bed*!' he roared, bringing up his hand and hitting her across the face.

The blow caused her to rock on her feet. She was stunned by his actions and she could only stare at him. He hit her again and there was an expression in his eyes that terrified her. She did not wait for the next blow to fall but fled up the stairs. He watched her go with a smirk on his face. Then went over to the front door and shot the bolts top and bottom before following after her.

Dorothy and Maggie stood on the front step. 'Why the heck doesn't our Betty answer?' asked Maggie. 'She's supposed to be letting us in. Surely she hasn't fallen asleep?'

'There's no point in us waiting any longer,' said Dorothy, giving a shiver. 'We're much later than we thought we'd be. Drag the key through the letter box and we'll let ourselves in.'

'What are you two doing out here?' demanded a familiar voice from behind them.

Dorothy turned and stared at her mother. 'We thought you were in bed!'

'No.' Elsie's expression was fixed. 'Teddy and I had words, so I decided to go out and visit an old friend. We haven't met for a while, so I wanted to see how she was getting on. Why are you two waiting on the doorstep?'

'Betty's supposed to be letting us in, but she's not answering,' said Dorothy. 'She must have fallen asleep.'

Maggie drew the key through the letter box and inserted it in the lock. It turned all right but the door didn't open. She frowned and tried again.

'What's wrong?' asked Elsie, leaning forward and peering at the lock.

'I don't know,' said Maggie, shaking her head.

Dorothy stepped forward. 'Let me try.' She did so, but the door still didn't open. 'I think it must be bolted,' she said.

Elsie swore. 'Betty wouldn't have done that. It's bloody Teddy. He must have woken up and done it just to be bloody awkward. We're going to have to go round the back.'

They walked up the side of the house only to discover that the back door was locked. 'How the heck are we going to get in?' asked Maggie, dismayed.

'The bathroom window could still be open,' said Elsie.

The three stepped back and looked up and saw that it was slightly open.

'Our Jared used to keep a ladder behind the shed,' said Dorothy. 'Let's go and get it.'

The sisters went and fetched the ladder whilst Elsie tried the back door again in the hope that it might just give. When it didn't, she lit a cigarette with a shaking hand. 'If I get pneumonia, he'll get it in the neck,' she muttered.

Maggie glanced at her mother as they placed the ladder against the wall. She held it steady whilst Dorothy climbed up to the bathroom window. She managed to push it wide open and moved aside the jar of bath salts, bottle of shampoo and tooth mugs. She clambered over the sill with some difficulty, but once inside, she didn't hang about but went downstairs. She opened the back door and let her mother and Maggie in.

'Well, I didn't expect to first-foot through the bathroom window, Mum,' said Dorothy, handing the coal, salt, bread and money to her. 'Happy New Year.'

Elsie did not answer but went through into the sitting room and threw the coal on the fire and placed the rest of the items on the table. 'Well, he's not down here, so he must have locked up and gone to bed,' she said angrily.

'But what about Betty?' asked Maggie. 'The wireless is still on. If she'd fallen asleep I would have thought she'd done so down here.'

'Perhaps she just got fed up of waiting,' said Elsie, warming her hands by the fire. 'How long were you away?'

'We bumped into several of the neighbours and they kept us talking,' said Dorothy.

'Then that's what happened,' said her mother. 'Betty probably thought you'd be able to get in by dragging the key through the letter box and went to bed.'

'That would mean Uncle Teddy must have come down after she did,' said Dorothy, frowning. 'She wouldn't have locked us out.'

'He did it deliberately to annoy me,' said Elsie in a tight voice.

She went over to the sideboard cupboard and took out a bottle of sherry and poured herself a glass. 'Well, being locked out wasn't a good start to 1953 but let's hope it gets better. Happy New Year,' she said, raising her glass and then downing the sherry in one go before heading up the stairs.

Maggie looked at Dorothy, who reached for the sherry bottle and filled two small glasses. She handed one to her younger sister. 'Here's to our Jared. May God keep him safe and end the war in Korea and bring him home.'

CHAPTER THIRTEEN

Spring 1953

'So what are you going to do?' asked Lila, sprawling on a blanket on Emma's lawn. The air was balmy and the scent of lilac wafted towards her on a light breeze.

'You mean about visiting Liverpool?' asked Emma, pegging out the last pillowcase.

'Aye, you haven't seen Betty since February and you said that she didn't seem herself.'

Emma frowned and placed the washing basket on the coal bunker before kneeling beside Lila on the blanket. 'I'm thinking of going next Saturday. Easter weekend was a washout but at least there were plenty of Easter eggs in the shops now sweets are off ration. Last weekend was good. Once sugar comes off the ration, as they mentioned on the wireless, I'll be able to make more cakes and hopefully more money. I've enough to afford the fare to Liverpool, but I'm going to have to think seriously about getting those missing slates fixed on the roof soon. It would have been more sensible of me to have had it done last autumn, but I really had set my heart on seeing Betty and couldn't afford both.' Absently she plucked a leaf from a nearby mint plant and chewed on it. 'She hasn't answered my last letter. I'm wondering if it's gone missing or there's something seriously wrong.'

'Surely Dorothy or her friend Irene would have let you know if there was,' said Lila, gazing up at her.

'I would have thought so, but perhaps it's something she can't talk about,' said Emma.

'She could be worried about her exams coming up,' suggested Lila.

'Maybe. I'll write to Irene and post the letter today. She should get it by Tuesday at the latest. If she replies straight away I should know what's going on before making the trip.'

'Will you be seeing Dougie?'

'He hasn't been in touch,' said Emma shortly.

'Have you written to him?'

'No. I'm not going to chase after him if he can't be bothered writing to me,' replied Emma, wishing her friend would drop the subject of Constable Marshall.

Lila turned over a page of the *Red Letter* magazine. 'I wonder if we'll ever see him again.'

'Well, that will be up to him. I suppose you'll be working on Saturday, so you won't be able to come with me to Liverpool,' said Emma, thinking that Lila's one and only trip to the big city seemed to have put her off going there again.

'Aye, I am working,' said Lila. 'It's a busy time of the year.'

'That's OK,' said Emma, getting up and balancing the washing basket on her hip. 'If you don't mind, I'll go and write that letter right now.'

Irene Miller picked up the envelope from the coconut mat and saw that it was addressed to her. She recognised the handwriting and so she placed the letter with the other letter addressed to Betty and called to her stepfather that she was off to school now.

She headed towards Bridge Road, hoping to see Betty at the bus stop. She used to always be there before Irene up until a few weeks ago. She nibbled on a fingernail, thinking that Betty hadn't seemed her normal self since January. Early on in the Easter school holidays, she had expected Betty to come round but there had been no sign of her, so Irene had decided to call at the Gregorys' house.

Never again!

Mrs Gregory had bitten off her nose and told her to bugger off. Irene had been shocked by her use of such language. But she had stood her ground and asked what she had done wrong to deserve being sworn at. She was told that she'd led Betty astray by encouraging her to go to the Gianellis'. Irene had protested and said that Dorothy had been there to keep her eye on them. For a moment she had thought Mrs Gregory would blow a gasket but instead she'd slammed the door in Irene's face.

To Irene's surprise Maggie was at the bus stop, standing a little away from the queue, looking anxious. 'What are you doing here?' asked Irene. 'This isn't your bus stop. Where's Betty?'

'She's been terribly sick for a week or more and Mum's been demented. She's been dosing her with stuff that's made her even more sick,' said Maggie rapidly. 'Mum wouldn't let me go out, saying I might be infectious. She asked me questions about who we've been mixing with in case she had caught it off them. I had to tell her about us going to the Gianellis' music evenings. She wanted everyone's names.'

'I called but she told me to b— off,' said Irene.

Maggie gasped. 'She shouldn't have sworn at you but she's been really worried about our Betty. I actually thought that she might die!'

221

Irene was horrified. 'She was that bad?'

'Yes!'

'Poor Betty.'

'I know.' Maggie sighed. 'She can get on my nerves at times but I don't want her to die. Fortunately Mum seems to think she'll be on the mend soon. I thought I might be infectious but she said enough time had passed to convince her that I wasn't, so I'm off to school. She's given me a note to give to you to take in to Betty's teacher. Truthfully, I was glad to get out of the house. I was fed up of being in and having to put up with Uncle Teddy, who's been in a right mood, expecting me to wait on him hand and foot.' She glowered at nothing in particular before continuing. 'Mum was paying him hardly any attention with her being so worried about our Betty.'

Maggie handed over an envelope and Irene took from her pocket the letter addressed to Betty that had arrived a couple of weeks ago. 'Give that to her. It's from Emma.'

Maggie thanked her. 'I'll give it to our Dorothy and she can give it to her. I'm still not allowed in our Betty's bedroom.' Her brow furrowed. 'It's odd that our Dorothy is and she's still going to work. I wonder if I should tell Mum about Emma, with our Betty being so ill?'

Irene turned on her. 'You shouldn't do that without speaking to Betty about it first! Anyway, don't you think your mother's got enough on her plate without getting her all worked up about Emma?'

'I suppose you're right,' muttered Maggie. 'I've been told I'm not to go to the Gianellis' anymore. I'm really miffed about that.'

'It's a blinking shame,' said Irene. 'But if Betty is still not well by Saturday, we could meet at the bridge on Saturday morning at ten and you can tell me how things are.'

Maggie's freckled face brightened. 'I'll do that. See you!'

Irene watched her as she went off to catch her bus to Litherland High School for Girls. Her own bus drew up and she climbed aboard. After she had paid for her ticket, she took out the letter from Emma and began to read it. She frowned, wondering what reply to give to Emma. The truth as she knew it? Maybe she should suggest that Emma put off her visit for a couple of weeks. Surely by then Betty would be better?

Dorothy stood beside the bed, gazing down at Betty. She was so pale that her freckles seemed to stand out. It was as if all the blood had been drained out of her. It was not since Aunt Lizzie's sudden death that Dorothy had seen her cousin looking so vulnerable. She knew what her mother was saying but she found it difficult to accept.

When she thought about those musical evenings and how she had enjoyed making the acquaintance of the Gianelli family and friends, she found it nigh on impossible to believe that any of the youths had been responsible for Betty being pregnant. She had never been alone with any of them for a start, and although the teenagers often left the house together, Dorothy always accompanied them, along with Nellie Gianelli's sister, Lottie, and her family.

'I'm determined to find out who was responsible,' said Elsie, her voice seething with anger. 'She is so stubborn. Why won't she tell me who did it to her?'

Dorothy said firmly, 'I've said it once, Mum, and I'll say it again, it's none of those lads who were at the Gianellis'.'

'You're determined to have your way, aren't you?' said Elsie, reaching for a cigarette. 'You should never have taken her to that Eyetie's house. I thought you'd have known better than to have mixed with Catholics.'

'You're wrong about them,' said Dorothy earnestly. 'They're lovely people.'

'Go on! Go against me! You always think you know everything and you know nothing.' Elsie lit the cigarette and sucked smoke into her lungs.

'*By their fruits you will know them,*' said Dorothy softly.

Her mother's eyes narrowed as she stared at her through the curling smoke. 'What's that supposed to mean?'

'Work it out yourself, Mum. Why don't you go downstairs and make yourself a cup of tea? I'll sit with Betty.'

Elsie gazed down at her niece. 'Good money, that's what she's cost me. Could have brought shame on this household if I hadn't acted quickly. Fortunately I knew a midwife and she has sympathy for the likes of Betty. Surely she must have known what she did was wrong, but is she saying anything? No!'

'Did you tell her how babies are made, then?' asked Dorothy, flicking back her blonde hair and sitting on the side of the bed. 'I had to explain to her what periods are. She was playing hockey when she started bleeding and had no idea what was happening to her. Fortunately she had the sense to come to me and ask. I found out from a book.'

Elsie reddened and blustered, 'You shouldn't be reading that kind of book. Anyway, that's no excuse. My mother never told me anything and I kept myself pure until I married your dad.'

'Then sex must have come as a terrible shock to you.'

Elsie gasped and slapped her face. 'Go and wash your mouth out with soap! You know far too much for an unmarried girl. Don't think I'll be here for you if you get into trouble.' She hurried from the bedroom.

Dorothy put a hand to her stinging cheek, thinking her mother would be the last person she would go to if she needed help. It was true that she had been through a worrying time with Betty, but it seemed she was more concerned about what the neighbours thought than poor Betty. What a thing to have to go through.

Dorothy reached out and took hold of her cousin's hand, thinking she would dearly love to know who had got her pregnant. She could only remember the crippled Marshall twin ever giving Betty more than a second glance and he'd only joined them six weeks ago. She felt her cousin's fingers tighten about her hand and as she watched, Betty's eyelashes slowly lifted.

A pang of pity shot through Dorothy and she remembered the stricken expression in Betty's eyes when Elsie had told her what ailed her.

'How are you feeling?' asked Dorothy.

Betty did not answer but withdrew her hand from her cousin's and turned her head away and buried it in the pillow. 'I want to be left alone,' she said in a muffled voice.

'Honestly?'

'Yes! I don't want to talk about it.'

Dorothy sighed. 'OK. But I have a letter here for

you from Emma. Irene gave it to Maggie. It came the other week but—'

'You don't have to say any more, just give it to me,' said Betty, holding out a hand without lifting her head.

Dorothy gave it over. 'Irene got a letter from Emma this morning, too. I don't know what hers said. Maybe she's thinking of coming to Liverpool. I thought I'd write to Emma and—'

'Tell her I've been ill and to leave meeting up in Liverpool for now,' said Betty, her fingers crushing the envelope.

'OK.' Dorothy stood up. 'Is there anything I can get you?'

'No, thank you.'

Dorothy left the bedroom.

Immediately the door closed Betty sat up, and as she did so she felt a rush of blood soak the sanitary towel. For weeks she had wanted to scream and smash everything in the room but she had kept her emotions rigidly under control. *It was him, him, his fault and she hated him!* She rested her head against the pillows, tore open the envelope and took out Emma's letter.

Dear Betty,

Are you all right? I've had this feeling lately that something is wrong. Perhaps you are worried about exams or something

else that you feel that you can't talk to your
Liverpool family about.

Betty was astonished by her half-sister's perception and felt a rush of affection for her. How could she have known that she was in such a state? She hadn't said a word to anyone about that filthy swine's behaviour. He had hit and threatened her, raped her and boasted that her aunt wouldn't believe her if she told her what he had done. After the way she had gone on about the lads at the Gianellis' musical evenings, Betty could believe that her aunt would never accept that her husband was responsible for her condition. She had wanted to tell someone but had felt so dirty and besmirched by what he had done that she had simply wanted to pretend it had not happened.

Her eyes were suddenly wet with tears. She had been stunned to learn that she was most likely having a baby. If the vomiting hadn't already been enough to cope with, her aunt's words had caused such an icy chill to seize her that she hadn't been able to think straight. Then her aunt had confused her by telling her that she had food poisoning and locked her in her bedroom.

The door suddenly opened and *he* entered and she was filled with fear. 'So here we are,' said Teddy, smirking at her. 'All better now, are we?'

She wanted to throw up but there was nothing

in her stomach to get rid of because she hadn't eaten that day. She managed to say, 'Get out!'

'Who d'you think you're talking to?' he said, his expression turning ugly. 'You don't give the orders round her. You're a disgrace. Getting yourself into trouble with boys. I bet there was more than one,' he said loudly. 'Tart!'

She gripped the bedcovers and pulled them up to her chin. 'You two-faced swine,' she shouted. 'Get out of my room!'

He approached the bed, and seizing her cheek, pinched it hard. She managed to turn her head and bite his hand. 'You little bitch,' he snarled, slapping her face.

Betty could scarcely believe this was happening after all she had been through. Would it all start up over again? Then she heard her aunt calling him and instantly he made for the door. 'One word out of place,' he warned, 'and you'll regret it.'

The door closed behind him and Betty sat, trembling, her mind dark with the horror of what had taken place on New Year's Eve. She could not stay here! Had to get out! She realised that she was still clutching her sister's letter and he hadn't even noticed. It had been crushed into a ball when she had pulled up the bedcovers.

Without reading further, she placed it under her pillow with Winnie the Witch and lay back, trying to bring order to her chaotic thoughts. She had to return to school and continue with her studies, had to do well in her exams, and only then would she feel free to leave this house. But she would write to Emma and tell her that she had been worrying about her exams and would see her once they were over.

CHAPTER FOURTEEN

'You OK, Betty?' asked Maggie, looking anxiously at her cousin as she picked up her jacket.

'Will you stop fussing over me. I'm fine,' said Betty in a brittle voice. 'I just want to get out of this house.'

'We're doing that. Got all you need?'

'Yes!' Betty wrenched open the front door and stepped outside. It was a month since the abortion and her nerves felt stretched to breaking point. Despite her determination to study and do well in her exams, she often found it impossible to concentrate. She walked down the drive, but as she reached the bottom she saw Teddy coming round the corner on the main road. Immediately she turned in the opposite direction and raced along the pavement.

Maggie hurried to catch up with her. 'Why are we going this way?' she asked. 'Was it seeing Uncle Teddy?'

'Why else?' gasped Betty, her heart banging away in her chest. 'Surely you didn't want him to keep us talking, nosing into our business?'

'Of course not,' said Maggie, breathless with rushing.

'Well, then,' said Betty, thinking she would kill herself rather than have him touch her again, 'let's stay out of his way.'

'OK! But you look wild.'

Betty thought, *You'd look wild if you'd been through what I've been through*. 'I was thinking of walking down Hatton Hill Road and then through the park and over the canal. It's not a bad day and it'll be a nice walk.'

'You mean you're going to walk to school instead of getting the bus?' asked Maggie.

'Yes. I feel like a good walk.'

Maggie gave her an uneasy glance. 'But you could be late, and what about meeting Irene? Are you sure you're feeling all right? I mean you've been acting a bit peculiar, since you've been ill.'

The muscles of Betty's finely drawn features tightened. 'Let's forget about that. I'm fine now. You don't have to walk with me. In fact, I'd quite like to be on my own.'

'OK! If that's how you feel,' said Maggie, tossing her head. 'But Irene's going to get annoyed when you don't turn up at the bus stop.'

Betty thought how she hadn't been able to talk about what had happened, even to her best friend. Without another word, she strode ahead. Now her thoughts were of the woman who had performed the abortion. She had been neither judgemental nor cruel, but rather, beneath her brisk no-nonsense manner, Betty had sensed sympathy for her plight. Her aunt had not told her the name of the woman, but there was something about her which convinced Betty that she could be trusted to know what she was doing. What a relief it had been when it was all over. Her aunt had bundled her out of the house in a furtive manner and into a taxi. Despite the pain, Betty was at least relieved to be rid of what her aunt called HER SHAME, capitalising all the letters.

'I don't know what Mum's going to say,' Maggie called after Betty. 'I'm supposed to stay with you and keep my eye on you to make sure you're all right.'

And I know the reason why she wants you to do that, thought Betty. She's convinced there's a lad I've been seeing and is determined that Maggie will let her know who it is. I can't cope with this anymore, she decided.

When Betty crossed the Leeds-Liverpool canal, instead of heading towards Beach Road she began to walk along the towpath northwards. There were ducks, coots and moorhens swimming in the water, some with young that were so cute that she felt her tension ease a little. The hawthorn was still in blossom and the grass verge was bright with buttercups and daisies. When she reached Netherton, she carried on walking, past Maghull and onwards. A barge passed her and the bargee waved to her. She waved back and continued on her way for what was surely miles. Her leg muscles were aching and so were her hips.

Eventually, she had to stop and rest and she chose to do so at a place where there was an elderly man fishing and a woman sitting on a rug, reading a book. Betty had no idea where she was but had it fixed in her head that if she kept on travelling north, eventually she would reach her sister's village.

'Can you tell me where I am?' she asked the woman.

'Halsall, dear,' she replied, without looking up from her book.

'Where's that?' asked Betty, wiping her damp brow on her sleeve.

'Not far from Ormskirk.' She gave Betty a curious look. 'Why, where are you heading?' Betty told her. 'Goodness me, love, you're miles away from there. It's up near Blackburn and you won't reach it by just following the canal. You'll have to come off and it'll take you ages to walk there.'

Betty's shoulders slumped. 'But I've got to get there,' she insisted. 'I can't walk all the way back. I have to see someone.'

'Who do you want to see? And why aren't you at school?' asked the woman.

'I've been ill and I need to see my sister. She lives in a cottage up north.' Betty named the village. 'I'm an orphan,' she added.

The elderly man glanced her way. 'You're not running away from an orphanage, are you, lass?'

Betty shook her head and looked longingly at the bottle of water poking out of the haversack on the ground. 'I'm running away from my uncle. He hits me and I can't cope with it any longer. I've walked miles to get this far.'

The elderly couple exchanged looks. 'Why don't you live with your sister?' asked the woman.

'Because she's my half-sister and we only got to know about each other last year.' Betty licked her dry lips. 'My father was married twice and he was killed at Dunkirk.'

'That must have been hard. You thirsty, lass?' asked the man.

Betty nodded.

She watched as the woman half-filled a mug with water before handing it to her. 'Thanks,' she said, and drank thirstily.

'I bet you're hungry, too,' said the man, smiling faintly.

'Yes, but don't worry about it. Now I've had a drink, I'll rest for a while. Then I'll see if I can cadge a lift from one of the bargees going north.'

'They'll probably only be able to take you as far as Wigan,' said the woman, 'and it could take some time, dear, before one comes along. Is there any way we can get in touch with your half-sister and let her know where you are? She might be able to send someone to pick you up from Ormskirk.'

Betty heaved a sigh. 'Emma doesn't have a telephone.'

'But there's bound to be a post office in the village. We have a telephone at home and I could ask the operator to put a call through and hopefully they'll get a message to her,' said the man.

Betty felt tears well up in her eyes. 'You'd do that for me?' she said in a husky voice.

'That's what we've been put on this earth for, lass,' he said kindly. 'I reckon you must be quite desperate to try to walk so far.'

'I am,' agreed Betty.

'So what's your sister's name?' asked the woman.

'Emma Booth. She lives in Honeysuckle Cottage.'

'Well, you come with us,' said the man, reeling in his fishing line. 'And I'll make that telephone call and we'll see what happens. Your name is?'

'I get called Betty, although my name's really Elizabeth, the same as my mother's,' she replied.

He nodded. 'We've a granddaughter, Elizabeth.'

He removed his reel and dismantled his rod. His wife was already collecting her things together.

'What's your name?' asked Betty.

'Molyneux,' he replied. 'Gerald and Hannah Molyneux.'

'Thank you, Mr and Mrs Molyneux. I'm really sorry I've spoilt your day out,' said Betty.

'Don't you be worrying,' said her elderly knight in shining armour. 'We've the whole of summer to look forward to. Now let's be going.'

Emma replaced the telephone in the post office, withdrew some money from her saving account, expressed her thanks and walked out into King Street. She'd dropped everything when she had received the message from the postmaster. Now she must prepare a bedroom for her sister and finish off the weekly accounts she had been in the middle of doing if she was to get them to her client on time. She had been prepared to make the journey to Ormskirk after listening to a babbled outpouring from Betty which Emma had difficulty untangling, but one thing was for certain, and that was that her sister was in a state and had come running to her for help. Emma had spoken to Mr Molyneux on the telephone, saying she would get in touch with him after she had visited the railway station and had the information needed from the stationmaster on which was the quickest route for her to take to Ormskirk. She had been completely overwhelmed by his thoughtfulness when he told her not to bother because he had a friend, a salesman, who had a van and travelled all round Lancashire. He would arrange for him to deliver Betty to her that evening. If she could just reimburse his friend for the petrol, that should take care of the matter.

Emma wasted no time getting home and decided to finish her paid work before preparing the spare bedroom. She found it difficult to concentrate because one sentence kept repeating itself in her head. Betty was running away from her wicked uncle. Presumably that was Uncle Teddy. Her eyes darkened with anger, thinking she would have the sorry tale out of Betty.

Emma managed to complete her work and then she went upstairs and into her former bedroom. She made up the single bed and shook the rug outside, polished the lino and then dusted the single chest of drawers and the bedside cupboard. She had settled on a boiled egg and bread and butter for her supper but thought that perhaps that wouldn't be enough for her sister, so she sliced potatoes, planning to fry them and make an omelette.

Then she decided that the man who was delivering Betty to her might appreciate a cup of tea and a couple of home-made scones, so she did a baking. Afterwards, she fished out the letter

Dorothy had sent to her, knowing she wouldn't find any mention of the wicked uncle in it. Still, she was hoping she might discover some clue to Betty's unexpected behaviour between the lines.

Reading the letter again, *restrained* was the word that kept coming into Emma's head. It was a bit like Betty's last letter. Her half-sister's letters were generally full of her doings and the occasional joke. Sometimes she even enclosed a cartoon cut out from the local newspaper, but there hadn't been a bright note in that letter. Emma remembered how she had thought something was worrying her sister before Dorothy had told her she had gone down with food poisoning. Had the uncle been hitting Betty? If so, why hadn't she told Dorothy about it? Why had Betty chosen to run away from her aunt's home to her, instead?

'How are you feeling now?' asked Emma, watching her sister curl up on the sofa with Tibby on her lap. Betty's face was flushed with the sun and she had even more freckles than when last Emma had seen her.

'Better now that I'm here,' said Betty, stroking the cat's head.

'Are you going to tell me what this is all about?'

Betty kept her head lowered. 'I thought I told you over the telephone.'

'You babbled something about a wicked uncle.

Am I to take it you mean Dorothy and Maggie's Uncle Teddy?'

Betty nodded.

'What did he do?'

Betty did not answer but Emma saw the muscles of her face tighten. 'Did he hit you?'

'Yes, but I don't want to talk about it.'

'We have to talk about it,' said Emma gently, feeling a curl of anger unfurl in her stomach. 'What's the point of your coming here if you won't talk about it? Why didn't you tell your aunt?'

Betty turned her head and the curtain of ginger hair fell so that it shielded her face. 'She wouldn't have believed me.'

'Dorothy, then. If you spoke to her about it, I'm sure her mother would have had to listen.'

'Aunt Elsie wouldn't believe her either because she knows we both don't like him and he knows it as well. He's sneaky. You've no idea how sneaky he is,' said Betty, a tremor in her voice.

Emma frowned. 'Surely there'd be bruises where he hit you? Did he hit you where they couldn't be seen?'

'Sometimes, but at others he'd slap my face or clout me on the side of the head.'

'That is so wrong,' burst out Emma, her fists clenching. 'A grown-up should never hit a child on the head! He could have knocked you silly. Surely he wasn't picking on you just because you don't like him?'

'Probably. He didn't like the way I talked to him. I bit him last time he hit me,' she said with satisfaction.

'Good for you,' said Emma, glad to see her sister show some spirit.

'He tasted horrible and I wondered afterward whether I would really get food poisoning.'

'You're saying that you didn't have food poisoning?'

Betty was silent. Emma stared at her, wishing her sister felt able to tell her everything. She was definitely holding something back. Betty lifted her head and gazed about the kitchen. 'I like it here. It's not as big as Aunt Elsie's kitchen but it's homely. I don't want you to spoil the atmosphere by asking me any more questions about him. I feel safe here and I want to put him out of my mind.'

'That's fine,' said Emma smoothly. 'Did you leave a note saying where you were going?'

'No! I don't want him knowing where I am,' said Betty, her face paling beneath her sunburn. 'It has to be a secret.'

'But surely your aunt will be worried about you?' said Emma.

Betty's expression hardened. 'It won't do her any harm. She thinks the worst of me as it is. She's convinced I flirt with boys and I don't.'

Emma thought a little flirting with boys at her sister's age was normal. 'It's probably because she doesn't want you to be distracted from your schoolwork. She is responsible for you and when you don't arrive home, she might go to the police and report you missing.'

A nerve flickered beneath Betty's left eye. 'I never thought of that. I was sure she'd be glad to be rid of me, so I wouldn't be a bother to her anymore.'

'Maybe, maybe not,' said Emma, wishing she knew more about Elsie Gregory. 'What about Dorothy and Maggie? They care about you.'

'I thought you could write to our Dot and let her know I'm here,' said Betty, getting to her feet, still nursing the cat.

'But she mightn't get the letter until the day after tomorrow.'

'But she might get it tomorrow. Can I go to bed now? I'm awfully tired after all the walking I've done.'

Emma nodded, but she was still concerned about Dorothy worrying about Betty. Somehow she had to get information to her quickly to prevent her mother from reporting Betty missing to the police. Maybe if she could get in touch with Dougie? She didn't like doing so having not heard from him for ages, but then needs must when the devil drives.

She escorted her sister upstairs to the small bedroom that overlooked the garden. 'I've put an old pair of my pyjamas under the pillow for you,' she said.

'Thanks,' said Betty, managing a smile. 'It's a nice bedroom. Not as big as mine back in Litherland but I'll feel safe here. Can I keep Tibby with me?' she asked anxiously, seeming a lot younger than her sixteen years.

'Aye, but don't force her to stay. You don't want her making a mess on the bed.'

Betty nodded.

Emma hesitated. 'Will you be all right here on your own for a short while? There's an errand I must do.'

'Yes, I'm sure I'll be OK here,' said Betty, heaving a sigh.

Emma put an arm around her sister's shoulders and kissed her. 'I'll come up and see you when I get back. If you're awake I'll bring you a cup of cocoa.'

'Thanks. That'd be lovely.' Betty sat on the bed. 'And will you make me a chocolate cake sometime?'

Emma's face softened. 'I haven't forgotten my promise the first time we met.'

Betty's eyes suddenly filled with tears. 'I didn't think you would forget,' she said in a shaky voice.

Emma sat on the side of the bed. 'Now, why are you crying because I said I'd make you a chocolate cake?' she teased.

'It's your not forgetting,' said Betty, resting her head on her sister's shoulder for a moment, and then she straightened up. 'You can go now. I'll be OK.'

'Are you sure?' asked Emma, reaching out and touching her sister's brightly coloured hair.

'Yes. You go.'

So Emma left the cottage and went to seek the help of the local bobby. Although it took some time to get the telephone number, she was eventually able to speak to the desk sergeant at the police station in Liverpool where she had spent the night in a cell. He remembered her. Unfortunately Dougie was off duty but the sergeant promised to get a message to him. Relieved, Emma returned to the cottage, wondering whether she would possibly see Dougie again in the near future.

CHAPTER FIFTEEN

Dorothy wrenched the front door open and stared at the policeman standing on the step. She should have been on her way to work but she was late because she had been to the Gianellis' to see if Betty was there, but had had no luck. The policeman was young, with fair hair and blue eyes.

'Oh God!' she exclaimed, placing a hand to her mouth. 'Something terrible has happened to my cousin, Betty, hasn't it? She's thrown herself in the canal and has drowned.'

'Calm down, luv,' he said firmly. 'It's nothing like that. Am I talking to Miss Gregory?'

'Yes!' Dorothy's lovely features relaxed. 'It's just that she's gone missing and I've searched everywhere but can't find her. I was all for getting the police last night but my uncle said to wait and that she's probably gone off somewhere just to annoy us. My mother agreed and so—'

He held up a hand as if to stem the rush of words. 'Betty's safe,' he said. 'I'm Dougie Marshall. I believe you know my brothers. I received a message from my station concerning your cousin. I was to tell you that she's with her half-sister, Emma, at her cottage up Lancashire.'

'What! You're Dougie Marshall and Betty's with Emma! How did she manage to get there? She hasn't any money as far as I know. I wish she'd told me she was going!' babbled Dorothy.

'Calm down, luv,' he said. 'Emma will be writing to you.'

'Is that all she said?'

'That's all I know, Miss Gregory.'

Dorothy put a hand to her head. 'I see. Thanks. Perhaps I should go and visit them. I'll have to check the train times.'

'Why don't you wait until you get Emma's letter?' suggested Dougie. 'It could be that your cousin will only be staying up there for a few days and will be back soon.'

'You could be right,' said Dorothy, feeling some of the tension drain out of her.

'Have you been to the cottage before?' asked Dougie.

She shook her head. 'But I know you have. Emma told me that you've visited her.'

'Lovely fell-walking country nearby. Do you walk?'

'No. I'm a real townie.'

He smiled. 'You should try it. Keeps you fit and is relaxing.'

She thought that he had the bluest eyes. No wonder Emma had fallen for him. 'Thanks for the advice and for letting me know Betty's safe,' she said, giving him a dazzling smile.

He flushed. 'All part of the job.'

'Even so, I'm ever so grateful.'

'My pleasure. See you around.' He raised a hand and hurried down the drive.

Dorothy stood, staring after him for a moment, and then she went inside the house. 'Who was at the door?' asked her mother. 'Was it one of our Betty's other friends come to tell us where she is?'

'No, Mum.'

'She'll get the edge of my tongue when she comes back,' said Elsie, exasperated, lighting a cigarette. 'She's doing it deliberately to annoy me.'

'What she needs is a good hiding,' growled Teddy. 'You're best rid of her. She's no good.'

Up until then Dorothy had given no thought to what she was going to tell her mother, but both Elsie and Teddy had so maddened her that she decided to keep them guessing as to Betty's whereabouts.

'I'm going to have to go to work now, Mum. I'll see you later. Let's hope Betty's returned by then. If not, then I really think you should start being less annoyed and a bit more worried about her!'

She picked up her swagger coat and handbag and walked out the room, thinking she would drop by at the Millers' house in the hope she might find Maggie there. Her sister had left the house early, so she and Irene could make their own search for Betty. It would mean Dorothy would be even later for work, but as she was already going to have money docked from her wages, what did it matter?

The Millers' door was opened to her by a man in a khaki shirt and trousers. He was well built and of medium height, with neatly cut mousy hair and straight eyebrows. His eyes were grey and they scanned her face and figure in one quick movement that brought a blush to Dorothy's cheeks.

'Can I help you, luv?' he asked.

'I hope so,' she said, checking the number on the door. 'I have got the right address, haven't I? Irene Miller's house.'

'My stepmother's name was Miller before she married my dad. I'm Billy McElroy,' he said, holding out a hand.

Dorothy stared at the workmanlike shape and texture of that hand and its cleanliness before touching it. 'Dorothy Gregory,' she said.

'Ahhh!' His expression was instantly serious. 'You'll be Maggie's sister.'

'Is Maggie here?'

He freed Dorothy's hand and rested a shoulder against the door jamb. 'You've just missed her and Irene. If you had your running shoes on you might be able to catch them. They're walking along the canal, hoping they might find a clue to Betty's disappearance.'

Dorothy heaved a sigh. 'They're wasting their time.'

He raised those straight dark brows of his. 'You mean she's been found?'

'Yes.'

'Alive?'

She nodded.

'Where?'

She hesitated.

'You can trust me, you know,' he said. 'I know all about Emma.'

'What!' She stared at him in annoyance. 'Did Irene tell you?'

'No need to get yourself in a twist,' he drawled. 'I'm stationed up north Lancashire and I heard Irene and Maggie talking about Betty having a half-sister living near Clitheroe this morning.'

'Damn!' exclaimed Dorothy, vexed. 'It's supposed to be a secret.'

'You can't expect schoolgirls not to natter to each other. Is Betty there?'

She chewed on the inside of her cheek, staring at him and comparing him with Dougie Marshall, thinking the policeman was more handsome but Billy McElroy was oh so much tougher-looking. 'Oh, all right, she is.'

He smiled and his face was completely transformed. 'I can go after the girls if you like and let them know she's safe. When will she be back?'

'I don't know,' replied Dorothy, shrugging a shoulder.

'Perhaps you'd like me to suggest to Irene that she tells the teacher that Betty's had a relapse and is having a week or so convalescence in the countryside,' suggested Billy.

Dorothy stared at him in astonishment. 'What a good idea! I see you know she's been ill.'

He nodded. 'As I said earlier, girls natter.'

'OK! Do what you suggested,' said Dorothy hastily. 'As long as Irene doesn't tell her form mistress where she's staying.'

'Does it really matter if the teacher knows Betty has an older half-sister living up north?' asked Billy, pulling the door closed behind him.

'She might mention it to my mother,' said Dorothy, beginning to walk up the street in the direction of the library.

He fell into step beside her. 'Isn't it time your mother knew that you're aware of Emma's existence? Especially now Betty's taken refuge with her.'

Dorothy dug her hands deep in the pockets of her swagger coat. 'What do you mean by refuge? What else has Irene been saying?' she asked, slanting him a challenging look.

Billy's grey eyes met hers. 'That Betty doesn't like your uncle.'

'Neither do I, so that's nothing new,' said Dorothy. 'He's a creep and Mum was a fool to marry him.'

'Does he know about Emma?'

'I've no idea. I hope not.'

Billy frowned. 'Let's think about this a bit more. If Betty is frightened of him, then she won't want him knowing where she is. She definitely won't want to come home. That's bad. After all, she's got important exams coming up and she'll need to be in school for them.'

A thought suddenly occurred to Dorothy and she felt her heart begin to thud. 'What else did Irene have to say about my uncle?'

'I got the impression he could be a bit violent. He might be clouting Betty while no one's around, and if he's threatened her with worse, then she might have been too scared to mention it to your mother. It's surprising what goes on in families, but secrets have a habit of coming out when you least expect it,' said Billy.

They had reached the corner of the street and paused there. 'You sound like there's been skeletons in your family cupboard,' said Dorothy, curious to know more about him despite finding his presence rather overpowering.

'I wouldn't deny it, but I'm not telling you what they are,' he said, a smile lurking in his grey eyes. 'I hope I'll see you again, Miss Gregory.' He raised a hand and walked away.

She gazed after him until he vanished round the corner of Bridge Road. Then, as a Ribble bus came into view, she crossed the road. As she climbed aboard, she thought of her uncle. Betty wouldn't talk to her, but was it possible she would do so to Emma about whoever was responsible for getting her pregnant?

Dorothy stared out of the window, watching people passing by without really seeing them, wondering if it would be worth mentioning her suspicions to her mother. She sucked the inside of her cheek, she had all day to decide what to do. One thing was for certain, and that was she was going to keep a careful eye on Uncle Teddy in future.

As soon as Dorothy entered the kitchen that evening, her mother pounced on her. 'What's this I hear about you knowing that Betty is safe and convalescing in the countryside?' she cried.

Dorothy darted a look at Maggie sitting at the table with an exercise book open in front of her and a fountain pen clenched in her fist. She watched her sister's face turn pink. 'What have you told her?' asked Dorothy angrily.

'I didn't tell her where she is or with who,' said Maggie, bravely meeting her sister's gaze. 'Mum was worried and wanted to know where the Gianellis lived. She thought Betty might be hiding out there.'

'I'd already been there,' said Dorothy, turning to her mother. 'I told you she wasn't.'

'You could have been lying. You could have been protecting someone.' Elsie thrust her face into Dorothy's. 'What have you got to add to the story?' she demanded.

Dorothy jerked her head back and went into the lobby and hung up her jacket. Her mother followed her out. 'Well?' she asked.

'Betty ran away, most probably because she was scared of your husband. She's gone to stay with her half-sister up north,' said Dorothy, facing her mother. 'And don't tell me, Mum, that you don't know who I'm talking about.'

Elsie stared at her in silence and then she returned to the living room and lit a cigarette. She stood in front of the fire. 'How did you find out?'

'Emma wrote to Betty when you didn't answer her letters last year.'

'You've known all this time and kept quiet about it?'

Dorothy could sense the fury simmering beneath

the surface of her mother's seeming calm. 'No! I didn't find out about her for months, and when I did, it was by accident,' she said, sitting on the sofa and easing off her court shoes.

'Why didn't you mention it to me at the time?' asked Elsie.

'Why didn't you answer Emma's letter? Why keep it secret from Betty?'

Elsie opened her mouth and the cigarette clung to the bright purplish-pink lipstick on her bottom lip but no words came out. She sat in a chair and stared into the fire. 'Betty didn't need a half-sister in a village up north. She had a family. She has us.'

Dorothy was flabbergasted. 'I don't think that's a good enough answer. She could have both, but you decided for her. As it happens, Betty was made up to have a big sister and the pair of them get on really well. Otherwise she wouldn't have gone running to Emma when she felt desperate.'

'Desperate!' cried Elsie, hitting the arm of the chair with her fist. 'I got her out of trouble! There was no need for her to go running off when it was all over.'

'Perhaps she didn't believe it was all over,' said Dorothy. 'Didn't you hear what I said, Mum? She was scared of Uncle Teddy.'

Elsie stared at her elder daughter and then flicked her cigarette stub into the fire and lit another cigarette. She dragged smoke into her lungs and broke into a spasm of coughing. It was several minutes before she had breath to say, 'What are you insinuating?'

'I believe I don't have to put it into words. I think you know what I'm talking about.' Dorothy flicked a glance in Maggie's direction. 'I've been thinking all afternoon about New Year's Eve.'

Elsie continued to stare at Dorothy for several moments before saying, 'I don't believe it.'

'That's because you don't want to accept you made the worst possible mistake, welcoming that man into our home. We hardly saw him when Dad was ill. Then afterwards he came calling and pestered Aunt Lizzie. Her death must have come as a real shock to him but that didn't prevent him from starting to pester you. Week after week he was here, then it was a couple of times a week, then three times. Once our Jared left to do his national service, he was scarcely ever away from the place. The next thing we knew was that you'd married him in a registry office.' Dorothy was trembling and she hugged herself. 'A real hole-in-the-corner affair. You must have felt guilty, because you didn't want us there.'

'So I made a mistake in marrying him,' said Elsie unevenly. 'But it's too late to do anything about it now. He might have his faults but I can't believe he would do what you're hinting at. He doesn't even like Betty.'

'But she's scared of him, Mum,' said Maggie, fiddling with her pen. 'I'm a bit scared of him, myself.'

'And so you both should be,' said Elsie. 'It's good for you young ones to have a healthy fear of adults, or goodness knows what's going to happen to society. Discipline will break down altogether. I have to listen to enough cheek from our Dorothy as it is, so I don't want you siding with her, Maggie.'

'Mum, I'm over twenty-one,' said Dorothy. 'I'm not a kid anymore, and our Maggie will be fifteen next year. I should be able to talk to you as an equal. The suffragettes fought for equal rights with men, nothing was said about us women all being equal and I think that's wrong. Older people don't always get it right.'

Elsie's face turned puce. 'While you're living under my roof, what I say goes,' she said indignantly. 'As for Betty, she can stay up there with Emma. Let her have the responsibility of keeping her on the straight and narrow.'

'What's our Betty done that's so terrible?' asked Maggie.

'Never you mind,' said her mother, her eyes glinting. 'It has nothing to do with you.'

Maggie put down her fountain pen and stared at her mother. 'You said a few minutes ago that Betty was part of our family. How can we be family if our Betty's been in trouble and you kept it from me?

And what about her exams? She needs to get back here to school.'

'I'm sure there's schools up north,' said Elsie harshly.

'But you know Betty had her heart set on getting good exam results and going to the Art School in Liverpool,' said Maggie, earnestly.

'And you know I didn't want her to go to art school,' said her mother, flicking her cigarette butt on the fire. 'Of course, I might have had second thoughts if she'd been a good girl. As it is, she's burnt her boats.'

'So you're saying that she's no longer a member of this family?' said Maggie.

'That's right.'

'Dad wouldn't have agreed and neither would Jared,' said Dorothy heatedly.

Elsie turned on her elder daughter. 'Keep your father out of this. He's no longer here.'

'More's the pity,' said Dorothy, getting to her feet. 'Will you be telling Uncle Teddy where Betty has gone? I hope not, although perhaps he already knows about Emma?'

Burning her fingers, Elsie swore and dropped the match she'd just struck to light another cigarette. Dorothy picked it up and threw it on the fire. 'You smoke too much. Your lungs must be all black inside.'

'Shut up! If you had my nerves and had to put

up with what I have to, then you'd smoke too,' said Elsie, her expression fierce.

'Well, does he know?' persisted Dorothy.

'Yes, he knows!' yelled Elsie. 'He's my bloody husband! He's known since Emma's first letter arrived and he thought that Betty should have nothing to do with her.'

'I should have known he'd had a hand in it,' said Dorothy, shaking her head. 'That's terrible, Mum, telling him and not us about Emma's letter. We're your daughters.'

'How can we trust you when you put him before us?' asked Maggie.

Elsie closed her eyes and rested her head against the back of the chair. 'You don't understand. Whatever our Dorothy says about your being fifteen next year, you're still my little girl. There are things that you're too young to know about. Things I want to protect you against.'

Maggie scooped up her homework from the table. 'I'm no longer your little girl. I want to be treated like an adult,' she said, and walked out of the room.

'See what you've done now!' cried Elsie, rounding on Dorothy. 'You've turned her against me.'

'Not me, Mum! You've done that all by yourself,' said Dorothy, suddenly pitying her. 'I'm going upstairs to change. I'll have my dinner later.'

Once she was alone, Elsie sat, staring into the fire. Could what Dorothy had hinted at about Teddy be true? No, no! He might have his faults, but surely he wasn't a child molester? But what was she thinking? Betty was no child but a young woman who would be seventeen in November. She could have been testing her feminine wiles on him. Men could be so weak. Her head began to ache. God! She was beginning to accept that her daughter could be right about Teddy getting Betty pregnant. What was she going to do about it? Confront Teddy? She could imagine him going right through the roof and then lashing out at her for suggesting such a thing. But it was possible that Dorothy was mistaken and was protecting one of those young men at that Eyetie's house. Maybe Teddy had just hit Betty for giving cheek and that was why she was scared of him? Elsie knew her husband could be violent on occasions. She had never told anyone about him hitting her when he'd been drinking and she'd refused to give him his marital rights. It was much too personal. What should she do? Keep quiet or bring the subject up that night when they went to bed? He might bluff it out, even if he was guilty. If it was true, then she wanted nothing to do with him. Yet she had married him for better, for worse. She had made promises. Her head was aching unbearably. God, she'd been a fool marrying him. He could have just lived with them. She'd thought of that at first but then reasoned that the neighbours would talk.

Elsie finished her cigarette and went upstairs. She stood on a chair to reach the shelf where she kept the box with all her important papers inside, as well as old photographs and suchlike. She lifted it out and sat on the bed with it and rooted through the contents. Her brow puckered as she realised that the photographs of her sister and William Booth were missing.

She could feel her heart thudding uncomfortably in her chest. Someone had been through her things and taken them. How thoroughly had they looked at the letters and documents here? She could only think that it was Betty who would have taken the photographs, but when had she done so? She might have found Lizzie's letters and the deeds to the house and she could have read them. It could perhaps be another reason why she'd gone off to her sister.

At that moment she heard the front door open, and recognising Teddy's tread, she swiftly placed everything back in the box and returned it to its place. She hurried downstairs before he could shout for her. As she reached the living room she made up her mind what she was going to do.

Teddy wasn't alone in the kitchen because Dorothy was there, eating her dinner at the table. 'Any news?' he asked, turning to face his wife as she entered the room.

'Yes.' Elsie glanced at Dorothy. 'She's gone to some friend's house but she hasn't given an address. Just sent a message saying that she's safe.'

'What friend?' said Teddy, his hand clenching and unclenching on the back of his niece's chair. 'Do you know, Dorothy?'

'Why should I know?' she replied, pulling away from his hands.

'Did the message say why she's gone?' he asked.

'You know as much as I do,' replied Dorothy, reaching for her cup and taking a sip of tea.

'What's that supposed to mean?' he snapped, flicking her head with a finger.

She shot up and glared at him. 'Don't touch me!'

His mouth worked and spittle appeared at the corners. 'I scarcely touched you. Don't you dare speak to me in that tone or you'll feel the back of my hand.'

'Shall we let this drop?' said Elsie hurriedly. 'We know Betty's all right, and no doubt sooner or later we'll hear from her again.'

'But what about school?' said Teddy, staring at her. 'You're responsible for her, Elsie. You've got to get her back.'

'You said we were best rid of her this morning,' said Elsie. 'That she was no good.'

'Yeah, but she's your niece, isn't she?' he said, shifting his gaze. 'You've got to keep an eye on her. What will people say if they find out she's gone off to stay with friends after not being well?'

'I'd say it's none of their business,' said Dorothy, getting up and placing her dirty plate and cutlery in the sink. 'But if you have to say something, you could tell them she's had a relapse and is convalescing.'

'Now, that's a good idea,' said Elsie, seizing on it. 'I'll send a note into school, saying just that.'

It was the following evening that Maggie handed a letter to Dorothy that Irene had passed on to her. She had waited until her sister had gone upstairs to her bedroom and followed her. 'I think it's from Emma,' she said. 'I was tempted to open it, but I thought you'd tell me what she's written anyway.'

'Of course I will,' said Dorothy, slitting open the envelope with a finger and taking out the single sheet inside.

> *Dear Dorothy,*
>
> *I do hope you received my message from Dougie but if you haven't I will ease your mind now by telling you that Betty is safe with me. Would you believe she set off to find me by walking along the Leeds-Liverpool canal. Fortunately she encountered a very nice elderly couple who took her under their wing and saw to it that she was delivered safely to Honeysuckle Cottage.*

I was shocked to discover that her reason for running away was because your uncle had been hitting her. When I asked why she hadn't told your mother about this, she seemed convinced that she would not believe her. No doubt you'd know if this is true or not. I did question why she did not speak of it to you but she seemed convinced that your mother wouldn't believe you either, because she knows that neither of you like him. I do feel that Betty is keeping something back from me and maybe you can throw a light on what's been happening at your house.

I plan to keep her here as long as she wishes to stay, although we're both concerned about her exams. Have you any ideas about what we should do? I will leave it to you to decide whether you tell your mother about Betty's accusations against your uncle. Do feel that you can come and visit us here at any time.

Love, Emma

'The swine,' muttered Dorothy, folding the letter.

'Can I read it now?' said Maggie.

'Of course!' Dorothy handed it to her sister and watched as she read it.

'Why did Uncle Teddy hit Betty?' asked Maggie.

'I think he probably more than hit her,' said

Dorothy, plucking the letter from her sister's fingers. 'What do you know about where babies come from?'

Maggie stared at her and her eyes slowly widened. 'No! Our Betty wasn't having a baby, was she?'

'Gosh, you are bloody quick on the uptake,' said Dorothy. 'Mum's blaming one of the lads who go to the Gianellis' musical evenings, but I've told her that I don't believe it. Betty wasn't saying anything.'

Maggie sat on the bed and nibbled on a finger. 'I'm glad you're not going to tell me that storks really do bring babies or that they're found under gooseberry bushes.'

'Don't be daft. It takes a male and a female of the species to—' Dorothy shuddered. 'When I think maybe *him* and our Betty.'

'Don't!' Maggie gulped. 'It is so wrong!'

'Yes,' said Dorothy, fiddling with the letter. 'You must never let Uncle Teddy touch you *there*!' She pointed and wondered if she needed to name bodily parts.

'Say no more!' Maggie twisted her hands together. 'I feel embarrassed saying this, but haven't you ever played doctors and nurses and been a patient?'

'What!'

Maggie's face went red. 'I wish I hadn't started

telling you this now, but a group of us kids did during a school summer holiday one year. We were only about seven or eight. Us girls were curious and so were the boys. We knew it was naughty but there was really no harm in it. One of the girls' mothers had had about ten children and she peered round the door when her mother was giving birth and saw where babies came from. She acted out what happened. Blinking heck, did she scream!'

Suddenly Dorothy found herself struggling to keep her face straight. 'I don't suppose you played mothers and fathers, too?'

'No, the boys didn't want to kiss us,' said Maggie.

Dorothy couldn't help it and burst out laughing.

Maggie looked relieved. 'Of course, since then one or two of the boys have wanted to kiss me during a game of "Catch the girl, kiss the girl!" in the park, but I'm not as ignorant as Mum thinks and know that a kiss is as far as it must go until I'm married.'

'When you can cuddle,' said Dorothy, controlling her mirth and giving Maggie a hug. 'But what we've talked about does have its serious side.'

Maggie nodded and said soberly, 'I know. I just wish our Jared was here.'

'Yes. He'd deal with Uncle Teddy.' Dorothy sighed. 'I can't even write to him about this. He's got enough to worry about fighting the Commies.'

Maggie agreed. 'You know what Emma doesn't mention, and that's our Betty's clothes and possessions.'

'That's true,' murmured Dorothy. 'I'll send them to her. If what I suspect is right, then she's best staying with Emma.'

Maggie heaved a sigh. 'Something should be done. Do you think Mum—?'

'No! I think she's scared of him.'

'I'm going to miss Betty. She won't be at the coronation party, will she? Irene will miss her, too. I suppose she'll make new friends up there if she stays, won't she?'

'I suppose she will,' said Dorothy softly, 'but it's not certain that she will stay. Anyway, we're still her cousins and can write to her. Maybe she'll eventually feel able to talk to us about what happened. Perhaps I should tell Emma my suspicions and see if she can get Betty to confide in her. That's if she hasn't already done so. We can go and visit them. In the meantime, don't forget what I've told you and make sure you're never alone with Uncle Teddy.'

'Y-you really believe he is responsible for Betty having been . . . ?'

Dorothy nodded, reminding her about their cousin having been alone in the house with their uncle on New Year's Eve. 'Remember Mum thinking he was just being spiteful in bolting the doors? I think he did it for another reason.'

Maggie clutched her stomach. 'I think I'm going to be sick.'

'No, you're not! Deep breaths,' said Dorothy, hurrying over to her sister. 'We mustn't let him get to us, so that we feel we have to leave this house. Now, I need you to help me pack Betty's things.'

Maggie took several deep breaths.

'Slowly,' said Dorothy. 'You don't want to hyperventilate.'

Maggie nodded. 'I'd like someone to cut it off him.'

Dorothy smiled grimly. 'I feel exactly the same, but stop thinking about him now. What do you think we should pack, apart from her clothes?'

'Her school exercise books, so she can revise. Maybe Emma will be able to arrange for her to do her exams up there.'

Dorothy nodded, and without further delay they went into Betty's bedroom and set about packing those of her possessions they considered essential for her needs.

CHAPTER SIXTEEN

Betty finished feeding the hens and then went and sat on a chair at one of the tables now placed in the garden. Emma had told Betty that she had managed to sell some of her grandmother's pottery to a second-hand shop, and with the money and some that she had saved, had bought a few second-hand folding chairs and a couple of card tables.

'What d'you think Dorothy is doing now? What did you say to her in your letter?' Betty called to her sister.

Emma shook the soil from the roots of a young lettuce. 'I told her your uncle had hit you and that you were staying with me for the foreseeable future. I said that she was welcome to visit us here any time.

I left it to her to decide whether to tell your aunt or not. I also asked her what she thought we should do about your schooling.'

Betty's shoulders sagged. 'I'm worried about my exams. I really do want to get some decent qualifications and attend art school, even if I have to get a job and attend night school. I so wanted Mum and Dad to be proud of me if they'd been alive.' Her eyes filled with tears and hastily she wiped them away on her sleeve.

Emma's brown eyes were filled with concern. 'Don't you worry. You'll get there. I'll write to the headmistress at your grammar school and explain the situation.'

'But she might think I deserve punishment for running away. Aunt Elsie will be furious and so will she!'

'I'm not concerned about them. It's you I'm worried about,' said Emma. 'Anyway, I'll give it some thought and maybe the headmistress will be able to suggest a hostel where we can stay in Liverpool whilst you sit your exams.'

'But it would still cost money and I need to be revising now.' Betty groaned and put her head in her hands. 'I should have thought before running away the way I did but I was in a panic. It's going to be extra expense for you having me here and for us to stay in Liverpool and I don't want to be a burden on you.'

Not for one moment was Emma going to let her sister start worrying about being a burden. 'Don't be daft. I'm glad to have you here,' she said, patting her shoulder. 'I'm sure you're going to be of help to me.'

The words were scarcely out of her mouth when the knocker sounded. Betty lifted her head. 'Will I go and see who it is? It won't be *him*, will it?'

'I doubt it,' said Emma, feeling a pang of pity. 'It could be a customer.'

But it was the postman and he had a parcel for them. When Betty felt it and saw the postmark, she had a pretty good idea of its contents. Her spirits lifted. After thanking the postman, she hurried inside to find Emma in the kitchen, washing the lettuce. She had already put eggs in a pan to boil.

'I think my clothes and possibly some books and other personal belongings are in here,' said Betty.

She was right, in part, and sighed with relief when she saw her exercise books. 'I'll be able to revise, but they haven't packed the Winnie the Witch doll you gave me. There are two envelopes here, though.'

'I can make you another doll,' said Emma.

Betty smiled. 'Thanks. One envelope is addressed to you and the other is for me. Mine looks as if it's from Maggie. I recognise her handwriting.' She unsealed the envelope.

'And mine's from Dorothy,' said Emma, placing

the letter in the pocket of her pinny.

'Aren't you going to read it now?' asked Betty, glancing up at her.

'No. I need to watch the eggs and make the sandwiches. I'll read it later, but you can tell me what Maggie has to say if you want.'

Betty sat down and spread the sheet of paper on the table. 'It's not very long and it's a bit of a scribble.' She fell silent, trying to decipher her cousin's handwriting. 'I think Maggie's trying to tell me that she's going to miss me and so is Irene and that they'll try and come and see us during the summer holidays,' murmured Betty. 'She also says that Dorothy called Uncle Teddy a swine for hitting me.'

Emma glanced at her sister and saw that tiny nerve twitching beneath her left eye. 'And so he is, but you mustn't get yourself worked up about him. He's not going to hurt you ever again.'

'He's not very big, you know,' whispered Betty, looking tragic, 'but he's strong.'

Emma put down the knife she was using and went and slipped her arms around Betty. 'Forget him. It's good that we can look forward to a visit from Irene and Maggie. I bet Dorothy will come with them.'

Betty said, 'Yes. I'd like to see all three. Maggie mentions my missing the coronation party and asks if we will be having a party here.'

'Oh, I should think so,' said Emma, dropping a kiss on her sister's hair.

'She doesn't say anything about Aunt Elsie,' muttered Betty.

'Perhaps Dorothy will do so in her letter,' said Emma, hurrying now to remove the egg pan from the heat.

She read Dorothy's letter over lunch and its contents shocked her, but she said nothing of that to Betty, only telling her that which she thought would not cause her sister worry or pain. She told her that her policeman friend, Dougie, had visited the house and that Dorothy had been fortunate enough to open the door to him. She pondered on whether to mention that her aunt did know that Betty was staying with Emma. In the end she decided that she was not going to keep it secret from her. Sooner or later it was bound to come out and might cause Betty to believe that she could not trust her.

'Your aunt knows that you're staying with me,' said Emma, glancing across at her, 'but your uncle doesn't. For reasons of her own, your aunt decided to keep that from him.'

'I wonder why,' murmured Betty. 'I'm glad she did, anyway.'

'Now, this is interesting. Your aunt is writing to your headmistress to tell her that you've had a relapse after your illness and you're going to be convalescing in the countryside for a while. Apparently it was Irene's stepbrother's idea. Dorothy spoke to him when she went to the house.'

'Oh, she must mean Billy McElroy, he must have been home on leave. He's in the army, stationed up north here somewhere. He teaches new recruits how to fight.'

'Fancy that,' said Emma, smiling. 'It's a good idea of his because it opens the way for me to write to your headmistress and explain who I am and my concern about your exams.'

Betty looked relieved. 'I will miss the old school and my friends, and especially art classes and going along to the Gianellis' musical evenings.'

'You can always play the piano here,' said Emma.

Betty grinned unexpectedly. 'You wouldn't want to listen to my playing. It was Mum who was determined I'd learn the piano but I don't have the aptitude. My creativity is with pencil, paintbrushes and paint.'

'You must continue with your art here. Dorothy has enclosed your paintbox, drawing pad and other paraphernalia, I notice,' said Emma, folding her letter and pocketing it. 'Practice makes perfect.'

She was glad that during that afternoon several people called in for cakes and tea. Betty did some waiting on and seemed to enjoy it. Emma was relieved to have other things to think about, so less time to dwell on Dorothy's shocking news and her suspicion that the uncle was responsible for Betty's pregnancy. No wonder she had run away, but how terribly sad it was that she had been unable to tell her aunt or Dorothy about what had taken place.

Yet in a way Emma could understand why. It was just too awful to talk about and, in the normal way of things, girls of Betty's age, or even hers and Dorothy's, weren't expected to know much about what went on when it came to sex. It was something that wasn't discussed openly. She had no idea how she was going to get Betty to unburden herself, when most likely she wanted to try and forget about it.

By early evening, the fine day had given way to drizzle, and after the evening meal Betty went up to her bedroom, having told Emma that she felt in the mood to do some painting. Lila dropped by, having heard on the grapevine that Emma had her half-sister staying with her.

'So Betty's come to visit,' she said, sitting herself down in front of the fire.

'Yes. She's been ill and has come here to convalesce,' said Emma.

Lila looked her straight in the eye. 'I see. How long is she going to be staying?'

'As long as it takes for her to get better,' said Emma, after a moment's hesitation.

'I heard that she ran away from an orphanage,

would you believe?' said Lila with a wry smile.

'Well, you know that can't be true because she wasn't in an orphanage. She has left home but that's because she hasn't been well,' said Emma.

'In what way not well?' asked Lila.

Emma rolled her eyes. 'As having been very sick and needing to convalesce. I'm just a bit concerned about her exams, but I'm sure we'll be able to work something out.'

'But will you be able to cope financially with having Betty here?'

'The repairs to the roof will have to wait,' said Emma, handing Lila a cup of tea.

'How did business do today?' asked Lila.

'Not too bad,' replied Emma, smiling. 'And Betty was a great help.'

'It's early days, though, isn't it?' said Lila, looking thoughtful. 'And you have to admit it's a lot duller here if you're used to the hustle and bustle of Liverpool.'

'I know what you're saying,' said Emma, her smile fading. 'But I'm sure she'll be able to occupy herself. And Dorothy, Maggie and Irene are planning to visit in summer. My roof might leak and the window frames are rotting but we've lovely countryside and the fresh air will do them good. Anyway, it's a while off yet and there's the coronation to look forward to before then.'

'So what are your plans for the coronation?'

asked Lila. 'I'll be listening to the service on the wireless with Dad. Mam's on duty at the hospital. They're having a party there afterwards. You can both come and listen to the radio with us if you like. Makes it more of an occasion than if just the two of us are on our own. Dad admires you and would enjoy your company.'

'What!' exclaimed Emma, surprised.

'He says you're a go-getter and that one day you'll have some brass.'

Emma smiled as she curled herself up in an easy chair. Tibby immediately jumped onto her lap. 'Didn't know your dad had a crystal ball,' she said, stroking the cat. 'I'll think about it. Do you want the last scone and another cuppa before you go home?' she asked.

Before Lila could reply, there came a knock on the back door and a male voice enquired, 'Anybody in?'

Lila and Emma exchanged looks and the next moment Lila was on her feet and opening the door. Outside stood Dougie Marshall. Instantly Emma waited for that rush of longing at the sight of him but it did not come. Absence had not made the heart grow fonder in this case. She guessed that he had come to check up on Betty. No doubt he would then relay the news that she seemed to be settling in OK back to Maggie, via his brothers, while she would let Dorothy know that she was all right.

Emma got to her feet. 'How nice to see you, Dougie. Step aside, Lila, and let the man in.'

'He'll be hungry. No doubt he's hoping you'll have a pan of soup on the boil and will whip up a batch of scones in no time at all,' said Lila dryly.

Dougie protested, 'I don't come here just to eat Emma out of house and home, you know. There is another purpose to my visit. How is your dad? I'd like to talk to him about my brother, Pete.'

'What about your brother, Pete?' asked Lila, giving him a startled look.

'I'd like some advice from your dad about what it's like having difficulty walking when you've been active.'

'I'll ask him.' Lila glanced at Emma. 'I think it's time I was going. See you soon, and think about what I said about Coronation Day.' She slipped out of the door and was gone.

Dougie stared at Emma. 'What is it about me that makes her rush off?' he complained. 'I could have gone with her. I bet her dad would enjoy seeing a new face.'

'She hasn't said she doesn't like you,' said Emma, returning his gaze. 'So are you just here to see Mr Ashcroft or is it for news of Betty that you can take back to Liverpool?'

He smiled and bent and kissed Emma's cheek. 'I came to see how you're getting on as well. You look great.'

'Thanks a lot,' she said dryly.

There was a pause.

'So how is Betty?' asked Dougie. 'Her cousin was in a right state over her. She thought she might have thrown herself in the canal. I was of the opinion that was a bit drastic in the circumstances, but then you never can tell what's going on in people's heads. The cousin's quite good-looking.'

'Yes, she is,' said Emma, wondering if he was going to turn his attention to Dorothy now. 'You can tell her that Betty's fine. She's upstairs doing some painting. I'll be writing to Dorothy to let her know how things are, anyway, and about the decisions I've made.'

'Will Betty be coming back to Litherland?'

'It depends on the replies I get to my letters.' She paused. 'Do you want a cup of tea? I've one scone left.'

'No, it's OK. I'll go after your friend. Where do they live?'

'Just outside the village.' Emma was thinking that his visit was very short-lived and told her much about his feelings for her. He was definitely not the one for her.

'Quiet spot, is it? Not much going on?'

'No.'

'Poor bugger. D'you mind if I—?'

'Of course not. You go after her. Turn left when you leave here. I might follow you on. I'll just have a word with Betty.'

She waved him away and, as soon as he had gone, she made for the stairs. She had only started up them when she heard Betty coming down. She looked pale. 'I heard a man's voice. Who was it?'

'Dougie Marshall.'

'You mean Norm and Pete's brother?'

Emma nodded. 'He came to see if we were OK and now he's gone chasing after Lila. I thought I might join them. See if Mr Ashcroft takes to him. D'you want to come? The walk might do you good.'

Betty hesitated. 'Perhaps I will. I've heard so much about him but never set eyes on him. I'll just put my brushes in water. Be with you in a minute.' She went back upstairs.

Emma washed her hands, tidied her hair, changed her shoes and grabbed a jacket. She was ready by the time her half-sister reappeared. Betty had changed into a clean skirt and blouse and looked smart. As soon as they had left the house, she linked her arm through Emma's and they hurried after Lila and Dougie.

They were walking at least a yard apart and Dougie seemed to be doing all the talking, which was no surprise to Emma. She caught up with them and Lila flashed her an odd little smile.

Dougie said, 'You were quick.'

'Do you think so?' she responded. 'This is my sister, Betty. She's heard that much about you that she wanted to meet you.'

'He doesn't look like the twins,' said Betty to Emma.

Dougie heard her. 'No, thank God, two of them is enough.'

'So how long can you stay, or are you heading back to Liverpool this evening?' asked Emma.

'Not sure yet,' said Dougie.

Lila hesitated. 'I don't want you staying long at our house. Dad's not used to visitors and he won't want your pity, you know.'

'He won't get it,' rasped Dougie, his smile vanishing. 'Your dad was wounded in the war. Mine was killed.'

Lila's face went blank with shock. Dougie stared at her and looked uncomfortable but he didn't apologise for the swift rebuke he had given her. Emma felt embarrassed by their exchange. Betty glanced at her sister and rolled her eyes. Emma pulled a face. The only sounds now were the breeze rustling the trees and of a blackbird singing.

It was not long before they reached the house. She could see Mr Ashcroft in the window as they went up the path. He must have heard them coming because he turned his head and looked down at them, with an arrested expression on his face. Emma thought how he did not often have visitors and that the unexpected arrival of two strangers must have taken him aback. She could only hope that he and Dougie would get on with each other.

Lila led the way inside and ushered the other three into the front room. 'Dad, Emma and her sister have come to see you with Dougie, the policeman I mentioned. He wants your advice. I'll be in the kitchen if I'm needed.'

Jack Ashcroft switched off the wireless and stared at Dougie. 'You must be the young man whose brother fell off a wall and is crippled. How can I help you?'

'I'd like to know what helps you to cope and what makes life harder for you in your condition?' he said without hesitation.

Emma decided to leave the two men alone and murmured to her sister that she was going into the kitchen. Instantly Betty followed her. They found Lila standing over by the window, staring out over the garden.

'They're talking. I think you were worrying about your dad unnecessarily,' said Emma.

Lila turned round with a sad expression on her face. 'They're two very different men. If only Dad had just a little bit of Dougie's confidence I think he would force himself to get out into the world, instead of sitting in here day after day making his models.'

Emma said quietly, 'Don't be so hard on your dad. I'll tell you something. Betty and I will come and listen to the coronation on the wireless with

281

the pair of you. I'll make a special cake for the occasion.'

'Thanks!' said Lila, giving a half smile.

'No trouble. You tell your dad after we've gone.'

When they returned to the front room, it was to find Dougie inspecting Jack Ashcroft's latest model. 'This is really good. What you need is a market for them,' said Dougie, picking up one of the ships Jack had made. 'I'd like to buy this one.'

Jack looked astounded. 'I did that from a photograph. It's the troopship that brought me home.'

Dougie nodded. 'Then you could do another one if I bought this. I've the perfect place for it in our house. I've one pound ten shillings on me,' he said.

Jack said gruffly, 'I'll take ten shillings. I could make you a new model as that one's been around for a while and is a bit dusty.'

'If you do that,' said Dougie, 'I'll pay you a pound and come back to pick it up. You or Lila could write to me and let me know when it's ready.'

Emma thought how nice Dougie was being to Lila's father and she warmed to him all over again. If only she knew where she stood with him. But he had given her an idea. 'Why don't I display some of your models in my front room where I serve teas, Mr Ashcroft?' she suggested. 'Could be that you might get more sales.'

Jack stared at her and his Adam's apple moved

convulsively. 'You'd have to take a percentage,' he said roughly.

'Of course,' she replied, considering his pride. 'I'll charge a bit more than the price you fix.'

'Mam'll be pleased if you do sell some of your models,' said Lila. 'Thanks for putting the idea into his head, Dougie,' she added, smiling up at him.

'I admire your father's skill,' he said, touching her cheek with the back of his hand. 'I'm sure there must be a bigger market for his models in Liverpool.'

Jack chuckled. 'I think you're being a bit too ambitious for me, lad,' he said. 'But I'll bear it in mind.'

'You can't be too ambitious,' said Dougie, glancing at Lila. 'I'd best be going. Don't forget to get in touch with me when it's ready.'

'It's unlikely to be before the coronation,' said Lila. 'I'll see the three of you out.'

'What a nice man he is,' said Betty, during the walk back to the cottage.

'Aye, not like some,' said Emma.

Betty guessed who she meant. If only Aunt Elsie had not married Uncle Teddy, then she could still be at home, seeing her friends and going to school. It wasn't that she didn't want to be with Emma, but she would have much preferred for them both to be celebrating the coronation with Irene, Maggie and Dorothy. She remembered how her younger cousin had hinted that her mother might actually rent or buy a television so they could watch the queen being crowned as it actually happened. Betty would have enjoyed doing that, but she would never return to her aunt's house whilst *he* was living under its roof. If only he could drop dead, it would make her day.

CHAPTER SEVENTEEN

'I hate this frock!' Maggie crossed her arms and dragged the short, puffed-sleeved gingham dress over her head and threw it on the bed. 'It's too young for me.'

'I thought you chose it,' said Dorothy, glancing over at her sister.

'You're joking! I don't get to choose anything now,' she said with a mutinous expression. 'I'll have to wear the last one I chose myself; at least the short sleeves are plain and the neckline is not so frumpy.'

'Mum will have something to say,' murmured Dorothy, brushing her hair.

'I don't care. It's all her fault! She's determined to treat me like a kid. I'd love to do something to shock her into realising that the world's moved on since she was my age.' Maggie removed a pink and white polka-dot frock with a sweetheart neckline from the wardrobe and put it on.

'She's had enough shocks lately, so behave yourself,' said Dorothy, placing her hairbrush on the dressing table. 'You'd better get a move on.'

Maggie began to brush her hair. 'I suppose you haven't mentioned Betty having gone to live with Emma in your last letter to Jared?' she asked.

'No, it would be difficult knowing what to leave in and what to leave out. Besides, Mum might have already written to him,' said Dorothy, reaching for the Max Factor lipstick she had treated herself to last Saturday.

Maggie nodded and fastened her hair into a ponytail. She cocked her head to one side. 'Did you hear the front door go then? That means another of the neighbours has arrived. I'm surprised Mum's asked so many to come as they might start asking more questions about our Betty. I know a couple of kids in the street have asked me where she's gone.'

'What did you tell them?' asked Dorothy, outlining her lips.

'That she's staying with her dad's relatives. It's true, isn't it?'

Dorothy nodded, dabbing 'Evening in Paris' behind her ears, wondering if any of the women would get the wrong idea and think that which her mother had done her best to avoid. 'I wonder what Mum's told them.'

Maggie shrugged. 'Let's forget it for now. The television's on and I think I've just heard the door go again! There's going to be quite a crowd in the living room.'

'Perhaps I should go on ahead,' said Dorothy.

'No! Wait for me,' said Maggie.

'Isn't it time you were downstairs, Dorothy,' said Teddy, thrusting his head around the jamb. 'Your mum can't do everything herself, you know.'

'I've already been helping out in the kitchen,' said Dorothy, an edge to her voice. 'Now, if you'll get out of the way, Uncle Teddy.'

He moved aside to let her through but then blocked the doorway so Maggie couldn't get past. He touched her shoulder and she shrugged off his hand. 'Don't do that!' she said.

He scowled. 'What's wrong with you, Maggie? I'm just being affectionate.'

'I d-don't want you being affectionate. Dorothy!' she called. 'Uncle Teddy is messing about and won't let me past.'

Dorothy poked him in the side with her elbow and, reaching round him, grabbed hold of Maggie's arm, so forcing him to move out of the way. 'If you don't mind, we've got things to do, Uncle Teddy,' said Dorothy. 'Come on, Mags.'

He muttered something beneath his breath that

they did not catch. 'We mustn't let him spoil our day,' said Dorothy, hurrying downstairs.

'I can't wait to see the queen in her golden coach,' said Maggie, her eyes sparkling, thinking that, according to the timetable in the *Echo*, the first procession would arrive at Westminster Abbey at quarter to nine, but it would not be until eleven o'clock that the queen would take the oath. She was due to be crowned at twenty-five to one. It was going to be a long service.

The sitting room was already occupied by a number of neighbours and the sisters realised they would have to grab a cushion and sit on the floor. Hopefully Elsie wouldn't expect them to make tea and carry it round with a plate of biscuits just yet.

'It's a blinking shame that it's raining,' said the woman from next door.

'Let's hope it goes off or it's going to spoil the street party,' said another.

'At least there'll be more food than we had for VE and VJ Day,' piped up an elderly gentleman.

Dorothy could remember VE Day. Her father had still been alive and so had Aunt Lizzie. Her eyes were shiny with tears, remembering her aunt saying that they must be glad that the war in Europe was over, even though her husband and thousands of other men wouldn't be coming home.

Dorothy wagered that the queen would be thinking of her father today of all days. It must be a very emotional time for her. She would be sad and excited at the same time and somehow she was going to have to smile, smile and smile for her subjects who'd be cheering like mad when they saw her in a golden coach, wearing a crown.

As the minutes ticked by, Dorothy was aware that her uncle had entered the room. The chair that had been her father's had been kept empty for him and that infuriated her. He appeared to be having a joke with one of the women, and even as she watched, he glanced her way and there was dislike in his eyes. She stared at him coolly and then looked away at the television screen.

The room grew silent as the deep, rich tones of Richard Dimbleby's commentary did justice to the occasion. Dorothy felt quite emotional as she watched her sovereign taking the solemn oath. Maggie said that it was as good as a play but that the small television screen didn't give the full spectacle of the occasion. 'I can't wait to watch it all over again in colour at the cinema,' she added.

As the two sisters handed around cups of tea and biscuits, Dorothy's thoughts were of her brother and cousin. She knew that Betty and Emma would have been listening to the service on the wireless at Lila's parents' house because Emma had written telling her so. Then they would be going to a party in the village. She had told her also that she was writing to Betty's headmistress and hopefully they could come to some arrangement concerning her exams.

No doubt Jared would be listening to the service, too. There had been mention of a possible armistice in the newspapers and she was praying her brother would live to see it come about. It would be terrible if he should go and get killed within months of being demobbed.

After they had finished the tea and biscuits, the neighbours left to make their own preparations for the party and the girls gave Elsie a helping hand. Fortunately the rain had ceased and the red, white and blue roses and streamers of crêpe paper that decorated doorways and gateposts had not been ruined. Chairs and trestle tables were set up in the street. Snowy-white tablecloths were spread over the table tops, and cutlery, dishes and cups put in place. Then came the sandwiches, jellies, cakes, biscuits, meat pies and sausage rolls. They were covered with napkins and tea towels whilst most people went to change into their glad rags.

Dorothy thought of all the food being eaten throughout Britain and the colonies to celebrate this special occasion, not to mention the drink that would be downed. Uncle Teddy had vanished as soon as there was work to do, but now he reappeared with a couple of other men, bringing a barrel of beer from the local pub. No doubt there would be a few sore heads in the morning, she thought.

'Well, well, well,' said Teddy, as soon as he had

a glass of beer in his hand. His gaze slid over his wife, Dorothy and Maggie. 'Don't you all look a picture. I must get a snap of the three of you,' he said, placing his glass on a table. He produced the Brownie camera that had once belonged to his brother, Owen, and tried to focus.

'Are you having trouble seeing us?' asked Elsie, who was wearing a new floral-print dress in red, white and blue.

'I bet he's already had a couple of pints in the pub,' Maggie murmured to her sister.

'Just bloody keep still,' ordered Teddy.

At last the picture was taken and then he thrust the camera in Elsie's hand and told her to take one of him with the girls. Before they could move away he'd thrust an arm around Dorothy and Maggie's waists, squeezing them as he did so.

'Don't do that!' said Dorothy, pulling away.

'Keep still!' cried Elsie, and pressed the button that operated the shutter. The girls immediately dragged themselves free and put as much distance between them and their uncle as possible.

The party was soon in full swing, and after people had eaten their fill and while the tables were being cleared, a piano was brought out of a house.

First, there was a game of musical chairs for the children to the tune of 'The Teddy Bears' Picnic'. After that a great deal of fun was had with a game of Blind Man's Bluff. Eventually, though, mothers took their young ones to bed and the pianist began to play dance music.

Determined to see what was happening in Irene Miller's street, Maggie slipped away unnoticed while her mother was talking to a neighbour and Dorothy was dancing with a young man she had known since they had moved to Litherland. Suddenly, Dorothy became aware that she was being watched by a tall, fair-haired young man. He seemed vaguely familiar, but she only realised when the music stopped and he came over and tapped her partner on the shoulder and asked if he could butt in, that it was Dougie Marshall.

He really was extremely tall and she had to tilt back her head to see his face clearly in the twilight. She felt a tremor go through her as their eyes met. Then the pianist struck up a polka and Dougie's arm went round her waist. He clasped her left hand and they were off. She had always enjoyed the polka, considering it one of the most lively and exciting dances she had ever learnt. She could hear him humming to the music as he whirled her round and she found herself laughing with the sheer joy of the moment.

It wasn't until the dance ended and the pianist struck up a leisurely waltz that he bent his head and murmured in her ear, 'That was enjoyable.'

'Yes, it was,' said Dorothy, smiling. 'Where did you learn to dance?'

'At the Grafton in West Derby Road,' he answered. 'Never had any lessons, just picked it up by watching people and having a go.'

'You must be a natural,' she said, enjoying being held closer to him as he twirled her around. 'I had lessons.'

'Lucky you.'

'I like dancing.' She paused. 'So why are you here?'

'I went to see Emma and I thought you might like to know that she and Betty appear to be OK.'

'It's kind of you to come and tell me but she did write and tell me of your visit. She told me that you went to visit Lila's father, too. Was he able to give you any useful advice on how to help your brother?'

Dougie nodded slowly. 'Advice I found difficult to accept, because when Dad didn't come back from the war, I had to take his place. Mr Ashcroft told me that I need to step back and let Pete do things for himself. It isn't going to be easy.'

'I can understand how you feel,' said Dorothy sympathetically. 'I feel I have to watch out for our Maggie more since Betty ran away.'

'Do you know why she went?'

Lulled into a sense of well-being by the music, a couple of glasses of port and lemon and their friendly conversation, Dorothy decided to tell him some of it. After all, he was a policeman and must be accustomed to keeping things under

293

wraps. 'My uncle took to hitting her. I didn't know anything about it until Emma wrote and told me. Betty spoke to her about it but didn't feel she could tell Mum.'

Dougie frowned. 'This uncle is your mother's second husband?'

'Yes. He's over there drinking. The short one,' said Dorothy.

Teddy was standing alone, drinking and watching a couple of teenage girls giggling as they tried to learn the dance steps.

'Dad never hit any of us,' she continued, 'but Uncle Teddy has a short fuse and is quick to react.'

'Tricky,' said Dougie, frowning. 'Now if he was hitting your mother and we were called in to what we refer to as a "domestic", then I could do something about it. As it is—'

'I wasn't asking you to do anything,' said Dorothy hastily. 'I was just explaining that he's the reason why our Betty ran away. Once my brother, Jared, comes home things will be different.'

'Jared doing his national service?'

'Yes. I suppose Emma or Betty told you about him.' She paused. 'Will you be seeing Emma again soon?'

He told her about Lila's father's model making and how he'd be going up there as soon as Lila got in touch with him. 'Perhaps you'd like to come with me,' he suggested.

'I'd like that,' said Dorothy, her eyes shining.

The music stopped and she felt a tap on her shoulder and turned to see her mother standing there. 'Are you going to introduce me to this young man?' asked Elsie, looking slightly the worse for drink.

Dorothy would rather have not, guessing that her mother would give her the third degree about Dougie. Yet she knew that she had no choice without being rude. 'This is Dougie Marshall, Mum. He's a policeman.'

'A policeman!' Elsie looked pleased and held out her hand. 'Pleasure to meet you, Mr Marshall.'

'Mrs Gregory.' Dougie inclined his flaxen head as he shook her hand. 'Your daughter is an excellent dancer.'

'Yes. Her father would be pleased to know that his money wasn't wasted. I've been watching you and your steps match perfectly,' she said, beaming up at him.

Dorothy wanted to say *Mum, don't!* but at that moment there were calls to the pianist to play the 'Hokey-cokey'.

'You're going to join in with this, aren't you, Mr Marshall?' asked Elsie, taking his arm.

'Actually, I'll have to be going,' said Dougie, tempering his refusal with a smile. 'I'm on duty very early in the morning and need to get some sleep. I also need to check up on my brothers.'

Elsie looked disappointed. 'Well, if you must go. Hopefully we'll see you again soon.'

'It was nice meeting you, Mrs Gregory,' he said, before turning to Dorothy. 'I enjoyed your company. See you again.'

'Yes, Mr Marshall,' she replied, his smile doing lovely things to her.

He walked away and mother and daughter watched him go.

'Well!' exclaimed Elsie. 'Good-looking, isn't he? And with a good steady job. Let's hope he does make the effort to see you again.'

'Yes, Mum,' said Dorothy, turning away and watching neighbours and friends gathering together in a circle. 'Come on, let's join in with the hokey-cokey.'

'Our Maggie could do this,' said Elsie, glancing about her. 'Where is she?'

Dorothy looked around but could see no sign of her sister and neither could she spot Uncle Teddy. Should she be worried? There were plenty of people about, so surely Maggie was safe from him. 'She's probably around somewhere.'

'I hope she hasn't gone to see that Irene Miller,' said Elsie, taking Dorothy's hand. 'Come on or we'll miss out.'

Dorothy allowed herself to be persuaded and soon she and her mother were *putting their right leg in and their right leg out, in out, in out, shake it all about!* After that there was a request for the conga, but there was still no sign of Maggie. Where could she be, and where was Uncle Teddy?

'I'd best be going,' said Maggie.

'OK!' said Irene, glancing across at her. 'Are you sure you'll be all right on your own?'

'It's not dark yet and there's still people about,' answered Maggie.

'I'll walk so far with you,' said a voice out of the dusk. The next moment Pete Marshall limped into view, leaning on two sticks.

'I appreciate the offer, Pete,' said Maggie in a soft voice, 'but it is a bit of a way for you to walk.'

'I need the practice,' he said gruffly. 'And I didn't say that I'd walk all the way.'

'So you didn't.' Maggie smiled. 'OK, come on, then.'

They set off towards Linacre Road and once there turned in the direction of the lift bridge over the canal. 'Where's your Norm tonight?' asked Maggie.

'At the Gianellis',' he replied. 'I said I'd meet him at the bus stop near theirs. Our Dougie is planning on catching the bus with us as well.'

Maggie nodded, slowing her pace to match his. 'It's a wonder Irene wasn't at the Gianellis' as well.'

'So she didn't tell you that her ma insisted on her staying put. Apparently she moaned that she hardly sees anything of her, and as this is a special occasion . . .' He raised his shoulders and let them drop.

'I wonder why she didn't tell me,' mused Maggie.

'You haven't long been there, so most likely she didn't see the need.'

They crossed the bridge and had just got to the other side when an unwelcome voice said, 'So there you are, Maggie! What the hell d'you think you're playing at, going off without telling anyone where you're going?' And her Uncle Teddy hovered into view.

Maggie found herself reaching for Pete's arm. 'There's no need for you to come looking for me, Uncle Teddy,' she said, a tremor in her voice. 'I've only been away a short time and I'm on my way back now.'

'Don't give me that rubbish,' snapped Teddy, thrusting his head forward. 'I can see you've a lad with you. You can tell him to bugger off.'

Maggie clung to Pete's arm. 'No! You're drunk, Uncle Teddy! Why don't you just go back to Mum, before she starts missing you?'

'No, you're coming with me!' snarled Teddy, grabbing hold of Maggie's free arm.

'Pete, don't let him take me!' she cried, hanging on to the youth.

Teddy tried to drag her away, but not only did Maggie hang on to Pete but he also dropped one of his sticks and kept hold of her. 'Listen, mate, you'll have the three of us over if you carry on the way you are,' said Pete, struggling to stay upright.

'Bugger off,' said Teddy, thrusting his free hand into Pete's chest.

The lad lost his balance and went down, pulling Maggie to the ground with him. She managed to kneel up, intending helping Pete to his feet, but her uncle seized her by the hair and yanked Maggie upright. She screamed.

'What's going on here? Is that you, Pete?' asked Dougie, appearing out of the gloom.

'Never mind me,' gasped Pete. 'Stop him from hurting her!'

Dougie glanced up and recognised the man that Dorothy had pointed out to him. He was dragging a screaming teenage girl along the road. Instantly, Dougie went after them and seized Teddy by the shoulder.

He brought him to an abrupt halt and forced him to let go of Maggie's hair. Teddy took a swing at him but his fist barely grazed Dougie's chest, and as Maggie collapsed to the ground, Dougie grabbed a handful of Teddy's jacket and lifted him off his feet. Beer and whisky fumes wafted into Dougie's face. 'I'm arresting you for being drunk and disorderly,' he said, 'and I'm taking you to the station.'

Teddy swore at him and Dougie brought up his fist and gave him a swift uppercut and he collapsed like a deflated balloon. Dougie turned and looked down at the two teenagers struggling to get to their feet. 'Get yourself to the bus stop, Pete,' he ordered. 'Norm should be there by now.'

The skin about Pete's mouth was white and he was obviously in pain. 'I'll go with him,' gasped Maggie, staring at Dougie. 'Thanks.'

He nodded and hoisted Teddy over his shoulder and made off at a run. Maggie picked up Pete's sticks and handed them to him. 'So that's your big brother,' she said. 'Gosh, he's not half strong.'

Pete said nothing but sought a secure hold on his sticks. She guessed from his expression that he was feeling angry and embarrassed by what had happened. She felt really sorry for him. 'I don't know what I'd have done if you hadn't been with me,' she said.

'You don't have to soft-soap me,' muttered Pete.

She fell silent, walking alongside him, and now she began to shake inwardly. They reached the bus stop where Norm was waiting, talking to a youth whom Maggie recognised as Tonio Gianelli. She paused only a moment to say 'ciao' and 'ta-ra' and then she took off at a run, barely able to believe that she had been rescued in the nick of time and that her uncle was on his way to jail. He was going to be hopping mad when he woke up in a cell with a sore jaw and a terrible hangover.

She found her sister and mother dancing the

conga with a line of people up the middle of their road and so she collapsed onto a chair to get her breath back and to wait until the dance eventually came to an end. She waved to her sister and saw the relief in Dorothy's face.

'You haven't been there all the time,' she whispered, collapsing beside her.

'Tell you later,' said Maggie, watching her mother stagger across the pavement to their house. She stood up. 'Come on, Dot, we'd best follow her in. I want my bed and I've something to tell you about Uncle Teddy that you just have to put in a letter to Emma and Betty. They'll be made up.'

CHAPTER EIGHTEEN

Elsie stared down at the letter from Betty's headmistress and knew she must not get annoyed with Emma or her niece for writing to the woman. But she'd had enough to contend with lately, having listened to Maggie's tale of Teddy's attack on her and the crippled brother of that nice-looking policeman who had danced with Dorothy. Then she'd had to cope with Teddy and his massive hangover, after his being let out of jail, and listen to his excuses. They hadn't satisfied her but she hadn't said so because she'd had to go to work. It wasn't until she had returned home later in the day to find him slumped in the armchair that they'd had the row. Yet she had been unable to bring herself to accuse him of raping her niece, scared that he might become even more violent. She fingered the bruise beneath her collarbone where he had gripped her and forced her down into a chair. She had not slept with him but spent the night on the sofa, thinking through what she must do. Now, here was this letter from the headmistress that must be dealt with right away.

She came to a decision and checked the contents of her purse and would have sworn there was ten shillings less than there had been last night. No doubt Teddy had taken it, but as he had already left the house, she could not ask him. She made sure she had her bank book in her handbag and, shoving writing pad and a couple of envelopes and fountain pen inside its capacious interior, along with her purse, she hurried out.

Emma picked up two envelopes from the doormat. She slit open the one that had her name typed on the envelope. On discovering it was from the headmistress of Betty's school, she read it through swiftly and then she tore open the other envelope. A postal order fell out as she opened the single sheet of paper. She picked up the order and saw to her amazement that it was for twenty pounds. Placing it on the table, she read the letter with growing incredulity.

> *Dear Emma,*
> *You are long overdue a letter from me but this will only be a short one. Hopefully*

you will have had a letter from Betty's headmistress concerning her GCE exams and I am enclosing a postal order, the sum of which should be enough for her to stay in Waterloo while she sits her exams. The headmistress has suggested a sensible widow woman who is prepared to have my niece stay with her. Tell Betty I wish her luck and hope to see her when she feels ready to come home again.

Yours sincerely,
Elsie Gregory

Emma could only wonder what had happened in the Gregory household for Betty's aunt to send such a letter. She wasted no time going into the kitchen where Betty was at the kitchen sink, washing strawberries.

'I've two letters here that you must read,' said Emma, her eyes alight. 'One's from your headmistress and the other from your aunt.'

'What!' Betty's face was a picture of amazement.

Swiftly, she dried her hands and took the letters from Emma. Sitting down at the table, Betty began to read. When she had finished she looked up at her half-sister. 'What's been going on at home, I wonder?'

'I'm sure we'll find out sooner or later. It wouldn't surprise me if Dorothy writes and lets us know. In the meantime, you're going to have to decide what to pack to take with you to Waterloo,' said Emma.

'Will you come with me?' asked Betty, her voice quivering.

Before Emma could answer, the door knocker banged vigorously. She hurried to answer it and pulled open the door to find Lila on the step. Her face was drawn and there were signs of tears on her cheeks.

'What's happened?' asked Emma, reaching out and bringing her into the house. She made her sit down in the front room. 'You look dreadful.'

'Mam's terribly ill,' cried Lila, twisting a crumpled handkerchief between her fingers.

Emma's eyes widened. 'What's wrong with her?'

Lila raised her hand in a helpless gesture and then let it drop. 'The doctor said it's food poisoning. Several people have already died up at the hospital. They're blaming the meat pies they had for the party on Coronation Day. It's touch and go.'

Emma was stunned and for a moment could not think what to say, and then she put her arm around her friend. 'Your mother's strong. She'll get over it.'

Lila shook her head. 'I've never seen her laid low like this and neither has Dad. We don't know what to do, but one thing is for sure, I'm not going into work. I'm only here now because I had to do some shopping. I can't linger.'

'Do you want me to come back with you?' asked Emma.

'No. It's OK. I just wanted to let you know.' She brushed a tear away.

'Can't you even have a cup of tea?'

Lila hesitated. 'OK. A quick one and then I'll have to go.'

Emma called to Betty to put the kettle on.

Lila glanced at the table. 'I thought you might be working on a client's accounts today.'

'I'll do that this evening. I'm making strawberry jam this morning. Something interesting happened today. I received two letters. One from Betty's headmistress and one from her aunt. She's sent money, so Betty can stay near to her school and do her exams.'

'Gosh, that is good news! Will you be going with her?'

Emma knew that if Lila needed her, then she must be there for her. 'I'll go with her, but not stay.'

Lila nodded. 'Look, forget the cup of tea. You and Betty have enough on your hands. I'll let you know how things go.' She stood up and hurried out of the cottage before Emma could stop her.

Emma returned to the kitchen, but there was no need for her to tell Betty what had happened because she had overheard the conversation.

'Gosh, Mrs Ashcroft's got food poisoning and might die!' exclaimed Betty. 'When Aunt Elsie put it about that I had it, I never realised it was so serious.'

'I know.' Emma hesitated. 'You don't mind if I can't stay with you in Waterloo?'

'Of course not, I'd like your company but I understand that Lila and Mr Ashcroft might need you.'

'Of course, I'll come with you as far as Liverpool.'

Betty shook her head and tilted her chin. 'No, it'll cost money. It's unlikely that I'll bump into Uncle Teddy if I keep away from Litherland. Somehow, I doubt Aunt Elsie will have told him that I'll be doing my exams.'

Emma gazed at her half-sister with a smile and thought, *You've grown up a bit more since you've been here. You seem to be recovering your confidence.* 'OK, luv, if you're all right with that, then we'd best carry on with the strawberries or they'll spoil. I must get the jam done today as tomorrow is going to be another busy day. You'd best write a letter to the widow woman and let her know that you'll be there on Saturday afternoon.'

The news came via the postman that Mrs Ashcroft had died. Betty told Emma not to worry about her, but to see what she could do to help her friend. Emma thought that was good of her, considering her half-sister must be apprehensive about the journey to Waterloo and her swiftly approaching exams.

There followed a difficult time for Emma,

and it was with almost a sense of relief that she accompanied Betty to the station and saw her into a carriage. At the last minute, she handed her a parcel. 'A little gift for your landlady and I hope all goes well with your exams. I'll be praying for you. See you soon.'

Betty put her arms around Emma's neck and hugged her. 'Thanks for everything. I'll be back.'

Emma kissed her cheek and then stepped away from the train. She waved until it was out of sight, then she returned to her cottage. She had agreed to do a buffet for the funeral guests, so there was plenty to occupy her, but she knew that she was going to miss Betty's presence in the house.

Emma glanced surreptitiously at her friend's pale face as they knelt side by side in the pew, and asked herself again how Lila and her father were going to cope without Mrs Ashcroft. He had a war pension and there were Lila's wages going into the house, but life was going to be more difficult for them.

The prayers came to an end and the vicar announced the final hymn. As the organist played the first chords of 'Abide with Me' the congregation rose. Even Jack Ashcroft managed to struggle to his feet, despite his obviously being in pain. When the time came to follow the coffin down the aisle, Lila had the task of pushing him in the wheelchair while Emma slipped out by a side door. Jack had wanted to go straight home and dispense with the niceties. For once his daughter had argued with him, saying that it wouldn't be right. Her mother had been a respected nursing sister at the hospital and a member of the WI.

As Emma's cottage came into sight, she was surprised to see three figures standing outside her door. As she drew closer, they materialised into the recognisable persons of Dougie, Dorothy and Maggie. Dorothy was wearing a red swagger coat over a red pleated skirt and yellow blouse, and on her blonde hair was perched a pillbox-shaped hat made of red feathers. Emma felt quite envious and wished she could look so smart.

At any other time she would have welcomed them with open arms, but right now they presented her with a problem. She wondered if they knew that Betty was in Waterloo, or had Mrs Gregory decided to keep that a secret? Still, it looked like she might discover soon what had happened to cause Betty's aunt to behave the way she did.

'Hello, you three,' called Emma. 'It's lovely to see you, but your being here isn't very convenient.'

Dorothy looked at her with concern. 'What's up? You look tired.'

Emma shrugged. 'I'm OK. But Lila's mother died and I'm providing tea for the mourners and Betty has gone off to Waterloo to do her exams.'

Dorothy blinked. 'What! How come?'

'You must be wishing us anywhere else but here,' said Dougie, frowning.

'We could give you a helping hand,' offered Dorothy.

Emma smiled. 'Thanks, but it's OK. The food's all prepared and a couple of women from the village are coming to help out.'

'So it's best if we're out of the way,' said Dorothy. 'But, before we toddle off for a walk, tell us how it came about that Betty is in Waterloo?'

Emma hesitated. 'I'll give you the bare bones of it. I wrote to the headmistress of Betty's school and she must have got in touch with your mother. She's sent a postal order for Betty's board and lodgings while she does her exams. We did wonder why your mother should suddenly get in touch and be so helpful.'

Dorothy smiled and glanced at the other two. 'We have an answer but we'll explain later because you're busy right now. We'll come back in an hour or two.'

'That's fine,' said Emma.

She was about to turn away, when Dougie said, 'If you don't mind, girls, I'd like to pay my respects to Mr Ashcroft and Lila.'

Dorothy could scarcely conceal her disappointment. 'Of course, you've met them.' She gave a wry smile. 'I confess I'd rather you showed us the village and the ruins but we'll have to manage without you.'

Dougie looked relieved. 'Thanks for understanding. You shouldn't have any difficulty finding your way around.'

Emma agreed, although she would have preferred not to have Dougie under her feet while she was getting things ready. 'See you later,' she said to the sisters.

They nodded and walked away.

Emma went inside the cottage, followed by Dougie. She removed her jacket, and after washing her hands, put the kettle on before taking milk from the larder.

'Is there anything I can do?' he asked.

She glanced up at him. 'You can pour milk into cups but don't be too heavy-handed with it.'

He was just about to do so, when there came a knock on the back door. It opened to reveal Emma's two helpers. 'Coo-ee! Can we come in?'

'Of course you can come in,' called Emma, smiling.

She introduced Dougie, knowing full well that they already had a fair idea who he was and were glad to have a closer look at him. She had little opportunity to see the effect he had on other people as they entered the house, but she did notice Lila's expression as soon as she caught sight of him. He wasted no time going over to her and Mr Ashcroft and stayed talking to them for quite a while.

Most people had departed by the time Dorothy and Maggie returned from their walk. Hearing their voices, Emma glanced out of the window and saw them looking at the hens. She opened the door and called to them.

A few moments later, Dorothy limped into the kitchen. 'Is it OK for me to take off my shoes, Emma?' she asked. 'I've gone and got a blister. You wouldn't have a plaster, would you?'

'I'm bound to have one somewhere,' said Emma, pulling out a chair. 'Sit down and make yourself comfortable.'

Dorothy sat in a chair and eased off her court shoes. 'These really aren't suitable for walking. Next time I come I'll be prepared and maybe Dougie will take me hill walking.'

'Fell walking, Dorothy, and you'll need a proper pair of boots,' he said, smiling at her.

'I know,' she said ruefully. 'Perhaps you can advise me on the kind I should buy.' She dimpled up at him.

'I'd be happy to,' said Dougie.

Lila glanced at him and then looked away.

'Cup of tea, Dorothy, Maggie?' asked Emma, after taking a tin of plasters out of a drawer and placing the tin on the table by Dorothy's elbow.

'Just what I need. You're an angel,' said Dorothy.

She glanced at Mr Ashcroft. 'I'm sorry about your wife. I know what it feels like to lose someone you love,' she said sincerely. 'I lost my father not long after the war.'

'Thank you,' said Jack Ashcroft gruffly. 'You'll be Betty's cousin. You don't look like her.'

'No, but my sister here does,' said Dorothy, smiling. 'Dougie was telling me that you make models out of matchsticks.'

'Aye, I do,' he said, glancing at Dougie. 'I hope he didn't build me up to be a marvel at the job.'

'Actually,' said Dorothy, leaning towards Jack, 'he did. And I've been wondering if you'd make one for my brother.'

'Your brother!'

'Yes,' said Dorothy, waggling her foot. 'It's his birthday in autumn and hopefully he'll be home from Korea by then. He's been doing his national service. Dougie told me that you were making a ship for him. I wondered if you could make a sailing ship for Jared. He used to enjoy reading the Hornblower books.'

Jack looked uncertain. 'I have done a sailing ship in the past but it mightn't be good enough for a birthday present.'

'Couldn't you try?' asked Dorothy in a persuasive voice. 'I'd really appreciate it. It would be something different.'

Jack hesitated. 'I'll see what I can do once I've got over this lot.' He switched his gaze to Dougie. 'You'll be wanting your model. You can come with us and fetch it if you like. I'll be glad to have it off my hands.'

'Fine,' said Dougie. 'I'll see you later, girls.'

Emma went with them to the front door and told Jack that she was still willing to have some of his models on display, if he was in favour of the idea. He agreed gruffly and she watched as Dougie helped Lila ease her father's wheelchair down onto the pavement. She waved to them as they headed off along the road before returning to the kitchen.

'Well!' she exclaimed, smiling at Dorothy and Maggie who were sitting on the sofa together. Dorothy had eased off her stocking and was gazing at her bloodied heel.

'Well what?' asked Dorothy. 'You're wondering how we come to be here with Dougie. That's easily answered.' And she told Emma about the events that had taken place during the evening of Coronation Day.

When she had finished, interrupted several times by Maggie, Emma was frowning. 'That probably explains why your mother wrote to me. But isn't it possible your uncle might become even nastier now he's been made a fool of?'

Dorothy pursed her lips and nodded. 'It could be the reason why she didn't tell us about Betty staying in Waterloo. Mum's not daft and she could be worrying about Uncle Teddy getting into the habit of following one of us when we go out. You can bet he'll be wanting to get back at Maggie for his ending up in a cell at the police station.'

Emma agreed. 'You're going to have to be on your guard.'

'Don't worry,' said Maggie in a sombre voice. 'I keep looking over my shoulder. If only we could get rid of him.'

'It's not going to be easy,' said Dorothy. 'All my hopes are pinned on our Jared coming home.' She glanced up at Emma and changed the subject. 'Could you let me have a little bowl of water and a cloth, so I can wash the blood away?'

Emma nodded, and while Dorothy dealt with her blister, she fetched some food from the larder and placed it on the table. Maggie had picked up a book about the Pendle witches and she told Emma that she had found Betty's doll but she had forgotten to bring it with her.

'Don't worry about it,' said Emma. 'She has a new one. There's some displayed in the front room, now: I call them "wise women".'

'You know what would sell,' suggested Maggie, turning over the pages. 'A book of spells and recipes. I bet they'd sell like hot cakes.'

Dorothy nodded in agreement, 'What about writing little individual recipes and placing them in their tiny hands and you could also do little herbal cures, as well.'

Emma nodded. 'You mean like use feverfew for headaches?'

'Do you have some in your garden?'

'Aye, and I suppose I could cut the odd herb fresh and place a sprig in the doll's other hand. It would be something different from those I've seen around Pendle and Clitheroe.'

The girls fell silent and got on with eating and drinking.

Emma offered more tea but they shook their heads. 'We'll have to be going soon,' said Dorothy. 'When do you think Dougie will be back? Is the Ashcrofts' house far?'

'Outside the village, but I wouldn't have thought he'd be much longer, knowing you've a train to catch and need to change a couple of times,' said Emma.

She was right. Dougie arrived shortly after with a cardboard box. 'So you've your model, then,' said Emma.

He nodded. 'Sorry if I seem to have been a long time. I haven't had a chance to talk to you, Emma.'

'It doesn't matter,' she said lightly. 'Dorothy's brought me up to date with what's been going on.'

'I thought she might. Lila was telling me you still haven't visited the registry office in Liverpool.'

'That's right,' said Emma. 'But I can't see me making it into Liverpool for a while. Now that summer's come, I'm going to be busy.'

'I could visit the registry office for you,' offered Dorothy. 'Just remind me about what you're looking for.'

'That's good of you,' said Emma warmly. 'But don't you worry about it. I'll get round to it one day.'

There was a silence.

'Are we going, then?' asked Dougie.

Dorothy nodded. 'Better had. Don't want to be too late, or when we speak to Mum, *Big Ears* might be there listening and we don't want him knowing what's going on.'

'You know you're welcome to come and visit, anytime,' said Emma.

Dougie said, 'Mam's been nagging me to get some decorating done and it's best done in the summer because paint dries quicker then.' He looked at Emma. 'I was thinking it would do Mr Ashcroft good to get out of the house. I even thought he could work here on his models when you're open for business?'

Emma agreed that there was something in what Dougie said. 'I'll speak to Lila and see what she thinks.'

'So what about Betty?' asked Dorothy.

'She'll be helping me out here during the summer,' answered Emma, 'but if she gets the results she needs and is accepted by the art school, I can see her trying to find a room nearby in Liverpool. I'm hoping it'll be a real good summer and that your mother might help me out with her living expenses. Betty will have to find herself some part-time work, too.'

'Well, after Mum sending Betty twenty pounds, I suppose it is possible that she will help out,' said Dorothy. 'I'd love to know where she got the money from. Our Jared perhaps? We'll soon find out, I suppose.'

CHAPTER NINETEEN

'Gosh, it's hot,' said Lila, fanning herself with a magazine. 'Aren't you glad you're not in Liverpool right now, Betty? It'll be stifling in the city streets.'

'It wouldn't be as hot down by the Mersey,' replied Betty, without looking up from the drawing she was doing of a sleeping Tibby under a bush. 'We'd be getting the sea breezes. Anyway, I'll be going back there any day now I've got my results. I wonder how the twins did. I need to find myself a bedsit and a part-time job.'

'At least you've had experience waiting on,' said Emma, her expression pensive, 'and you're not a bad little baker. You've been a great help to me.'

Betty glanced at her and smiled. 'You're a good instructor.'

'Your lessons aren't finished, my girl,' said Emma, smiling. 'I was thinking of going blackberrying this evening. With sugar off the ration, I'll make lots more jam. What do you say? There's still a chance we might have some customers this afternoon, so it's best going later.'

Emma knew she was going to miss her sister but she had known that if Betty did well in her exams, then she'd have to help her to fulfil her dream of becoming an artist. She had written to Mrs Gregory informing her of the situation, although she had sent the letter to Irene's house, wary of the uncle getting his hands on it. They'd had a couple of brief letters from Dorothy, Maggie and Irene but there had been little of importance in them. Uncle Teddy seemed to be keeping a low profile and Maggie and her mother had had several days out during the school holidays, visiting New Brighton, Chester and Southport. As for Dorothy, she had seen nothing of Dougie but had had a couple of dates with a young man she had met at a dance hall with one of her friends from work, but the romance had fizzled out.

'At least we've got Dad out of the house,' said Lila, glancing over to where Jack was sitting at a table, having nearly finished the model of the sailing ship that Dorothy had wanted. For weeks after his wife's death, he had been unable to settle to anything, but between them, she and Lila had eventually coaxed him to get started again by moving the models he'd already made here.

Suddenly Emma heard the sound of voices. Customers, she thought, rising and hurrying towards the house. Her wise women had gone a treat during the summer months and she'd knitted a few more. She had also sold a couple of Jack Ashcroft's models, which had been encouraging.

There were several people crowding into her front room and one was dressed in army uniform. Emma welcomed them and asked if they wished to stay indoors or sit out in the garden. Most chose indoors in the shade, but the soldier chose to go out into the garden.

Betty heard the sound of voices and put down her pencil. Time to see if Emma needed her help, she thought. She glanced up and instantly recognised the man who had come outside.

'Billy McElroy!' she exclaimed.

He smiled across at her. 'Betty Booth. Irene said that I would find you here.'

'Did she?' Betty grinned at him. 'Is that why you're here?'

'That's right. I'll be leaving the army this week and I've bought myself a decent little motor. Irene put it to me that I could take you and your luggage to Liverpool.'

Betty's mouth fell open and for a moment she couldn't speak. Then Emma appeared and said, 'I need your help, Betty.'

'Coming,' she croaked. 'Only wait a minute. I must introduce you to someone.' Seizing Emma's hand, she said, 'This is Irene's stepbrother, Sergeant Billy McElroy. He's stationed up here but he's going home soon and has offered me a lift in his motor. What d'you think?'

Emma looked the soldier up and down and realised he was giving her the once over, too. Their eyes caught and she saw the amusement in his. 'Do I pass muster?' he asked. 'You can trust Betty to me. I've known her for several years.'

'It's not that,' said Emma hastily, knowing she was telling a fib. 'It's just that she has nowhere to stay in Liverpool yet.'

'We'll find her somewhere,' said Billy confidently. 'You leave it to my dad and me. He's a bobby and has his ears to the ground.'

'I-if you say so,' said Emma, wishing she had half his confidence.'

Betty said, 'You do make me feel anything is possible, Billy. Now what about a nice slice of home-made strawberry jam sponge with cream?'

'It sounds just the ticket,' said Billy with a chuckle.

Betty and Emma vanished inside.

He sat down and glanced over at the young

woman in a deckchair and caught her looking at him. 'Lovely afternoon,' he said.

'Aye, it's a real nice day,' said Lila, blushing beneath his bold eyes.

Her father glanced up and nodded in Billy's direction. 'You stationed up here?'

'Not for much longer. You live here?' asked Billy.

Jack nodded.

'Lovely country.'

'Bit too quiet at times,' said Jack, 'and it's a bloody forsaken hole in the winter. Going to be worse this one because my wife died not so long ago, and what with Lila here out at work all day, I'm going to be stuck once Emma closes down her tea room.'

Billy looked at Lila. 'Your dad, is he?'

'Aye. He were wounded in the leg during the war and can't get about. You'll have to forgive him for grouching,' she said.

'If he's unhappy where he is, then he should up sticks and move. You only have one life. What do you do to earn a crust?'

'I used to work in the mill but got a bit fed up, so I changed jobs and work in a shop in Clitheroe now,' said Lila, seeing no reason why she shouldn't tell him.

'Plenty of shops in Liverpool. Your dad would see plenty of life there.'

'It's not easy to get a house, though, is it?'

said Lila. 'I was listening to what you said to Betty and Emma. You and your father must be miracle-workers if you can find her somewhere so quickly.'

'A bedsit, that's all she needs,' said Billy, 'and she's young, so if it's on a second or third floor, it won't matter as much to her as it would to your dad.'

Lila said, 'Tell me something I don't know, soldier boy.'

A smile broke over his face. 'Don't be so touchy. What he needs is a ground floor flat and a friendly charwoman, who'd come and do for him.'

'We couldn't afford a charwoman,' said Lila, flushing.

'He should remarry, then.' He glanced up. 'Good, here's my cup of char and the promised delicious cake.'

Emma placed the tray on the table in front of him. 'Did you really mean what you said about taking Betty to Liverpool?' she asked.

Billy took the mug and spooned in two sugars. 'Miss Booth, besides your excellent cake that was my only reason for coming here. Irene's missed Betty and I like her to be happy. If you feel you can't trust me, then why don't you come along for the ride?'

'I didn't say I didn't trust you,' she retorted hastily.

He smiled as if he didn't believe her. 'Can you be ready the day after next?'

She nodded, her head in a whirl, and then hurried away.

Billy left half an hour later. Emma, Betty and even Lila went out front to have a look at his motor and to wave as he zoomed away in a cloud of exhaust fumes. 'Well,' said Emma, smiling. 'There's plenty of life in him.'

'You can say that again,' said Lila wryly. 'He as good as said that me and Dad should move to Liverpool.'

'And why not?' said Betty, raising her eyebrows. 'Your dad has his war pension and you shouldn't have any trouble finding a job there.'

'Easy for you to say,' said Lila, sighing. 'He and his dad are going to find you a place.'

'Aren't they just,' said Betty, smiling. 'I think he's the bee's knees and his dad is a lovely man, as well. I know I'll be safe with either of them.'

Lila and Emma exchanged looks but didn't say a word.

Two days later Emma and Betty were ready by nine in the morning. Billy hadn't told them what time he would arrive and they didn't want to keep him waiting. After about an hour, they heard the sound of his motor from way down the road and had the front door open before the car came to a halt.

He switched off the engine and got out and smiled at them both, standing there with Betty's luggage. 'I see that the pair of you are raring to go. There was me, hoping you'd give me a cup of tea and something tasty to go with it before we set out.'

'I've made us a picnic and I've a flask,' said Emma, wondering what it was about Billy McElroy that put a smile on her face.

'Good girl, I'll settle for that,' he said. 'I'll just use your lav, if that's OK, and we'll be on our way.'

He didn't keep them waiting long and soon he had Betty settled in the back seat with her luggage. 'The boot's filled with my stuff,' he explained. He helped Emma into the front seat and then they were off.

She soon discovered he wasn't one for small talk whilst he was driving, which surprised her because she had the impression he was one of those chatty men, not full of himself but having plenty to say on a variety of topics. Within the hour he brought the car to a halt on top of Parbold Hill and encouraged Emma and Betty to get out and look at the view of the Lancashire plain that stretched out before them. He took out the picnic and a waterproof which he spread on the ground.

'Sit down, girls,' he said.

Obediently they sat and Emma took packets of food from a shopping bag. Betty poured out the tea and handed Billy his cup first. Emma plied him with food and then the three of them ate in silence. Only when they had finished did Betty wander off down a path, saying she was going to stretch her legs. Billy began to ask Emma about herself and her village and how often would she be able to get to Liverpool to keep an eye on Betty.

'Not very often,' she admitted.

'You haven't thought of moving to the port?' he asked.

Her lips curled in a smile. 'I've been asked that question before and I admit, I'd find it difficult leaving my village. It's my home, just as Litherland is yours.'

His grey eyes were thoughtful and a lock of mousy hair had fallen onto his forehead. 'I'm not planning on staying there for ever,' said Billy, stretching out on the ground. 'I'd like to move further out, but I need to find myself a job and a place of my own. It's time I settled down and got married.'

'You have a girlfriend?' asked Emma.

Billy's smile faded. 'I've already seen the one I want, but whether I can get her to fall in love with me, now that's something else. I'm going to have to work on it. No rushing her but I'd like to be married six months from now,' he said seriously, gazing at her.

Only for a few seconds did Emma wonder if he

meant her. She felt extremely flattered if that was so, but she was not the least bit in love with him and that meant he wasn't the one for her. She smiled. 'I call six months after meeting rushing it. Don't you think that you need to get to know someone really well, before settling down with them for the rest of your life?'

'You obviously don't believe in love at first sight, Emma,' he said, taking out a packet of cigarettes and a lighter. 'Mind if I smoke?'

She shook her head. 'Even if I did believe in love at first sight, I still think a couple should take time to get to know each other,' she replied.

His brow knitted as he inhaled. 'I wouldn't argue but a man can get impatient and I'd settle on courting for three weeks, then an engagement for another three weeks and then comes the wedding.'

'But that's only six weeks, not six months!' Emma shook her head. 'Much too soon. You could believe yourself in love and then discover after a while that you've fallen out of love.'

Billy stared at her. 'That's happened to you?'

Emma hesitated and then nodded. 'So I'm going to wait until I'm sure I'm really in love before saying yes.'

'And what if love strikes you like a thunderbolt?' asked Billy.

'I'd rather it didn't,' she said, beginning to collect empty paper bags together.

'But you don't always have control over these things,' said Billy.

Emma made no comment because she had spotted Betty coming back up the hill. Emma glanced at Billy. 'Are we ready to go?' she asked.

'Let me finish me ciggie and we'll be on our way,' he said.

They arrived in Liverpool about an hour later. Billy parked his car in Hope Street at the back of the unfinished Anglican cathedral. He opened the passenger door and helped Emma out. 'Why have we come here?' she asked.

'I telephoned Dad yesterday and he's come up trumps. Nice bedsit in one of those houses across the way in Gambier Terrace,' said Billy.

'Gambier Terrace! I can't believe it,' said Emma, gazing across the road.

'Why not?' asked Billy.

'Because Gambier Terrace is where the registry office is and I've been meaning to visit it for ages.'

Billy opened the back passenger door and Betty slid along the leather seat and got out. 'I must admit I'm feeling nervous. If I take this bedsit I'm going to be all on my own,' she said.

'Rubbish,' said Billy. 'You'll make new friends once you start lessons, and our Irene and Maggie and your Dorothy will soon come visiting.'

Betty rested her hand on his arm and placed her other hand on Emma's. 'Isn't he cheerful, Emma?

He makes it sound like everything is easy and will turn out fine.'

'And why shouldn't it?' asked Emma, quashing any doubts she might have. She almost added, *And there's no reason why Uncle Teddy should find you here,* but she kept that thought to herself. She had never mentioned knowing that Betty had been pregnant, hoping that her half-sister would confide in her, but she never had. So Emma was not about to remind her of it. Instead, she thought of money. She had paid Betty for the work she had done during the summer and was prepared to add to it from her small savings, so hopefully here was enough at least for a month's rent. Betty would have to find a part-time job, whether her aunt was prepared to help out her niece or not.

Billy locked the car and they crossed the road. The houses loomed up. Some were of yellow brick and several storeys high. They were set back from the main road that ran the length of the terrace.

She and Betty allowed themselves to be led to the address that Billy had written on a slip of paper. He rang a bell and a few minutes later they were being welcomed inside by a middle-aged woman. She led them up a couple of flights of stairs to an attic that had not only a dormer window but a window in the roof as well, so that the furnished room was filled with light.

'It's perfect,' said Betty, her eyes sparkling.

'Except for those stairs,' said Emma, also thinking that the furniture was sparse and not the least bit attractive. There was a sink, two gas rings, a single bed, shelves, a desk, a chest of drawers and a curtained-off alcove with a rail to hang clothes. Still, her half-sister did not seem to worry about material things. Emma remembered that she had been perfectly content with the small bedroom back at the cottage. This room was much bigger and had an interesting view of the sunken cemetery in the shadow of the cathedral.

The formalities were dealt with and soon the moment came for Emma to take her leave of her half-sister. She hugged her and said, 'You will write regularly?'

'Of course I'll write,' said Betty, sounding surprised that Emma should think that she might forget about her. 'You've done so much for me and I'm really grateful for the money. You must come and stay. I'll sleep on the floor and you can have the bed. I'll definitely try and visit you in a few weeks' time.'

'Sounds great,' said Billy, who was leaning against the door jamb. 'I'll give you a lift, Emma, to Lime Street.'

'Thanks,' she said, taking his words as a hint that he wanted to be on his way.

Betty turned to him and held out her hand. 'Thanks for all you've done. I know you didn't have to do any of it,' she said shyly, 'and I know I have Irene to thank, as well, but I really appreciate the trouble you and your dad took in finding me this place. It's amazing that you did.'

'That's all right, kid,' he said, shaking her hand. 'I'll tell Irene you're in residence and I'm sure the pair of you, and Maggie, will be nattering away ten to the dozen hidden away up here under the roof at weekends.' He released her hand and turned to Emma. 'You ready?'

She nodded, kissed Betty and then left the room without looking back.

Neither she nor Billy spoke as they went downstairs. They crossed the road to the car and only then did she turn round and gaze up at the top windows of the houses. She thought she caught sight of Betty and waved. The figure waved back. Emma had a lump in her throat and tears pricked her eyes.

'You OK?' asked Billy.

Emma nodded, wiped her eyes on her sleeve and got into the car.

Neither of them spoke until he drew up outside the side entrance to Lime Street station. 'Thanks for all you've done,' she said, holding out her hand.

He surprised her by leaning forward and kissed her lightly on the mouth. 'My pleasure. If I wasn't already in love with someone else, then I think I could really fancy you, Emma. Have a good journey.'

She smiled at him. 'I wish you lots of luck with your love life, Billy. Bye!'

He saluted her before driving off.

She turned and hurried into the station to buy her ticket and catch the train home, wondering about the woman who had captured his heart.

CHAPTER TWENTY

'Is that a new frock?' asked Elsie.

Dorothy glanced at her mother who had just come into the bedroom. 'Yes. Why, is there something wrong with it?' She gazed down at the pink waffle-weave rayon dress that she had bought last Saturday, especially for tonight.

'Don't you think the neckline is a bit low?'

'No. This deep U-neckline is fashionable.'

'Fashionable or not, you don't want to look tarty,' said Elsie. 'I don't know what our Jared will say if he sees you dressed like that, but I do know what Teddy will and I'd rather he didn't give you the once-over.'

'You're not the only one, Mum, and that is why

I plan to be out of this house before he comes in. Once our Jared's home we won't have to give a damn about Uncle Teddy. He'll soon be running scared, because if you don't tell Jared what's been going on here, I intend to do so.'

Elsie reached for the cigarettes in the pocket of her pinny with a trembling hand. 'I don't want to lay this on his shoulders as soon as he gets home. He's had enough to contend with in Korea. Teddy's my husband and nothing can change that.'

Dorothy raised her pencilled eyebrows. 'You could get a legal separation. I've heard you arguing and it wouldn't surprise me if he belts you when we're not around. Anyway, when are you going to visit our Betty?' She picked up a lipstick and gazed at her reflection in the mirror. 'Has Uncle Teddy asked lately if you know where she is?'

'He's given up asking,' said Elsie, straightening the corner of the candlewick bedspread and sitting down to light her cigarette. 'He knows none of us are going to tell him. You and Maggie are going to have to be really careful about visiting now she's living in Liverpool. I worry about him following you two and me. That's why I haven't been to visit Betty, but I have given you money for her, so I feel a bit better about myself.'

'That's all right, then,' said Dorothy in a tight voice. 'As long as *you* feel OK about not seeing her.'

Her mother flushed. 'At least I'm doing

something to help the kid. I did before that friend of hers, Irene's, stepfather and stepbrother helped her out. I don't know why they felt they had to interfere.'

'Because Irene asked them to! I'm grateful to Billy and his father. It was really good of them. Anyway, it's half-term this week and Betty's gone up to stay with Emma for a few days.' Dorothy finished with her lipstick and placed it in her handbag.

'Good,' said Elsie, forcing down a cough. 'Anyway, where are you going wearing a new dress?' she asked in a croaky voice.

'I'm going to a dance, if you must know.'

'With that good-looking policeman?'

'Yes, as it happens. We both like dancing.'

'I remember watching you on Coronation Day. Perhaps he'll ask you to marry him one day.'

'Perhaps he will,' said Dorothy, a wistful expression in her eyes. She glanced at the clock. 'Anyway, I must go or I'm going to be late.'

Dorothy was halfway down the street when she spotted a dark-haired young man with a lean, sunburnt face striding along the pavement towards her. For a moment her steps faltered and then she let out a scream and ran towards him. She flung herself at her brother, catching him off balance. For a moment they teetered on the kerb in danger of falling off the pavement, then he dropped his kitbag and steadied them both.

'It is you, Dot?' he said, smiling.

She placed a hand on his shoulder and looked up into his face. 'Of course it's me, you noggin! I can't have altered that much and I recognised you straight away.'

'Yes, but you were just my plump sister when I left and now you're a lovely young woman,' he teased.

Dorothy laughed. 'I was a young woman then, you idiot. It's just that I went on a diet after you left.'

'Well, you look marvellous. The person I remember has gone and instead here's the new you.'

Her throat felt suddenly tight as she noticed the lines on his face that had not been there before. 'I'm still the same old me but you've changed. You look older. Was it terribly bad? You always made a joke of things.'

A shadow darkened Jared's eyes. 'It can't have been any worse than what millions of soldiers put up with during the last two wars. By the time the King's got there, it was trench warfare and we were up against the Chinese. General McArthur should never have invaded North Korea.'

'Well, I'm glad you're home. I feared that you mightn't make it,' she said, her voice husky with emotion.

Jared touched his sister's cheek where a lone tear

trickled down. 'There's no need for tears. You don't have to worry about me anymore.'

'I hope not.' She hesitated. 'Mum can't wait to see you.'

'And Uncle Teddy?' he asked, releasing her.

'The serpent in Eden,' she said in a hard voice.

'That's strong!'

Her eyes glinted. 'You don't know the half of it. But you'll get to know and then we'll have to do something to get rid of him.'

'You're serious,' said Jared, frowning down at her.

'Indeed I am! Betty isn't living with us now, by the way,' she said lightly. 'Didn't tell you at the time because I didn't want to upset you. She ran away last May. Went up north to live with her half-sister, Emma. Betty's back living in Liverpool now, but that's a secret that must be kept from Uncle Teddy.'

Jared's eyes narrowed. 'Ma told me that the half-sister was dead! Why did she lie?'

'What! You knew about her?' said Dorothy, startled.

'Aye, but I was sworn to secrecy because Ma said it would upset Betty, knowing about her.'

Dorothy punched him lightly on the arm. 'You've kept secrets from me, you horror.'

He rubbed his arm absently. 'Sorry. Anyway, tell me what you know.'

'I haven't time now. I've got a date,' she murmured.

'So that's why you're all dolled up.'

'Yes, I'm going dancing. I'd cancel, but he'll be waiting for me and I can't have him thinking that I'm the sort of girl who lets a bloke down. His name's Dougie Marshall and he's a policeman.' Her tone was suddenly animated. 'Mum approves because she sees him as having a steady job, but there's no way I want to bring him home just yet. She'd embarrass me by asking him all sorts of questions.' She paused and sighed. 'Besides, I'm not sure how he feels about me. He was Emma's friend first and he does go and see her, but I can't say I've noticed anything lover-like in his behaviour towards her. Besides, he has responsibilities. A mother and twin brothers. His dad was killed in the war.'

'He sounds like an OK bloke.'

Dorothy's face glowed. 'He's blonde and blue-eyed and he's mad about exercise. He likes the great outdoors, walking on the fells and cycling.'

'The fells?'

'You know! Hills up Lancashire.'

Jared chuckled. 'I can't see you climbing hills, so what d'you have in common? Besides dancing, I mean.'

Dorothy's eyes twinkled. 'I could get to like climbing hills. Just need the proper footwear.'

'You in walking boots! Don't make me laugh. You're a townie.'

Dorothy protested. 'I can change.'

Jared said, 'I won't argue. I'd like to meet him sometime. See if he's good enough for my sister.'

'That would be nice. I'm sure you'll like each other.' She glanced at her watch and gasped. 'I'd best be going or I'm going to be late!'

'I hope you have a good time and I'll see you later,' said Jared, picking up his kitbag.

'It's great to have you home.' She reached up and kissed his cheek, hurrying away before she came over all emotional again.

Jared watched her for several moments before slinging his kitbag over his shoulder and heading for the house where he had not felt comfortable in years. It was bigger than the one they'd lived in in Liverpool, but for him it had never had the warm, cosy atmosphere of their previous home. Perhaps that was partly due to his father being so ill when the family had moved in, along with Aunt Lizzie and Betty. Then, what with his father dying and not long after Aunt Lizzie being killed, there had been an atmosphere about the place. And, to top it all, his mother had to go and marry his dad's brother.

Jared remembered coming home on leave and talking to his mother about Teddy. He'd been convinced that she had been crazy to make such a move. He hadn't changed his mind, and the little his sister had told him convinced him that he was right. What had happened to cause Betty to go and live with her half-sister? How had that come about?

He decided that instead of letting himself in with the key on the string, he'd best knock on the front door, as he didn't want to give his mother a shock by walking straight in on her. He knew he'd made the right decision when Elsie opened the door and let out such a screech that several sparrows flew up from the garden.

'You're here, you're here!' she cried, clutching his jacket. 'I knew it wouldn't be long once the King's Regiment disembarked.'

'Calm down, Ma, and let me in,' said Jared, grinning.

'Of course I'll let you in, son.' She pulled him inside. 'You've just missed our Dorothy.'

'I saw her.'

'What did you think of the frock she was wearing?'

'She had her coat on, so I didn't see it. What I did notice was that she's really grown-up now,' said Jared. 'Got a fella, so she told me.'

'Yes, a policeman, so respectable. But you want to hear the way she speaks to me sometimes.' Elsie rolled her eyes. 'She has far too much to say for herself.' She led the way into the living room, which was deserted.

Jared glanced about the room and his eyes fell on the television in the corner where there had once been a bookcase. He wondered where the money

341

had come from for such a luxury item. 'Is our Maggie in?' he asked.

'No, she's taken over from Betty doing messages for an old woman. She should have been home by now, but I bet she's gone off to meet her friend Irene.' Elsie moved a couple of comics from the best chair by the fireplace. 'Sit down, son. You look well, got yourself a tan. I'll put the kettle on. It's not long boiled, so I won't be long.'

Jared dropped his kitbag by the door, but instead of sitting down, he prowled around the room, thinking about what Dorothy had said. When his mother returned, he asked, 'Where's Teddy?'

His mother stiffened. 'What's our Dorothy been telling you?'

'Not much.'

Elsie placed the tray on the table and looked at her son as if she didn't believe him. 'Normally, Teddy and I would be going to the second house at the pictures tonight, but now you're here, I'll be staying in so you can tell me what your plans are now you're home,' she said.

Jared's eyes narrowed. 'Where is he now? Round the pub?'

'Yes, but at least he's out the way, so I've got you to myself.' She smiled as she poured the tea. 'So, tell me your plans.'

Jared sat down. 'I'm going to call in and see my old boss later. He wrote to me regularly while I was away.' *More than you did*, he thought.

'Then he'll be taking you back,' she said, looking relieved.

'Why shouldn't he? There'll be plenty of work around for plasterers with so many houses having been destroyed or damaged during the Blitz,' said Jared, taking the cup and saucer from her.

'Good,' said his mother. 'Do you want a bite to eat? I could make you a sandwich. If I'd known you'd be arriving today I'd have saved you some dinner.'

'A sandwich will be fine,' said Jared impatiently. 'If I feel hungry later, I'll drop in at the chippy.'

'I'll just be a minute, then.' She vanished into the kitchen.

When she reappeared with a plate of cheese-and-pickle sandwiches, he waited until she was sitting down before saying, 'So what's this I hear about our Betty running away to live with her half-sister up north?'

The cup shook in his mother's fingers and tea spilt into the saucer and onto her skirt. She muttered beneath her breath and dabbed at the fabric with the sleeve of her cardigan. She stared at him with a wary expression in her eyes. 'So our Dorothy told you that much? Of course, it wouldn't have come as much of a surprise to you because you knew about Emma. William told you.'

'Yeah, but you told me she was dead,' said Jared,

with an edge to his voice, 'so how did Betty get to know about her and why did she run away to live with her?'

Elsie put down her cup on its saucer and placed it on the table. 'Her behaviour got out of hand and I had to do what was necessary. Then suddenly out of the blue she disappeared. I had no idea where she'd gone. She's just like our Lizzie, doing things without thinking about the consequences. The three girls had kept it a secret from me that they'd been meeting Emma Booth. It doesn't surprise me that our Betty did, because she's just like our Lizzie, secretive. But my own daughters keeping it from me, I was really angry and hurt.'

Jared said patiently, 'Aunt Lizzie wasn't secretive. I could read her like a book.'

Elsie's eyes darkened. 'You didn't know her!' she shot back at him. 'If it wasn't for me, then she'd never have married William Booth. But I made sure that she did or she'd have caused a scandal and been in a right mess.' She took a packet of cigarettes and matches from the shelf nearby and lit up.

Jared stared at her. 'What kind of mess?'

His mother took in a lungful of smoke and began coughing. When she got her breath back, she said, 'Never you mind. Why don't you go up to your bedroom and unpack your things? You'll be wanting a wash before seeing your old boss.'

Jared guessed that he was not going to get any more information out of her right now. Still, he would like to know more about Betty's reasons for running away. No doubt his sisters would tell him. Right now, his mother was right, he needed a wash and change.

Jared's old boss, Mr Bridges, was glad to see him and, after a short conversation about what had been happening since they had last written to each other, it was decided that Jared would have a week's holiday before starting work on the following Monday.

Although it would soon be dark, Jared decided he needed some fresh air and so made for the towpath of the Leeds-Liverpool canal, thinking there should be hardly anyone about at this time of day. He was feeling the strain of putting a good face on things. He had made light of his time in Korea to his sister but there had been moments on night patrol when things had got really bloody. He'd been wounded slightly but his best mate had been killed. They had promised to watch each other's backs, but bullets could seemingly come out of nowhere when it was dark.

He felt the tears on his cheeks and told himself not to be such a bloody sissy. Crying would not bring Harold back. He turned round and began to retrace his steps, oblivious to his surroundings as he relived that night.

'Jared!'

The sound of someone calling his name caused him to whirl round, but he couldn't see anyone on the darkened towpath. Then he looked ahead and realised that he had walked further than he had intended and had come to the lift bridge by the Red Lion. The voice came again and he glanced up and saw a girl waving to him. It was Maggie and she was not alone – another girl and two lads accompanied her. He thought of what his mother had said and knew she'd have a fit if she could see Maggie with a couple of lads. He waved and headed for the steps leading up to the bridge.

'We're coming down. Stay where you are,' called Maggie.

The next moment his younger sister was hanging onto his sleeve and the other girl and one of the youths had stopped a few feet away. The other youth was slowly descending the steps with the aid of a stick.

'Irene, twins, this is my brother, Jared,' introduced Maggie. 'Remember my telling you that he's been away fighting in Korea and would be home any day now?'

The lads nodded in Jared's direction. 'Pleased to meet you,' they said. 'I'm Norman Marshall,' said the one next to Irene, 'and that's my brother Pete. Our older brother has a date with your sister tonight.'

Jared looked at them with interest. 'The policeman?'

'That's right,' said Norman, pulling a face. 'He's a good one, though,' he added hastily. 'Really conscientious, although he's inclined to think he knows it all and we know nothing.'

There was a pause.

'So where have the four of you been?' asked Jared.

'Nowhere, really,' said Maggie, fiddling with a strand of long ginger hair. 'Just walking and talking. We're not doing anything wrong.'

Jared said easily, 'That's OK, then.'

'We'd best be going or Mam'll start worrying about us,' said Norm.

'I'll see you again sometime,' said Jared, and headed for the bridge.

Maggie called, 'Will you wait for me the other side?'

'Yeah!' he shouted without looking back.

When Maggie caught up with him, he asked, 'So how did Pete get the limp?'

'He fell off a wall doing what he shouldn't,' she said, slipping her hand through her brother's arm. 'He was in hospital for ages. He's got a job now working in a shipping office. Norm's at Riversdale College the other side of Liverpool, studying to be a marine engineer.'

'And what about you?' asked Jared, gazing

down at her. 'How are you doing at school and what d'you want to do when you leave?'

Maggie said mischievously, 'You remind me of Irene's stepbrother, Billy, when he's making an effort to show interest in what I'm up to and about the family. He always asks after our Dorothy because they've met. He left the army not so long ago and brought our Betty and Emma to Liverpool in his car.' She stopped abruptly and darted Jared a sidelong glance. 'Do you know about that?'

'I've been told that Betty ran away from home to live with her half-sister up Lancashire,' said Jared. 'But tell me a bit more about this Billy who's showing an interest in our Dot and brought Betty back to Liverpool.'

Maggie hesitated, before saying slowly, 'He fought in the war, but was only young at the time and stayed on in the army afterwards. His father's a policeman and Billy's thinking of doing something in security. Our Dot thinks he's OK.' She paused. 'So what did Mum have to say when she saw you? Have you seen Uncle Teddy?'

'I believe he's propping up the bar at the local,' drawled Jared, shortening his stride so his sister did not have to hurry to keep up with him. 'I gather our Dot wants him out but she hasn't explained why. I'm guessing it has something to do with Betty?'

'So they haven't told you everything?' said Maggie, shooting him a glance.

'Dot didn't have time and Ma was finding it difficult to give me answers. So you tell me,' he added softly.

'Oh hell,' muttered Maggie, then was silent for several moments before saying, 'Betty was really scared of him and I don't blame her. I'll tell you a little bit. He's a bully and had been hitting her but she kept quiet about it.'

'Why didn't she speak to Ma?' rasped Jared.

'She thought she wouldn't believe her.' Maggie glanced up at her brother and then away again. 'Then, after Betty had left, on coronation night he got drunk again and I'd wandered away from the street party to go and see Irene. I met Pete there. He was walking part of the way home with me because he was meeting Norm at the bus stop close to the Gianellis' house.'

'The Gianellis? Sounds Italian.'

'It is. Uncle Teddy is so prejudiced against Mr Gianelli, although he's half-Scouse. He's got a lovely tenor voice and his son, Tonio, has a really nice voice, too. They play musical instruments, as well. Me and our Betty and Dot really used to enjoy going to their house for musical evenings,' she added wistfully.

'OK!' said Jared, looking amused. 'Can we get back to the evening of the coronation?'

Maggie nodded vigorously. 'Sorry. Uncle Teddy made a show of me and got really violent. Pete tried to protect me, but he was on two sticks then, and Uncle Teddy pushed him over. Then the swine got me by the hair and was dragging me along the road. Then, thank God, Pete's brother, the policeman, who our Dot's gone out with, came along. He biffed him and arrested him for being drunk and disorderly.' A giggle escaped her. 'I wish you could have been there to see it. Anyway, he was locked up in a cell for the night and wasn't very happy the next morning. He knows for certain now that we all loathe him and want to be rid of him. I think even Mum feels the same, because she's kept Betty's whereabouts a secret from him.'

Jared's frown deepened. 'So how did Betty find out about Emma?'

Maggie told him some of what had taken place last year, and by the time she had finished they had arrived home. 'Are you going to have words with Uncle Teddy when we get in?' she asked, her eyes gleaming in the lamplight.

'I'll have more than words to say to him,' said Jared grimly, sensing that his sister had not been completely honest with him. But he would have it out with his uncle before the night was out.

But when they went indoors, Elsie was all alone, staring at the television screen. 'Where's Teddy?' asked Jared harshly.

Elsie looked at him and Maggie and he saw fear in her eyes. 'So you found her. What's she been saying to you?'

'Enough to make me want to give that husband of yours a punch on the nose to start with,' answered Jared, clenching his fist. 'Where is the cowardly swine?'

'He went back to the pub when I told him you were home,' said Elsie, her voice quivering. 'And perhaps that's just as well, because I really can't cope with more violence.'

Jared gazed down at her and then touched her face, where there was a fresh bruise. 'He's been hitting you as well, hasn't he, Ma? Why the hell didn't you report him to the police?'

'The neighbours would all be talking about us. It was bad enough when Betty ran away,' she said.

Jared swore and left the house without another word. He was determined to find his uncle and give him the hiding of his life. But Jared never reached the White House pub, because coming along Sefton Road was his sister, Dorothy. He hadn't expected to see her this early and stopped in front of her.

'Something wrong?' he asked, gazing into her miserable face.

'He didn't turn up.' Her voice cracked on the words.

'What! He must be mad to let you down!'

'Oh, he sent a message,' she said. 'A sudden police emergency with them needing extra men.'

'I'm sorry, our kid,' he said, putting his arm

around her. 'But at least he let you know and he'll probably be in touch.'

'I know,' she murmured. 'But then some bloke tried it on as I was standing there and it really shook me up. He was drunk and I thought he was going to get violent. Fortunately the doorman realised what was going on and stepped in.' Dorothy clutched her brother's arm. 'Don't go telling Mum. She'll blame me for the way I dress and for putting on a bit of lippy, when it's nothing to do with that.'

'Of course I won't tell her.'

She looked relieved and managed a smile. 'So where are you going?'

'To have a few bloody words with Uncle Teddy for using my family as punchbags,' said Jared, drawing in his breath with a hiss. 'I don't get Ma! What did she ever see in him after being married to someone like Dad? I remember Uncle Teddy clouting me across the head when I was a kid and smaller than him. I told her, but she said I must have done something to deserve it. He never did it again once I grew bigger, though.'

'He sweet-talked her. Remember how his visits started after Aunt Lizzie was killed? He'd come and be as nice as pie to Mum, take her to the pictures and bring her flowers,' said Dorothy. 'Well, she knows now that she made a mistake. Aunt Lizzie would have told her not to marry him because she had his measure and never wanted him in the house.'

'Ma was moaning about Aunt Lizzie, saying that she made her marry Uncle William. Do you remember him?' asked Jared.

'Yes. You will, of course.'

'I remember him talking about his family before the war, and how during the last century they'd originally come from a small village near Clitheroe, when the factory closed down,' said Jared. 'Apparently his great-grandfather did well here. Then, didn't William go and marry a lass from the same village after meeting her in Liverpool?'

Dorothy smiled. 'Go on. What else did he tell you?'

'That he had a daughter who lived with her grandparents. He'd painted a picture of this toddler and I asked who she was. I saw quite a few of his paintings. I know Aunt Lizzie sold some, and one was exhibited in the Walker Art Gallery in Liverpool.' Jared's brow puckered in thought. 'I wonder what happened to the rest? Went up in smoke during the war, perhaps.'

Dorothy stared at him wide-eyed. 'The toddler, of course, was Emma. I wish you'd told me.'

'Ma told me that there was no point in raking up the past.' Jared frowned. 'She lied to me. Why?'

'I don't know,' said Dorothy.

She was about to say *Let's ask her,* when Jared said, 'Guess who's coming along the road towards us right now.'

'Uncle Teddy?'

'Yeah. You stay here.'

Jared took off.

He knew the moment his uncle saw him because he did a double take, crossed the road and beetled off in the opposite direction, disappearing up one of the roads on the other side. It was surprising how swiftly he could move for a man so small in stature.

Dorothy had ignored her brother's order and followed him, and now she seized his arm. 'Do you think it's worth going after him? There's people about and they might look at the height of you and the size of him, and not knowing what it's all about, give you hassle. You know how he can rouse people's sympathy.'

Only too well, thought Jared angrily. 'OK! I'll wait until he sneaks into the house when he thinks we're all in bed,' he said.

Dorothy smiled. 'I've a better idea. Bolt the doors. Let him sleep outside.'

Jared grinned. 'Maggie told me about his locking you out on New Year's Eve.'

'What else did she tell you?'

Jared told her as they retraced their steps and headed home. When they arrived there, it was to find downstairs deserted, but no sooner had Dorothy put the kettle on, Maggie came into the kitchen in her pyjamas. 'What happened? Where's Uncle Teddy?' she asked.

'He saw Jared coming and beat it,' said Dorothy. 'Mum gone to bed?'

'Yes. She said that she couldn't face any more talk tonight.'

'Well, Jared is going to bolt the doors, so there won't be any violence,' said Dorothy, a smile lurking in her eyes.

Maggie grinned. 'Let's hope Uncle Teddy doesn't wake the whole neighbourhood when he discovers he's been locked out.' She yawned. 'I'm going back to bed. I've got a library book I want to finish.'

Dorothy made some cocoa and wondered how to tell Jared what else they suspected their uncle of doing to Betty. But the words wouldn't come, and as she thought her brother's features were looking drawn, she decided to give talking a rest for now. They both went to bed shortly after.

Sunday dawned bright and sunny but there was no sign of Teddy waiting outside on the doorstep to be let in. 'Not really surprising,' said Dorothy. 'Perhaps he decided to stay away.'

A disappointed Jared agreed. As for their mother, she looked relieved, and an hour or so later she went off to St Philip's Church with Maggie, leaving Dorothy to put the Sunday joint in the oven and to prepare the vegetables.

Jared watched her whilst having a second cup

of tea. 'So what's your opinion of Emma Booth?' he asked.

'I like her. She's friendly and really cares about Betty. The countryside is lovely round about where she lives and she's working hard to make a little business out of having a tea room in her cottage during the fine weather. She's a smashing cook and also does part-time work as a bookkeeper.'

'Maggie told me you'd been up there,' said Jared.

'Yes. I went with Dougie and our Maggie, but we didn't spend much time with Emma because her best friend's mother had just died and she'd done the catering at her place.' Dorothy put the potatoes in a pan of salted water and then faced her brother again. 'When are you starting work?'

'I've a week off. I was thinking of maybe going up to Emma Booth's place. I'd like to meet her and I'd enjoy some country air.'

'Betty's up there right now,' said Dorothy. 'She could come back with you. If I wasn't working, I wouldn't mind joining you.'

'Another time,' said Jared. 'No doubt Betty will be visiting Emma again before the year's out.'

'It's possible that Emma will come to Liverpool around Christmas, like she did last year. If Uncle Teddy stays away, then she could come here.'

'I'm hoping he'll come back,' said Jared, drumming his fingers on the table. 'I want to have it out with him.'

But Teddy did not arrive home that day or the next. Elsie insisted on Jared visiting Teddy's favourite drinking haunts with her and they spoke to the men who knew him but drew a blank. None of them seemed to know where he had gone.

'You've obviously put the wind up him,' said Elsie when they arrived back home that evening.

'He's terrified of what Jared will do to him because he's acted like a monster,' said Dorothy, yawning.

Maggie glanced up from reading the *School Friend*. 'Perhaps he'll never come back and our Betty will feel safe here again.'

'Perhaps she's happier where she is,' said Elsie.

'I'll find out, shall I?' said Jared. 'If you all think you'll be all right for a couple of days, I'd like to take a trip into the countryside.'

Dorothy suddenly remembered the birthday present she'd asked Mr Ashcroft to make for her brother. 'I think I'll take a day off and come with you,' she said.

CHAPTER TWENTY-ONE

'How much is that doggie in the window?' sang Betty, as she shovelled more dead leaves onto the bonfire.

'It amazes me,' said Emma, leaning on the yard brush, 'how a song like that can have topped the charts this year.'

'Well, there are probably robbers around with flashlights that shine in the dark.' said Betty, smiling across at her half-sister. 'And Lita Roza wants her lover not to be lonely.' She took a deep breath of smoky air and coughed. 'Gosh, it's great being out in the fresh air in the country,' she croaked. 'I just hope that we don't get any really nasty fog in Liverpool this winter or I'll end up with a bad chest. Did you know that Lita Roza is a Liverpudlian? She was the first female artiste to top the charts. It says something about us Liverpudlians as performers, doesn't it? Frankie Vaughan is another one born in Liverpool, just like me and you.'

'I know that,' said Emma, gazing fondly at Betty, relieved to see her so happy. 'You've reminded me, I must get round to visiting the registry office on Gambier Terrace next time I visit you,' she added.

'I could do it for you,' said Betty.

Emma was about to say that she'd enjoy finding the information out for herself when a voice called, 'Anybody there?'

Emma started and turned to see Dorothy walking across the grass towards them. She was not alone but accompanied by a man who seemed vaguely familiar.

'I've brought a visitor,' said Dorothy, smiling. 'Emma, this is my brother, Jared.'

Before Emma could greet him, Betty shot past her and flung herself at him. 'Oh, I'm so glad you're home,' she cried. 'If only you'd never gone away.'

He hugged her to him and grinned down at her. 'But I'm back now, so there's nothing for you to worry about,' said Jared.

Emma smiled as she watched them, pleased to see Jared Gregory in close-up. She noticed that his fine-boned face was tanned and just as attractive as Betty had told her, with a straight nose and a firm chin. Suddenly he winked at her and she felt herself grow warm, conscious that his eyes seemed to be taking in her appearance from head to toe in one sweeping glance. She felt a tingle down her spine and was glad she was looking halfway decent in a pair of brown slacks and a Fair Isle jumper that she had knitted herself.

'I love the smell of a bonfire,' he said, over Betty's head. 'I hope you don't mind us surprising you like this, but I wanted to see Betty and to meet you, as well.' He untangled himself from Betty's embrace and held out a hand. 'I've heard a lot about you, Emma Booth.'

'I could say the same about you,' she said, smoothing a hand over her untidy hair and then wiping her hand on the seat of her slacks, before holding it out to him.

Immediately, it was swallowed up in a grip that was strong and firm, if slightly rough-skinned. 'I'm glad to meet you at last,' he said. 'I can still see glimpses of the portrait Uncle William did of you.'

'W-what portrait?' she asked, taken aback.

'The one he painted of you as a toddler,' said Jared, continuing to hold her hand. 'I liked your father.'

'You did?' she said, delighted. 'You can't imagine how that makes me feel.'

'He was a tolerant man, prepared to put up with having a nosy, overactive nephew in his studio.'

She beamed at him. 'I never expected this when Betty and Dorothy talked about you. Do come inside. You must be hungry, I'll get you something to eat.'

'That's just what I was hoping you'd say,' said Jared, gazing down at their hands and slowly releasing his hold on her fingers. 'I've heard all about your cooking . . . your hotpot, your scones and jams. I couldn't wait to get here.'

The colour deepened in Emma's cheeks. 'You don't want to believe everything you hear.' Her eyes twinkled up at him. 'We all have our off days.'

'Harrumph!' said Betty, staring at both of them. 'I think you've forgotten about me. Can I get a look in? I'd like another hug.'

Jared switched his attention to his cousin and held out his arms to her. She went into them and he hugged her and murmured something in her ear that made her smile. Emma felt an unexpected pang of envy.

Dorothy whispered, 'You can see why he's popular with the female members of our family, can't you? He's just like Dad, doesn't have a grumpy bone in his body. It's just so good to have him home and all in one piece.'

'Let's go and put the kettle on,' said Emma.

They went up the garden to the house and Emma

kicked off her old shoes just inside the kitchen and padded across the floor in her stocking feet to deal with the kettle. She washed her hands and asked, 'What does he know about Betty?'

'Not all of it. Without Betty confirming my suspicions, I decided to keep quiet about it for now,' said Dorothy, removing her gloves and holding her hands out to the fire. 'Uncle Teddy has gone off, by the way. He took one look at Jared and made a run for it. That was on Saturday and we haven't seen him since. We've looked in a few of the pubs, but there's been no sign of him.'

'Have you reported him missing?' asked Emma.

'In the circumstances, no,' answered Dorothy. 'We're hoping he'll stay away and never come back.'

'Perhaps he's had an accident and has no identification on him and is dead,' said Betty from the doorway. They turned and looked at her. She smiled. 'Jared's just told me that Uncle Teddy's run away. I hope he's as frightened of our Jared as I was of him.'

'You know what this means, Betty,' said Dorothy, smiling. 'You can come back and live at home.'

Betty hesitated. 'I know it costs money, but I do like my little nest at the top of the house in Gambier Terrace. I'm close to college and, living in town, I feel as if I'm at the centre of things. I'll be seventeen in November, and with Christmas coming up, I should be able to get more hours working in a shop, so will be able to deal with some of my living expenses.'

Jared exchanged glances with his sister. 'Perhaps it's best for Betty to stay where she is for now.' He switched his attention to Emma. 'I thought she could come back with us and I'll be able to see where she's staying.'

'But I'm not going back until tomorrow,' said Betty, glancing at Emma. 'Isn't that right? You're prepared to put up with me until then.'

Jared leant against the wall and folded his arms. 'Let's think about this. Dot's got to go back this evening because she can't afford to take another day off work. But I don't, because I don't start work until next Monday. If there's an inn or a B&B where I can stay, then—?'

'You can stay here,' interrupted Betty eagerly. 'Can't he, Emma? I can sleep with you in the double bed and he can have the single in the back room.'

There was a silence.

Jared stared at Emma. 'What do you say?' he asked.

She felt her cheeks warm again under his scrutiny. 'I don't see why not. You're family after all.' To hell with her reputation, she thought.

'That's settled then,' said Dorothy cheerfully. 'I don't mind travelling back on my own. I can read my magazine in peace.' She paused. 'Right now, I wouldn't mind taking a walk to the Ashcrofts' place. Mr Ashcroft has something for me.'

'Who's Mr Ashcroft?' asked Jared.

'You'll find out later,' said Dorothy, winking at Emma and heading for the door.

'I'll go with her, shall I?' said Betty hastily. 'I haven't seen her for a couple of weeks and there's something I need to tell her.'

She did not wait for their response but followed her cousin out. The door closed behind her, leaving a silence that, to Emma, felt loaded with expectation. She wasted no time occupying herself in making tea and putting jam on scones.

'I like these walls,' Jared surprised her by saying.

She glanced over at him and saw that he was running his hand over the peeling paint on the outside wall. 'The whole place needs decorating,' she said.

'This wall needs more than decorating,' he said. 'They built them strong in those days, but I reckon you need a damp course put in here. Your plasterwork definitely needs redoing.'

'I wouldn't deny it,' she murmured. 'Of course, with you being in the building trade, you'll be interested in buildings.'

He nodded. 'Being a plasterer wouldn't have been my first choice of job, though, but my dad was a brickie and he told me that I should become a plasterer. He had it mind that, one day, we'd be in business together with a plumber friend of his. Only Dad became ill and everything went for a burton. As it turned out, there was much more to my apprenticeship as a plasterer than I thought there'd be.'

She looked at him with interest. 'What do you mean?'

He pulled out a chair and hitched up his black corduroys and sat down. She was aware that he was watching her as she went over to the dresser and took down two plates. There was that tingle down her spine again.

'There's more to plastering than just plastering walls,' he replied. 'The journeyman plasterer who taught me helped repair the plasterwork in St George's Hall, which was damaged during the Blitz. Plaster flowers. He'd spent his war in the artillery, coast-watching down in Kent. He has a wife and four kids and supplements his income by making decorative plaques, which he designs and paints himself. He's artistic, just like your father was.' He paused. 'Ever been to Speke Hall on the outskirts of Liverpool?'

She smiled. 'No.'

'You should. It's Elizabethan. They had time to be really creative in those days, as long as the aristocracy were paying their wages. A lot of these mansions have marvellous ceilings,' said Jared, his eyes alight with enthusiasm.

'I know what you mean,' said Emma, placing

the scones on the table in front of him. 'There's an old manor house not far from here and you can see that it was once beautiful, but sadly the whole place is looking the worse for wear now. Its last owner was killed in the war and I hear the solicitors are still looking for his next of kin.'

He nodded. 'It's a blinking shame. Trouble is, there isn't the money around at the moment to afford the repairs that are necessary. It's a time-consuming job is renovation.'

'Is that what you'd like to do? Make something that was beautiful, lovely again?' she asked.

Jared said, 'You bet. As it is, I have to be where the work and the money is. Right now, people need homes. My old boss told me that the Liverpool Corporation sites at Kirkby, Speke and Aintree represent some of the most valuable building land in the country. That's why the building industry is in competition to rebuild Liverpool.'

'That's understandable,' said Emma. 'I saw some of the devastation caused by the bombing.' She hesitated. 'You mentioned a portrait of me painted by my dad. Have you any idea what happened to it?'

'No.' Jared got to his feet and began to prowl around the room.

'How can you be so certain it was me?' asked Emma, wishing he'd keep still. She had to keep turning her head to look at him.

'He told me about you living with your grandparents in the countryside,' said Jared. 'I presume that would be here in this house. He and Aunt Lizzie hadn't been married long. I saw some of his other pictures. They were mainly seascapes. He told me that one he had painted of shipping in the Mersey had won some prize and been bought by the council and put on display in Liverpool's Walker Art Gallery.'

Emma felt a swell of pride. 'Honestly?'

He glanced over his shoulder at her. 'You really should go there and see if they've hung it back up again.'

'What do you mean "back up again"?'

'The paintings were all taken away and hidden during the war; it was feared they could be destroyed in an air attack on the city,' he said, coming and standing in front of her, so close that his breath fluttered a lock of her chestnut hair. 'The building was used by the Ministry of Food during the war, issuing ration books and that kind of thing. It was only opened again in 1951 due to it needing essential reconstruction work.'

'I presume you haven't been to see if the painting is back in place, yourself?' she asked, her heart racing due to his nearness.

'Not yet.' He smiled down at her. 'Perhaps we can go there together when you're not so busy.'

'I'd like that,' said Emma. Their faces were

only inches apart and she felt quite breathless. She thought he might kiss her and wished he would. That shocked her, because it had not been so long ago that she had wanted Dougie to kiss her and believed herself in love with him.

Jared moved away and she breathed easy again. 'I'll pour the tea, shall I?' she said. 'You can help yourself to scones.'

'Thanks,' he said, smiling faintly at her.

They were silent as they ate and drank. She waited for him to pass comment on her baking, but he was gazing about the room again. She thought he was probably comparing her cottage to his own home, thinking his was much better.

Suddenly, he said, 'Would you mind showing me around after?'

Emma gave a start. 'I-I don't mind at all. I'd need to show you where you're sleeping, anyway. S-so what do you think of my scones?' she added.

Jared smiled. 'I wouldn't have eaten most of them if I didn't think they were a bit of all right. Lovely fruity jam and the pastry nice and light.'

Emma was relieved because she had done something that he liked. 'Betty and I picked the blackberries only a few weeks ago.'

'I remember blackberrying during the war. I was evacuated to Anglesey for a while. The farmer's wife used to make blackberry jam but it wasn't as good as yours.'

Emma murmured, 'All compliments gratefully accepted.'

'You'd make some lucky man a good wife. Although, I suppose with your running your tea shop as well as doing bookkeeping, you're not really looking for a husband.'

'No – not actively looking,' said Emma, picking up the crockery and carrying it over to the sink.

'Let me wash up.' said Jared, getting to his feet.

'No!' She sounded shocked. 'Men don't wash dishes in this house.'

'I washed many a crock whilst in the army.'

'Well, you're not washing any here,' said Emma firmly, putting in the plug and running water. 'If you need the lavatory, by the way, it's outside. I haven't got a posh bathroom like you have at home.'

'I didn't expect you to have,' said Jared, sounding amused. 'This is a two-up, two-down, isn't it, luv? No room for a bathroom, unless you built on.'

She glanced over her shoulder at him. 'I would love to build on. You've seen the size of the garden. There's plenty of space but I don't have the money. They weren't too fussy about hygiene and cleanliness when this was built. Growing food was more important, hence the large garden. I'd love a bathroom and a bigger kitchen with all mod cons. I could do with a fridge. I'm fussy about cleanliness. I have to be if I'm handling food and serving customers. Did Dorothy tell you that I also sell souvenirs for the tourist trade?' She realised that she was babbling.

'What kind of goods?' he asked, looking only mildly interested.

'Go in the front room and have a look. I'll be finished here in a few minutes and then I'll show you upstairs.'

He left her at the sink and went into the front room. A few minutes later she found him tinkering with the piano. 'Do you play?' she asked.

Jared rose from the stool. 'Self-taught. You?'

'Granddad was all in favour of my learning to play, but I'm not brilliant.' Emma put down the lid and stared at him. 'So what do you think of Mr Ashcroft's models and my wise women?'

He smiled. 'Different. But this room is north-facing, and with winter coming on, they could get damp. It's obvious to me that you live mainly in the kitchen, so you'd be better moving them into there.'

Emma agreed. 'They'll make the kitchen look even more crowded, though.' She sighed. 'I really do need an extension, but expense is the problem. I've been able to put aside enough money to repair the roof before winter but that's all.' She sighed.

Jared raised an eyebrow. 'Your roof leaks?'

'When it rains the water plinks into the bucket

and almost plays a tune,' she said with a wry smile.

'Let's have a look,' he said.

'The room where you'll sleep is the worst,' said Emma, leading the way upstairs, conscious of his closeness on the narrow stairs.

She opened the door of the back room and indicated that he should go in first. His eyes were instantly drawn to the damp patch in the corner of the ceiling. 'I'll get the materials and come back later in the week and fix the roof for you,' he said.

'You mean it?' she asked, taken aback.

'I wouldn't have said it if I didn't mean it,' said Jared.

'But you're not a roofer.'

'No, but I helped out on various jobs during my apprenticeship. If you've a ladder, I'll take a look at the roof in the morning.'

Her face lit up. 'It's behind the shed.'

He crossed to the window and gazed out. 'I see you keep hens.'

'Aye, I'll probably have one for Christmas.'

He grinned. 'I remember Ma plucking a chicken for Christmas. I was tormenting my sister with one of its claws. You know there's a sinew you can pull on that makes the claw move?'

'Aye!' She laughed. 'You must have been a terrible brother.'

His eyes twinkled. 'I chased Dorothy all around

the house with it. You ask her about it. I bet she hasn't forgotten.'

There was a sudden silence and they stood there, looking at each other. Then he said, 'Are you going to show me the front bedroom?'

'Sorry, I was thinking of something else.' She led him across the tiny landing and opened the door of the main bedroom.

'Now, this is a good size,' he said, going inside.

'There's a tiny room just off it, no bigger than a decent-sized cupboard,' she said, crossing the wooden floor and opening a door. 'It's just big enough to take a baby's cot.'

He gazed at the space, nodded and then said, 'You probably slept here when you were a toddler.'

'Most probably so did my mother, and my uncles who were killed in the Great War,' said Emma, feeling very conscious of those who had lived in this house.

'Let's not get miserable,' said Jared, as if reading her mind. 'What do you do with yourself in winter?'

'I work, I knit and I sew and I go to the cinema and to church and to concerts and dances put on at the assembly rooms. I have neighbours and a close friend, Lila.'

He smiled. 'So you keep yourself busy, but even so, you must get lonely now you're living on your own.'

She agreed. 'I miss Granddad, but I do have a cat.'

'I presume you don't have a broomstick, as well.'

Emma chuckled. 'Only to sweep up the leaves. I have a book of spells, though. I found it in a second-hand shop in Clitheroe, so just you be careful I don't put a spell on you.'

'I think you already have,' said Jared under his breath as he left the room.

Emma was not sure she had heard him aright but her heart felt light as she followed him downstairs. He suggested that she might want to go back to burning her garden rubbish and offered to help her.

She said with mock seriousness, 'I never turn down a willing volunteer.'

So it was that Dorothy and Betty found the two of them in the garden, working in companionable silence. 'Did you get what you wanted?' asked Jared.

'Yes,' said Dorothy, smiling as she held out a box to him. 'Your birthday present. I hope you like it.'

'I'll need to wash my hands before I look at it,' he said, obviously pleased.

The three girls watched him take the model sailing ship from the box. Instantly, Emma knew from his expression that he liked it. He didn't say so right away, just as he hadn't done about her scones, but inspected the model and then nodded. 'Clever.

373

This will have pride of place in my own home one day. I must thank the man who did it.'

'Mr Ashcroft would really appreciate that,' said Dorothy. 'By the way,' she added, glancing at Emma, 'Dougie visited them, you know?'

'No, I didn't know,' said Emma, surprised.

'A few weeks ago. He had a couple of orders for models from some of the bobbies at the station.' Dorothy added lightly, 'He never said anything about it to me when we bumped into each other and he asked me to go dancing.'

'Perhaps he'd forgotten,' said Emma, suspecting Dorothy was hurt that Dougie had not done so.

Dorothy shrugged. 'It doesn't matter,' she said.

Emma changed the subject. 'You must be hungry. I'll make us something to eat before you have to catch your train.'

Soon there was a tantalising smell of something frying.

'What is it you're cooking?' asked Jared, peering over her shoulder.

'Nothing exciting,' said Emma, her face flushed with the heat from the range. Her chestnut hair hung in wisps about her ears. 'It's just bread dipped in a mixture of egg, milk, onion and cheese.'

'The way to a man's stomach,' murmured Dorothy. 'I really should get you to teach me to cook, Emma.'

'Never mind about that,' said Betty, setting the

table. 'What did Jared have to say about our dad?'

Emma gave her a smiling glance. 'He told me that one of Dad's paintings won a prize and used to hang in the Walker Art Gallery in Liverpool.'

'What! Our dad's famous!' Betty put down the knives and forks and did a dance around the kitchen.

'Stop acting daft,' said Dorothy, laughing as she grabbed her arm and pushed her onto a seat. 'You're frightening the cat.'

Betty gazed at her cousins and Emma from dazed eyes. 'I'm the daughter of a real artist and nobody can take that away from me. Wait until I tell them at college. I feel that everything is just going to get better from now on.'

Over their meal, Betty bombarded Jared with questions about William Booth. Emma listened with close attention to everything else that he had to say, learning much about her father that was of interest. She had never known, for instance, that he had worked in a theatre, painting scenery, and it was there that he had met her mother.

Soon after they had finished eating, Dorothy said that it was time for her to make a move. The others decided to accompany her to the railway station. She hugged the three of them.

'I'll tell Mum to expect you tomorrow night, Jared,' she said.

'OK!'

He, Emma and Betty waited until the train pulled out, before leaving the station and returning to the cottage.

When Dorothy arrived home, she was relieved to find Elsie and Maggie sitting on the sofa together, watching television. Dorothy went to speak but her mother put her finger to her lips, so Dorothy went and put the kettle on before sitting in an armchair and staring at the screen. It was at least ten minutes before the programme finished and by then Dorothy had made the tea.

'So how did things go?' asked Elsie, lighting a cigarette.

'Jared and Emma really took to each other. He's staying there tonight and coming back to Liverpool with Betty tomorrow.'

Elsie said, 'You mean he's staying at the cottage?'

'Yes. Betty will sleep with Emma and he'll have the back room,' said Dorothy, amused by her mother's expression. 'There'll be no hanky-panky, Mum. Emma's not that sort of person.'

'Will you keep your voice down, remember who's here!' Elsie jerked her head in her other daughter's direction, who was toasting a round of bread on the fire.

'Oh, Mother!' sighed Dorothy. 'She's not a child. Anyway, has there been any sign of Uncle Teddy?'

'No.' Elsie frowned, and lowering her voice,

asked, 'Did Betty say anything about you-know-what?'

Dorothy whispered, 'I mentioned it to her when we were on our own. She said that if I had half a brain I'd know who it was and she was thinking of knitting a little doll of Uncle Teddy and sticking pins in it.'

'What!' exclaimed Elsie. 'That's voodoo, isn't it?'

Dorothy arched her eyebrows. 'Never mind that! She's as good as admitted he was responsible.'

'But that's witch country up there, and you don't mean to tell me that it doesn't brush off on people,' said her mother.

'Don't be daft, Mum,' said Dorothy, exasperated. 'You should meet Emma and you'd realise what a nice person she is.'

'I've written to her. Let that be enough,' said Elsie, flicking ash into the fire. 'I'd feel embarrassed meeting her after keeping quiet about her all these years and ignoring her letters.'

'But you wrote to her during the summer,' put in Maggie, who had been listening. 'It would be a really nice gesture if you invited her to stay at Christmas.'

'Christmas!' exclaimed Elsie, aghast. 'You must be joking.'

'What's wrong with Christmas?' asked Dorothy, kicking off her shoes. 'If Uncle Teddy continues to stay away, we could have a really good time. See what our Jared has to say when he comes home. I'm sure he'll be in favour of it.'

'She still mightn't want to come,' muttered her mother.

'I'm certain Emma has a forgiving nature.'

'Then she must take after her father,' said Elsie. 'I'll tell you what. I'll think about it.'

CHAPTER TWENTY-TWO

Emma stood, holding the ladder, gazing up at Jared as he descended. Her expression relaxed and she moved aside as he reached the bottom.

'Well?' she asked.

He dusted his hands on the back of his trousers and nodded slowly. 'I should be able to manage it.'

'That's a relief. Do you have any idea of how much the materials will cost, so I can give you the money before you leave today?'

'I'm not short,' he said, lifting the ladder and balancing it on his shoulder. 'You can pay me when the job's done.'

'Are you sure?' Emma hurried round to the other end of the ladder and got a hold on it. 'How are you going to get the materials here? Will you be coming on the train with them? I suppose we could have ordered them locally,' she said, trying to keep up with him as he made for the shed.

'You'd pay more. My boss will give me a discount and he'll probably lend me one of the work vans,' said Jared.

'You can drive?'

'Yep. I learnt when I was eighteen so I could ferry material from the yard to different sites. I'm thinking of buying my own car soon.'

Betty, who had been feeding the hens, chimed in, 'That would be useful. Don't you find it peaceful here, Jared? And it's lovely in summer.'

Jared put down the end of his ladder and eased the rest of it over his shoulder, dragging it rung by rung as Emma released her hold on the other end. 'Do you walk the fells, Emma?' he asked.

She eased her back and met his gaze. 'I used to when Granddad was alive, but I haven't done so since he died. My weekends have been taken up trying to get the tea room off the ground during the best of the weather.'

'But at this time of year, surely you'll have the time?' he asked, holding her gaze.

'If the weather is fine, but it can get pretty nasty during the winter up on Pendle,' she said, wanting to be honest with him. This, despite thinking it would be great to have him visiting her and going for walks together. She imagined them coming back from a day out in the fresh air on a crisp, cold, sunny winter's day and having a hot meal together in front of the fire.

Betty interrupted, 'But you don't have to go to Pendle for a bit of peace and quiet, you can get that here. It's just what us townies need every now and again.'

Jared agreed. It really was peaceful at the moment, despite the hens squabbling over the last of the chicken feed. There was the distant sound of the River Calder running over the rocks, and sheep bleating, the smell of woodsmoke and damp vegetation. He found it difficult to imagine Emma in a different setting. He had only known her for twenty-four hours and yet he wanted to marry her, but that would mean taking her away from here to the city, where his work was.

Emma sighed and then said abruptly, 'How about us going for a walk before you two have to catch the train?'

Betty glanced up at the sky. 'It looks like it might rain.'

'A bit of rain won't harm us,' said Emma.

'I'm game,' said Jared, smiling down at her.

They headed towards the house and Emma put on an old waterproof of her grandmother's and tied a scarf around her head.

Jared grinned at her. 'I don't suppose you've a waterproof that would fit me?'

Emma's heart lifted at the sight of that smile of his; she must look a sight, dressed as she was. Oh, she really did like him! 'You can borrow Granddad's. I never did get round to getting rid of it when I sold the rest of his clothing.'

He reached for the waterproof and put it on and found it too short in the arms. 'I bet I look like a scarecrow,' he said with a wry smile. 'All I need is a battered hat and some straw sticking out of my neck and sleeves.'

Emma giggled. 'We'll find a field to put you in and see if you frighten the birds.'

'Stop messing about, you two,' said Betty with mock severity, 'and let's be on our way. I want to be back in Liverpool before dark.'

Emma had a sudden idea as they set off along the road. 'Let's go and see Mr Ashcroft, Jared. You said that you wanted to meet him.'

'That's fine with me,' said Betty. 'I like Mr Ashcroft.'

As they left the village behind she showed Jared where she went blackberrying in the autumn. 'I must give you a pot of jam to take home for your mother,' she said. 'Food for free, that's what my grandmother used to say every time we went blackberrying,' she added, filled with a sense of well-being as she strode along beside Jared. 'Granddad used to say it wasn't true. We put time and effort into picking the blackberries and we ended up with purple-stained fingers and tiny, irritating prickles in our skin.'

'I've been blackberrying in my time. Ma insisted on us all going after Dad died. We went along the canal, loads of berries there.'

She looked at him and caught an expression in his eyes that caused her heartbeat to quicken. 'I'll have to enlist your help next year when it's jam-making time,' she said boldly.

'I'll be glad to be of service,' he said, with the slightest of bows.

'Will you two stop talking and do more walking or we'll never get there,' said Betty over her shoulder. 'I reckon it could rain any minute now.'

She was right.

The heavens opened and the rain sheeted down. 'We'd better make a run for it,' cried Emma, putting on a spurt.

It did not take them long to reach the Ashcrofts' house. Emma spotted Jack's face at the window and he signalled that they went round the back. The three of them hurried round the side of the house and in through the kitchen door and hung their waterproofs on the hooks there.

'Are you all right?' called Mr Ashcroft.

'Aye, we're coming through,' said Emma.

She led the way and was glad to see that there was a fire burning in the grate. She thought Lila's father looked worried. 'Are you OK, Mr Ashcroft?'

she asked with concern. 'Would you like me to make you a cup of tea?'

'Aye, thanks, lass. I'm just a bit worried about our Lila and Dougie.'

'Dougie Marshall's up here?' she asked, remembering what Dorothy had said yesterday about his having visited and not mentioned it.

'Aye. He'd arranged to come last time he was here and so our Lila took the day off. He's bought a blinking motorbike and has taken her over to Pendle. In this weather the mist could come down and the pair of them could get lost.'

'How long ago is it since they left the house?' asked Jared.

'Several hours,' replied Jack. 'You must be Dorothy's brother.'

Jared said that he had that pleasure and Emma vanished into the kitchen to make tea. She wondered what Dougie was playing at, supposedly going dancing with Dorothy and letting her down and then coming up here and taking Lila out on a motorbike up to Pendle. Of course, as far as she knew, he'd made no promises to either one. It was a good job that she, herself, had got over the crush she'd had on him.

Betty suddenly appeared at Emma's elbow. 'Mr Ashcroft asked could you make him a sandwich. He also offered us something to eat, as well. What do you think? We don't want to eat him out of house and home because he's not well off, is he?'

'No, luv, he isn't. The trouble is that he might feel insulted if we refuse his offer,' said Emma. 'We don't have to eat much.'

They made some sandwiches and took them in. Jared was frowning as he listened to Jack Ashcroft. Shortly after, Jared drew Emma aside. 'It seems to me as if your friend, Dougie, is two-timing my sister. I'll have something to say when I see him.'

Emma said, 'I know how you feel but don't create a scene, Jared! It's obvious both have something that he likes and he can't make up his mind between them.'

Jared glowered. 'Maybe not, but I wouldn't behave the way he does towards you and I only met you yesterday. I can tell you now, Emma, I feel like I've known you for ages.'

She felt a warm glow inside. 'I feel the same,' she said, touching his hand. 'But be that as it may, people are different, Jared. Because of his mother and brothers, Dougie might be in no rush to make up his mind when it comes to choosing the girl he'd like to spend the rest of his life with.'

She had no sooner finished speaking than there came the roar of an engine outside, growing ever closer. The next moment Jared had left her and was out of the house. 'No, wait,' she called, and followed after him.

She heard the engine cut out and then a skidding

sound and a crash. She ran and came out onto the road to find Jared flat on his back and Dougie a couple of feet away, gazing down at the motorbike on the ground, its wheels still spinning. She wondered where Lila was and then saw her picking herself up off the road. She seemed OK, so Emma gave all her attention to Jared.

She knelt on the ground, 'Are you all right?' she asked anxiously, kneeling on the damp ground beside him. He opened his eyes and winced. 'Thank God, you're not dead,' she said.

He reached up and brought her head down and kissed her. 'What was that for?' she asked, lifting her head.

'It seemed the right thing to do to reassure you that I was very much alive,' he said, smiling.

'Dafty,' she said, returning his smile. 'Can you get up?'

'Of course I can, but no thanks to him,' said Jared, scowling in Dougie's direction. Jared got to his feet and said, 'You're a bloody fool!'

'Sorry. I didn't see you there,' said Dougie, having removed his goggles.

'Have you forgotten about me?' asked Lila, coming up behind him.

Dougie turned and smiled at her. 'You're a game girl. You've enjoyed today, haven't you?'

'Aye, but I'm not sure about the motorbike. It's a dangerous contraption and you should get 'rid of it,' she said, a tremor in her voice.

'But, Lila! I bought it so I could come and see you more often,' he said, looking dismayed.

'That's very flattering,' she said, rubbing her bottom. 'But you were plain daft coming down the hill at that speed with the road wet. We could have both been killed.'

'But we weren't,' said Dougie unnecessarily.

'No, but we could have been, and who would have looked after me dad then?' said Lila, who was looking a mess. Her clothes and boots were sodden and there was a smear of mud across her pretty face.

'I'm sorry,' said Dougie.

'So you should be,' she retorted. 'I'm going in and you can go home.'

'Go home!' exclaimed Dougie. 'You're not serious?'

'Of course I'm serious,' said Lila, shivering. 'See you another time, maybe.' She limped past him and paused in front of Emma and Jared. 'I suppose you're Jared,' she said.

'That's right.' His tone was brusque.

Lila said, 'I'm sorry you were knocked down. Dorothy told me you were here. Have you been inside?' She jerked her head in the direction of the house.

'Your dad was a bit worried about you, Lila,' said Emma. 'We'll be leaving now you're here.'

Lila sighed. 'He would, wouldn't he? I don't

know what I'm going to do about him and Dougie.'

'We'll leave you to it,' said Emma hastily. 'We'll just get our waterproofs and be on our way. Jared and Betty have to go back to Liverpool today.'

Lila nodded and limped up the path.

'Lila, wait!' shouted Dougie, going after her. 'I'll get rid of the motorbike. I'll do anything to please you. I love you. I want to marry you.'

Lila stopped, turned round and stared at him from wide eyes. 'Y-you want to marry me?' she stammered.

'Yes!'

'B-but what about my dad?'

'I'll marry him, too,' said Dougie, running his hand across his face. 'I mean he can come, too.'

'Y-you mean to Liverpool?' asked Lila in disbelief.

'There'll be more life for him there.'

'B-but where would we live? Isn't it hellish difficult to get a house in Liverpool?'

'If I get married, I can probably get a police house. Don't have to live right in the centre of the city. There are newer housing estates a bit further out,' said Dougie.

Lila's face lit up. 'I think you really mean it. OK, then . . . I mean, yes! You'd better come and talk to me dad about it.' She linked her arm through Dougie's and glanced over her shoulder at Emma and winked. 'You will be my bridesmaid, won't you?'

Emma nodded, completely flabbergasted.

Betty suddenly appeared with their waterproofs. She said something to Lila, who nodded, and then the younger girl came towards Jared and Emma. 'You coming?' she asked them.

Jared blinked and shook his head as he stared after Lila and Dougie. 'I feel like giving him a punch,' he said, 'but I suppose that's hardly civilised.'

'No,' said Emma, smiling. 'I know it's tough luck on Dorothy, but I am glad for Lila. I'm sure your Dorothy will have no trouble finding someone else.'

Jared said, 'I'm glad you don't still fancy him.'

'How can you even think that, after . . . ?' She blushed.

Jared reached for her hand. 'It really is lovely countryside around here. I can't imagine you ever wanting to leave it.'

'I'd have to have a very good reason for doing so,' said Emma, gazing up at him, knowing that it was unlikely that he'd leave Liverpool to come and live up here. He needed to be where his work was, and what would she do about her cottage? But she was thinking too far ahead to a future with a man she had only met yesterday. The way the pair of them felt about each other could just be a passing phase.

CHAPTER TWENTY-THREE

Elsie placed a bowl of scouse on the table in front of her son and then sat down opposite him. 'I thought you'd have been home earlier,' she said.

'I saw Betty back to her bedsit and then went to the yard and spoke to the boss. I needed a favour from him,' said Jared, letting out a yawn. 'I'll be going back to Emma's tomorrow. Her roof's leaking and I promised I'd fix it for her.' He reached for the bottle of HP sauce and unscrewed the top.

'That's generous of you,' said Elsie, reaching for a cigarette. 'But don't forget you've got a family here who needs you.'

He frowned. 'I haven't forgotten, Ma. Has there been any sign of Teddy?'

'No, but even so, who's to say that he mightn't suddenly turn up?' said Elsie, lighting up. 'I'd prefer it if you were here when he does.'

'So would I,' said Jared, his eyes darkening.

'I don't think he's going to come back,' said Maggie.

'Wishful thinking,' said her mother, without looking at her. 'So, who does Emma look like?'

'I'd say Uncle William,' said Jared, 'but then I never met her mother. Emma has his colour hair and his eyes.'

'William had lovely brown eyes,' murmured Elsie. 'I remember he was good with you. It would have been nice for him to have had a son. His first wife was in digs with a neighbour of ours in Liverpool, you know, so we knew his first wife, Mary, before he did. Our Lizzie used to lodge with us and she and Mary got quite friendly, with our Lizzie loving the theatre and doing a bit of singing herself. Mary invited us along to the Royal Hippodrome on West Derby Road when it was still a theatre. She had a lovely singing voice and did a bit of dancing and acting, as well. We were invited backstage and that was when we met William for the first time.' She paused to have a quick puff on her cigarette before continuing. 'Our Lizzie got friendly with a member of the cast, but he was only there off and on. Like a lot of actors and actresses, he was often on tour or out of work.

It could be months before she saw him again. This went on for ages, and then one year he didn't come back.' She fell silent.

'Carry on, Mum,' said Dorothy, glancing up from filing her fingernails. 'This is really interesting. Why didn't you tell us about it before.'

Elsie's eyes narrowed and she waved the cigarette smoke away. 'Because it was the past and didn't involve you. Where was I?'

'Aunt Lizzie's bloke didn't come back,' said Maggie.

Elsie flicked ash from her cigarette. 'Well, never mind that for now. We were really talking about Emma's parents. Anyway, William married Mary but they weren't happy for very long. She had to give up the stage when she started with Emma. She resented having a baby, wasn't at all well during the pregnancy. She liked you, though. You were a good-looking little lad. You had such lovely curls and she thought you were just like the little boy in the painting of *Bubbles*. Your hair was fairer then. Strange the way it can change as one grows up.' She paused. 'Where was I?'

'Our Jared having lovely curls,' said Dorothy, smiling at her brother.

'Right. If Mary had to have a baby, she wanted a boy just like our Jared. Only she didn't have a boy, did she? She had Emma. So what did she do?'

'What?' asked Jared, listening intently.

'She couldn't cope. Still hadn't got her health back after the birth. We didn't realise then that she really was ill. Anyway, I remember our Lizzie telling me that Mary had told her that she and William had had this big row. Apparently, he wanted her to go and stay with his grandmother who had a big house in Formby within a mile of the pinewoods. But Mary wasn't having any of it, because she didn't like the old lady, so she left him and went home to her parents, taking Emma with her.'

'I think we know what happened next,' said Jared.

Elsie gave a wry smile. 'Then tell me what happened.'

'William found out where they were and he visited them, only to discover that Mary really was ill and dying. Emma's grandparents blamed him and told him to go away. He felt sorry for them because it looked like they were soon going to lose their daughter. He didn't like taking Emma from them, so he left her with them.'

'You're near-enough right,' said Elsie. 'What happened was, his grandmother also became very ill at the time and his sister was trying to cope with her all on her own. She wasn't a well woman herself. Anyway, he went and stayed with the grandmother and his sister. The old woman died and then the sister was ill and he needed to look after her. He did get in touch with Mary's parents, only to be told that she was dead.'

'I suppose that's when Aunt Lizzie tried to console him,' said Dorothy.

Elsie nodded. 'It was a difficult time for everyone, but especially William and our Lizzie.' She fiddled with her cigarette. 'Her young man, whom she hadn't seen for about two months, died of blood poisoning: caught his hand on a rusty nail in a tea chest containing stage costumes. Anyway, she and William consoled each other and were married within the year. There were rumours of war flying around even then and they only had a few years together.'

'It's a really sad story,' said Dorothy in muted tones.

'Yes,' said Elsie, sighing, 'but this century has seen a lot of sad stories and heartbreak.'

'Now I've listened to all this, Ma,' said Jared thoughtfully, 'how about inviting Emma to stay here for a weekend? I'm sure she'd be interested to hear whatever you have to tell her about her parents. It would be a good opportunity, too, to have Betty here and to break the ice, seeing as how you haven't seen her since May.'

Elsie was silent for what seemed ages to her waiting children. Then she said, 'OK, if you really believe that Emma will come.'

'I'm sure she will, if I tell her you've invited her,' said Jared positively.

Elsie took a deep breath. 'All right. You tell her that I'd like to meet her and she doesn't have to wait for Christmas as the girls suggested.'

'No?'

'No, best to get it over with,' said his mother.

'Then, how about this weekend?' urged Jared. 'I could bring her back tomorrow evening in the boss's van.'

'You don't think that's too soon?' said Elsie, suddenly looking nervous and puffing her cigarette.

'It's never too soon to make things right,' said Dorothy.

Emma was in the middle of totting up a column of figures, when she heard a knock on the back door. She got to her feet and hastened to open it. As she hoped, it was Jared. 'You're earlier than I thought,' she said, trying not to appear too overwhelmingly delighted to see him.

'That's because I want to get the job done as soon as I can,' he responded with a smile.

'You'll have a cup of tea first?' she asked.

'You should know now that builders never say no to a cup of tea.' He watched her cross the floor with a grace of movement that really pleased him. He bet that she would be a good dancer and couldn't wait to hold her in his arms. Perhaps they could go dancing tomorrow night if she agreed to come home with him. 'I've something to ask you,' he said.

Emma glanced over her shoulder. 'What is it?'

'Ma has invited you to stay for the weekend,' said Jared.

Emma's face lit up, and then her mouth drooped and she said slowly, 'That's really kind of her, but I don't think I can.'

Jared placed a hand on her shoulder. 'It won't cost you anything. I can take you in the van and bring you back. It's much quicker by road than having to change trains several times.'

'But won't it be a bother to you having to make the journey so many times in a few days?' asked Emma, hoping he would say that it was no bother at all.

'I'll have your company on two of them and I've a lot to tell you,' said Jared, squeezing her shoulder gently. 'Things that my mother told me about your parents. She was keen to talk about the past last night, and I didn't want her to stop once she got going. I won't tell you now because I must make a start on the roof. I need the daylight to work.'

'I won't keep you, then,' said Emma swiftly, despite wanting to hear what he had to tell her. 'Do you need my help with the ladder?'

'It would make it easier for me.'

She nodded, pleased that he hadn't turned her offer down. 'Can I help you get the materials out of the van, too?'

He shook his head. 'No, they'll be too heavy for you to lift and I'd rather you made the tea. I'm parched.'

He let her go and went out the back way.

After he had drunk his cup of tea, she helped him fetch the ladder and then stood at the bottom, holding it steady, while he carried all he needed up onto the roof. 'Now, Emma, you don't have to stay there,' he called down. 'Go back to doing what you were doing when I came and I'll shout for you when I need you.'

She would much rather have remained there, making certain he was all right, but she did have her own work to do, so she went indoors, having decided that she would make some warming lentil soup.

It was beginning to get dark by the time Jared finished the job, and he'd only had a short break to eat the steaming soup with a couple of slices of crusty bread. 'Best soup I've ever tasted,' he had said, placing the crockery and cutlery in the sink. 'You're good.' He had brushed his lips against hers and then went outside again.

Emma was still thinking of that kiss when he was washing his hands at the kitchen sink, promising he would come back and sort out the damage the water had made to the ceiling and wall once they had dried out, although it could take some time.

'Thanks, I really appreciate what you've done,' she said reaching for her handbag. 'How much do I owe you?'

He told her a price that appeared ridiculously low in comparison to the one she'd been quoted a few weeks ago. 'That seems really cheap,' she said. 'Are you sure you're not robbing yourself?' she asked, counting out the money.

'Not at all. As you said the other day, I'm family,' he said easily, reaching for a towel and drying his hands.

'Does your mother think of me like that?' asked Emma.

'I don't think she's thought about it,' he said, taking the money and pocketing it. 'How soon can you be ready? I'd like to be on our way as soon as possible.'

'Aren't you tired? Wouldn't you like a rest first?'

'No, what I need is a bath and I can have one of them at home.' He rolled down his shirtsleeves and buttoned them, before reaching for his jacket. 'Have you packed for the weekend yet? I hope you've included a dress suitable for dancing.'

'Dancing?' she asked, her eyes startled.

He smiled. 'I thought we could go tomorrow evening if you feel in the mood.'

'Oh, I'm sure I'll be in the mood for dancing,' she said, her eyes sparkling now. 'Just let me go and pack a dress and shoes and stockings.'

She vanished up the stairs, before he could add that in the morning they could drop by at Betty's place and see if she'd like to go to the Walker Art Gallery with them. The afternoon could take care of itself.

It was not until they were driving south along the A59 that Emma asked Jared what his mother had told him about her parents. He told her, but was careful to avoid mention of Mary resenting getting pregnant and having a daughter when she had wanted a son.

He caught the gleam in Emma's eyes as she turned her face towards him. 'I must go to the Royal Hippodrome. I'd just love to sit in the auditorium and imagine both my parents being there. Mam on the stage and Dad in the stalls admiring her.'

'We can go there tomorrow afternoon if you like,' suggested Jared. 'I thought that in the morning we could visit Betty and the three of us could go to the Walker Art Gallery and see if we can find your dad's painting.'

'Oh, Jared, I'd love to do that!' she cried, wanting to fling her arms around his neck and kiss him.

'I'm dead chuffed that you do,' he said, his voice warm with pleasure, 'because I'm really looking forward to it, myself.'

'I'm so glad that your mother decided she wanted to see me and invited me to stay,' said Emma happily.

'You tell her so, because I reckon she's still going to feel awkward about meeting you.'

'Well, I'm prepared to forgive her anything.'

'You do realise that she must have known you when you were a baby?' said Jared, aware of the flashing headlights of cars coming towards them on the other side of the road, so not looking at her.

Emma had gone very still. 'I never thought of that, but I suppose she must have. Do you think she might have an idea what happened to Dad's painting of me?'

'I could ask.'

Emma thanked him. 'I do feel sorry for your Aunt Lizzie, though. For her first sweetheart to die of blood poisoning and then for her to lose my father in the war. It must have been really tough for her.'

'She was only in her thirties when she was killed,' said Jared. 'Terrible.'

'Aye, terrible,' murmured Emma, glancing at his shadowy, lean profile and feeling a catch at her heart. It seemed impossible that she had known him only a short time. 'How different mine and Betty's lives would have been if that actor she loved hadn't caught blood poisoning. She would never have married Dad. Betty wouldn't have been born and you and I would never have met,' she said in a low voice.

'But Aunt Lizzie did and you found her letter, so

400

here we are, together,' said Jared, glancing at her.

'It must have been fate,' murmured Emma, knowing she had probably given her feelings for him away. She remembered her and Billy McElroy's conversation about love at first sight and what she'd said about a couple waiting a decent length of time before getting married, so they could really get to know each other. Yet here she was in love with Jared after only three days. She was so happy to be in his company and was already dreading Sunday when he would deliver her to her front door and leave her all alone.

Elsie looked at herself in the mirror and wished she didn't feel so depressed and nervous. Her children were being really nice to her because she was behaving in a way they wanted her to behave. They believed she had been completely honest with them about the past, but she hadn't and it lay on her conscience. Yet it would really put the cat among the pigeons if she told the whole truth. She supposed it all depended on what she, herself, thought of Emma.

At that moment there was a banging on the door. Was it Jared and Emma or had Teddy returned? Just the thought of her husband caused a sudden stabbing pain in her chest and she felt frightened, as if she was about to die.

'I'll get it,' said Maggie.

Elsie was glad that Dorothy was there although she had said that she would be going out later. She felt better having her elder daughter to help break the ice and share in the conversation in a way that Maggie couldn't. At least she did not have to face Betty this evening. She heard voices in the hall and felt a need to sit down. Yet how could she be sitting when Emma came into the room? She ought to be on her feet to greet her. She told herself the pain was nothing serious, just indigestion, and she reached for her cigarettes, only to decide that she could hardly be holding a fag either when her son introduced her to Emma. She took a deep shaky breath and pinned on a smile as Dorothy and Maggie came through the doorway, followed by Jared and a young woman with chestnut-coloured hair, an oval, pleasant face and apprehensive brown eyes.

'So here you are,' said Elsie, slightly breathless. 'I'm glad you've arrived safely.'

'Ma, this is Emma,' said Jared, smiling down at the woman at his side. 'I think you'll agree that she's changed since last you saw her.'

'You can say that again,' said Elsie, holding out a hand. 'You've got a look of your father, Emma.'

'Thank you! I'm really pleased to meet you at last, Mrs Gregory.'

'I'm sorry about the delay,' said Elsie, waving her to a chair and sitting down swiftly before her legs gave way. 'If I'd answered your first letter, I could have saved us a lot of trouble and . . . and heartache, but I did have my reasons.'

Emma smiled. 'It doesn't matter now. It's the past and we have to move on.'

'Actually it does matter,' said Elsie, surprising herself as well as her children and Emma. 'When I get to know you better, maybe we can talk about certain matters to do with your father, that my lot don't really need to know.'

'Why don't we need to know?' asked Jared, placing Emma's overnight bag on a chair.

'Never you mind,' said Elsie, placing a hand to her chest. 'Would you like something to eat, Emma?'

'No, Mrs Gregory. I'm fine. Don't put yourself to any trouble.'

'A cup of cocoa, then?' suggested Dorothy, smiling.

'Aye, I'd like that,' replied Emma, returning her smile before giving Elsie all her attention once more. 'Jared was telling me what you told him about my mother performing at the Royal Hippodrome. He's promised to take me there tomorrow.'

'You should enjoy that,' said Elsie, feeling slightly dizzy. She needed to go upstairs, getting up again and leaving the room.

Jared exchanged looks with his sister. 'Is Ma OK?'

'I think it's all a bit much for her,' said Maggie, and left the room.

'Sit down, Emma,' said Jared. 'You look tired.'

'I'm OK. Just feeling a bit strange,' she said, sitting on the sofa.

Jared sat on a chair opposite her. 'I was thinking we could go and see a film at the Hippodrome tomorrow afternoon.' He searched about him for the *Echo* and found it down the side of his chair. He looked for what was showing at the cinema tomorrow on the front page. 'It's the musical *Calamity Jane*,' he said, glancing across at Emma.

'I've heard about that,' said Emma, looking pleased.

'It stars Doris Day and Howard Keel,' said Jared.

'That's great,' said Emma. 'I like them both.'

'Then that's settled,' said Jared, folding the newspaper. 'If you don't mind, Emma, I just want to nip upstairs and see if Ma's OK.'

'Don't worry about me,' she said easily. 'I'll be fine. I'll have a word with Dorothy.'

Jared went upstairs, and as the door of his mother's bedroom was open, he went inside. He found her sitting on her bed with a box on her knee, reading what appeared to be a document. 'What have you got there, Ma?' he asked, sitting beside her.

'The deeds to the house,' she murmured.

Jared frowned. 'Why now, with Emma only just having arrived?'

'Because, seeing her, made me decide what to do,' said his mother in a voice barely above a whisper. 'I'm going to have the house signed over to you.'

'What!' exclaimed Jared.

The document shook in her hand and he reached out and placed his hand over hers. 'Calm down, Ma. Emma wouldn't like to see you upset like this. Is it that seeing her has brought back bad memories?'

Elsie swallowed. 'Something like that, and besides, I don't know when I might pop off. I'd hate Teddy to turn up at my funeral and lay claim to this house because he was still my husband,' she said in a trembling voice.

'Ma, you're not about to pop off,' said Jared firmly.

She gazed into his face, and reaching up a hand, placed it against his cheek. 'You were always a good lad. I hope you're right, but I want to do this. You're my only son and you're my eldest, too. I know you'll see the girls right, not letting them go short or be without a roof over their heads.'

'Of course I'll look after them, Ma, but don't talk like this,' he said, his face wearing a worried expression.

She patted his cheek and then dropped her hand. 'I haven't always done what's right and I want to make sure I don't make a mess of this. I'll need to see a lawyer.'

'Do you want me to get one for you?' he asked.

She got to her feet. 'No, no! I'll deal with it myself. Now you go downstairs to Emma. I'll be down in a bit.'

When Jared entered the living room, he found Maggie and Emma drinking cocoa. Maggie glanced at him. 'You'd better have yours quick, Jared, before it gets cold,' she said.

He sat down beside Emma and she handed him his mug. 'Is your mother OK?'

'She'll be down in a minute,' he replied.

Emma took that to mean that Mrs Gregory was all right. 'Maggie has just been telling me that she's convinced that her and Betty's friend Irene's stepbrother, Billy, fancies Dorothy. I'm interested because I've met him. He's the one who took me to see the bedsit with Betty.'

'What did you think of him?' asked Jared.

She gave a sleepy smile. 'He's got a lot of life in him.'

Jared turned to his sister. 'Where is our Dorothy?'

'She told me that she was going to the Gianellis'. Dot likes Mrs Gianelli and besides Billy used to work in her garden during the war, so she knows him reasonably well. She's younger than Mum and easy to talk to,' replied Maggie, kicking off her slippers and curling her feet beneath her. 'I'd love to go back there again,' she said dreamily. 'Their musical evenings were fun. D'you think, Jared, that you could ask Mum about it for me? She'll listen to you. I thought if our Betty does come tomorrow, we could go along there together.'

'OK! I'll see what I can do,' he said, seeing no harm in his sister and cousin enjoying a musical evening.

Emma stifled another yawn.

'Are you tired?' he asked, his expression softening.

'Sorry,' she said hastily. 'It's been a long day, and didn't you say that you wanted to have a bath?'

'I did.' He got up and held down a hand to her. She took it and he pulled her to her feet. 'Seeing as Ma hasn't come down yet, I'll take you up and she can show you where you're sleeping.' He picked up her overnight bag.

Emma followed him upstairs, too tired to be curious about the house that was so much larger than her cottage. Elsie suddenly appeared in a doorway. 'You ready for your bed, Emma?' she asked.

Emma nodded. 'I'm sorry, but I'm feeling really sleepy.'

'Nothing wrong with that, love,' said Elsie.

She opened a bedroom door and switched on the light. 'I hope you'll be comfortable.'

'I'm sure I will,' said Emma, gazing about her.

She noticed the pretty floral bedcover on the single bed and the Michaelmas daises in a vase on the chest of drawers. The curtains matched the bedspread.

'Our Dorothy made the curtains and bedspread,' said Elsie. 'She's quite talented that way.'

'They're very pretty,' said Emma, watching Jared place her overnight bag on a chair.

'I'm glad you like them,' said Elsie, looking relieved. 'I put a hot-water bottle in your bed earlier. I think a bit of warmth helps you to sleep when you're in a strange bed.' She hesitated before saying, 'Your dad was a good man, you know. It's a pity you didn't see more of him when you were a child.'

'I'd like to have done, but at least you've told Jared some of what you remember about him, and I appreciate that,' said Emma sincerely.

'I hope you have a good sleep,' said Elsie. 'Come on, Jared,' she added, 'let Emma get to her bed.'

Jared winked at Emma, wished her goodnight, and left her alone.

At least they were under the same roof, thought Emma, wishing she could have said a proper goodnight to him. She remembered that she needed to clean her teeth and go to the lavatory. She opened the door again and saw Jared standing on the landing, leaning against the wall.

Before she could speak, he said, 'I'll show you.'

'Fancy you guessing,' she whispered.

He led her along the landing and opened a door. Then he lowered his head and kissed her. 'I hope you sleep well.'

She reached up and put her arms around his neck and returned his kiss. 'Thank you. I hope you sleep well, too.' She went inside the bathroom and closed the door.

CHAPTER TWENTY-FOUR

'Look, see that bombed hollow,' said Jared, pointing to the stretch of derelict land, opposite the Linacre Methodist Mission, as they passed it on the bus. 'Bryant & May match works used to be there. It received a direct hit during the war. Fortunately for men like Mr Ashcroft there's another match works the other side of Liverpool,' he said seriously.

'You've reminded me about Lila,' said Emma.

'I wonder where they'll live in Liverpool? Maybe he'll get one of the houses that was built in the Thirties,' said Jared.

Emma had no idea. 'I'm more interested in when they'll get married and where. You might get invited, and if you do, will you come?' she asked.

'If you want me there,' he said, taking her hand. 'Maybe our Maggie will get invited as well, seeing as she's friendly with his brothers.'

Emma sighed. 'Irene might be invited, too, because I believe her mother knows the family.'

'This is going to be a big wedding,' said Jared dryly. 'Could be that the Gianellis will be there, too. Our Dot was in late last night. It seems she had a good night round there.' He fell silent.

'Go on,' urged Emma. 'Did you remember to ask your mother what Maggie asked you to?'

'I did.'

'And?'

Jared smiled. 'I persuaded Ma to think about going and visiting Mrs Gianelli. I told her that she had no right to judge her, when she hadn't even met the woman.'

'And what did she say?'

'That she'd think about it, but if our Dot was going round there, then she'd allow Maggie to go as long as she kept her eye on her.'

Emma was pleased. 'Good. I know Betty loved going there. I hope she'll want to visit your mum this evening.'

'So do I, but let's not worry about that now,' said Jared. 'We won't get many days out like this together once I start work.' He squeezed her hand, raised it to his lips and kissed it.

Emma sighed with sheer pleasure, enjoying the

warm secure feeling that his attention gave her. 'I hope Betty's in,' she said.

'If she's out, then we'll just have to go to the art gallery without her,' said Jared firmly. 'After all, she can go any time she likes with living in the city.'

As luck would have it, they didn't get an answer at Betty's bedsit and were told by one of the other tenants that they'd just missed her by half an hour. At any other time Emma might have suggested visiting the registry office, seeing as how they were in Gambier Terrace, but she knew that would take time up that they did not have, if they were to fit in everything they wanted to do that day. She had on her best frock but sensible shoes, having her dancing shoes in a bag.

So they made their way down past the Anglican cathedral, along the Georgian terraced houses in Rodney Street and into Leece Street, with Jared telling her some of the history of Liverpool, especially of its seafaring past and the part the School of Tropical Medicine had played in researching tropical diseases. Emma found it all very interesting and when she spotted a ruined church, tugged on Jared's arm. 'Is that St Luke's?'

Jared nodded. 'Beautiful stonework.'

'I believe it was left standing in memory of those killed in the war,' said Emma.

He nodded. 'It's a blinking shame so many fine buildings were destroyed in the bombing. I know

412

the loss of lives was worse, but even so . . .' He shrugged. 'Anyway, let's get a move-on if we want to get to the Hippodrome this afternoon. We might be tempted to spend more time in the art gallery than we planned.'

Emma had a huge lump in her throat as she stood, staring at the setting sun reflecting off the waves. She liked the way the sunlight caught the bow of a white liner, loved the fussy little tugs towing the vessel. There were other ships, whose function she had no idea about. Jared had pointed out a dredger and the pilot's boat. He told Emma how, hundreds of years ago, Chester was the more important port, but then the Dee had silted up and Liverpool had taken over that prime position. Even so, the port had problems with sand silting up the Mersey, hence the need for dredgers and the pilot boat to guide the big ships safely through the channels between the sandbanks in the river.

Emma's eyes scanned the painted blue sky with streaks of apricot-tinged clouds above the Liverpool skyline before the war. She wished that she could take the painting home and hang it on her wall, but she felt so proud when she read her father's signature in the corner of the painting, and thought it only fitting that it should be here on show in the city that he had obviously cared about.

'Don't you just love it?' said Betty's voice behind her.

Emma whirled round and smiled. 'How did you know I'd be here?'

Betty slipped her arm through Emma's. 'I didn't. I come here every day and look at it. Unfortunately I can't stay long, I just thought I'd nip in here and see it again.' Her eyes shone as she gazed at the painting. 'Doesn't it make you feel proud that our dad did this? I could look at it for ever and ever.'

'Me, too,' said Emma. 'Jared stayed for a few minutes, then he went off to have a look at some of the other paintings. I think he sensed that I might want to be alone for a while.'

'I'm glad you like each other,' said Betty, squeezing her arm.

'I really do like him. We called in at your place but you were out. I'm staying at your aunt's for the weekend and she said that you could come and stay if you wanted.' Emma smiled. 'I'm going to the pictures with Jared this afternoon and dancing this evening, so you'd have to make your own way,' she added.

Indecision flitted across Betty's face but eventually she said, 'I'm glad she's invited you there, but I couldn't go this weekend. Not only do I not feel ready to return there yet, but I've got a shift at the café and then, this evening, Irene is coming into town and I'm taking her along to meet some of the friends I've made. They've got a little music group going and we're going along to support them.'

'Sounds fun,' said Emma, thinking that, by allowing her half-sister some independence, Emma could lose Betty when she hadn't long found her. 'I'll tell Jared and explain to his mother.'

'Thanks,' said Betty, looking relieved. 'I'll have to go. I hope to see you soon, and don't forget to write.'

'Of course I won't,' said Emma.

Betty hurried away. For a few more moments, Emma continued to gaze at her father's painting, then she went in search of Jared.

When they arrived at the Royal Hippodrome, Emma saw that it was a very different building from the Majestic where she and Betty had watched *An American in Paris*. When she commented on this, Jared said, 'Different periods. The Royal Hippodrome is typical of the Victorian era when the music hall was so popular. The Majestic was built at the end of the Twenties and is art deco.'

Once they were inside, an usherette led them to a couple of seats near the back. They settled down to watch the supporting black and white feature. Emma found her mind drifting, trying to imagine the mother she only remembered as pale, sickly and bedridden, coughing up blood and complaining in a thin, reedy voice, up on the stage, singing her heart out.

Not easy.

It really wasn't until Doris Day appeared on the

screen, singing 'Secret Love', that Emma was able to transpose her mother's image onto the blonde-haired film star.

'You OK?' asked Jared in a low voice.

'Yes, just thinking,' she replied.

He reached out for her hand and she shifted a little closer to him. She could have sworn that he kissed her hair. She felt caught up in a romantic dream as the love stories on the screen culminated in a double wedding.

When they left the cinema, Jared put an arm around her and danced her over to the bus stop, bringing her to a laughing, swinging halt. They weren't the only cinema-goers to come out singing and dancing. She was reminded of that evening she and her granddad had seen Fred Astaire and Jane Powell. She thought how much he would have liked Jared and she wished they could have met.

'Good film,' said Jared, smiling down at Emma. 'Helps you to forget the horrors of war, and the atom bomb, for a while.'

Emma's brown eyes glowed. 'I love a good musical. So what are we going to do next? Surely it's a bit early to go to the dance hall?'

He smiled down at her. 'I thought we'd go for a Chinese. I bet you didn't know that there's a Chinatown in Liverpool. I know a restaurant that serves pretty decent food in Nelson Street, and after that we'll catch the bus back along here and go either to the Grafton, which has a dance floor that bounces, or the slightly snazzier Locarno, almost next door to it.'

'Two dance floors so close together. How did that happen?' asked Emma.

Jared smiled, 'You could say it resulted from the Yanks coming over here during the war and being mad about dance, especially the jitterbug. There was only the Grafton on West Derby Road then, and it was strictly ballroom; jitterbugging and jiving were looked upon with horror by the older generation, just as the Charleston was in the Twenties.'

'So tell me about the Locarno,' said Emma.

'The Locarno started out as a theatre, the Olympia, but didn't do as well as the Hippodrome and eventually became a cinema. I think it became a depot during the war.' His brow was creased in thought. 'What I do know for certain is that it was bought by Mecca and turned into a ballroom. Before I did my national service, I tried out both places and discovered the Locarno generally caters for a younger clientele. I don't know what it's like now, but we can give either a try.' His eyes twinkled, 'But bear in mind, when you're a teenager, over twenty-one is old.'

She laughed. 'You're telling me that we're regarded as old by someone of Betty and Maggie's age?'

He nodded. 'I reckon we'd best wait and see

what the length of the queues are like and pretend we're younger if we end up in the Locarno. Now for the Chinese restaurant,' he added.

Emma could not have been more delighted that he was making such an effort to make her visit to Liverpool such a treat. She was fascinated by the decor in the restaurant, with its paper lanterns and small statues of Buddha. She had never had a Chinese meal before and asked Jared to choose for her.

'You'll like this,' he said, when the food came. 'It's not spicy, although you might find it a little hot, but that's the ginger in it.'

She raised an eyebrow and stared at him across the table. 'Ground ginger?'

'No, the real root. It's good for you to try different foods, Emma,' he drawled, with a faint smile.

'I suppose you got used to oriental food in Korea,' she said, ruefully.

He shrugged. 'You have to be careful if you eat native food. You can end up with a real nasty bellyache.'

'Is that what happened to you?'

'Yes, and I was ill for days, but it didn't put me off curry.'

'I can't see me serving up curry at my place,' said Emma seriously.

Jared smiled. 'No. You stick to what you're

good at. Eat up and then we'll have coffee, a drink at the pub opposite the Grafton, then head for the dance floor.'

Emma had never been in a pub, but did not like saying so. As it happened, she need not have worried, because by the time they reached West Derby Road, the pub opposite the dance halls and the one on a street corner a short distance from the Grafton were filling up with men. Jared made the decision that perhaps it was best if they had a drink once inside the dance hall, although the drinks would be dearer there.

Having already noticed that there were queues forming outside both places, that came as a relief to Emma. As it turned out, they ended up in the Locarno. She had never jived in her life and was a little worried about it, yet she was impatient to be held in Jared's arms and to be twirled around the dance floor in whatever fashion.

They did not immediately get up and dance but had a drink, sitting at a table a few feet away from the dance floor. She was surprised and glad to see that there was a proper big band playing. No jazz or jive, but a quickstep. She could manage that, she thought, and was pleased when Jared stood up, bowed to her and said, 'Shall we dance?'

Soon they were whirling around the dance floor and she thought nothing could be more delightful. A swirling, shiny mirrored ball hung overhead and she was part of a bigger crowd on the largest dance floor she had ever stepped onto. She was glad that Jared did not talk while they danced, because she wanted to immerse herself in the music and the sensations roused by being in his arms. She lost track of how many times they danced, as they were seldom off the floor, but occasionally they sat out to get their breath back. Then she found it fun to sit back and watch other people enjoying themselves. She could not help noticing the young men that grouped together in various places around the dance floor and the girls that did the same. As she waited for Jared to bring her a drink, she saw the band leaving the stage and a smaller group taking their place.

In no time at all the tempo of the music had changed: it was much faster. Even though some people were quickstepping, some of the youths had found themselves girls and were jiving to the music. A song that she had never heard before, called 'Crazy Man, Crazy', was being belted out by a young man on the stage.

Jared placed her shandy on the table in front of her and said, 'Do you want to dance?'

'To this?' asked Emma, startled.

'Too tired?' he asked, his eyes daring her to have a go.

Emma rose to the challenge. 'If you can do it, then I can do it!'

She gulped down half her shandy and stood up. As soon as she was on the dance floor, she realised this was not Jared's first experience of jiving. He seemed to know exactly what he was doing and twirled her this way and that. She stood on his toes a few times, apologised, and was told that she would soon get the hang of it. When he swung her between his legs and then up into the air, and then over his hip, the move left her gasping and laughing. By the time the music came to an end, she was leaning against him, with her head resting on his shoulder, and definitely needing to cool down.

'Have you had enough?' murmured Jared against her ear.

She lifted her head and smiled up at him. 'For now,' she said in a breathless voice.

He bent his head and kissed her, then taking her hand he led her off the dance floor. 'That's a Bill Haley & His Comets song,' he said.

'American?' asked Emma.

Jared nodded. 'Met Yanks when I was in Korea, and over here after the war.'

'Is that when you learnt to jive?'

He smiled. 'There were dances in some of the parks during the war and you'd find Yanks there jiving. I used to watch them and have a go. A lot of liners sail backwards and forwards from Liverpool to New York and it wouldn't surprise me if Jimmy Miller, Irene's sailor brother, has brought that record over and she plays it on her record player, because our Maggie can jive.'

Emma did not doubt it and she wondered if maybe this music group Betty and Irene were supporting would soon be playing it. 'Did the Yanks stay long in Liverpool?'

Jared said, 'They were based at Burtonwood airbase, near Warrington, but they often came into Liverpool. They left after the war, but returned when the Russians blockaded Berlin, to airlift food, fuel and equipment into the western sectors of the city.' Jared downed half his beer. 'Ready for another dance yet?'

She smiled. 'I wouldn't mind a nice slow one.'

The big band had returned to the stage, and when they struck up 'It Had to Be You', Emma could not say no. She felt as if she was floating as Jared held her close and sang the lyrics in a low voice against her ear. The words were some of the most romantic ones in the world in her opinion. But surely he could not mean them after such a short acquaintance? Because if he did, then she knew that there would be sacrifices to be made, and most likely it would be she who would have to make them.

CHAPTER TWENTY-FIVE

Elsie placed a tray on the coffee table and gazed at Emma's glowing face. Jared had just gone upstairs and the older woman was glad of that because it gave her the opportunity to talk to Emma alone. 'It looks to me like the pair of you had a lovely time. I presume from Betty's absence that she couldn't face coming to see me,' said Elsie.

'No, it wasn't that at all,' said Emma hastily. 'She wasn't in when we arrived at her bedsit.'

'I see.' Elsie paused. 'So did you find your father's painting?'

Emma's face lit up. 'Aye, it's there all right. I thought it was marvellous.'

'I'm glad,' said Elsie, looking relieved. 'And the Hippodrome?'

'I found it hard to imagine my mother up there on the stage. The film was great, though. You should go and see it. It makes you feel good.'

'Perhaps I will. It's a while since I've seen a film,' said Elsie. 'I haven't mentioned, Emma, that your father used to help paint the backdrops at the theatre. I think that's how he and your mother met.'

Despite having already been given that information by Jared, Emma thanked her. 'We then had a Chinese meal and afterwards went dancing.'

'You enjoy dancing?'

Emma's eyes shone. 'Oh aye! Jared's a good dancer. He seems to have a natural rhythm.'

'He takes after his father.' A sigh escaped Elsie. 'You have to make the best of every minute, because you never know when it's going to come to an end, Emma,' she added earnestly. 'My first husband, Owen, was a good man and a good provider,' she went on, sitting down beside Emma and picking up her own cup of cocoa. 'And patient! He had the patience of a saint. He never flew off the handle like his brother, and he'd had it tough, but in a different way from Teddy. He'd gone hungry and without shoes as a boy, but being the eldest he fared a bit better than the younger ones. But it also gave him a sense of responsibility, and that's what Jared has. Owen was never sorry for himself despite the muscle-wasting disease that killed him, and he was never envious of what other people had. His brother Teddy, though . . .' Elsie rolled her eyes.

Emma presumed that Teddy was all the things that his brother was not and she could understand why Jared, Dorothy and Maggie would never accept any kind of excuse as a good reason why their mother had married their uncle.

'Well, Teddy's gone now and I certainly don't want him back,' continued Elsie. 'Now come on, luv. Drink your cocoa,' she said, changing the subject.

Emma picked up her cup and sipped the steaming brew and was surprised by its creaminess. 'You make a good cup of cocoa, Mrs Gregory.'

'That's the Jersey milk,' said Elsie, looking pleased. 'I always treat us to a pint at the weekend. I've seen the cow and know the farmer. We're not far from the country here, you know, luv. It's not like when we used to live in Liverpool. You get real fogs there. I remember how my mother didn't dare go out when they came down; so bad, you couldn't see your hand in front of your face. Her chest was something chronic. In the end it was the bad air attacking her bronchials that killed her. It's time the government did something about cleaning up the air.'

'That's a cheerful conversation you seem to be having with Emma, Ma,' said Jared, causing the two women to jump at the sound of his voice.

He picked up his cocoa and sat down on a chair facing them. 'I was thinking, Ma, that perhaps we should try and find Teddy.'

Dismay crossed his mother's face. 'Why? I thought that would be the last thing you'd want.'

'I'd like to know where he is, so we can keep an eye on him. Perhaps it's time you reported him missing to the police,' said Jared.

'They'll wonder why I've waited before doing so,' said Elsie.

'I thought our Maggie could ask Irene to mention it to her stepfather. He's a policeman,' said Jared.

'I'll think about it,' said Elsie, draining her cocoa cup. 'Anyway, it's time we were all in bed. Drink up, Emma. I'll go up with you. We can leave our Jared to check the doors and windows and make sure everywhere is locked up.'

'Thank you, Mrs Gregory,' said Emma, finishing her cocoa. 'Perhaps I can wash the cups?'

'No, the first time you visit, you'll be treated like a guest. Leave your cup there and say your goodnight to Jared. I'll see to it later.'

Emma stood up and smiled at Jared. 'Goodnight, and thanks for a lovely day.'

'I had a great time, too. See you in the morning.'

A quarter of an hour later Emma was in bed, lying on her back with her hands behind her head, reliving her day. It had been the happiest one she had spent, ever.

CHAPTER TWENTY-SIX

'Gosh, have you seen this in last night's *Echo*?' said Maggie. 'A man threw his own son under a bus in Bootle.'

'Was he killed?' asked Dorothy.

'No, but his leg was damaged. The police are saying it was attempted murder.' She glanced up. 'Fancy trying to kill a member of your own family!'

'It's not so unusual,' said Dorothy. 'If you read the history books, you often get fathers killing sons, and sons their fathers and brothers, and how many men murder their wives? Think of Crippen.'

'Enough,' said Elsie. 'Isn't there anything cheerful or funny you can tell us?'

'Not funny, but I find this interesting,' said Maggie. 'A deckhand was remanded for selling *Royal Iris* whisky during a private cruise. Fancy being able to afford to hire the *Royal Iris* for a get-together.'

'It would be great,' said Dorothy, getting up from the table. 'For a wedding, that would be nice.'

'Talking about get-togethers,' said Elsie. 'Where do the Gianellis live?'

Dorothy and Maggie exchanged glances. It was a month since Emma had visited and the topic of visiting the Gianellis had been raised. Emma was due to stay for the weekend this Saturday, as it would be Christmas in a few weeks and apparently Jared was taking her shopping.

'Why are you asking?' said Dorothy.

'Because I've decided to visit Mrs Gianelli and see what she's like for myself.'

'You've taken your time,' said Dorothy, shrugging on her coat.

'I've had a lot on my mind,' said Elsie, humping a shoulder and reaching for a cigarette. 'I've had several visits to make to various places.'

'Where?' asked Dorothy bluntly.

'To visit my solicitor, for starters,' said Elsie, fiddling with her cigarette and then putting it away, unlit.

'Your solicitor! I didn't know you had one. What for?' asked Dorothy, leaving her coat unbuttoned and resting her hands on the table and staring at her mother.

'I'm in the process of having the house made over to Jared and I'm also having my will drawn up.' Elsie reached for the teapot and removed the hand-knitted cosy and topped up her teacup. 'I don't suppose you'll like the idea.'

'You mean you're making it over to him now?' asked Dorothy, stunned.

'Yes. I don't want to pop off and for Teddy to claim it,' said Elsie. 'You might think it's unfair, but he's the one who's most likely to get married first and he'll need a home to bring his bride.'

Dorothy shrugged. 'Just because Dougie Marshall isn't available, it doesn't say I won't date someone else and get married before our Jared. I know what you're thinking: that he and Emma might make a match of it, but he's only seen her once since she was here, and she mightn't want to leave her cottage.'

'We'll see,' said Elsie smugly, sipping her tea. 'I'd like a grandchild before I die. Hopefully, your future husband will provide you with a roof over your head, as that's what husbands are supposed to do.'

'Mum, you must know how difficult it is for married couples to find a home of their own since the war,' said Dorothy, in a tight little voice. 'But putting that aside, there's something that's puzzling me. Where did you and Dad get the money from to buy this house, or is there a whopping mortgage on it?'

Elsie's cheeks turned a dull red. 'That's none of your business.'

'It's our Jared's business,' said Dorothy heatedly. 'Is it that you can't afford to pay the mortgage and are landing him with it?'

'That's not it at all,' snapped Elsie. 'There isn't a mortgage. The house is paid for.'

'Well, that's a relief. It still leaves a question unanswered.'

'And it'll remain unanswered until I'm ready to give answers,' said Elsie.

Dorothy took a deep breath. 'Honestly, Mum, you are the most frustrating person to deal with. I admit I'm really glad you've come to your senses about Uncle Teddy. It's just a pity you couldn't divorce him.'

'I did actually mention about getting a legal separation to the solicitor.'

'I'm glad to hear it, but solicitors do cost money,' said Dorothy.

'You leave the worrying about money to me,' said Elsie.

Dorothy said, 'Have you won the pools or something?'

'That's my business,' said Elsie, reaching for the newspaper.

'Oh, I'm going to work,' snapped Dorothy, tying a scarf about her head. 'Are you coming, Maggie? We might as well walk to the bus stop together.'

Her sister nodded and collected her things and they left the house.

Elsie guessed that they'd have their heads together talking about her, but she wasn't going to worry what her daughters thought about her right now. And hadn't they gone and forgotten to give her the Gianellis' address? Well, perhaps it wasn't meant for her to go there.

She cleared the table and washed the dishes before combing her hair, putting on a bit of face powder and lippy and her outdoor clothes. Then she locked up and set off to catch the bus for the solicitor's office in Crosby.

That evening the family were all sitting round the table together, having their meal. 'So what time is Emma coming on Saturday?' asked Dorothy.

Jared glanced up and put down his fork. 'Early afternoon. I'm going to meet her at the station. She wants to go and look at her father's painting again.'

Maggie said, 'Will you be seeing Betty?'

'She has her Saturday job, so I doubt it,' said Jared. 'Why do you ask? Is there something you want to say to her?'

Maggie shrugged. 'Nothing in particular. I was

just wondering, that's all, if she was coming here for Christmas.'

'She's been seeing Irene Miller, so why don't you ask her?'

'I thought Emma might know.'

Jared smiled. 'You can ask her yourself, when you see her.' He turned to his mother. 'I was thinking, Ma. Is it possible some of Uncle William's other paintings survived the war?'

'If they did, then our Lizzie would most likely have put them in the loft,' said Elsie. 'But I would have thought she'd have sold them for the money.'

Jared grimaced. 'You could be right, although it's possible she might have wanted to hang on to a couple, thinking they could be worth more years later. The money could help pay for Emma's damp course and possibly an extension to the rear of the house.'

His mother gave a snort. 'You're getting carried away, aren't you? Think they'd be worth hundreds? If there are any pictures, they'll be filthy and not worth looking at. Believe me, son, it'll be a waste of your time going up there.'

'Even so, I wouldn't mind having a butcher's,' said Jared, his eyes alight.

Elsie pushed her dinner plate away and reached for her cigarettes. 'Well, if you fall between the joists and crash through the ceiling, don't blame me.'

'Give me some credit, Ma,' said Jared, grinning. 'I'll give it a go tomorrow.'

The following day he was home by four o'clock. At this time of year his working hours were always shorter, and as the weather had turned foggy, the boss had told them they could knock off early. The house was empty as his mother was at work and his sisters wouldn't be in until later.

He didn't bother changing out of his working overalls, which were speckled with plaster and paint, and he kept on the cap that protected him from the worst of the plaster dust. He went down the garden to fetch the ladder from behind the shed and carried it upstairs. Then he took a torch from a drawer in the kitchen and a pair of old gardening gloves from under the sink and went upstairs.

He nipped up the ladder and unlocked the bolt on the trapdoor. He was whistling as he did so, thinking of Emma and looking forward to meeting her tomorrow. He shone his torch into the loft, and odd dark shapes immediately revealed themselves as all sorts of paraphernalia that had been discarded for one reason or another, but kept, as they might come in handy one day.

Placing his torch carefully on a joist, he heaved himself into the loft. He reckoned if there were any of his Uncle William's pictures here, then most likely they would have been placed out of the way. The loft was a fair size, so probably they'd be over by one of the walls, out of harm's way. He picked up the torch and shone it around, thinking as he did so that, with a couple of windows in the roof and a proper floor and the rubbish removed, this space could be made into a decent room. The torch's beam passed over what appeared to be rectangular newspaper-wrapped packages, leaning against the wall to his right. Stepping carefully, he went in that direction.

There were four of them and they felt as if they could be canvases. He decided to carry just two at a time, not wanting to overbalance and put his foot through the ceiling below.

He was in the act of carrying the last two across the loft when he thought he heard a noise down below. He poked his head out of the opening, wondering if his mother and the girls had come home early due to the fog. He could not hear any voices, only the sound of a chair being moved. Then there came footfalls on the stairs.

Carefully, he eased himself out of the opening and was halfway down the ladder when he caught sight of his uncle on the first-floor landing. He was wearing an overcoat that Jared recognised as once having belonged to his father. It was much too long for Teddy, but maybe it was the first thing he'd found to hand, and the foggy weather was freezing outside. Jared noticed his uncle was carrying a box beneath his arm and recognised it as belonging to his mother. Jared was furious and drew in his breath with a hiss.

Teddy must have heard him because he looked about him in alarm. He spotted Jared and the next moment was scuttling down the stairs. Jared dropped the last couple of feet and raced after him. He would have caught up with him if the carpet runner on the landing hadn't been rucked up by Teddy's feet. Jared tripped on it, lost his balance and fell headlong down the stairs. He managed to slow his descent by grabbing hold of the banister. He swung round, slid down backwards and caught his arm with a whack on the newel post. The pain was excruciating and his fingers slid off the banister, causing him to land with a thud on the hall floor, his head catching the vestibule door, leaving him stunned.

The front door slammed and Jared managed to stagger to his feet. He had a struggle with the vestibule door, fumbling with a shaking hand for the doorknob. At last he managed to open it. The front door had been left wide open and Jared made his way down to the gate and onto the pavement, but what with the fog, he could see no sign of Teddy. He mustn't have half shifted himself, thought Jared, furious with himself for falling. He felt sick and dizzy with pain, and cursed his uncle.

Suddenly he heard female voices and recognised them as belonging to his sister and a neighbour. He called Dorothy's name, and there must have been something in his voice that brought her running.

'Did you see Uncle-bloody-Teddy?' he asked, when he could make out her features.

'No! Why? Has he been here?'

'He was in the house. I was up in the loft, heard a noise, spotted him and ended up falling down the bloody stairs.'

'Damn!' exclaimed Dorothy, looking upset and angry as she stared at Jared. 'You look terrible!'

'I feel bloody terrible.'

'Your face is filthy and you're bleeding, and what's wrong with your arm?' Her voice was filled with concern.

Jared said savagely, 'I think I've broken it due to that bloody man.'

'Oh no!' she exclaimed in dismay. 'You're going to have to go to the hospital and get it X-rayed.'

'I know. But I'm more worried about Uncle Teddy getting away. He was carrying Ma's box with her documents in.'

'How did he get into the house?' asked Dorothy.

'I can only think I must have left the back door open when I carried the ladder inside,' groaned Jared.

'But how would he know that?'

'Perhaps he's been watching the house, waiting for an opportunity like that,' said Jared, leaning against the gatepost.

Dorothy shivered. 'Ooh, that's creepy.'

'Well, I'm not going to go off to the hospital and

leave you alone. I'll wait until Ma or Maggie comes home,' he said, his mouth tight with pain.

Dorothy put an arm round him. 'Let's go inside. I'll make you some hot sweet tea. D'you think you'll still be able to meet Emma off the train tomorrow?'

'Of course I can. I might have broken my arm, not my leg,' said Jared, realising with a sinking heart that he wouldn't be able to sort out Emma's back bedroom, or do his paid job, for weeks, if it was broken. Perhaps it was only jarred. Within hours he knew the latter was just wishful thinking.

'You should never have gone up there,' said Elsie, much later that evening.

She placed a cushion on the arm of the sofa, so her son could rest his plastered arm on it if he wished to do so. 'The bloody nerve of Teddy coming into this house without a by your leave.' Her expression was strained.

Jared gazed at her from beneath drooping eyelids. 'I know. That's how I felt. He must have been watching the house. I'm sorry he got away with your box, Ma.' He closed weary eyes.

His mother stiffened. 'That's the first time you've mentioned a box. You mean to say it was the one from my bedroom?'

'I didn't get a good look at it but I'd swear there was a picture on the lid.'

Elsie swore. 'I bet you're right.'

'But why should he have taken that?' asked Dorothy. 'You didn't keep money in it, did you?'

'Some, but not a lot,' said her mother, 'but it's got all the insurance policies and birth, marriage and death certificates in! As well as my bank book. The bloody swine!' She started to her feet, a hand to her chest. 'There's private letters in there, as well as photographs of you kids when you were young, and the little chalk drawing you did, as well as the first birthday card your dad ever sent me,' she gasped.

'What would he want them for?' asked Dorothy.

'Just to make life bloody difficult for me.' Elsie's hand shook as she reached for her cigarettes. 'We've got to get it back.'

'He's probably burnt the lot,' said Dorothy.

'No! He wouldn't burn everything,' said Elsie, lighting a cigarette. 'We need to call the police in. We've talked about it but haven't done it. He can't be far away.'

'At least the deeds to the house weren't in it,' said Jared, glad that he'd taken them from his mother yesterday and placed them in the metal box he'd had since he was a kid. It contained shells he'd picked up off Formby beach, his champion conker, a Victorian double-headed coin and the toy car that his dad had bought him for his eighth birthday.

'I've just remembered that there was a copy

438

of my new will in there,' said Elsie, paling. 'He'll discover that he doesn't even get a mention in it, and Emma does.'

'Emma!' exclaimed Dorothy, staring at her. 'Why Emma?'

Elsie did not immediately answer because she was puffing on her cigarette as if her life depended on it. 'You get a mention, as well. You all do – even Betty.' She hesitated. 'But there's a typed letter paper-clipped to my will, explaining why Emma's included.'

'I don't understand,' said Dorothy, her green-blue eyes bewildered.

'I owe Emma a lot. I wouldn't have a penny if it wasn't for her,' muttered Elsie.

Jared groaned and rested his head against the back of the sofa. 'Uncle William's money!' he exclaimed.

His mother stared at him. 'What do you know? Did the solicitor say something to you or have you been prying?'

'Have I hell,' said Jared, glaring at her. 'I worked it out for myself. You and Dad didn't have the kind of money to buy a house this size. Especially once he took ill. Aunt Lizzie must have helped you out, and where did she get the money? Uncle William must have left it to her and his daughters.'

'One daughter,' said Elsie.

There was a silence.

'What do you mean?' he demanded. 'Come on, Ma, spill the beans.'

Elsie was visibly trembling as she lit another cigarette from the one she was smoking. 'Y-you're to keep this to yourself, both of you,' she said in a whisper. 'Although, if Teddy's been through my stuff, he'll know everything. Having said that, he's a poor reader, so he'll have difficulty understanding every word of the letter.'

'He could get someone else to read it to him,' said Jared, his eyes never leaving his mother's face. 'Come on, Ma, what does the letter say?'

Elsie took a deep shaky breath. 'Betty isn't William's daughter. Her father was that actor our Lizzie was mad about, only, as I told you, he went and died. She told me she was pregnant and I hit the roof. She ran out the house, straight into the arms of William, who had come to tell us that Mary was dead. She told him that Johnny was dead, too. When I learnt that, I felt terrible, but I was so annoyed with her for being so stupid. I told her that she had to go away, have the baby and give it up for adoption. She refused because she wanted Johnny's baby, so I persuaded her to make a proper friend of William and be a comfort to him.'

There was a heavy silence.

A couple of minutes passed before Jared asked, 'Did Uncle William know Betty wasn't his child?'

'I'm sure he guessed,' said Elsie. 'Anyway, I

might as well tell you about the money. William didn't trust banks and kept his money in a safe in the house. Of course, being a soldier in wartime he had to make a will. He wrote Lizzie a letter, saying that he'd left everything to her, because he didn't want Emma's grandparents to get their hands on his money. No one knew about it but our Lizzie. He trusted her to do what was right by Emma. She knew the combination of the safe and removed the money and deposited most of it in Martin's Bank after his death. I certainly didn't suspect he had so much money. It was a good job she did do that, because you know what happened to the house.'

'So she tried to get in touch with Emma, but her grandmother ignored her letters,' said Dorothy.

Elsie nodded. 'So she gave Owen the money to buy this house on the condition that one day it would be sold and half given to Emma. Anyway, she and Betty came to live with us, as you know. Of course, Lizzie was entitled to some of William's money herself because she was his wife, so after her death her share belonged to Betty.' She paused to drag on her cigarette.

'I would never have believed it of Aunt Lizzie,' said Jared. 'Why couldn't she have gone up north to see Emma?'

'At first it was because it was wartime,' said Elsie.

'But afterwards!' said Jared, his face set.

'I know, I know! She should have done it, and after she died I should have tried to find Emma, but I was on my own, grieving for her and your dad.' Elsie fell silent.

'So when Emma wrote to you out of the blue,' said Jared roughly, 'it must have given you a helluva shock.'

'It did! Especially when I knew Emma wasn't really Betty's half-sister. Our Lizzie never told Betty about Johnny, so she believed that William Booth was her father.'

Jared put his head in his hands and said in a muffled voice, 'I'm going to have to mortgage this house and give Emma her share of the money.'

'Don't be daft!' said Elsie, alarmed. 'Why do you think I made the house over to you? When I listened to you talking about Emma, and then saw you with her, I knew you'd fallen for her, and it was obvious to me that she'd fallen for you. I could see the pair of you getting married and living here, so in a way she'll get what's her due.'

'If you really believed that, Ma, then why is Emma in your will?' asked Jared.

Elsie sighed. 'I couldn't be *certain* you'd marry her. Besides, I haven't been well lately and I don't know when I might pop off.'

'You'd be as fit as a fiddle if you gave the ciggies up,' said Dorothy. 'You are devious, Mum.'

'Never mind that now,' said Jared, frowning.

'How much money are we talking about you leaving in your will, Ma?'

Elsie hesitated before saying, 'A substantial amount. Me and our Lizzie invested some of the money William left and it brought us in a nice little income, without us having to touch the capital.'

Dorothy gasped. 'When I think of the way you made me hand over most of my wages, I could walk out of here right now!'

'When I pop off you'll get it back with interest,' snapped Elsie.

'I could do with it now. Anyway, why the heck did you bother getting a part-time job when you and Aunt Lizzie were loaded?' asked Dorothy.

'I didn't want people suspecting I had money,' muttered Elsie. 'Besides, if I'd come clean, I'd have had to explain where the money came from and that would mean Betty knowing the truth about her father. As it is . . .' She paused, gulped and the colour drained from her face.

'As it is – what?' demanded Jared.

Elsie put a hand to her breast and took a shaky breath. 'Teddy might know everything now. Pass me my handbag. I need my pills.'

'What pills?' asked Dorothy, getting up and fetching the handbag.

Elsie only said, 'Get me them. I'll need a drink of water.'

Dorothy fetched water and she and Jared

watched their mother open a container and remove a little blue pill and take it with the water. She leant back against the back of the sofa and was silent for several minutes. Then she looked at Dorothy. 'You've got to talk to that policeman friend of yours and get him to find Teddy.' Then she turned her gaze on her son. 'And you've not to tell Emma the truth. The house is yours. She'll get her due when I die.'

CHAPTER TWENTY-SEVEN

Jared stood at the other side of the ticket barrier, watching the passengers pour out of the train from Manchester. He still hadn't made up his mind about what he was going to say to Emma about his mother's revelations. Suddenly he spotted Emma and his heart lifted, in spite of all that bothered him. He saw her face light up when she saw him, and then her brow knit and she came running.

As soon as she was through the barrier, he moved towards her and stretched out a hand for her overnight bag. 'Are you OK?' he asked.

'Never mind me,' she said, holding on to her baggage. 'What about you? What have you done to yourself, luv?' Her voice was as gentle and soothing as a caress.

In that moment he knew what he must do, even though it was going to be difficult and would upset her. 'Let's go to Lyons and have a cup of tea and a toasted crumpet and I'll tell you all about it.'

Emma linked her arm through his undamaged one and they began to walk towards the side entrance of the station. 'Don't keep me in suspense,' she said. 'Start now.'

He told her about going in to the loft and bringing down what he had hoped were her father's paintings. 'What are they like?' she asked excitedly.

'I haven't looked. I thought we could do that together,' said Jared.

She looked pleased and squeezed his arm. 'I hope they are his paintings.'

'So do I, because if I hadn't gone up there, then I would have caught Uncle Teddy in the act, burgling our house, and wouldn't have fallen down the stairs and broken my arm. As it is, he got away.'

Emma frowned. 'That's awful. Does your arm hurt much?'

'Not as much as it did,' he said, smiling wryly.

She kissed the side of his face. 'I wish it hadn't happened.'

'So do I. You do realise I won't be able to finish the job at the cottage now?'

'That can wait. You can still come and visit me, though.'

He paused and kissed her on the mouth, and for a moment their lips clung before parting. 'You are understanding. I'm annoyed with myself that I left the back door open and that's how he got into the house,' he said crossly. 'He stole Ma's box with all her important papers inside.'

'Oh Lor'!' Emma's eyes widened in dismay. 'That'll inconvenience her. Is there anything you can do to find him and get them back?'

He told her what his mother had suggested and she said, 'So what are you going to do about notifying the police? Your mother might have trouble explaining matters to a policeman who doesn't understand the family situation. He's still her husband, after all, so he isn't like an ordinary burglar, is he?'

Jared said grimly, 'No, he isn't. But there's more I have to tell you and I'd rather wait until we're sitting down to do that.'

She stared at him. 'What is it? You look—'

'I'll explain later,' he said.

Emma had to be satisfied with that, but she had started to worry.

They walked along Lime Street until they came to Lyons café and went inside. It was busy but they managed to find a table for two and sat down. Jared waited until a waitress had taken their order before

447

reaching out for Emma's hand that lay on the table and clasping it.

'I'm going to tell you something now that will shock and disappoint you, but I feel it would be wrong to keep it from you.'

She moistened her lips and cleared her throat. 'You look so serious, you're frightening me. It's not that you've got an old girlfriend tucked away somewhere and don't want to see me any more?'

His expression relaxed. 'No, of course not! What kind of person do you think I am? I love you, Emma. I want to marry you. I know there are difficult choices ahead, but I'm sure we can sort them out.'

Her eyes glowed. 'You really love me?'

'I wouldn't say it if I didn't.'

'I love you, too, and of course I want to marry you and for us to be together for always.'

He let out a long breath. 'Good! I just hope you'll still feel like that when I tell you about the bombshell Ma dropped on Dorothy and me last night.'

She stared at him expectantly.

There was a long pause and then he said, 'Your father left a lot of money, Emma, with my Aunt Lizzie. Some of it was meant for you, but she lent it to my father to buy the house where we live now. I've decided to mortgage the house and hand over half the money to you.'

Emma gazed at him for what felt an age and then said, 'You don't have to do that if we get married. The house can belong to both of us.'

'That was Ma's idea.' He hesitated and held her hand tightly. 'But there's more; shall we wait until the tea comes before I tell you?'

She raised an eyebrow. 'Why? Do you think I'm going to need plenty of sugar in it for further shock?'

He did not answer but glanced around for the waitress.

'You're getting me worried again, Jared,' said Emma in a low voice.

'Sorry.' He gave her his full attention. 'It's to do with Betty and—' He stopped short, thinking this was much more difficult than he thought it would be.

'Go on!' urged Emma.

'She's not your half-sister,' he said in a low voice.

Shock seemed to pierce Emma's soul. 'W-what do you mean? Of course she's my half-sister.'

'Not according to Ma she isn't. Aunt Lizzie was in love with an actor called Johnny. They must have been lovers at some time and then he went away and died of blood poisoning. She discovered that she was pregnant and told Ma. She thought Aunt Lizzie should go away, have the baby and get it adopted. Aunt Lizzie refused because she wanted Johnny's baby. Around the same time, your father

449

came to tell Ma and Aunt Lizzie your mother had died. Your father and Aunt Lizzie comforted each other and the next thing is they were married.'

Emma's face quivered. 'H-he knew she was pregnant?'

'Ma thinks that most likely he did know.' Jared squeezed her hand. 'I'm sorry. I can imagine how you must feel.'

'How can you? You have two sisters and a mother. You can't possibly understand what it meant to me to find someone of my own flesh and blood.' Emma's voice trembled and she withdrew her hand from his, snatched up her handbag and blundered away from the table.

'Emma, come back!' Jared was on his feet, not caring what people thought, and would have followed her, only the waitress carrying their order got in his way. He took some money from his pocket and threw it on the table and then went after Emma.

'Hey, you've forgotten your overnight bag!' called the waitress.

Jared hesitated. 'Look after it for me,' he shouted. 'I'll be back.'

Emma didn't see the man who suddenly appeared in front of her and collided with him. 'I'm sorry,' she said, pulling back.

'You want to watch where you're going, Emma,' he said.

She started, wiped her eyes with the back of her hand and stared at the man. He was short and middle-aged and there was an expression in his eyes that she did not like at all. 'Who are you?' she asked.

'That would be telling,' he sneered.

Suddenly, she had a feeling about him. 'You're Uncle Teddy!' she exclaimed.

'Clever girl!' He seized her arm, but she wrenched it out of his grasp and turned back towards the café. She felt a shove in the small of her back and she hit the café door with such force that it knocked the breath out of her and she slid to the ground.

The door opened cautiously and Jared appeared. 'Emma, what happened? Are you all right?' he asked anxiously, attempting to hoist her to her feet with his one good arm. Fortunately she was able to struggle to her feet with his help. 'The last thing I wanted to do was hurt you, but I believed that having secrets from you wasn't a good way to start our married life.'

'Your uncle was here,' she croaked, hanging on to Jared's arm. 'He must have followed you.'

Jared swore and looked about him, but the pavements were thronged with people and there was no one who looked remotely like his uncle. 'What did he say to you?' he asked.

'He knew who I was,' she gasped. 'I didn't like the look of him at all.'

'That doesn't surprise me,' said Jared, furious that this should happen to Emma after her being so upset by his news about Betty.

'He warned me to watch where I was going,' said Emma. 'Then he grabbed my arm. I dragged myself free and turned to go back in the café; h-he pushed me so hard that I crashed into the door.'

'Come on, let's go back inside. With a bit of luck that waitress might have left our tea on the table,' said Jared.

She had left the tea but there was no sign of Emma's overnight bag. 'You pour and I'll go and check if the waitress has put your bag behind the counter,' said Jared.

The woman had done so and Jared took it back over to the table. Placing it on the floor, he sat down at the table and gazed at Emma with concern. 'So what do you want to do next? How are you feeling? Did you hurt anything when you banged into the door?'

'It knocked the stuffing out of me, that's all,' she said in a shaky voice. 'I want to go home.'

'Home! You mean right now?' he said, taken aback.

'Aye.' Emma's eyes filled with tears. 'I know what you're thinking. But I can't stay. What am I going to say to Betty when I see her? I can't tell her what you've just told me. She's convinced that she gets her artistic talent from my father and is determined to follow in his footsteps. I need time to come to terms with what you've just told me. Don't you understand?'

'Of course I do!' He ran a hand through his dark hair, raising it up in a crest. 'If you want to go home, then I'll come with you.'

She lowered her gaze. 'I need to be alone. I have to think, and your being there will be a distraction.'

He flinched, and she felt as if a hand squeezed her heart as she watched him struggle to regain his composure.

'What about my Uncle Teddy? What if he's still hanging around somewhere and follows you?' said Jared.

'Why should he follow me?' she asked.

'If he has read, or someone has read to him, the papers that were in Ma's box, then he'll know you're in her will and he's completely out of it. He'll also know the truth about Betty. If he's been watching the house, then he might have seen us together. He'll have put two and two together and worked out that I care about you. He'll know the way to hurt me is through you.'

Emma thought about that and said, 'If he follows me home, then he'd stand out like a sore thumb in the village because he's a stranger. I'll speak to our local bobby and have him keep an eye open for him.' She placed her hand on his arm. 'I know it's not your fault, but please, let me be alone for a while.'

Jared said stiffly, 'If that's what you want.'

She hesitated. 'I tell you what – walk with me to the station and wait until the train leaves, just in case you're right and he has me in his sights.'

Jared said, 'I planned to follow you there, anyway, to make sure he wasn't doing so.'

'Then let's go now.'

He was about to suggest that she drank her tea first, but already Emma had picked up her overnight bag and was on her feet.

They did not speak as they made their way to the station to find that the Manchester train was due in a quarter of an hour. Jared purchased a platform ticket and kept looking around for any sign of his uncle. Then the train came in and he saw Emma into a carriage.

'I'll write,' she said.

Jared nodded and touched her cheek but made no attempt to kiss her. He remained on the platform, keeping an eye open for anyone that looked even remotely like his uncle, until the train departed.

He wasted no time catching the bus, wanting to get home as soon as possible. He was expecting to find his mother at home. Hopefully Dorothy would be with her. In the meantime he could only hope that his mother had made sure that both front and back doors were firmly locked.

Dorothy banged the knocker, hoping that this time someone would come. She heard footsteps and the door opened and Billy McElroy stood there.

'Oh, it's you,' she said, sounding disappointed.

He smiled down at her and drawled, 'We're going to have to stop meeting like this, Dorothy Gregory. What can I do for you this time?'

'It's your father I wanted, Mr McElroy,' she replied, a flush on her cheeks.

'I'm sorry about that,' said Billy. 'He's just retired and he's gone away for a few days' fishing.'

She could not conceal her dismay. 'Have you any idea when he'll be back?'

'Tuesday.' He added with a serious note in his voice, 'Look, if you give me an idea what the problem is, perhaps I can help. Unless you want to go to the police station, so you can talk to someone else.'

'No, I don't want to go there. I-it's difficult,' she said.

'In what way?'

'I need a policeman, a figure of authority, who can put the wind up someone.'

Billy's eyes crinkled at the corners. 'I can do that. Just tell me who this someone is.'

'This isn't funny, you know,' said Dorothy indignantly. 'It's a very serious matter.'

'I didn't say it was funny,' said Billy, his smile fading. 'Look, why don't you come in and explain what your problem is?'

'No thanks.'

'I won't bite.'

'I didn't say you would, but I need to get home and see if Mum's OK,' said Dorothy, turning away.

She was at the foot of the step when he said, 'This wouldn't be to do with your uncle, would it?'

She whirled round. 'What d'you know? Have you been eavesdropping on the girls again?'

'They have such piercing voices,' drawled Billy. 'Come in and have a cup of tea and I'll tell you what I know.'

Dorothy hesitated. 'I've a better idea. Why don't you walk me home? Mum could be there all alone and worrying about me.'

'I'll just get my jacket,' he said.

Elsie put the key in the lock and pushed the door open and went inside, shutting it firmly behind her. 'Anyone home?' she called.

There was no answer and she stood a moment, listening to the silence. Then she went into all the downstairs rooms and checked there was no one there, before dumping the shopping on the kitchen table and putting the kettle on. She went upstairs to check out the bedrooms and change her shoes. She noticed that the rectangular packages that Jared had brought down from the loft were still leaning against the wall of the upstairs landing. She carried one into her bedroom, took a pair of scissors out of a drawer and snipped the string.

Then she removed the newspaper wrapping to reveal a portrait of her sister cradling a baby, surely Betty. Tears filled her eyes and she covered it up again before opening the other one that was of a similar size. It was of a curly-haired toddler with a toothy grin and smiling eyes. *Emma!* Elsie thought it was natural for Lizzie to have put that one away, but why the one of herself and Betty? It seemed a strange thing to do, but then there had often been times in the past when she hadn't understood her sister at all.

Suddenly she smelt burning and hurried downstairs. Without thinking she picked up the kettle, only to drop it with a scream. She switched off the gas, unlocked the back door and flung it open to let out the smoke. Then she turned on the cold tap and thrust her hand beneath it. She swore beneath her breath, telling herself that she was stupid. Butter, she needed butter to put on the burn.

She went into the larder and brought out the butter dish; she removed the lid, ran a finger through the surface of the butter and spread it on her blistering fingers. Her heart was thudding in her chest and she knew that she had to sit down. It really hurt! She pulled out a chair from the table and sat down. It was then she realised that the kettle was still on the floor, where she had dropped it. Most likely it would have cooled down by now. She got up and bent down to pick it up. As she did so she heard a slight sound. The next moment she was sent sprawling on the floor. She groaned and attempted to push herself up, only to feel something slam into her back and crush her to the floor.

'How does it feel, Elsie, to be down and unable to get up again?' said her husband.

Her heart banged against her ribs. 'Is that you, Teddy?' she gasped.

'Who the hell, d'you think it is? You're going to rewrite that will, Elsie, or you'll regret it, girl.'

She could not believe this was happening. He must have been spying on them to have been able to get in just at that moment. Well, she was not going to do what he told her. 'Go to hell!' she wheezed.

'That money is mine. Your Lizzie should have married me. I asked her often enough, but she was forever throwing my words back in my face.'

'I didn't know that!'

'No? Well, she got her comeuppance. I lost my rag one day and went for her. She hit me in the face and then ran out of the house. Bloody fool! I would have made her a good husband. I really wanted her, but instead she ran straight in front of a car.'

'You were responsible for our Lizzie's death?' gasped Elsie.

'I didn't mean for her to die, but that's life, isn't it? We both grieved for her. Betty was so like her mother. Bloody hell, did she put up a struggle on New Year's Eve, but I enjoyed that. She was a fighter, just like Lizzie.'

Elsie felt such a rage building up inside her. She placed her hands flat on the floor and tried to push herself up in an attempt to throw him off and get her hands on him. But it was too much for her and she collapsed onto the floor.

The back door slammed against the wall, causing Teddy's head to swivel round. In the doorway stood Maggie. 'What d'you think you're doing, you pig? Get the hell off Mum!' she said, charging towards him.

He scrambled to his feet and gazed at his niece and the youth who had limped in after her, leaning on a stick. 'Not you two again,' he muttered. 'Get out of my way, both of you. Elsie's blacked out and she needs a doctor.'

Maggie glanced at Pete.

'You go for the doctor and I'll stay here and watch him.' Pete slid his hand further down the stick and grasped it midway, his face hardened as he stared at Teddy.

Maggie backed away from her uncle and turned and left the kitchen. Then she ran. As she reached the front gate, she saw her sister and Billy McElroy coming towards her. 'Thank God,' she said, running straight for her sister and falling against her. 'Uncle Teddy's in the kitchen. Pete's watching him. He was on top of Mum and she's blacked out. I'm going for the doctor.'

'Well go then!' cried Dorothy, pushing her sister in the direction of the main road before running towards the house.

'Get out of me bloody way,' snarled Teddy. 'Or I'll knock you down, lad, and you'll never get up again.'

'Try it,' said Pete, gripping his walking stick with both hands. 'I hate your bloody sort, picking on women and girls.'

Teddy went for him. Pete swept his feet from beneath him. As the man went down his head hit the floor, but he managed to grab one of the youth's legs. Pete toppled backwards against the wall. Teddy groaned and staggered to his feet and stumbled out of the kitchen, only to find Dorothy blocking his escape.

'G-get out m-me way,' he stuttered.

'What have you done to Mum, you swine?' she asked, pushing him hard in the chest.

'Sh-she's my wife an-and sh-she had it coming.' Teddy blinked at her. 'Sh-she's dead. Now out of my way!'

Dorothy's face went blank with shock. 'I don't believe it!' She barged past him in a hurry.

Teddy staggered forward, only to find his way barred now by Billy. 'Come on, little man,' he said, beckoning him with a crooked finger.

Jared was coming down the road and had just reached the gate, so he saw what happened next, but at the inquest he was unable to tell the coroner exactly what it was that caused his uncle's knees to buckle and for him to collapse onto the ground. He swore that Billy did not touch him. One thing was for certain, Uncle Teddy never got up again.

Sadly, neither did his mother.

CHAPTER TWENTY-EIGHT

13th February 1954

Emma was only half-listening to one of her favourite radio programmes, *Journey into Space*, because she was unable to take her eyes from the envelope propped up against the clock on the mantelpiece, beneath the painting her father had done of her as a child. The envelope had come that morning, and as it had SWALK where it had been sealed, she had decided to leave opening it until tomorrow.

She had known it was from Jared as soon as she picked it up from the coconut mat. It wasn't the first time he had written to her since they parted in Lime Street station. His first letter had arrived on Christmas Eve, along with the parcel containing her father's painting of her. The letter had informed her that he was putting his house up for sale. By then she knew of the deaths of his mother and Uncle Teddy, because Betty had arrived on her doorstep within days of that eventful Saturday. Emma had been at a low ebb, feeling that she should not have run away but remained with Jared and faced his mother.

But it had been too late for that, and she had sat listening to Betty, who was full of the news. She had talked incessantly, until Emma's head had ached even more than it did already. It was obvious to her that neither Jared nor Dorothy had told Betty that William Booth wasn't her father. At least Emma could be glad of that, and also that none of them had to worry about the uncle any longer. Yet knowing Betty was no sister to her had still felt like a bereavement. Despite being extremely fond of her, Emma could not help but feel differently about her. She hoped in time that she would get over it, but for the moment she had to consciously pretend that nothing had changed between them.

Emma's feelings towards Jared, however, had not gone away. If anything, she missed him more than she had done when she had been ignorant of the fact that his aunt and mother had used money that rightfully belonged to her. Despite still loving him, she had felt the need to keep a distance between them: that meant he stayed in Liverpool and she in her village, although she had written to him several times, thrilled that he should have sent her the portrait of herself.

It had seemed like a long winter and it was not over yet, but the snowdrops were flowering in her garden and the days were lengthening out. Now here, on the mantelpiece, was what she felt certain was a card, not a letter. She longed to open it and read what he had written but had decided to wait until St Valentine's Day. The radio programme came to an end and, switching it off, her patience suddenly snapped. She was unable to bear the suspense any longer. She reached for the card and slit it open.

A red satin heart bordered by flowers was on the front, as well as the words *To my Valentine with love*. She opened it and did not bother with the printed words, her eyes going immediately to those in Jared's handwriting. She laughed because the two lines of verse were so corny, but her face was soft with tenderness as she read them: *Roses are red, violets are blue, sugar is sweet and so are you. Can we meet?*

She had wanted to send him a Valentine card but the difficulty was that he had sold his house despite her having told him that she did not wish to deprive him, Dorothy and Maggie of their home. She had received a letter in January saying that it was too late for that and he already had a buyer.

Emma turned the card over to see if there was

a new address on the back; suddenly she was disturbed by a rat-tat-tat on the back door. Swiftly she shoved the Valentine card behind the cushion and got up. At the back of her mind was the hope that it might be Jared, but on opening the door, it was Lila who stood there.

'Why didn't you come?' asked Lila, looking upset.

She had obviously been rushing because her cheeks were flushed and her hair was in a tangle. 'Come in! You're getting my house cold,' urged Emma, dragging her inside. 'What did I forget?'

'You're hopeless,' said Lila, shaking her head as she shrugged off her coat and hung it up. 'Your bridesmaid's dress! You were supposed to be coming for a final fitting.'

'Sorry,' said Emma guiltily. Perhaps she had forgotten because what she wanted was to be a bride, not a bridesmaid. 'Anyway, the dress fits me perfectly. I'm not on a diet like you.'

Lila rolled her eyes. 'The excuses you give for not doing things. You know you've lost weight, without even trying. It's time you made up with Jared.'

'But I haven't fallen out with him,' protested Emma, putting the kettle on. 'Cup of cocoa?'

'Thanks,' said Lila, plonking herself down in a chair and closing her eyes. 'I never thought that getting married and moving house would be so exhausting. Only a month to go.'

'If I was getting married, I'd want to be a June bride,' murmured Emma.

Lila opened one eye. 'But you'd lose tax perks if you did that.'

'I don't care,' said Emma, smiling.

'That's because you're coming into money. I am glad for you, although I am the teeniest bit envious, as well,' said Lila wryly.

'Well, you're going to have a husband with a good steady job and a nice police house and I will buy you a smashing present,' responded Emma, spooning cocoa into cups.

Lila smiled. 'Thanks. I will miss you. Will you miss me?'

Emma stared at her. 'Of course I'll miss you – and your dad – although I don't know how long I'll be here myself.'

Lila sat up straight. 'You mean you're going to sell up and get a bigger place with your inheritance?'

'It depends how things work out. If they don't, then I'll get a damp course put in and an extension built on the back here,' said Emma, gazing out the window. 'But before I do any of that, I'll need to write a letter to Betty.'

Betty stared out of the window, and as soon as she saw the van park on the other side of the road in the shadow of the cathedral, she went downstairs. Jared and Maggie got out and Betty skipped across the road, wearing pants with the bottoms rolled up and a thick Aran sweater, that Emma had knitted her, over a pink blouse.

'I have a letter for you,' she said, brushing Jared under the chin with it.

He snatched it from her, gazed at the address on the envelope and grinned. He placed it in his overcoat pocket. 'I hope you're not going to be too overcrowded with our Maggie's stuff, Betty.'

'It's only temporary, so I think I can cope,' she said, hugging herself. 'How long, Jared, before the rest of the lovely dosh comes through?'

'Not much longer,' replied her cousin, going round to the back of the van and opening the doors. 'Come on, you two, I'm not lugging all this upstairs myself.'

Maggie, who had lost some of her bounce since her mother's sudden death, hurried to help him. He locked the van and followed the two girls across the road, carrying an almost brand-new Voice of Music 'Playtime' record player that had been Maggie's Christmas present from him and Dorothy, and a cardboard box of records. The player had been meant to cheer her up but it had only partially succeeded. Hopefully, living with Betty would do the trick.

They were all feeling the loss of their mother, but it had been worse for Maggie, because she had been the closest to Elsie. It came as a relief to hear the girls twittering like a couple of birds as they went upstairs ahead of him.

Only when he entered the bedsit did he gather that they were talking about the jukebox that had come straight from America, and had pride of place in Betty's favourite snack bar. Apparently there was also the promise of watching the students from the university jousting with mops this coming Saturday to raise money for the hospitals.

He didn't linger because he wanted to read the letter from Emma, so he said, 'Ta-ra,' and left the two girls to sort things out and returned to the van. He slit open the envelope and read what Emma had to say. It was brief and to the point. *How can I meet you, if I don't know where you are?*

He smiled faintly and dropped the letter on the other seat, started the engine and drove off, whistling 'No Other Love Have I', which had been a hit for Perry Como the previous year. Once he'd had a word with Dorothy, he would go to the post office and send a telegram to Emma.

Emma was reading about meat and bacon coming off the ration at the end of July and felt even more cheerful than she had done earlier. Her eyes skipped the next article to the news that hundreds had fainted at the queen's garden party in Sydney. She glanced through the window at her rain-soaked garden and tried to imagine such heat, but couldn't.

The door knocker sounded and she got up and went to see who was there. Perhaps it would be Jared? But it was the telegraph boy and her heart flipped over. 'Telegram for you, Miss Booth,' he said, holding out a yellowish envelope to her.

She took a thruppence from her pocket and handed it over, thanking him. This, despite her belief that telegrams were generally bad news. She went into the kitchen, tearing open the envelope and extracting the sheet of paper inside.

Meet me Saturday 20th in the Walker Art Gallery at two o'clock in front of your father's painting, love Jared.

So she was going to have to go to him, thought Emma with a twist of the lips. Yet, how could she refuse when he had chosen a place in Liverpool that she longed to return to? He had still not given her an address, so he must be trusting her to turn up. She began to think about what she should wear for her date with him. If only it had been summer, then she could have worn something light and feminine, with lots of material in the skirt and a shiny, black patent leather belt to cinch in her waist. Instead, she decided on slacks and sweater and her thick winter coat, woolly hat and gloves. The next two days seemed to drag by. It was a relief when Saturday dawned and she was able to set out for Liverpool.

Jared had arrived at the meeting place too early, impatient to see Emma. He feared that perhaps she might not come after all. He need not have worried, because she turned up at ten to two, sensibly clad. He felt a rush of love and moved towards her, taking her hand and squeezing it gently. 'Hello, you,' he said.

'Hello, yourself,' she said, returning the pressure of his fingers.

He brushed his lips against hers and then they both turned and gazed at her father's painting of the ships on the Mersey. 'You do realise that it was your dad who really brought us together,' said Jared. 'If he hadn't stayed in Liverpool and eventually married Aunt Lizzie, we would never have met.'

'I see what you mean,' said Emma. 'When I look at this picture, I see what was important to him. He loved this city,' she said.

Jared turned to her. 'And how do you feel about it?'

'It's where I was born,' she murmured. 'Can we go down to the river?'

He smiled. 'If that's what you want. It'll make it easier for me to bring up an idea of our Dot's.'

'And what is that?' asked Emma.

His dark eyes were serious as he brought her close to him, not caring about the other two people in the gallery, who glanced their way. 'You do still want us to spend the rest of our lives together?'

'Aye, and I know that will mean us being where your work is.'

Relief spread across Jared's face and he brushed his lips against hers, before taking her hand once more and leading her downstairs. They paused a moment on the steps, flanked by the statues of Raphael and Michelangelo, and gazed across at the Wellington Monument and St George's Hall, and then down past the Mersey Tunnel and the roofs of the buildings of the city's business centre towards the river, where the Liver birds could plainly be seen. Then he said, 'Come on, I've a lot to tell you, and hopefully, you'll agree that our Dorothy's idea is a good one.'

CHAPTER TWENTY-NINE

June 1954

Emma stood, white-laced elbow against white-taffeta elbow, with Dorothy on the upper deck of the ship, gazing over the Mersey as the evening sun reflected off the surface of the water. They were taking a breather from dancing in the saloon below. She could hear the strains of 'That's Amore', made famous by Dean Martin, being sung by Michelangelo Gianelli. He had a voice as seductive as the famous Hollywood star. Mr Gianelli and his wife, Nellie, were musically talented and just as friendly and caring as Betty and Maggie had insisted they were. Emma felt that it was a shame that Jared's mother had never got round to meeting them; she felt certain knowing them would have enriched her life.

Dorothy glanced at Emma and there was a dreamy expression in her eyes. 'Isn't it a perfect evening? Aren't you glad that I persuaded you and Jared to have a double wedding and then the evening do here on the *Royal Iris*? I know it cost more than a bob or two, but what's money for, if it isn't to spend and get pleasure out of it?'

'It's been lovely,' said Emma fervently, 'and it's a real pleasure sharing mine and Jared's special day with you and Billy.'

'I feel the same,' said Dorothy. 'And to think that there was a time when I wasn't even sure I liked Billy, but eventually I realised he was one of the good guys and I could trust him. I wasn't sure whether he had a romantic bone in his body at first, but his Valentine's Day card persuaded me that maybe, given a push, he could make the right gestures.'

Emma chuckled, remembering Dorothy telling her that Billy had written on her Valentine card: *O my darling, do not falter, quickly lead me to the altar.* But she had made him wait, because just like Emma, Dorothy had set her heart, not only on a June wedding, but a cruise on the Mersey.

There was also the fact that their new home would not be ready until summer. Emma thought back to that day in February when she had met Jared at the art gallery. Instead of taking the bus, they had walked down Dale Street and Water Street, passing beneath the overhead railway and eventually ending up at the Prince's Landing Stage. On the way, he had told her that he'd gone into partnership with his boss and bought land on the outskirts of Formby village along the coast, approximately fifteen miles north of Liverpool. There they planned to build a dozen semi-detached houses and two detached ones for sale. Jared had it in mind that one of the detached ones could be for him and Emma, and the other for his sister and Billy.

'You wouldn't be far from the shops and a church, Emma,' he'd said in an attempt to reassure her that it wouldn't be that much different in its way from her own village. 'We'd also be close to the sea and the pinewoods, and there's a railway station with a direct line to Liverpool, so you'd be able to see Betty as often as you liked.'

She had remained silent for several minutes, thinking that she had never expected him to build them a house. Then Jared had added, in a slightly worried voice that caused her to believe that he felt he needed to throw an ace on the table, 'You don't have to sell your cottage, you know. We could have a damp course put in and build an extension on at the back and you could rent it out.'

So for the moment she still owned her cottage up north. Just how long she would hang on to it, she did not know. She heard footsteps behind her and recognised them. Turning, she saw her husband standing there. Their eyes met and he stretched out his hand. 'They're playing our tune,' he said.

As Jared took her in his arms and whirled her round, causing the hem of her white lace gown to brush the deck, Emma could hear the strains of 'It Had to Be You' and they both began to sing.

AUTHOR'S NOTE

Readers often ask where I get my ideas from and I often answer that it can be from what someone has said, or something I've read, or often it can come from research and real-life experiences. What fiction writers do is ask *What if?* and let their imagination take over.

During the past year I've been tracing my ancestry, a fascinating and addictive hobby. When I was growing up in Liverpool it was still part of Lancashire, not the separate entity known as Merseyside. I discovered that the further one goes back, the more ancestors one has, and I possess more than one set of great-great-grandparents and so on, who came from what is known as Lancashire today. During the hard times of Queen Victoria's reign, several of my ancestors came south and settled in Liverpool. For which I am grateful. If they had not, I wouldn't be here to tell this tale.

This story is set in one of my favourite eras, the Fifties, and I thought, what if my heroine, Emma Booth, living in a village in the Clitheroe area, discovers that she has a half-sister living in Liverpool?

Some readers might recognise that village as Whalley. I have stood on the spot in the lovely old parish church where my great-great-grandparents were married and spent several hours in Clitheroe library. For those who know the area so much better than I do, I ask that you forgive me any errors I might have made, and remember that these characters bear no resemblance to anyone living or dead.

Warmest wishes,
June Francis

If you enjoyed *It Had to Be You*, read on to find out
about more books by June Francis . . .

To discover more great fiction and to
place an order visit our website at
www.allisonandbusby.com
or call us on
020 7580 1080

ALSO BY JUNE FRANCIS

'Played out with flair and passion . . . Terrific!'
Books Monthly

'All the atmosphere and colour that romance fans have
come to expect'
Liverpool Echo

'Real people. Real emotions . . . June Francis is good at
evoking the reality of life in wartime'
Historical Novels Review